Wise Wo

By R A Forde

Women of the Dark Ages, Book 1

Also available in this series:

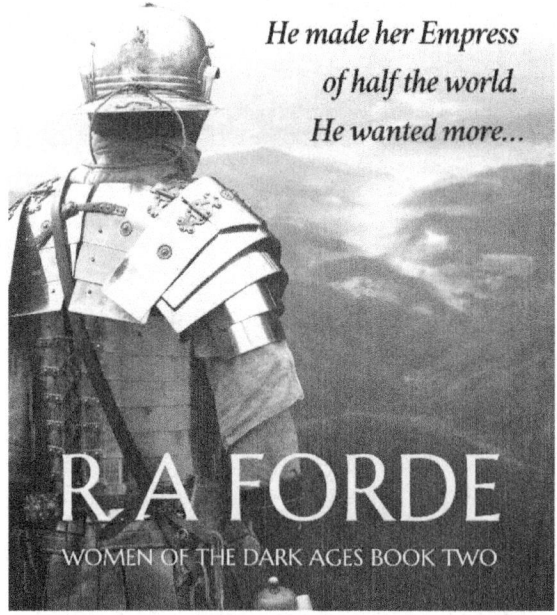

The Dream of Macsen

Women of the Dark Ages, Book 2

Magnus Maximus (known to the British as Macsen) was a real historical figure. He was born in Spain and rose through Rome's military to become commander of its forces in Britain. He is said to have married a British princess called Helen, and his story is told in heroic and romanticised form in the Welsh collection of traditional tales, *The Mabinogion*.

In reality, he was a ruthless military campaigner, and fought with other Roman forces for leadership of the Western Roman Empire (there were three emperors at this time, sharing sovereignty). He was also an orthodox Christian and persecuted "heretics" mercilessly.

His story is told here from the point of view of his wife, starting from her childhood and leading up to her time as Western Empress and Macsen's ultimate bid for total power. Her story is one of love and tragedy, and eventual peace. Like many others, she clings to the old religion, and Macsen's conversion to Christianity places great strain on a marriage already weakened by his inexplicable lack of attention to her. Amid civil war and religious strife, is there any hope for the future?

Details of other books appear at the end of this story
Wise Woman: background

The story of the lost city of Ys is a Breton legend which comes from the same period of history as the Arthurian legends of Britain, which are also found in Brittany. There are many different versions of the legend, and the one that I have given here has drawn on some of them. However, I have also drawn on historical sources from the same period. It was a period of religious and political instability, the effects of which were felt all over Western Europe. The Roman Empire was collapsing in chaos, the Barbarians were invading in their hundreds of thousands, and the Christian church was trying frantically to preserve the position it had attained as the only permitted official religion of the Empire. This had been declared by the Emperor Theodosius only a few years before, but there is evidence that even as late as the eighth century the authorities were not always able to enforce it, even at the centre of the Empire. We know that votive offerings continued to be made at pagan sacred sites long after Christianity was supposedly universal throughout Europe.

Names

At this time a multitude of languages were spoken in Western Europe, but Latin was widely used as an international language, especially by educated people. The Roman naming convention was often used for personal names, men usually having three and women two, although the convention was beginning to break down at this time.

Place names were complicated, many places having old Celtic names as well as Latin names. Some were even acquiring Saxon names as the Barbarians advanced! I have generally stuck with the Celtic names wherever possible, using Latin names for large cities which would have been generally known by these at the time. Spellings often varied, whichever language was being used.

The name "Ys" is pronounced to rhyme with "fleece" today, and probably was in the fifth century too.

Official titles might be either Celtic or Latin. I have tried to avoid them altogether, apart from one. This is the title '*Domina*', meaning roughly 'lady' or 'mistress'.

Wise Woman

Chapter One

After the Saxon raped my mother nothing was ever the same again. For ever afterwards I had a sense of the frailty of civilised life, and all the things we women used to take for granted.

My Uncle Lucian had ridden out that day in answer to a summons from Colchester. A small party of Saxons retreating after Hengest's defeat in the North, had raided a farm just outside the city. It was typical of many incidents which took place. The Saxons were starving, and seeking food rather than plunder. Some of the farmworkers fought and were killed. Most fled. The incident at our estate was also typical.

It was a cold, crisp autumn day with a little mist. I had begged to be allowed to go out and play in the courtyard. Uncle Lucian's house was once a Roman nobleman's villa, built around three sides of a cobbled square. The fourth side had a high wall and a gated entrance. The gates were closed these days except when someone was passing through, but it was little protection.

I played for a while with a wooden doll, as girls everywhere play. I could hear some of the men at work outside in the fields, and smell the smoke from the bonfire where they were burning the end-of-season waste. I suppose a child pays little attention to these things, but I remember becoming suddenly aware that the men were no longer singing or calling to each other. Perhaps too, I had a vague idea that there had been some shouting, and the clash of metal. After so many years it is not always easy to tell what is the simple memory of a child, and what is the adult filling in the childish omissions with what she knows must have happened. I do know that at some point I heard the scrape of boots on brick, and looked up to see a man sitting astride the courtyard wall.

He was clearly a big man. He seemed almost as broad as he was tall. His hair was the fairest I had ever seen, in spite of being dirty and uncombed. His full beard and moustache mingled with his head-hair, which fell to his shoulders and lower. His clothes were obviously foreign, even to my childish eye. Lucian and my other male relatives favoured the Roman style. I had never seen trousers before, nor the leather tunic he wore above them, its belt studded with iron. He had no armour, but looked every inch a warrior. All at once there came to mind all the tales I had heard of the blond giants from the Saxon Shore. Letting my doll fall, I backed away and tried to scream. No sound came, so I wet myself instead.

Ignoring me, he leapt down with ease and strode towards the gate. Finding my legs if not my voice, I turned and fled into the house, where I ran headlong into my mother.

'Whatever is the matter, Keri? Gods, child, you're wet! You haven't done such a thing since –'

'Mamma! Giants, Mamma! Giants!' I broke into incoherent sobs of terror. Nonplussed, she went to the door dragging me with her as I refused to let go of her skirt.

The courtyard was filling with Saxons, perhaps twenty of them. She took in the situation at a glance and slammed the great front door, ramming the bolts into place and calling the servants.

'Naso! Constans! Bar the window! Lock every door! The Saxons are here! Move, by the Gods! Move, if don't want us all killed!'

Naso was a boy and Constans an old man. Mother had laid a heavy responsibility on them. They ran around locking doors and window-shutters, but the house was too large to defend, even if the defenders had all been able-bodied. In any case, the Saxons had other ideas. We heard them smashing the doors of the outbuildings, searching for horses or equipment to aid their escape. After a while they stopped, and there was a muttered conference. I was huddled by my mother's side as we waited silently, praying for Lucian's return with his men. Then we heard boots stamping up the short flight of steps to the front door, and a heavy fist crashed upon it three times.

'Open!' A heavily accented Germanic voice. Probably one of those who lived on the Saxon Shore and had learned some Celtic.

'You open! We want food!'

Mother replied, her voice loud and steady. 'Open the door, and be murdered?'

'No kill! We have hunger. You give us food, we go. I have said! Now open door or we burn house.'

My mother turned to Naso and the elderly Constans.

'Don't believe them, Olivia Galeria. They are barbarians.'

'Constans?'

'*Domina*, if we anger them by refusing, they will certainly burn the house. Then we shall have to open the door anyway, and face their anger. If we trust their word, there is a chance. Even the Saxons keep their word sometimes.'

'Perhaps.'

Naso broke in, 'I would rather fight, and die honourably, than be butchered like a rabbit!' Then he remembered who he was talking to, and finished lamely: 'But it is for you to say, *Domina*.'

'You are a young man, Naso, and with only yourself to consider. I have my daughter also. I will do as Constans advises.'

'God will protect us,' said the old man.

'If your god is interested in protecting anything he's missed plenty of chances.' Even in extremis my mother could not resist a jibe at the religion she despised.

She went down the hall, having disentangled my fingers from her robe and handed me to Constans. The old man put his arms around me and made comforting noises. Fourteen times a grandfather he had had plenty of practise. Mother composed herself before the great oak door, and then nodes to Naso.

'Open it, Naso, and be alert for the first sign of treachery. Not that your dagger will serve much against twenty swords.'

I felt Constans' grip on my arm tighten. He appeared to be muttering a prayer as we watched the door swing open.

Standing in the doorway was the man I had seen on the wall. Now he was carrying a huge double-headed axe, and was clearly the leader of the group. He nodded to my mother, and indicated the rest of us with a sweep of his arm.

'All? Only four?'

'Yes. The other servants and slaves were in the fields.'

He grunted at that, but did not enlighten us as to their fate. He crossed the threshold and his men followed behind. Most carried fearsome weapons, and some were wounded. All were dirty and they stank – of sweat, animal hides, and the dust of the road. One sported a number of trophies – crucifixes on chains or thongs – draped around his shoulders. He seemed particularly taken with my mother, fingering her robe as he passed and slapping her on the behind. She gazed at him stonily before turning away with a snort of contempt.

The crucifix collector giggled, but one of the others nudged him and nodded towards the leader. It was obvious that we were not to be touched. In the corner Constans was busy thanking God. A little prematurely, as it turned out.

The leader turned to address his men. We did not understand a word, but we guessed from the gestures he made that some men were being posted as guards, and others as foragers. Finally he turned back to Mother.

'You go in your room, now. Take the child. One of us brings food. No harm if you stay quiet. I have said.'

'What about my servants?'

'Another room. No harm them too, if quiet. I, Edric son of Ethelwulf, have said!'

He seemed irritated that my mother doubted his word.

She inclined her head quickly, picked me up and carried me down the corridor to her room. One of the Saxons escorted us. His sword scraped the wall as we went, and his metal-studded boots rang on the stone floor. When we got to the room the man went in with us and checked the possible exits. Satisfied that the windows all gave on to the courtyard, where men were still posted, he retired to stand guard outside the door. There was no lock, save for a bolt on the inside only, so they could not leave us unattended. Mother promptly busied herself, cleaning me up with water from a pitcher in the corner.

'Poor Keri. What a fright you must have had. Never mind, child, it looks as though we may yet come through without harm. I think these Saxons don't wish to hurt us. If they did, they know the soldiers would hunt them down without mercy. A little food we can easily spare.'

With these and other soothing words she put me to sleep in her big bed – a real wooden bed with a proper feather mattress – and I slept for some time.

When I awoke it was nearing evening, for the room was shadowy. Someone had come in, and the banging door had woken me. It was the crucifix collector. He and my mother were standing at the foot of the bed, and he was saying something low and unintelligible in his barbarian tongue. She did not understand the words, but I could see she was uneasy at his attitude. The ostensible reason for his visit, a plate of bread and cheese and a pitcher of wine, stood on a table near the bed. From the sounds of merriment it was clear that the others were drinking the rest of our wine store. But this one had other things in mind, whatever his leader had ordered. I watched uncomprehendingly as he slid the bolt on the door, and turned to Mother with the same inane smile I had seen before. She stepped back towards the table, and raised a hand.

'Wait.' She was obviously thinking on her feet. 'Let's be reasonable. If this has to happen, then it may as well be with as little unpleasantness as possible. Here, have some wine.'

She poured some into a cup and handed it to him, smiling. He looked puzzled at her change in tone, but took it anyway. Still smiling at him, she reached up to her hair and removed the pins and ribbon which held it in place. She draped the ribbon over his free hand, and followed it with the sash from around her waist. Then, while both his hands were occupied, she moved.

The wine pitcher hit him full in the face and broke. She drove the jagged remnants into his face for good measure. Then she grabbed me one-handed and ran for the door heedless of the Saxon's roars of pain and fury.

The bolt stuck. Mother swore as I had never heard her do, then he was on us. As he hit her cheek I beat uselessly against his tunic. He raised one foot and sent me skidding across the tiles into the corner. Through my streaming tears I saw him punch her in the face and throw her half-stunned on the bed. Then he hooked his fingers in the neck of her robe, and tore it from her.

Nakedness was not a remarkable thing in our household. It is the Christians who regard it as sinful. I had seen men and women without clothes. I had seen male animals with their mates on the farm, and heard the guffaws and jokes of the labourers as they brought the bull to the cow, the stallion to the mare. But nothing had prepared me for this. Even animals court their mates. They strut before them, dance, compete, in order to win their acceptance. There is even affection sometimes, or so it seems. I thought of sex if at all, as something to do with making nests and making babies. Making love I could have understood. If I had chanced upon a loving couple I think I would have known what was happening and been intrigued, no doubt, but not damaged.

This was the same act corrupted out of recognition. Instead of love, or just plain joy in living, there was nothing but viciousness and humiliation. An instrument of pleasure was turned to an instrument of torture. She was impaled, violated, and I was helpless. I watched his scarred and bleeding face as he exacted his revenge, surrounded by his other war-trophies.

To this day I cannot bear the sight of the crucifix.

When it was finished he stood up, putting his clothing to rights. Hers he picked up and used to wipe some of the blood and wine from his face and hair. His smile had changed. It was triumphant now. He muttered at her the while – words of abuse, no doubt. Then came the knocking at the door, and the voice of Edric, the Saxons' leader.

'Open!' Then something else, presumably the same order in Saxon. A muttered conference. Then a yell and a crash, and the door burst inwards, the bolt sent flying.

Edric stood at the door, his other men filling the passageway behind him. He knew the scene for what it was. Who could not? He glanced at me, sobbing in the corner. There was an exchange of yells, Crucifix justifying himself, Edric demanding to know why his order had been disobeyed. He turned to the bed and covered my mother's nakedness with the twitch of a blanket. Thus distracted, he did not see the other's dagger until too late.

The blade entered high on his right side, and Edric staggered back to the wall, blood welling up and gushing down his tunic. Crucifix raised his bloody dagger and yelled. I think he was trying to proclaim himself leader instead, but the others would have none of it.

The wounded man reached out a hand and someone thrust his war-axe into it. He stepped unsteadily forward from the wall and swung the axe slowly, testing Crucifix's reactions. Crucifix lunged this way and that; if he delayed long enough the other would die on his feet. But his eyes were anxious. A man does not become a Saxon war-leader without proving himself many times over. Crucifix's life might be at stake, but so was his leader's honour. Both are equally important to a fighting man.

Suddenly Edric staggered backwards to lean against the wall. Crucifix charged forward and got the axe end-on in his midriff. Winded, he reeled gasping away. Edric slowly lifted the axe above his head, and as Crucifix turned again to face him brought it down with the force he had left. The heavy weapon sank deep into Crucifix's forehead. For an instant he seemed to stand, staring cross-eyed at the haft sprouting from his head like a horn. Then he fell with a clatter, spilling blood and brains across the tiles.

A sound like a sigh went up from the onlookers, and then Edric slid to a sitting position against the wall. One hand was clapped to his chest, and blood trickled out between the fingers. He had enough strength to speak to his men, and after a few moments Constans was ushered in.

'Old man, I am sorry. I did not want this. I have said. The lady is avenged. And my honour.'

I found myself sidling closer. I knew now that he was dying, and because he had taken my mother's side.

'Don't die, giant. Please.'

In spite of his pain a smile flickered in his greying face.

'No giant, little one. Cry not for me. I go to the gods. It is a good death.'

He lifted his arms up as far as he was able, and took one last breath as he looked at the ceiling.

'*Wotan! Ic cume!*'

The effort brought a stream of blood from his mouth, and he slid on to the tiles.

After this the Saxons were thrown into confusion. Some looked ready to panic and some stunned by the manner of their leader's death. Several of them came and knelt by his body for a few minutes to pay their respects, kissing his cheek. Some had tears on their own cheeks, and were not ashamed to show them in these circumstances, warriors or not. Then there were mutterings, and veiled gestures towards us. It seemed, though, that Edric's word still held.

Meanwhile Mother had stirred, and pulled the blankets around her. She said nothing, but gazed at the bed in front of her, shivering and uttering the occasional dry sob. I cuddled up to her, puzzled and frightened. She seems to be very cold, and I remember asking Constans to fetch more blankets. The Saxons seemed not to notice him as he scurried past them to the cupboard in the hallway, so busy were they in discussing their plans. They were still talking nineteen to the dozen when he came back with the blankets.

And also when Lucian's cavalry troop thundered into the courtyard.

There was the briefest of battles on the cobbled yard. Demoralised by their internal squabbles, and more than a little drunk, the Saxons were not in good fighting condition. Most were cut down at once. Six prisoners were taken, but when Constans told him what had happened my uncle ordered them killed. My first sight of Lucian was when he entered Mother's room, exhausted, one arm hanging uselessly at his side. She spoke without looking up.

'Lucian, I am leaving this place. Keri and I are going to Armorica!'

Chapter Two

I was born in troubled times, and as things are I will die in troubled times. When Maximus crossed from Britain into Gaul, in pursuit of his claim to the throne, the beginnings were already there; rival claimants like himself were appearing after every imperial funeral like seedlings after a spring shower. Indeed, by taking away so many men he left the country open to the Angles and Saxons who were already raiding from their homelands across the North Sea. The situation proved impossible to remedy, and within thirty years the Romans had left for good after four hundred years of occupation.

Maximus is still loved by the Welsh of course. His deeds have passed into legend, and some say that Arthur is his heir, come to rid Britain of the Saxon invader and restore the Roman peace. Well, perhaps. If I had not been barred by my sex from military service I should have been there myself, to see the new legend and avenge my family's humiliation.

Alas, it was my fate to see another legend in the making.

When Maximus was defeated some feared that his followers would be slaughtered by the Emperor, but not so. Indeed, Theodosius was praised for his mercy in allowing the rebels to settle in Gaul, although his purpose was probably more political than charitable. One of the rebels was my great-grandfather and our family was soon established on both sides of the Narrow Sea. So that is how my people came to be there, and how Armorica, the north-western part of Gaul, became British. So much so that these days it is called Lesser Britain almost as often as Armorica, especially since more and more of our people flee there before the Saxon Terror. How many more go depends on whether Arthur can stem the tide of the steel-helmed invader.

It was that tide that took us there, my mother and me, washed up on the Gallic shore like driftwood thrown up at Ocean's edge, supplicants at the court of King Gradlon. His grandfather and his family owned lands on both sides of the Narrow Sea.

Gods, what a journey! I have never been one to entrust my safety lightly to the sea. The power of Ocean is something to respect, and a thin wall of leaky wood is no protection against it. Yet the voyage awoke something within me which has always remained – a kind of sympathy with the sea. Next to the Saxon attack that seaborne journey is the most vivid memory of my early years.

After a prolonged series of arguments, my uncle had realised that there was no gainsaying my mother. In any case, she was a grown woman. She had property of her own – although this was rapidly being devalued as the Saxon encroached. In the last analysis he had no right to rule her life. Besides, perhaps he pitied her for what had happened. In later years she told me that fear of our relatives and neighbours was one reason for our emigration. She thought they would regard her as unclean. Better to have been killed, they would say, than to be dishonoured by a Saxon. Then again, she feared she might be pregnant, and what would the wagging Christian tongues make of that?

'I would have gone to a wise-woman,' she told me, 'and had the thing aborted. No Saxon blood would have sprung inside me, I can tell you.'

But then, Christians were against that, too. From the first they have tried to eliminate our ancient traditions, or assimilate them into their own. These days a wise-woman must be careful not to be taken for a sorceress, and put to ordeal. The priests will not admit to any power but their own. I wish a few of them had been with us on that ship to witness the power of the sea!

We had travelled overland to the coast under an escort provided by my uncle. Not that there was much danger from the Saxons in that direction, but there were robbers. The roads had not been safe since the Romans had left Britain. Each petty king tried to keep law and order in his own territory, but the borders were often vague, and poorly guarded. After what had happened to my mother, Lucian was taking no chances, and he managed to provide our wagon with a guard of twenty cavalrymen under the command of one of his best officers, Valerian.

The roads were dry, and we made good time. Our journey lay largely along the old roads which the Romans had built for their armies. Badly in need of repair as they were, they were still the fastest routes anywhere. Say what you like about the Romans, they could build. Indeed, looking at our soldiers one could almost believe the Romans had never left. Their uniforms and armour were just like those in the mosaics at Uncle Lucian's house. As I peeped between the canvas hangings at the back of the wagon, I tried to imagine myself a member of Maximus' army, bound for the coast – and onward to Gaul and the heart of the Empire.

It was a whole new world to me for I had seldom left my uncle's estate before. I looked on avidly as we passed by hamlets and farmsteads. Whole families were working to get the harvest in, perhaps to save it from the weather, perhaps from the Saxons. Suddenly I realised for the first time what the invasions really meant. I had a vision of all these thriving farms and peaceful villages being swept away on a tide of blood and fire – the scene at our own estate multiplied more times than one mind can imagine. For a child it was too much, and I burst out in a fit of uncontrollable weeping.

'What is it, Keri?' My mother, rocked into half-sleep by the swaying of the wagon, was taken by surprise.

I could tell her nothing. I just wept for all the farms and villages. For Uncle Lucian's estate, for my giant, for my mother's lost honour. For a Britain perched on the edge of an abyss. When no more tears came I drifted into sleep, my head resting on mother's breast. She did not need to ask me what was wrong again.

We arrived the next day in the southern port of Clausentum, which is on the River Itchen, just a few miles downriver from Venta Belgarum. Arriving at night, we had seen little of Venta, which is a lively, bustling place. Or was. God knows what it is like now the Saxons have it. They have even changed the name – Uintancaestir, or Winchester, they call it now.

Clausentum was not much of a port. The ships just pulled in at the riverside, where wooden landing stages had been built. It was nothing like the great stone harbours I have seen since. Even the fishing ports of Armorica can boast better. Still to me at that age it was all an adventure. I watched the merchants haggling on the quayside, as the slaves loaded or unloaded their cargoes.

The buildings of Clausentum were well suited to its standing – wattle and daub huts for the most part, although there was a small wooden fort in the Roman style. Valerian, thinking it might take some time to find a ship with a trustworthy captain, wanted to find suitable lodging for us. Mother, on the other hand, was anxious to get on with the voyage. She did not want to waste precious days lodging in some filthy tavern, surrounded by drunks and whores.

'Besides,' she said, 'the winter will be upon us soon. Once the weather turns no captain will venture out. I have no wish to be stranded in this backwater for the winter, nor to return to my brother's house.'

Valerian grumbled. He was against our going, for he thought the sea and sailors more dangerous than the Saxons. Still, he had his orders, however crazy he thought them, and Mother was a formidable commander! Shaking his head at the follies of women, he went the rounds of the harbour, asking each captain where he was bound next, and trying to gain some impression of his character. At length we began to get hungry, and Mother decided to retire to a tavern for at least the midday meal.

It was a fairly low place, but clean enough, and some very appetising smells were wafting from the kitchen. The owner, a swarthy Welshman, was delighted to have such distinguished guests. Nothing was too much trouble, and he soon had plates of steaming food in front of us. It was a meat pie, I remember, with herbs and vegetables to his own recipe (well, probably whatever he had over from yesterday). He was as generous with information as with his attention.

'Lesser Britain, is it? If you want my advice – begging your pardon, *Domina* – I could recommend Meriadauc. He's a fine sailor, they say, and he's honest.

I don't give credit to many, but he always pays up. He'll sell a cargo for a fair price, and bring every denarius back. Not many will do that these days. There's highwaymen on the seas as well as the roads.'

'Could you fetch this Meriadauc to us?'

'Why, surely, *Domina*. I have a boy I can send. Here, boy! The lady wants you to run an errand!'

Meriadauc duly arrived. He was a young man, about twenty-five, I think, and looked strong – in character as well as body. He had fine features for a common man, and his skin already permanently bronzed by the sun and wind. His black hair was cut short in the Roman style. He spoke to Mother politely but without the obsequiousness of the innkeeper.

'You are the lady who seeks passage to Armorica?' His voice was velvety and deep.

'I am Olivia Galeria, yes. I seek passage for myself and my daughter.'

He looked at me without comment. I saw his eyes were as deep a blue as the sea he sailed in.

'Just the two of you? No man?'

'My husband was killed by the Saxons. We are going to relatives in Kemper.'

'Every year there are more. I'm sorry for your misfortune, Olivia Galeria, but be careful it doesn't lead you into another.'

'I don't need your advice, Master Captain,' said Mother in irritation. 'Just your ship.'

'Maybe.' He paused a moment. 'If you're emigrating you'll have valuables with you.'

'What is that to you?'

'I'll tell you, Olivia Galeria. My safety, perhaps. Oh, and yours.'

'*Domina*, if you take ship with me you are in for a week's voyage. Some of my crew are new men, not well known to me. I'd rather know what is under my protection, lest anyone should be tempted.'

'Your... protection?' I think Mother was insulted. She shot an exasperated glance at the innkeeper, whose choice the captain was.

'Olivia Galeria, once at sea the ship and all in her are my responsibility. I have never lost a ship or a passenger, and I don't intend to start now. That's why I use the word "protection". It is a matter of honour.'

'I'm sorry. I understand.'

To hear Mother apologise to someone was a new experience. I decided that Meriadauc was worth watching.

'Well, *Domina*, if you are dead set on sailing with me we will need to arrange things quickly. I sail on the afternoon tide.'

'This afternoon? But surely the tide was going down when we arrived. It cannot be high tide again so soon.'

He looked impressed with her observation, but smiled.

'Not in most ports, but I see you have not heard of the four tides of Gueid Guith.'

'Gueid Guith?'

'You probably know it by the Roman name – Vectis. The Saxons call it the island of Wiht. Further downstream this river joins another, and they flow into a wide estuary called the Soluente. However, the Soluente splits again into two arms, running to the sea in both directions around two sides of the great island of Gueid Guith. When the high tide moves down the Channel it comes up one arm of the Soluente and goes down. Then, having moved around the seaward side of the island it comes back up the other arm of the Soluente and gives us a second tide. Thus, the harbours here have twice as many tides as any other place, and if we time it right we can almost fly down the Soluente, especially when the wind is right also, as it is today.'

'Why is there not a great port here, then?'

He smiled, 'It is too far west. The crossing is too wide here, or was before the Saxons barred us from Kent. Now we use it because we must. Even so, sailors do not like to stray too far from the land.'

Just then Valerian came in, grumbling because everyone he spoke to was recommending some fellow called Meriadauc, who was nowhere to be found. He was not entirely pleased to discover that Meriadauc had been with us all the time, but soon mellowed when he saw what kind of man the captain was. After twenty years of military command Valerian was a good judge of men, and Meriadauc's air of quiet strength obviously impressed him. They soon settled on terms, Uncle Lucian having charged Valerian with buying a passage for us. He was still unsure of our safety, and continued to say so. Finally it was Meriadauc who suggested the answer.

'Sir, why don't you send a couple of your men across with the lady? Two armed professional soldiers ought to be protection enough. I can bring them back on the return journey, or find some other ship for them.'

Lucian had planned this himself originally but Mother had refused to be nursemaided. Now she caved in, anxious to get things settled before we missed one more tide. 'Oh, all right! Do as you think best – you will anyway! I don't know why I bother arguing with men. Come on, Keri, let us go and look at the ship.'

'To the right,' said Meriadauc, grinning. 'She's called the *Boreas*. Handsomest ship in the harbour.'

She certainly was a handsome vessel. Her hull was black with the pitch used to seal the timber against the sea, but she had a smart nameplate at the bow with her name in proud Roman capitals: *BOREAS,* the North Wind. The letters were burned in with a hot iron in contrast to the faded paint on the other ships. She was obviously well cared for. The decks were scrubbed, all ropes neatly stowed, and some barrels on the deck firmly lashed down.

'It looks a well run ship,' said Mother. 'We should be comfortable enough for a few days.'

Soon we were joined by Meriadauc and Valerian. The soldiers were bringing our baggage, and trying not to appear too conspicuous lest they be chosen to sail with us. Meriadauc hailed his second in command, a rotund smiling Armorican with a beard and an enormous moustache. He had a proper name, but was known by all as Snorebeard. He was an old friend of Meriadauc's from his earliest days at sea, and the two men, though different in many ways, were very close. Snorebeard came down the gangway – a broad plank – and was introduced. He nodded to Valerian, bowed to Mother, and saluted me most solemnly. When I shyly hid behind Mother he roared with laughter.

'Never mind, little one! Old Snorebeard may be big, but he doesn't bite!'

'That's not what the girls at Branwen's say!' commented Meriadauc, but Snorebeard only laughed again, and began shouting orders to the crew about stowing our luggage. Meanwhile we were led on board by the captain and shown our cabin.

It was a tiny affair, but as comfortable as any. There was one bed, which we would have to share. Underneath was stowage for some of our luggage and the essential chamberpot. ('The men must hang over the side,' said Snorebeard, 'but it would hardly be seemly in your case.') There was very little space, but it was not intended to be more than a sleeping place. In good weather there was space on deck, in bad weather the ship would put in at the nearest harbour. Somehow it seemed a very small thing in which to brave the ocean. Nonetheless we did so that same afternoon, and flew down the Soluente on the receding tide, passing the dark form of Gueid Guith in the fading light as we headed for a new life.

There was a fresh breeze blowing down the Channel, and the few clouds sped along towards the setting sun, which floated above the misty western horizon like a ball of polished copper. The whole of the west was shrouded in veils of light – red, pink, mauve and orange.

'A fine sunset,' said Snorebeard, who had quietly materialised at the rail by my side. 'It will be a fine day tomorrow.'

'Do you think so, Captain?'

He chuckled. 'Bless you, little one. Don't let Meriadauc hear you say that. There's only one captain here, and that's him. Plain Snorebeard is good enough for me.'

'Why do they call you Snorebeard?' I had been dying to ask him this, but had only now lost my shyness.

'Because of my beard, and because I snore like a lion roaring, they tell me.' Again he chuckled.

'And how does Meriadauc come to be captain of the ship? He seems only a young man'.

'He seems....? Ha, ha!' Snorebeard guffawed loudly. 'By Neptune, there's a bit of your mother in you, young lady! Always questions. And a few straight answers, I'll be bound.'

'I only wondered.'

'Ah, of course you did, little one. Well, since you've asked, Meriadauc owns this ship. His father was a merchant in Namnetum. That's on the river Liger on the southern borders of Lesser Britain. It's a great river, and runs for miles and miles back into Gaul. They grow vines there, and corn, and make fine cloth, so there's plenty of work for traders, even in these times. Anyway, the tribesmen there – the Veneti – they're a wild lot at times. The country isn't safe. Meriadauc's father was killed by robbers near there, and a good deal of his money taken. Meriadauc put what was left into buying the ship. He was already a good sailor, and liked the life. Anyway, he says he'd rather have a good ship than a house any day.'

'You mean he lives here? All the time?'

'Hey, it's not so bad. His cabin is a good deal bigger than yours. He's more comfortable than many with houses. Anyway, he stays ashore during the worst of the winter. Then he lodges at a little place in Kemper, where you're going. Mind you, one winter when the money was poor he sailed us all down south where it was still fair weather and we traded all the winter as well.'

'You must have sailed everywhere.' My eyes were wide as plates.

'Not quite. Some places we've left for next year!' And off he went into one of his mighty laughs.

'Keri!' My mother was calling. 'Here you are! I hope you haven't been keeping the sailors from their work.'

Snorebeard laughed. 'Not a bit of it, *Domina*. She's a pleasure to talk to, that one, and I've nothing more urgent right now. Not until we anchor.'

'Anchor?'

'Anchor for the night, *Domina*. There aren't many places we can sail after dark these days. The Romans used to have lighthouses on the Kent coast, but the Saxons don't bother. Down here we're best anchoring in a sheltered spot until dawn, and then getting across the Narrow Sea tomorrow. The way the wind is, we'll be well sheltered here on the lee shore of Gueid Guith.'

Well sheltered! I had cause to remember that remark during the night. The rocking of the ship was enough to make me queasy when the sea was calm. But in the night the wind freshened and the waves rose, and I began to be very ill. My mother soon followed, partly from having to cope with my sickness in the confines of our cabin. At one point she dragged me up on deck, hoping that a breath of fresh air would make us both feel better. All that happened was that we both got damp from the sea spray and had to change when we went below. Finally, totally empty and totally exhausted, I fell asleep.

Chapter Three

I awoke late next morning. For a while I lay dozing, unclear as to where I was. Then I opened my eyes fully and saw the wooden wall of the cabin, and remembered. The rocking of the ship was much less now, and the creaking of her timbers had a slower, more purposeful rhythm. The water was rushing, rather than lapping the sides, and the sails flapped regularly in the breeze. The sun was bright, as I could tell from the little that crept in past the shutter on the tiny window-hole. Snorebeard's 'fine day' was here.

Apart from the occasional shouted order there was no human sound. I lay there a while, taking in the atmosphere. Then a loud rumble from my stomach reminded me that it was empty, and I now felt well enough to eat. I hopped out of the narrow bunk and put on a plain linen shift. Then, realising it might be cold on deck, I pulled a shawl around my shoulders and went out.

For a moment the light hurt my eyes, but when they were able to see I gasped in astonishment. There was no land in sight at all! All around us was the tossing ocean. The restless waves heaved and fell away, their tops crowned with wisps of spray as the wind brushed them. I was enthralled. Never had I imagined anything like this. I saw Snorebeard and my mother talking by the rail. She looked haggard, as if her sickness was still with her.

'Ah, little one, you are awake!' Snorebeard greeted me cheerfully. 'And hungry, I'll be bound.'

I nodded.

'Well, I'd tell you to see the cook, but he's an ugly old man, not a handsome fellow like me, and the sight would only turn your stomach again.'

This brought a shout of pretended rage from the youth who doubled as cook when there was nothing more urgent. He was particularly good-looking. Snorebeard only laughed, as usual, and went to get me some bread and fruit.

'Well, Keri, I hope you are feeling better.'

'Yes, Mamma. I think the sickness has gone.'

'You are lucky. I wish mine had. I think I could never get used to this. How the sailors do it for a living I just don't know. It's not natural, all this being thrown about on the water.'

'It's not so bad like this,' I said. 'Now we're underway it's different, as if we're really going somewhere.'

'Under way? You're talking like a sailor already.'

'Snorebeard says that. He's been everywhere, Mamma. Well, almost everywhere. He's saving some places for next year.'

In spite of the state she was in she laughed out loud.

'Don't listen to everything the sailors tell you. Sailors are terrible liars! They all have tales of sea monsters, sirens, and the like. I should take them with a pinch of salt.'

'You slander us, *Domina*!'

My mother wheeled round. 'Oh, Meriadauc, I didn't mean it like that!'

He was smiling, and held up his hand to ward off her apology. 'I understand. And anyway you are probably right. For the most part I place little trust in travellers' tales myself. Usually the man telling them wants to make himself seem important. If not, a few questions can often show up how little he is really certain of. How big was the thing? How close was he? How good the light? People love to make mysteries, though.'

'You might solve one mystery for me by telling me how long you think we will be at sea.'

He laughed. 'Had enough already, *Domina*? Well, unless some god drops by to tell me about the weather over the next few days I'm afraid that's one mystery I can't entirely clear up. But I can say that if this weather holds we shall cut a couple of days off the journey. Once round the Armorican Peninsula, though, the coast turns south. We could do with a change of wind then.'

'And if the wind doesn't change?'

'Then we must wait for it, or sail against it. Either way it will take much longer than I would like, so perhaps we had better pray for favourable winds.'

While this conversation took place I got on with eating. I felt quite steady this morning, and ready to fill the aching gap where my stomach used to be. I had been engaged in this for some time when I noticed that there was a change of atmosphere. Meriadauc was talking busily to some of his men, and our two soldiers were examining their swords with more than casual interest. I stood up, looking for the cause of this sudden seriousness.

Not two miles away, I suppose, there was another ship. She looked bigger and heavier than ours, but the spray made it difficult to see details. Meriadauc shielded his eyes against the sun every so often and tried to get a better view, but then turned and shook his head. Snorebeard who was near him, just shrugged and passed on order to the crew.

'Olivia Galeria!' Meriadauc called. My mother appeared as if in answer from down below, where she been lying on her sickbed again.

'There is another ship not far off. We are under full sail, but she is gaining slowly.'

'Is it pirates?' said my mother. 'Good. I'd rather die than go on with the sickness.'

'We don't know who it is. She looks too big for a pirate – usually they are only local chiefs with small ships – but one can't be sure. She's not long and low enough for a Saxon, the gods be thanked.'

'So who else could it be?'

'She could be a laburnian. When she's close we'll see.'

'What's a laburnian?' I asked.

'A Roman bireme, little lady,' said Snorebeard, much to my mother's interest.

'Roman? Here?'

Oh, yes. Aëtius still holds the northern part of Gaul in the name of Rome, though he's hemmed in by the Armorican British on the west and the barbarian tribes on every other side.'

'Not the Saxons again?'

'Their cousins the Franks and the Alamanni to the east, and the Burgundians and Visigoths to the south. The Visigoths have most of southern Gaul and northern Spain. Aëtius is a good general, though, and he knows how to play one off against the other. They're all meant to be federates, of course.'

'Federates!' When the barbarians couldn't be kept out, Rome allowed them land inside the Empire. They called them federates and tried to use them to defend the frontiers against further attacks, and against each other. The trouble was, they soon got ideas of their own about how much land they wanted and where. By the time of our voyage there was still a Roman Empire in the west, but in name only. Vortigern repeated Rome's mistakes in Britain with his Saxon federates, only a few years after the barbarians had sacked Rome for the first time.

We watched as the other ship slowly overhauled us, and at last it became apparent that she was indeed a Roman ship. Although larger than the *Boreas* she had much more sail to put to the wind, and was thus making a better speed.

'Well, that's all right, surely,' said Mother when she heard it was a Roman.

'Maybe,' said Meriadauc, 'Maybe. I don't like warships, though. The treatment you get depends very much on who's at war with whom.'

'Not with Britain, surely?'

'Not as far as we know. Anyway, which part of Britain? Britain isn't a province now, nor yet a recognised nation. Aëtius might well have a quarrel with some British chief. Anyway, legally speaking both Britain and Armorica are in revolt against Roman rule. You can't be sure that they'll never try to reimpose it.'

The issue was soon to be resolved, however, as the Roman ship drew within hailing distance. Someone who evidently had lungs of steel bellowed a greeting.

'Ahoy, there! *Boreas*!'

Meriadauc nodded to Snorebeard, who cupped his hands around his mouth to reply.

'Who hails the *Boreas*?'

'Quintus Flavius, tribune, and commander of the *Draco Maris.*'

'*The Sea Dragon*?' mused my mother. 'That's a very Saxonish name for a Roman ship. And every petty official calls himself tribune these days.'

'Quintus Flavius!' roared Snorebeard. 'You are a snail-eating bastard son of a Gaul, and as good a sailor as my grandmother!'

We were astonished at this outburst, which was met with a silence from the other side. Meriadauc and Snorebeard were chuckling together and shaking their heads, while watching the other ship drift closer. We could see that their spokesman had climbed down from the rail, and another man had climbed up. From his bearing and ornate military dress it appeared to be the tribune himself.

'Snorebeard,' he called in a rather more cultured voice than his spokesman. 'Is that grinning pirate Meriadauc aboard?'

Snorebeard laughed. 'He is, your honour, although it was you we feared might be the pirate at first.'

'Where are you bound?'

'Kemper and Namnetum, And you?'

'The same, and on south to the Mediterranean.'

'To Rome?''

'Hardly. Rome is being run by the Goths nowadays, and the Emperor has retired to Ravenna. Damn the barbarians to hell. Those that aren't pagans are heretics, which is worse. Anyway, we are bound to the Emperor's court at Ravenna. Aëtius doesn't trust the overland route at present, with the Burgundians and Alamanni running all over it.'

'Who can blame him? These are difficult times.'

'Yes. I suppose you'll want a free naval escort now that we've met?'

'An escort? Whatever makes you think so? Don't you know an Armorican is worth ten Romans any day? As a matter of fact, we thought we might escort *you*!'

This cheeky assertion was met with peals of laughter from the other ship, and a chorus of catcalls and rude gestures from the crew. At the age of five I was mystified by the way these men demonstrated respect and friendship by trading insults, but my mother told me it was usual amongst men. The shouted conversation drew to a close with Quintus Flavius saying he would sail ahead of us and lead us in to a safe anchorage for the night. He also invited himself aboard for the evening, saying that there were things that Meriadauc ought to know. On this ominous note he turned to give orders to his crew, the sails bellied out, and the laburnian forged ahead.

Before long the coast of Gaul was in sight. Meriadauc and Snorebeard had a hasty conference about our position, and followed in the wake of the Roman ship, now two or three miles ahead. She seemed to maintain that distance no, as if Quintus Flavius was not too anxious to lose us. As the light was fading we swung into a bay that Meriadauc obviously knew well, and found the laburnian already at anchor there.

I was rather frustrated to find that my first close sight of the Gallic coast was to be in the dwindling twilight. I could hardly see anything. There were no lights visible on shore, so presumably this bay was just a sheltered spot rather than a port. Soon both ships had lights showing, so the captains considered it an anchorage safe from pirates as well as tempests. I wandered the deck long after most of the crew had gone below, peering into the gloom and trying to make out shapes. I was still there when Mother called me below for supper and bed.

'Why are you not eating, Mamma? You're not still sick, are you?'

'I am much better, although I doubt if I could eat much. But no, that's not the reason. I am dining with Meriadauc this evening. He has a guest.'

'I know. Quintus Flavius.'

'There, you know it all already!'

'What is he like, Mamma, this Quintus Flavius?'

She laughed. 'Now, how should I know that? I never met the man before. Meriadauc knows him, and thinks he is a good man. It seems they fought together when Meriadauc was younger.'

'Was it a big battle?'

'Perhaps you should ask him yourself. Gods, I care little enough for tales of war. Anyway, I am to dine with them tonight in Meriadauc's cabin, so you must cease your chatter and get ready for bed.'

Soon I was tucked up in the little bunk and Mother made herself ready. Poor as the circumstances were, she said, it was her first social engagement since before the battle at Lucian's villa, and she was not going to appear like some peasant. She stripped off her dress, despite the cold, and washed in the bowl of cold water which was all we could get for the purpose. Then she took her little case of toiletries and rubbed her skin with oils and perfumes until it glistened. In our little cabin the perfume was overpowering and I wrinkled my nose. She smiled.

'When you are a woman you will know why sometimes these preparations are necessary. The fact is, we may have been driven from our home and our country, but ours is a good family. We have standards to maintain. When I go to dine with the captains I want them to see that we are people of substance, and deserving of their respect. For that I must feel right, look right and' – picking up another perfume jar – 'smell right. However, since we cannot bath here, I am afraid that artifice must do what cleanliness can't.' And with a look of distaste she applied the perfume liberally under each arm. Then she opened one of our boxes and found a plain white linen robe which she pronounced fit to wear. Having slipped this on, she tried to arrange her hair with the help of a little piece of polished copper which was her travelling mirror. She was less than satisfied with the result, but said it was the best she could do. Then she brought out a blue-dyed woollen shawl and threw it round her shoulders, fastening it with an enamelled brooch.

'Well, Keri, how does your mother look?'

'You look pretty, Mamma, but you would look pretty if you had only a sack to wear.'

'Bless you, child, you're worth your keep! Now, shall I leave the candle? You must be very careful not to knock it over.'

'No, Mamma, there is a bright moon, I will be all right.'

'Very well. Try to sleep. I think I will be late tonight.'

Goodnight, Mamma.'

And so I lay in the darkness, thinking how strange it must be to be a grown-up woman. A soft, cushiony chest, and hair on your body, and oil and perfume, and dining with men ...

I awoke much later, still in darkness. From outside the ship came the sound of wavelets lapping against the timbers. The ship was steady as a rock. As I lay dozing I became aware of another sound – the murmur of approaching voices. It seemed that Meriadauc's guests were departing. At least, one of them was. I could hear the voices of Quintus Flavius and Meriadauc.

'Take care, then' Meriadauc. All is not well in Lesser Britain, nor in the rest of Gaul. Aëtius is an honourable man, and knows the barbarians well. He bears the Armorican British no malice. But the Emperor's will is difficult to gauge. He is a wily old man, and one who strikes the weak before they become strong. That is how he has survived so long. He has had scores of rivals, or suspected rivals, murdered. I can't tell what his intentions may be towards Aëtius, or towards Armorica.'

'Well, Quintus, you've done me a service this evening in telling me so much. I shall be that bit better prepared.'

'I hope so, my friend. It may be some time before I see you again, so God be with you. And with that fine lady of yours.'

'Mine?'

'Don't sound so surprised. I know you of old. Anyway, she's a beautiful woman and you're a handsome enough fellow. Why not?'

'She's a noblewoman. And a relative of King Gradlon.'

'*Was* a noblewoman, and only a distant relative. Besides, you're far from a pauper. Maybe not patrician, but your family is known and respected in Armorica. What is she? A young widow of moderate means, and with a child.'

'Yes and a child who sleeps behind that door there, so perhaps we'd better talk elsewhere.'

They moved away, and their voices faded to a low murmur, in which I could make out nothing. I think I must have dozed off again, for it seemed almost immediately after that i heard my mother and Meriadauc saying goodnight outside the door. She seemed to be a little giggly, and I wondered if she was tipsy.

'I hope you enjoyed our evening, Olivia Galeria, and that all the political talk was not too boring.'

'You mustn't assume that I have no brain just because I am a woman, captain.'

There was a low chuckle in the darkness. 'Indeed, I would never assume that of you. And I doubt if you would let it be assumed!'

'Well, then, as it happens I did have a good evening. It is a long time since I enjoyed the pleasures of the dinner table.'

There was a noticeable hesitation on Meriadauc's part, the first time I had heard him sound less than confident.

'And are those the only pleasures you have not enjoyed for a long time?'

Now my mother giggled. 'Meriadauc, I think you have grown bold with too much wine.'

'I'm sorry if I have offended you.'

'Gods, man, you have done no such thing. It is a man's right to ask.'

'I was thinking of the difference in our social positions.'

'Sweet man! I am well aware of my social position, Meriadauc. I am from a patrician family. But that will count for little now. Oh, I want to keep up standards, but that is pride rather than any idea of my own importance. Have no fear, you haven't presumed.'

'But?'

'You asked me a question, and I shall answer it. I have not enjoyed the pleasures of which you speak since my husband was killed.'

'Is his memory sacred to you, then?'

Mother laughed out loud, and then stifled her laughter. 'We mustn't wake the child. Sacred to me? Gods, that sounds like a lovelorn maiden. No, it wasn't a love match, only the poor marry for love. He was a good enough husband in his way, but it is not for his sake I lead a chaste life now.'

'What then?'

'Well, at first the pleasures of love were not widely available on my elder brother's estate. He is a devout Christian, though a soldier, and more used to handling his sword than any other weapon.' They both giggled here, although I could not see why. 'Then the Saxons came.'

'You told us of that this evening.'

'I did not tell everything. After ...what the Saxons did to me, I am not sure I will ever be able to taste those pleasures again.'

There was a silence.

'I see.'

'What do you see, Meriadauc? An unclean woman?'

'What on earth do you mean?'

'That was what my brother saw. I should have died, you see. Defending my honour, and all that. Actually, I was beaten senseless and hardly knew what was happening, so I could not have defended an ant. None the less, glad as he was that I had not been killed, my living presence was an embarrassment to him. So now you know the truth about the woman you have just propositioned.'

'Olivia, I am not your brother. All of that makes no difference to me.'

'Then you are a good man, and you will realise that it has made a difference to me. I ... I cannot see certain pleasures as I did before. I am not sure the damage will ever be undone, but if it is, it will not be here, in a few snatched hours. It will take time, and patience.'

'Sometimes, when you are beating against the wind in a rough sea, there is a temptation to give in, to seek some safe anchorage and wait until the wind changes. But then at last you round the headland, and suddenly the wind is behind you and the struggle has been worth it. A sailor learns patience, Olivia. May I visit you when you are settled in Kemper?'

'Bless you, Meriadauc. Of course you may. Only, I have not promised anything.'

'That's understood.'

'Is it? I don't want you to deny yourself for my sake. I mean – '

'Bless you, too, then. I know what you mean. Goodnight to you, Olivia Galeria.'

'Still so formal? I liked it better when you just called me Olivia.'

'That was a slip. On board I will stick to the formality, crew's gossip being what it is.'

There was a short silence then, and I wondered if they had kissed. Then the door opened and my mother came in stealthily, trying not to wake me. She was asleep herself soon after snuggling into the warm bed beside me, but I lay awake pondering on the conversations I had overheard. I decided in the end that I knew too little of both politics and love to understand either, but I resolved to remember it all, for one day I would know.

In the morning I said nothing about it, and nor did Mother. Besides, there were other things to think about. We set sail at first light, and the sea turned rough almost at once. Both of us were very sick again, and kept to our cabin most of the time. The cook brought us some herbal concoction which he swore was a sovereign remedy, but it stayed down no better than anything else. All that day we were tossed on Ocean's broad shoulders. And the next. At night we had little sleep, and after two days of stormy weather we were nearly exhausted.

On the morning of the following day I awoke to find the ship steady. The light filtering through our window was dull, and from somewhere came a slow, rhythmic sound, like a sighing or a low chanting in the distance. I quickly threw on some clothes and ran up on deck, to see that we were entering the mouth of a river. On both sides were wooded banks, set back from the water by mud flats. Only a few yards in front was the *Draco Maris*, her sails now struck and her double-banked oars dipping in time to the rowers' low chant. On the left bank was a small village, with strange-looking people going about their business. Strange, because they were slant-eyed and had long black hair and sallow skins. I fairly flew below decks again.

'Mamma! Mamma! We're there.'

My mother, looking still very much the worse for wear, came on deck and watched with me, as we slipped silently by the village on half sail. And so, drifting gently under a leaden sky, we came on up the Odet to Kemper, and hope of a new life under the protection of King Gradlon.

Chapter Four

Our arrival in Kemper got off to a bad start. The fact that my mother arrived with two soldiers was instantly remarked upon by the crowds at the harbour. It was not that it was unusual for the better-off traveller to go with an armed escort, but soldiers in what looked like Roman uniform were another thing altogether. The crowd which always greeted the arrival of any ship was especially large, and some individuals called out insults to the men, until my mother asked them to go below out of sight. None the less, a detachment of troops soon arrived from the palace to see what was going on, rumours having reached them within minutes of our arrival.

The *Draco Maris* was an object of even more interest, although a Roman ship was no stranger to Kemper. For fear of offending Aëtius, Gradlon had apparently agreed to let his ships take on supplies at Kemper, provided weapons were not brought ashore. However, a laburnian was the largest class of vessel to be seen there, and visited only rarely.

I was still on deck with Mother when Gradlon's soldiers arrived. There were only a dozen or so, and although armed they were not in full battle order. A slim red-haired man of about forty in a white tunic and purple cloak seemed to be in charge of them. He bore no weapon, but the way that the crowd parted before him testified to the authority he carried. Meriadauc knew him, though I sensed that he did not like him much. His manner towards the newcomer was too formal for that. Still, he indicated his acceptance of the other's authority by leaving the ship to meet him on his own ground.

'I greet you, Tiernan. I trust His Majesty is well?'

'Indeed, as well as ever.' This seemed a strangely noncommittal thing to say, but it was explained later. 'Meriadauc, you know well that His Majesty does not relish the sight of foreign arms here, yet I understand that you have soldiers aboard.'

'Only two, Tiernan. They are a private escort for a passenger we have carried from Britain.' He indicated my mother, still standing on the deck. 'Her brother is a military commander fighting the Saxons, and also a kinsman of His Majesty. She has come to ask permission to settle here.'

'Indeed? I know nothing of this.' But he inclined his head towards Mother, to be on the safe side.

'There was no time to write and wait for a reply before the winter gales,' Meriadauc went on, but Mother breezed down the gangway and interrupted him.

'I am Olivia Galeria. My grandfather and the grandfather of King Gradlon were cousins who crossed the Narrow Sea together in the time of Maximus. I have a letter-tablet here from my brother and protector to the King. And who, may I ask, are you?'

The man was evidently disconcerted. His hazel eyes indicated his annoyance, but he managed a taut smile.

'I greet you, Olivia Galeria. I am Tiernan, His Majesty's steward. If you will give me the letter I will see that it is delivered promptly to His Majesty. In the meantime, it would be best if a lady such as yourself were to stay aboard, I think, rather than go ashore to mix with the hoi-polloi.'

'Thank you for your advice, Tiernan, but please do not leave us waiting too long. I have not come all this way to be kept at the quayside. The sooner we step on to dry land the better, as far as I am concerned.'

'Indeed, Olivia Galeria, I understand.'

He turned on his heel and barked an order at the soldiers, two of whom stood guard on the quay while the rest followed him away.

'Who is that arrogant little toad?' asked my mother benignly. Meriadauc laughed.

'He is called the King's steward, but you might almost say regent. He has considerable power, and it is not always used for the best.'

'Regent? Is King Gradlon away, then, or in his dotage?'

'Neither, *Domina*. He is rarely seen in public, but they say he is afflicted with a deep melancholia. Almost madness.'

'Gods, I wish someone had told us before we left Britain! Is the situation here no better than there?'

'Oh, I shouldn't worry too much about that. Gradlon is a popular king because of his stout defence of the people in the past. He has stood up to Aëtius at times, and fought off pirates from Friesia and Ireland. Before his melancholia struck him he was set to become a real power in this part of the world.'

'And now?'

'Only time will tell. He still appears to dispense justice, and does so pretty well by all accounts. But the steward tends to run things day to day, and he's not a pleasant man. A great one for the ladies, they say, but not much of a following outside the bedchamber, if you'll pardon my frankness.'

My mother giggled. 'It seems I shall have to get used to it.'

He shot her a quick glance, and then went on, 'Tiernan has no real power amongst the people and little amongst the army, so I don't think there's much risk of him deposing Gradlon. He's unpleasant, but not dangerous. He'll advise Gradlon against letting you stay.'

'How do you know that?'

'Because you stood your ground. You put him in his place instead of kissing his, er, feet.'

'I see.' Mother pulled a face.

'Oh, don't worry, *Domina*. Gradlon can hardly refuse your request. A lady in distress, and a kinswoman at that?'

'A distant kinswoman.'

'Makes no difference. He's honour bound to take you in, and he's an honourable man, melancholic or not.'

And so it proved. Within the hour a messenger came from the palace – not Tiernan this time – who said that His Majesty would be pleased to receive us. He brought slaves with a litter to carry us, too, so it was more than mere politeness! Mother turned to Meriadauc to say goodbye, but he merely said that he would soon see us again, as he was bidden to call at the palace tomorrow.

I saw little of the town on our journey. Mother kept the litter curtains closed against the curious. Occasionally they would flap open a little, and I would catch a glimpse of the bustling streets. There were stalls and open-fronted shops selling everything from sandals to wine, meat and bread. There were strange fruits and vegetables, and both strange and familiar smells filled the air – fresh and rotting fruit, frying meats, and the yeasty smell of freshly baked bread. On every side the vendors cried their inducements to buy this or that, and declared the superiority of their own stock over that of their neighbours. At one place I even saw a number of women hanging out of windows and calling to passers-by. I asked my mother what they were selling, but she drew the curtain shut and said nothing. I was too young then to realise that they were selling themselves.

All of this was new to me, not only because of our recent arrival, but because I was so unfamiliar with city life. I had been brought up mainly on my uncle's estate in the country, only visiting Camulodunum occasionally. Even then it had always been in some style, my uncle being who he was, and I had not been allowed to see the life of the streets at such close quarters. It was overwhelming in its colour and variety. I was fascinated by it, and immediately resolved to return and see it all properly.

We were going up a hill now. The litter was tilted slightly, although the poor slaves were struggling to keep it steady as they laboured up the slope. As was usual in these times, Gradlon's palace was a much a fortress as anything else, and the proper place for a fortress is on a hilltop. With the curtains closed we saw little of the outside walls, but soon the litter was in the shadow as we passed through the gate into the palace grounds. We were carried a little further, and then came to rest. The messenger, who had been walking alongside all this time, drew back the curtain.

'*Domina*, we have arrived. If you will be so good as to step down I will show you to the audience chamber.'

'The audience chamber? Gods, man, his Majesty may be ready to see me, but I am hardly in a fit state to see him! May I not at least wash my face and run a comb through my hair?'

'I am sorry, *Domina*, I did not think. My instructions were to take you straight to His Majesty, but I daresay a few minutes will make no difference.'

He called for a servant to take us to a guest room, and provide us with water. I soon realised that Mother was less concerned with washing than with her face-paints. She was a noblewoman by birth and upbringing, and she was jolly well going to look like one before the King, kinsman or not. After only five minutes' attention, she had brightened her face, emphasised her eyes and lips, and tidied her hair. In another three she had scrubbed me in all the parts that showed, and brought some order into my own tousled auburn locks.

'There, that'll have to do. Right, girl' – this to the servant – 'we're ready, or as ready as may be.'

The girl led us back down a series of passages to the entrance hall, where Tiernan was waiting for us.

'Olivia Galeria, may I apologise for our lack of hospitality. If you are ready?'

His appraising glance was enough to tell us that Mother's cosmetic preparations were worth their price. She smiled at me and took my hand as Tiernan led us down a long corridor towards a set of carved double doors. These were tall and strong, and evidently a Roman relic – we British do not generally go in for that sort of cumbrous ornament. An inscription in Latin was carved over the lintel, but I could not see it properly. I was about to ask Mother what it said when the doors swung back and we were ushered into Gradlon's audience chamber.

I don't know what I expected. Something grand and colourful, I think. Perhaps a golden throne, and a canopy of rich tapestry, with courtiers dressed in fine clothes and jewels. That, I had been led to believe, was how kings lived. I was disappointed.

The room was large, with a raised dais at the far end. On the left was an outer wall, with a row of windows. Most of these, however, were shuttered. Only one was partially open, allowing a little light to penetrate the gloom. In front of this was a small table where a scribe sat, stylus and wax tablets at the ready. Mother's firm step faltered for a moment, then she pressed on down the length of the room. The shadows on the right side seemed empty, but as our eyes grew accustomed to the half-light we saw that there were one or two shadowy figures there. It was impossible to see who they were, even if we had been familiar with the notables of Gradlon's court. At first it seemed as if Gradlon himself was not there. Then there was a movement in the shadows ahead. Tiernan, three paces in front, stopped and bowed.

'Your Majesty,' he said quietly. 'I present to you Olivia Galeria.'

Mother curtsied to the floor, and waited for Gradlon to come forward and raise her, according to the custom. At her side I did likewise. There was a moment's silence; then a weary voice spoke from the shadows.

'Rise.'

Mother replied from her kneeling position. 'I am sorry if our presence here displeases you, Your Majesty. We have observed the customs as well as we are able.'

There was a flurry of whispers from the right, and Tiernan protested.

'Olivia Galeria!'

The King himself only chuckled.

'Well, even a king has no right to be rude to a guest, and a kinswoman at that.'

He shuffled across from his throne and stepped down from the dais. As he passed through the shaft of sunlight I was startled by my brief glimpse of him. His hair was dark, though speckled with grey, and he had a straggly beard. I could not see the colour of his eyes, which appeared as two sunken black pits. What appalled me was his air of degeneracy. His hair and beard were greasy and tangled. His skin was as pale as that of a prisoner who has lain long in a dungeon without sunlight. He wore a simple linen tunic with a belt of leather, the buckle missing, tied in a knot at his waist. As he leaned over me a rank musty smell assailed my nostrils. From his sleeve a bony hand protruded to take my mother's wrist and raise her up.

'Please rise.' He said quietly, and she did so. He shuffled away again to his shadowed throne and sat down.

'Your brother Lucian writes well. He is a cultured man. He says you have suffered greatly at the hands of barbarians, and asks that I give you sanctuary here. Well, there is no telling whether the barbarians may even reach here, but such sanctuary as I can offer is yours.'

'Thank you, Your Majesty.'

'On one condition.'

'Condition?'

'That you continue to speak your mind.' He snarled at the shadowy figures on our right. 'I've got enough arse-lickers! Oh, saving your child's presence, Olivia Galeria.'

He leaned into the light, peering at me.

'She's a fine-looking daughter. How old is she?'

'Thank you, Your Majesty. This is Keri. She is almost six. She is my only child.'

The King looked to me.

'Hmm. I too have a daughter. You must meet her. If you are to stay in the palace you will be a fine companion for her. She's nearly eight, but she has no one else of her own age.'

'Your Majesty!' Mother sounded alarmed. 'We are asking for permission to settle in your kingdom, not to be a burden on your household!'

'Burden? I fear it is we who will be a burden on you. This is not Rome, you know, nor even the court of Ambrosius. There is no sparkling high society here. No, I do not mean to burden you with us for long. You are free to settle where you will, but you may stay as long as you wish until you decide what to do.'

'Your Majesty is most kind.'

'His Majesty is a blubbering old fool.' said the King. 'But he hasn't forgotten all the decencies, I hope. Tiernan! See that our kinswoman is properly housed and attended.'

'At once, Your Majesty.' And we were ushered away through the huge doors and down a maze of passageways. In another hallway Tiernan thankfully handed us over to a servantwoman, who was introduced as Menevia. She curtsied prettily to my mother, and led us in her turn to a guest room.

'Your luggage will soon be here, *Domina*. Do you wish for anything?'

'Yes I do. Menevia, can you get me a bath, and hot water?'

'Why certainly, *Domina*.'

'That's all I need right now. I want to soak in hot water and wash off the salt and the dust.'

Menevia was a small dark woman of about my mother's age. She was darker-skinned, black-haired, and short and stocky. She looked like a Welsh mountain dweller, and was probably descended from just such people. Indeed, her accent was strong, and we found it difficult at first to understand some of her Celtic. Her Latin was poorer still, so we settled for the local tongue in the end.

She told us that she was descended from one of Magnus Maximus's soldiers, who had been settled here by the Emperor Theodosius. Her family tradition had it that they hailed from Wales near Isca. She prattled away harmlessly and gently, telling us all the gossip of the palace. How Tiernan was not well liked, but respected for his efficiency. How the king was hardly seen, except when public occasions demanded it. How he had fought in his youth, and been every young maid's hero. By this time Mother had been led to the stone bath in an adjoining room and was reclining in it while I played with the water.

'Tell us, Menevia, why is the King so melancholic? He is a comely enough man, well liked, secure. What is the matter with him?'

'Well, *Domina*, they do say that in his youth he was not so. But they say he mourns for his lost queen.'

'Lost? I didn't realise he was a widower.'

'These many years, *Domina*, longer than he was ever married. It was before my time here at the palace, but they say he met this most beautiful foreign queen when he sailed north to punish some sea-raiders.'

'He chased them home? Gods! I wish we had men like him in Britain!'

'They say he did, *Domina*. They say he found their homeland and attacked it, killing their king, who was this beautiful lady's husband. As soon as he saw her he fell in love with her and took her for his own queen.'

'Like a trophy? Gods, I'd hate to be a prize of war!'

'Begging your pardon, *Domina*, they say that it was a true love match, this lady's husband having mistreated her so much. Anyway, they started home, but were led astray by storms and were a year getting home. In the meantime, the queen died in childbed, although the child survived, bless her.' She smiled fondly as she mentioned the Princess.

'Where is the child now?'

'Oh, she's in the palace. She is the King's only child, the Princess Dahut.'

'Dahut? What kind of name is that?'

'I don't know, I'm sure, *Domina*. Perhaps the Queen chose it. It would be an outlandish name, her being a Northwoman of some sort. Well, so they say.'

'Who are "they"?'

'Oh, some of the men who were on the voyage are still here in the King's service, *Domina*. They could tell you.'

'Yes,' said Mother. 'I daresay.'

She leaned forward in the water. 'Menevia, scrub my back, there's a good girl. And stop this gossiping before I come to believe the half of it!'

Afterwards I took my turn in the bath, and Mother sat wrapped in a huge towel and chatted with me and washed me down. Menevia clearly expected to do this herself, and was shocked that a gentlewoman should bath her own child. But then, one of the reasons I loved my mother was that she always had time for me. And one of the things I admired was that she never did a thing just because it was the custom, if her own inclination was different. Perhaps I was lucky, being her only child, and often enough her only companion. Sometimes she said things to me she might otherwise have kept to herself.

'Mamma, why don't you want to stay here in the palace? If there is another girl here I'd like to stay.'

'I don't mind being here for a while, Keri. I just don't want to be part of the King's household.'

'Why not?'

'For several reasons. For one thing, as I said, I don't want to be a burden. We are not beggars, you know. For another, well, grateful as I am to the King for allowing us to stay, I think I would prefer to be in charge of my own house. It's what I'm used to, I suppose, although I couldn't afford the sort of household your Uncle Lucian had.'

Menevia asked to be excused for a time, and Mother gave her leave to go. Then she turned back to me.

'There is another reason, though I didn't want to say it in front of a servant. You see, Keri, if an unmarried woman lives at court the King has great power over her. He acts as her father if she has none of her own. He can even marry her to someone, maybe someone she doesn't like. The King was polite enough to us today, but if he got tired of my face I wouldn't want him to marry me off to some noble to get rid of me.'

I pondered this for a while.

'Do you want to marry again, Mother?'

'I don't know, little one. Perhaps one day. But if I do it will be someone that I want, not someone chosen for me. For the first time in my life I have an existence in my own right. If I marry, then under the law everything I have becomes my husband's. I'm not giving everything up unless it's to someone I trust, and maybe not even then.'

'You don't want another orange marriage, I suppose?'

'Orange?' Mother's face was a picture. 'You mean an "arranged" marriage. No. I don't. Your father was a good husband, but I would still prefer to choose my own. Besides, I don't want you to have a marriage arranged for you either, and that's another thing I'd lose control over if I married again. Anyway, who's been talking to you of arranged marriages?'

'Oh, I heard you talking to Meriadauc one night on the ship.'

She reddened a little. 'Oh. What else did you hear?'

'Not very much.' I hesitated. 'Mamma, do you think Meriadauc is in love with you?'

She went quite scarlet now. Then she broke her embarrassment with a laugh. 'Really, Keri, in love indeed!'

'Well, he might be! You're a very nice person!'

She kissed me. 'He might be, for all I know. Still, Keri, as you grow older you'll realise that there are plenty of men who can fall in love easily enough at dinnertime and fall out of it again before breakfast! Now, enough of this, let's wash behind your ears!'

Chapter Five

Gradlon's daughter was the most beautiful girl I had ever seen. My mother was beautiful, of course, but the beauty of a child is the beauty of a spring rosebud, full of promise and unbruised by the harshness of a bad summer. We met in her nurse's room, where Mother and I had been led by Menevia, specially for the purpose. As the nurse held the door back, I saw the Princess sitting at a table behind, sewing. She stood up as she saw who was there.

Dahut was tall for her age, with her father's shiny black hair – only in her case it fell in curls to her waist. Her skin was pale and unblemished. As she moved forward her sleeve brushed against the sewing table and knocked a bobbin onto the floor. As she bent to retrieve it I saw that her movements were already elegant and flowing. When she looked up suddenly I experienced a strange feeling which is difficult to describe. It was a sort of thrill without the ecstasy, or a shudder without the disgust. Even now I cannot put a name to it.

It was her eyes, I think. They were a deep grey, like pools of mist, but the pupils were surprisingly small. If the eyes are the windows which bring light to the soul, then it seemed that Dahut had the blinds drawn against it. But she smiled as she approached, and it was impossible not to smile back. Her good nature was infectious at sight. I will always remember Dahut the child as open, generous, and loving, no matter what she became later.

'You are Keri,' she said, in a voice like a songbird's. 'I'm glad you're staying with us. It's so lonely here sometimes.'

'Well,' I faltered. 'I'm not sure exactly.'

'Oh, you'll stay I know. Even if you leave the palace, you'll be somewhere near. Here, come and look at this.' And she led me over to the table where her sewing lay.

When we had examined her work for a while — it was only an apron, but beautifully made — Dahut showed me round her nursery. I had never seen so many toys before. Many of them had been made as birthday presents by servants of the King's household, and others had been presented by court notables trying to ingratiate themselves with him. Dahut seemed perfectly well aware of their motives, but saw no reason to despise the gift as well as the giver. She seemed to know a great deal about the intrigues of the court.

'Have you met Tiernan?'

'Well, yes.'

'I see you don't like him, either. Still, he does a lot of work for poor Papa, so I suppose we need him. Oh, dear! I wish Papa would get better.'

'Has the King been ill for a long time?'

'All my life.' A shadow crossed her face.

We went through the treasure of the nursery. There were wooden toys – animals, carts, ships. There were dolls of earthenware and others of cloth. In one corner stood a beautiful model of a ship. It was a Roman trireme, complete with its three banks of oars and little wooden figures for the oar-slaves.

'Meriadauc brought me that. All the way from Rome. He is a very kind man. He and Snorebeard come here a lot between voyages. They often bring a present, but not usually like that one.'

I thought back to the ship, and our trip up the Odet – was it only that morning?

'Your Highness,' I began, and then we both collapsed in giggles.

'It makes me sound like a grand old lady, doesn't it? If you are to be my friend – '

'Oh, yes please!'

'Then call me by my name.'

'Well, then, Dahut, when we were coming up the river this morning we passed a village with funny people in it.'

'Funny?'

'They had sort of slanty eyes and long black hair. And lots of the men had long moustaches, but not beards. They looked sort of foreign.'

'I expect that was Trefarzan. The people there are mostly Huns.'

Huns! The children of today will not know with what terror that world filled us. The Huns were a savage barbarian tribe, a byword for ferocity and cruelty. 'The King of the Huns will come to get you' was a threat used by parents to keep naughty children in line. But I always pictured them galloping wild horses across dusty plains, not settled in peaceful fishing villages.

'They were brought here by the Romans to put down a rebellion in Armorica. That's what my nurse says. They had no wives, though, and after the rebellion there was a shortage of men amongst the Armoricans, so they married and stayed here. Now they are just like the rest really. We have all kinds of people here, you know.'

'How exciting!'

'I suppose so. Only, I hear a lot about the outside world. I don't go out to see it much. Maybe that'll change, now you're here.'

Dahut was not the only one who could spot an ulterior motive. I realised that she hoped to make my arrival an excuse for more trips out, but I could hardly complain at that. I was as eager as she was. We got on so well that day that my mother and the nurse agreed to leave us together. Dahut normally dined with her nurse, and I would join them. Mother would join the adults at the King's table in the big hall. Later my things were moved into the nursery, and I took up residence with Dahut, the nurse looking after both of us. Mother would still spend a lot of time with us, though, and old Berta, the nurse obviously appreciated what she did.

'A find lady, your mamma,' she would say. 'Not afraid to lend a hand. And she doesn't talk to you like you're dirt, either. Not like some I could name, but better hadn't. There's some that could take lessons from her. Some that thinks too well of themselves.' We always assumed she meant Tiernan, but she never said.

Meriadauc and Snorebeard, true to their word, came to the palace on the day after our arrival. They spent most of the time enclosed with Tiernan, discussing business and probably passing on some news, but they came to see us in the afternoon. Old Berta and Mother had taken us out into the palace garden. This was a well-kept walled space with lawns and paths and flower beds behind the main palace buildings. Around one corner at the side of the palace was a kitchen garden, which was mostly given over to culinary and medicinal herbs. The vegetables were brought in from farms outside, although there were some fruit trees against the garden walls. Dahut and I were eyeing them with interest, hoping to spot a last lingering apple or pear, when we heard Snorebeard's unmistakable tones.

'What's the matter, Princess? Don't they feed you properly here?'

We turned and ran to him gleefully, and he made much of bowing low before Dahut. Meriadauc followed him, grinning, and Tiernan followed them both, scowling.

'And how is my little Keri?' Snorebeard asked.

'Very well, thank you. Meriadauc was right. King Gradlon has allowed us to stay.'

'There. Didn't we say he was a man of honour? Tell me, did you meet the King himself?'

'Yes, for a little while.'

'And was he well? We have not seen him ourselves this time.'

'He seemed ... sad.'

'Hmm. We must hope that he's better soon. The way things are shaping no king can afford to be at less than full strength. Kingship is a heavy enough burden for a healthy man. I'm glad to see you and your mother settled. It must be a great relief to her.'

Meriadauc had gone straight to say a few words to Mother, and Berta had drawn aside to give them privacy. It seemed to me that they were talking very earnestly, and looking the whole time into each other's face. Ah well! If I had to have a stepfather I could think of plenty I would like less. Stepfather! That was taking a little too much for granted. My attention returned to Snorebeard.

'When are you leaving?'

'We catch the tide tomorrow early. Then it's Portus Namnetum. Quintus Flavius is going, too. We shall be glad of his company. There are pirates all the way from here to Italy.'

'Have you ever fought the pirates?' Dahut's eyes were wide open.

'Only once, Princess. We beat them off that time. The crew are good archers, you see. We all practise hard. That way we can hope to beat pirates off before they get close enough to jump aboard. Anyway, we're only a small ship, not rich enough pickings for most of them.'

Meriadauc approached.

'I'm sorry to spoil things, but we have much to do before nightfall. Farewell, Princess. The steward has asked us to seek certain items for him, so we will call in the spring, on our return journey.'

'Gods and pirates permitting,' added Snorebeard. Then he laughed like an earthquake and he and Meriadauc took their leave. We watched them go with sadness, for they seemed to us the best of men. Always cheerful, brave as lions, and never condescending to children!

Later in the nursery we tried to get some news from Berta. Dahut was sure that the visits of Meriadauc and Quintus Flavius meant important news from the outside world. We had been able to tell her of the news from Britain, and Ambrosius' uphill struggle against the Saxons, but this was less urgent to her. Britain was a place she had only heard about. Armorica was officially still part of the Roman Prefecture of Gaul, and the news brought by Quintus Flavius was of far greater interest. Her father might be recognised as King by the British in Kemper, but to the Romans he was only the Comes, commander of some British auxiliaries. It suited them to have a tough seafaring people to guard against the Saxon pirates, but British Armorica existed only at the whim of Aëtius, the military commander in Gaul. If the Emperor, or even the Prefect of Gaul, changed Aëtius' orders then it was a poor lookout for Gradlon.

Berta knew as well as anyone what Gradlon's position was, and that such matters were not deliberately kept from Dahut. Still, she was evasive when we pumped her at the dinner table.

'Now, then, Princess, you don't want to worry about things like that. Your father is a fine man. He can take care of such matters.'

'Yes,' said Dahut wistfully. 'But I'd like to know all the same.'

Berta just laughed. Indeed it was soon clear that she knew nothing anyway, but didn't like to admit it.

Later, huddled in the little bed which we shared, Dahut and I talked until we heard Berta's snores coming from the next room. The old woman always retired early and slept sound. It was a fact of which we shamelessly took advantage.

'Keri.'

'Mm?'

'Are you really sleepy?'

No-one ever asks that unless they are about to suggest something better. I was instantly wide awake.

'Why? What is it?'

'Can you keep a secret?'

'Yes, of course.'

'I have a secret hiding place.'

'Where?'

'It's part of an old passage that no one uses now. I sometimes go there when I'm hiding from Berta. I can show you it if you like.'

'What, now?'

'When better? Berta's asleep, and the rest of them are down in the big hall. They'll be eating now, and talking too much with the wine.'

'What of it?'

'We can get some news that way. We can see them.'

'From your hiding place?'

'Yes! Look, you must come.'

Nowadays the idea of wandering about on a winter's night wearing only a thin cotton shift seems the height of lunacy. Then I don't think we felt the cold – at least, not until we got back to bed and felt each other's chilled skin. On that first night the magic of the adventure gave us warmth enough. Looking back, it seems that ramblings at night came to be the essence of my relationship with Dahut, but later on they were not always so innocent.

We crept out of the nursery and down a dark corridor. There was a rush lamp on the wall but it gave a feeble light, just enough to save us from breaking our ankles. A few yards from the nursery the corridor turned a corner, and we peeped round it to make sure the coast was clear. Seeing no one we went on, another rush lamp further down flickering in some draught. On the left there was a pair of narrow doors, like the doors of a cupboard.

'In here!'

It was indeed a cupboard, a blanket store with heavy stone shelves. These barred the way and were built into the walls at either end. I was momentarily at a loss. When I turned to Dahut there was no sign of her.

'Dahut?'

'Here!'

The voice came from floor level. With a giggle she popped her head out from under the bottom shelf.

'There's a hole at the back of the cupboard!'

There was indeed, and a passageway beyond it. Beginning to be fearful now, I crawled through after her.

'Wait for me, Dahut!'

'It's all right. It's quite safe.'

She waited for me on the other side, and felt for my hand in the dark. Clasping it in hers, she reassured me.

'We can stand up here, but just wait for a minute. You'll see better when your eyes get used to it.'

And so it was. Gradually, I saw that there was a square of faint light a few feet away. Beneath our feet there was solid floor, albeit very dusty. The walls were peeling and hung with cobwebs, from which I shrank in distaste. The ceiling was lost in the gloom. From somewhere nearby I could hear the murmurs of many voices.

'What is that square of light?'

'Come and see.'

I inched forward until I reached the hole in the wall. It was at a convenient height for a child to peer through if kneeling, and there was a blanket on the floor to cushion our knees. Whether it was intended to be a secret window or whether it was just the gap where some bricks had fallen out I could not tell, but the effect was the same. I raised myself up and looked through.

There is something delectably naughty about watching something you are not supposed to see, especially when you are a child and things have actively been kept from you. At any rate, my heart was beating hard as I looked down upon the assembled adult company. Our little window was obviously close to their ceiling, and no one ever noticed it in the dim light thrown by the candles and torches below. I could see the three long tables, the top table across the ends of the other two. Gradlon himself sat in the middle of this one, with Tiernan and various other notables near him. I could see my mother some way down one of the side tables, surrounded by a gaggle of women. Just the sort of company she hated. From our vantage point we were looking straight down the gap between the tables, towards the King's place. It was precisely the view that someone would have on entering the hall, except for the difference in height. The kitchen entrance was through the doors at the other end, behind the King, although the food was being cleared away at the moment. Wine was still being poured, I noticed, and there was a lot of the noise and laughter which sometimes goes with drunkenness.

'Oh, no,' groaned Dahut. 'Father's glugging it down again. Look at him.'

It was true. Gradlon, still dressed as I had seen him before, was swaying in his seat and waving his goblet around. I was disappointed to see that it was not gold, but merely pewter. A servant refilled it at his command, and he quickly drank it down. The servant hovered at his shoulder, having clearly decided that it was not worth going away just yet. Gradlon then stood up, and a hush fell on the company.

'I think you should hear some news I have had today,' he announced, his speech a little slurred with the wine. 'As you know, Quintus Flavius, one of Aëtius' officers, has been here. You will hear rumours, so I think it better that I tell you what we know. Firstly, the Alans. As you know, they put down the rebellion around Namnetum, and we feared they might move against us too. But it seems that Aëtius realises we British were mostly not involved, and the Alans are already on the road back to Spain.'

'Who are the Alans?' I whispered to Dahut.

'Federates. Aëtius sent them to punish the rebels.'

More federates! Was there no end to it? Gradlon's announcement was met by cheers, and there were some very relieved faces around the hall. Evidently the Alans were as fierce as the rest of the barbarians. He went on.

'Other things are not so good to hear. It seems that the Vandals, who we thought had been defeated in Africa, rose in force almost eighteen months ago. They have now taken control of the whole province and their king, Geiserich, has been recognised by the Emperor as an independent sovereign. Not a federate, you understand, but king of an independent nation.'

There were some puzzled looks at the table, and after a few moments one young man gave them a voice.

'Africa is a long way off, sire. Why should we care who owns it?'

The King smiled. 'It is a king's job to look ahead, Cador, to look for ... implications.'

'I don't understand, your Majesty.'

'That, Cador, is why I am a king and you ... you are not!'

Cador looked thoroughly uncomfortable by now, but he was not the only one to be baffled.

'You see,' went on the King. 'Rome has for centuries obtained most of her corn from Africa. This gives the Vandals a stranglehold on her.'

'There are other cornfields,' someone said.

'Yes. There are Corsica and Sardinia. However, the Vandals realised that too. They had built a fleet in secret, and after they fell on Carthage, they sailed for Sardinia. Corsica and maybe even Sicily now lie in their hands. So where will Italy look for corn?'

There was a silence. Gradlon took another draught of his wine, and I saw Dahut shake her head fearfully.

'Well?' Gradlon seemed intent on his answer. 'There are thousands of German mercenaries all over Italy – Goths, Gepids, and the gods know who else. They need food. Where will Valentinian get it for them.? Not eastwards, Attila and his slant-eyed hordes are trampling all over Greece. Not northwards. There are only more barbarians there, and again all subject-allies of Attila. Southwards is only the sea, controlled by Vandal pirates. So what's left? Eh?'

'Is there any news of Valentinian's intentions towards Gaul?'

'Aha! You've got there at last, Cador. No, there isn't. Not yet. But that is one reason why Quintus Flavius is going to see him, I'm certain.'

'Surely the Emperor will not seek to plunder Gaul?'

'The Emperor will seek to keep the army happy, and to preserve Italy before anywhere else.'

'What about Aëtius?' asked someone else.

'Ah, you may well ask. Loyal Aëtius, servant of the Emperor, saviour of Gaul. He has played off the barbarians against each other for years now, in order to maintain the Roman way of life in Gaul. Will he see it swept away? I doubt it. Anyway, it seems not. He has resettled the Burgundian federates along the River Rhodanus, from Geneva almost to the sea. He says it's to guard the Alpine passes. But against whom, eh? I'd say he's just fallen out of favour in imperial circles.'

There were some nods and murmurs of assent at this. Then Cador spoke again.

'Well, perhaps the Emperor and Aëtius will finish each other off and leave us in peace.'

The ensuing laughter was broken into by a suddenly enraged Gradlon.

'Peace? Peace? Imbeciles all, do you not understand what is happening? The Western world is falling into an abyss! Civilisation is collapsing! Here am I trying to ensure that here on the edge of the world the storm passes us by, and you ... Don't you realise what Aëtius is? He is our shield! Behind him are the Franks, the Burgundians, the Visigoths – so you want to fight them again? – even the Saxons. Ask my kinswoman Olivia Galeria about the peace the Saxons will leave you!'

He was bellowing now. I shot a quick glance at Dahut, and saw tears well up in her eyes. She paid them no heed as they rolled down her cheeks. In the hall below, Gradlon threw his goblet at Cador, but it missed and clattered across the stone floor. Some of the dinner guests moved further away from him in case they were next.

'Olivia Galeria!' the King turned to my mother, 'Am I wrong about the Saxons?'

'No, your Majesty, you are not. If the way is left open for the Saxons to come then we are lost.'

'There!' He snarled at the company in triumph, snatched a flagon from his servant and began to stalk around the room, drinking straight from it.

'You are not worthy to be saved from the barbarians! Perhaps none of us are! Perhaps it's a judgement. While you sleep sound in your beds at night I plot and plan to protect you. Do you care? Do you even think? No, you just accept it all. Well, it will serve you right if it does all fall apart. At least then there'll be rest.' There was a great deal more in similar vein, becoming more maudlin as Gradlon became more intoxicated. At last he sat down at the top table again having apparently run out of abuse and self-pity.

'Go,' he said quietly, 'All of you.'

When they failed to disappear at once he found strength to yell again.

'Go on! Bugger off, the lot of you!'

His head sank to the table as the room emptied. His body shook. When I looked at Dahut she was still crying silently, and to my surprise I found that I was too.

'Come on,' I whispered, 'They'll be up here in a minute. We must get back to bed.'

She made no move until I took her arm. It felt cold, and I suddenly realised we were both shivering. As we crept away from our hiding place I heard Gradlon's voice raised in a groan.

'Oh, Malgven, Malgven ...'

We crept back through the gloomy corridor just as the first adults appeared at the far end, and slipped into the nursery to the accompaniment of Berta's ear-splitting snores. Once in bed I held Dahut to me, for warmth and in order to comfort her.

'I wish he didn't do such things,' she sniffed. 'It makes him seem so wicked, and he isn't – really he isn't.'

'I know,' I said, although he had frightened me. He had seemed dangerously sad, as if he might do dark things when driven by madness. Yet I remembered his gentle speech to us on our arrival. He had accepted a rebuke from my mother and he had given us sanctuary. Even in his rage tonight he had been worried for his people, trying to fathom how the great events in the world might bring them harm, and how that might be avoided.

'I know he is a good man,' I said. 'Snorebeard said the ... burden of kingship was hard for anyone to bear, and your father bears it alone.' That was not quite true; there was Tiernan, but I was looking for something comforting to say.

'Tell, me, who is Malgven?'

She stiffened in my arms. 'That was my mother's name.'

'Oh. He spoke it as we were leaving. Did you hear?'

'No, but he does call on her when the madness takes him. Once I even heard him talking to her. As if she was still alive, I mean, as if she was in the room with him. He didn't know I had come in.'

The memory saddened her again, and she fell silent. I held her close, thinking how strange it was that I was the one to give comfort, although two years the younger. Later on I was to comfort again and often be comforted in my turn, the threads of our lives woven together into one cloth until the one was indistinguishable from the other. But that first time still stands out in my mind, as if the basis of our affection was laid down then. For the first time I felt important to someone other than my mother. Dahut needed me.

I was almost asleep when she suddenly spoke.

'Your mother won't want to leave, will she, because of tonight? I couldn't bear it if you went now. Please don't leave us.'

No,' I said, stroking her hair gently. 'Go to sleep and don't worry. I won't leave you.'

Chapter Six

'You must leave Kemper.'

We were in the King's audience chamber, that place of gloom and shadow. It was about six months after our arrival, and Gradlon's promise that we could stay as long as we liked.

'Papa, you promised!' Dahut and I were now closer than sisters, and the prospect of separation appalled us.

'I mean all three of you to go, and Berta your nurse, and servants and a proper household.'

'But go where?' my mother broke in. She caught the King's eye. 'Your Majesty, please tell us what has happened.'

'Of course, if you will let me.' He grinned, his spirits a little higher of late. 'Fear not, I am not anxious to get rid of you. But I have had worrying news. It seems there is plague at Condevincum, just beyond Portus Namnetum. In fact, the plague has been active in Italy since last summer, and only paused a little during the winter months. It has moved westward and is now reported throughout Gaul. I want my only child out of harm's way as far as is possible. It would be cruelty to separate her from the friend who means so much to her, and cruelty again to separate the friend from her mother. Therefore, I ... ask you to go. I have an estate by the sea – well, a villa really. It is a healthy place, not frequented by travellers. If the plague should come this far, there is little likelihood of anyone taking it to you there. And it is a wonderful place for children. I have not been there for some years – I do not care for the sea since ... I do not care for the sea any more. But the girls will like it there.'

'When do we go?' Mother wasted no time on pleasantries, and Gradlon looked grateful.

'In three days. I will send an escort with you, of course, although to be honest the roads are safe enough these days. Still, I think you should have a small guard with you while you are away.'

So it was settled. We began packing at once.

'Have you been to this place?' Mother asked Berta at the first opportunity.

'Years ago, *Domina*. It was well enough then, an old Roman villa. Not so dilapidated as some of them are now, though of course it's been some time. Who knows? It's on a hillside, looking out over the Atlantic. A wild place, but beautiful if you've an eye for natural things. I only hope the winter storms don't set my rheumatism off.'

Mother laughed. 'Berta, it's only spring now!'

'Yes, well, if it's the plague we're hiding from we'll be gone more than a month or two. You mark my words. His Majesty won't call us back until the danger's well and truly over. He won't take any chances, not where my little princess is concerned.'

She was right, of course. We could expect to be gone for at least a year, but Dahut and I could hardly take this in at the time. We were so excited at the prospect, and relieved that we were not to be separated after all. Dahut was a little downcast when she realised that her father was not coming with us, but she knew that a king has his duty.

'And just think,' she said. 'No Tiernan for ages and ages.'

We both laughed.

Tiernan had been distinctly surly of late. He greeted us with the barest politeness, and was plainly irritated by our presence. We returned his coldness with equal frostiness, and yet were puzzled by it. Did he just not like children, or had we done something to offend him personally? We would often see him turn away at our approach, and pretend that he had not seen us. Sometimes, I caught him staring at Dahut with a far-away look, as if he were seeing something else. Once, just once, I thought I saw his eyes watering as he left the room hurriedly. Ah well, perhaps he had a cold. Anyway, children accept that some people are nice and some are nasty. We were not going to lose any sleep over it. He was one of the nasty ones, and that was that.

The day of our departure was on us in no time. We had a wagon with our effects on it, and ten soldiers for an escort. Old Berta rode beside the wagon driver, but Dahut and I were to ride our very own ponies. This was a further cause of excitement for us, as it was the first time we had ridden them on a proper journey, rather than just for fun. Mother was mounted on a fine grey, and there was another wagon-load of servants and baggage. The journey would take some time, as there were no Roman roads in this direction, and progress was expected to be slow.

I reflected, as we rode through the awakening streets, that I had hardly had a chance to see Kemper properly. The hopes of Dahut that my arrival might prove an excuse for more excursions had not been realised. At least she had some company now, though. The life of a princess, so far from being the glamorous and free thing I had imagined, seemed now to be more like that of a prisoner. Indeed, Berta even worried about us going out in the garden too much, in case we came to look too weather-beaten.

'A lady's skin should be fair as milk. Who will want to marry a princess with brown wrinkled skin and hands all roughened from climbing trees?'

Dahut would tease her. 'If he gets as much choice in the matter as the princess, I expect he'll have her, even if she has the skin of a lizard and the hands of a blacksmith.'

When Berta was especially tiresome Dahut would go further. 'Anyway, who says I will marry? Perhaps I shall be Queen in my own right, and spurn the attentions of all who crave my hand.'

Berta would pretend to be scandalised, but she would smile knowingly. 'Ah, you'll change your tune when you grow up.'

If she grew up, that is. She had been betrothed at six to the son of Riothamus of Darioritum, a neighbouring British king. It was a political match, intended to cement peace between the two kingdoms, after a history of feuding. But the boy had died the following year, and his elder brother was already betrothed to someone else, so the opportunity had passed. Dahut was unconcerned; she had never met either of them. Now there was peace anyway, and an agreement to punish those who sometimes raided along both sides of the border. Ironically, this meant the plague was more likely to reach Kemper, because travel was easier in peacetime.

Dahut broke in on these morbid thoughts. 'I wonder how long it will be before we see Kemper again?'

There was no answer to that. I took a last look around as we neared the town gates. 'There will be time to explore it again – when we are older.'

We thought then that adulthood would solve all our problems, unaware that it would bring a host of its own.

'I am not going to be sad today,' I announced, 'I haven't seen the sea since last year, and I think it's exciting. Let's look forward to this place.'

'Ker-Is,' supplied my mother. 'It means "low town", that's all. That will be by the sea, because the people live mostly by fishing.'

That ride through the town only served to awaken my curiosity further. We passed the marketplace, with the traders already setting up their stalls. They looked at us in surprise as we went by. Excursions by the royal household were a rarity since the onset of Gradlon's depression. Besides, they usually took place for an obvious reason – whether hunting or for some official purpose. I guessed that news of our departure – and rumours about the reason for it – would be all round the town before most of its inhabitants had finished breakfast.

After leaving the old centre of the town – Roman Aquilo – we came to the city wall, where Budic, the captain of our guard, had to identify us to the watch. We were through in a matter of moments, and the gates closing behind us. As they crashed shut I turned in the saddle. The city looked almost black against the silvering sky, and black crows wheeled above the walls, their hoarse cries suddenly shattering the dawn silence. Some scrap of garbage or carrion had no doubt attracted them. It did not seem like a favourable omen.

We rode on in silence, past the hovels which the very poor had built outside the walls. Gradlon, it was said, had ideas about helping the poor to build better houses, but there was nothing to show for it yet. It seemed that here, as at home, there was an undercurrent of decay, as the world's greatest civilisation crumbled to its doom.

'Sad to leave, young lady?' It was Budic, riding up after his business with the watch.

'Yes, a little. But sad for the world, really.'

He gave a surprised laugh. 'The world, is it? Little lady, those are deep thoughts and sorrows for one so young. What has the world done to deserve a child's pity?'

I didn't see, as a child doesn't, why my pity was less valid than anyone else's.

'Is Rome not the greatest empire in history, then?'

'Well, perhaps it is. But why the sadness?'

'The Empire seems to be falling to pieces. Is that not reason for sadness?'

He grinned. 'It is, if you're a Roman. Meaning no disrespect, young lady, but some classes of people are more Roman than others.'

'You are not?'

'Well, perhaps not. Those who love the Empire are mostly those who see that their power and position depend upon it. Ask a peasant and a patrician, and I daresay you'll get different opinions.'

'I see.'

'Mind you, one blessing which the Empire has brought us is the true religion. Thanks to the Emperor Constantine, who saw God's sign in the sky.'

Dahut was also nearby, and broke in. 'Can you tell us the story?'

'Well, I have to speak to the guards.'

'Oh, please, Budic!'

'Well, perhaps just quickly, then. You see, Constantine was at war with Maxentius, who had also claimed the Emperor's throne. They were to meet the next day at the Milvian Bridge for the battle which would decide who would be Emperor. Constantine followed the state religion at the time – the worship of the Unconquered Sun. As the sun was going down, they say he looked up to the sky and offered a prayer for victory. However, instead of the sun he saw a shining cross, which he knew was the symbol of Christ. Suddenly, he heard a voice in his heart telling him that if he put his trust in the Lord he would win the battle and reign long as Emperor.'

'And did he?' Dahut's voice seemed strangely dull, as if she were used to fairy tales.

'Indeed he did. After the battle he was baptised in the true religion and all the persecution of the Christians was stopped. He even returned to the churches the wealth which earlier emperors had taken from them. In time, Christianity was adopted as the state-approved religion, and the worship of the Sun put down, as other pagan cults are being today.'

'I'll tell you.' Mother had approached without our noticing. 'It means that peasants making harmless offerings to their gods are ambushed and massacred by those who claim to follow the god of peace. Their sacred groves are cut down and fired. Their shrines are desecrated, their altars smashed with hammers. That's what it means.'

Budic went scarlet in the face. '*Domina*!'

'You can't deny it, Budic. It was beginning at home before we left, and I understand that here it is already widespread.'

'The Church has ordered all its bishops to combat paganism, Olivia Galeria.'

'Yes, so I hear. But I find it ironic that you Christians are now meting out to others the persecution which was once meted out to you. Why can't you leave well alone? What harm is there in a few peasants following the traditions of their tribe?'

'They worship demons, *Domina*.'

She looked at him through half-closed eyes. 'Budic, they can worship a cow's arse for all I care, just so long as they don't expect me to do the same.'

Budic turned his mount abruptly and rode to the head of the column to speak to his guards. We were left flabbergasted.

'Mamma, do the Christians really do those things?'

'Yes.'

'But that's terrible!'

'Yes. A child can see it. It is terrible.'

'But why do they?'

'Keri, there are many religions in the world. Many others have arisen, stayed a while – perhaps a few hundred years – and gone again. Most of us believe that there are different gods in different places, that spirits or demons – or what you will – have their dwelling places as we have. To make them a little offering as you pass by does no harm, and may do good. It is really only being polite to the occupier of the place, as you would be to anyone whose home you entered. But the Christians do not believe this. They think there is only one god, and that they have a duty to stamp out the worship of all others.'

'My father is not a Christian.' Put in Dahut.

'No, he isn't. And there are few Christians at his court. As far as I'm concerned, it makes it much easier to live in!'

She laughed, and we joined in with her. I saw Budic, riding at the head of the column, turn and regard us for a minute. He obviously thought we were laughing at his expense, which perhaps we were. He muttered something to the man next to him, and this one also turned to look. Then he scowled, and faced the front again.

We began to run into heavy mud on the road. Hooves, feet and wheels had churned up the surface until it was a swamp. By the time we had gone a few hundred yards we were already spattered with mud thrown up by the wagon wheels and the horses' hooves. To make matters worse, the horses began to slip, and Budic ordered the troops to dismount and lead their horses over the worst patches. When this happened the rest of us did likewise, which meant that the whole column could only move at the walking pace of a child. At one point one of the wagons slipped into a rut, and it took the combined efforts of the dray horses and soldiers to get it moving again.

By the time we stopped for lunch both the men and the horses were tiring, and Dahut and I were exhausted. We had sat down next to Mother on an outcrop of dry rocks, and were tucking into bread and cheese when Budic strode up.

'The going is harder than we anticipated, *Domina*.'

'Yes. Do you know of a suitable place to stop? I don't think we should go on too late today.'

'Well, I'd suggest the two children ride on one of the wagons when we move on. It is too dangerous for them to ride on this ground, and too tiring, I should think.'

We agreed without protest, which is an indication of how true it was! In the meantime, lunch was finished and nature had to be attended to, so Dahut and I ventured off the track and into the woodland at one side. We were under Mother's orders not to stray too far, so we followed a little worn path between the trees. After only a few yards it led into a clearing, surrounded by trees whose branches had grown unchecked for years and threatened to cover it over again. Looking up, we saw a ragged gap in the leafy canopy, and a small patch of blue sky growing there.

A god stood in the centre of the clearing. He was a short figure carved in wood and placed upon a tree stump for an altar. His body was detailed with shameless precision, and there were antlers on his head. On the stump around him there were the traces of offerings long past, now just a stain on the wood. His face bore a thick-lipped grin, as if smirking at some coarse joke. We approached slowly, aware that the grove, although long since abandoned, had once been sacred to somebody. We stood for a while and looked at the odd figure. He was cruder by comparison with the Roman stone figures which we were more used to, but somehow that didn't matter. They represented art as well as devotion: he was a thing of the earth, as if he grew out of the soil and was rooted in it like the trees. He was part of something which had been here before the Romans, and would be here still when they were forgotten. Dahut giggled.

'I'm going to make an offering,' she said, and lifting up her shift she squatted in front of the altar stump.

'Dahut! You can't!'

'It's only a statue. No one even comes here any more. You can tell that by looking at the place.'

'I don't care, it doesn't seem right!'

'You're so serious, Keri. I wouldn't do it on a real altar.'

None the less I wandered into the edge of the wood to find another place to sully. I had just finished when I heard Dahut's cry.

'Keri! Help!'

I ran back through the undergrowth to the clearing. There I saw a strange and frightening tableau. Dahut was standing, leaning against the altar. On the far side of the clearing was a large wild pig. It was an old female, with tusks like a boar. Her belly was swollen, and her nipples enlarged with milk. She had a litter somewhere near, no doubt, and was all set to defend it.

'Dahut. Move over to the path. Slowly, now. We don't want to startle her. I'm sure she won't hurt us if we just go away quietly.'

'That's right. We'll just go away quietly. We won't hurt your piglets. We'll just – '

The sow grunted threateningly and took a step forward. We backed away rapidly, and sidled back along the path. The animal just stared at us, and then took a few more steps.

'Oh, no, Keri. She's coming!'

Our orderly retreat became an undignified rout. We ran screaming back towards the road, the sow following at a leisurely pace. If she had been charging in earnest she would already have killed us both, but we didn't realise that. We burst on to the road screaming hysterically, and several of the soldiers ran up carrying spears and swords. They saw the pig at once, and ran toward her. This time she really did charge. The leading man met her head on with his spear, and she transfixed herself upon it. The others closed in and stabbed her thrashing body with their weapons. She went on struggling, squealing in agony. Blood flew everywhere as the men hacked her to pieces. Dahut and I watched aghast as the animal was finally done to death, her screams subsiding into whimpers and then silence. The whole thing happened in less time than it takes to tell.

'Are you all right?' Mother was there, an arm round each of us. Berta had climbed off her wagon and was waddling towards us.

One of the soldiers had investigated the clearing, and came back to report to Budic. He went to see it for himself, and then reported in turn to my mother.

'*Domina*, there is a pagan shrine in the wood.'

'So?'

'Clearly, the children disturbed the demon whose dwelling place it was, and it took the form of the sow in order to attack them.'

We all three looked at him in disbelief. Dahut and I even stopped crying. Only Berta nodded sagely.

'Such things do happen, so they say.'

'It's obvious,' declared Budic flatly. 'What else could it be?'

'A nursing sow?' suggested Mother. 'Defending her litter?'

Budic only snorted and turned away. After congratulating the man who had speared the animal, and excusing him duty because of the bruised arm he had sustained, he wandered off into the wood again. By the time he came back we were ready to move on. I wondered what he had been up to, but as we drew away I saw the smoke rising from where the altar had been. First the 'demon', then its dwelling. I told Mother, but she was not surprised.

'Another Christian desecration,' was all she said.

Chapter Seven

In the event, we stayed two years at Ker-Is, waiting for the plague to subside. Those years were amongst the happiest of our lives. The villa at Ker-Is was perched on a cliff overlooking the sea. The coast here was rocky and wild – storm-tossed in winter and cooled by gentle breezes in summer. The villa itself was not very large, but it had a cosy feel. There were great fireplaces in all the rooms, and no shortage of firewood to be found in the windblown forest just back from the shore. I do not remember that we were ever uncomfortable there, in spite of the modest household. There was a small walled garden, and in good weather we would sit there with my mother or Berta, sewing or helping to prepare the food. My mother always felt that, ladies or not, we should know how to look after ourselves if need be.

The village of Ker-Is lay about a quarter of a mile northwards along the coast. It existed largely on fish, and scores of little boats went out every day to catch what they could. If they caught more than they needed the extra was salted or smoked to keep it for a time when the catch was poor. There was little farming, for the land would not support very much. Still, each cottage had a little plot for vegetables, and perhaps a few chickens. Some kept a cow for milk, and there were pigs and goats too. The villa had its own vegetable garden, kept by an ancient gardener who was himself as wrinkled and brown as an oak tree, if rather less substantial. He took a distant but grandfatherly attitude to us, and could be relied upon to provide the occasional treat from the orchard. A farm nearby served the villa, and kept sheep for wool and meat.

My mother adapted well to the life, although it was not what she was used to. So little was, these days. At least she was sheltered and provided for, and so was I. Perhaps that was all she hoped for. Well, not quite all. Once in charge of her own household she began to make some changes. Contrary to tradition, and to Gradlon's practice up to now, she decided that even daughters needed to be educated. Roman families educated their daughters, at least the better-off ones did, and she had been brought up in the Roman style. She decided that at the very least we must learn to read and write — which meant in Latin, of course — and learn something about the world outside our own narrow lives. She took this task upon herself at first, for there was no tutor to be had.

So it was that we began to spend our mornings learning more than just the genteel domestic concerns of the noblewoman. My mother had very few books — Uncle Lucian had a fine collection, but they remained with him. Still, what she had she let us see, and what she knew she told us about. I was fascinated by the old parchment scrolls. We learned a good deal of history from her, and much about the world around us. She had her own views about the present world crisis, and we heard them in full. We were too young for some of it, but she could sense when our attention was wandering, and would change to something else.

She took us out most afternoons. We would walk along the clifftops, breathing the sea air and feeling the spray from the breaking rollers cool on our skins, for the vapour would reach us even though we were fifty feet above the shore. Dahut had never known her own mother, of course, but she took to mine.

Old Berta would grumble and complain when Mother took us out in the sun. She tutted discreetly at the fact that we were being taught to read. She plainly disapproved of my mother, but was in no position to say so. I think now that she was not so much disapproving as jealous. Mother had usurped her role in a way, and was doing things that Berta would never be able to. The old woman was increasingly rheumatic these days, and could not walk with us, unless it was a straight trip down to the village. And she was illiterate, and so quite incapable of giving the education she claimed to despise.

We were not completely out of touch at Ker-Is. For one thing the guards had to be replaced at intervals – I was not sorry when Budic had to go back. Then every week a rider came from Kemper with a letter from Gradlon, and every week Mother sent the same wax tablets back with a reply. She said she was giving a report on how things were with us, and she would read out messages to Dahut from her father. Gradlon had no idea that Dahut would soon be able to read them for herself. We decided to keep it a secret for now, so that one day Dahut could surprise her father with a letter written by her own hand. Indeed, Mother had doubts about the wisdom of telling him at all.

'He might not approve, like Berta,' she said with a laugh. 'But then it'll be too late, I suppose.'

Dahut seemed to think she could handle her father. 'He's always wanted the best for me. I'm sure he would have had me taught if I'd asked him. Anyway I'm so grateful, Aunt Olivia.' Dahut, who had no aunts, always called her that now.

She was grateful, too. Amongst the few books in my mother's chest were two volumes of Latin poetry, one of them Horace and one of Martial. Dahut was fascinated by them. When we were supposed to read a little for a lesson she would read pages ahead. She loved Horace's rich imagery and Martial's dry satire equally. Literature was a new world to her, as it was to me. But the difference was that she was excited and captured by it. I have never really acquired the same feel for words. I can write a letter at need. I can see the poet's art, but I can live without it. A song is a different matter. That to me is alive, especially if it is a song of the people, not one of those parlour poems set to music. A fisherman's work-song, an epic ballad, these are history plucked from the air.

Another delight was the all-pervasive presence of the sea. Ever since my one sea voyage I had developed a fondness of the water. For Dahut it was a new world. She had been brought up largely within the walls of the palace, and an occasional glimpse of the harbour with its odour of rotting fish had been her only sight of free water. The real thing was a revelation to her. We saw the Ocean's every mood, from the days of brilliant sun and blue water to the sullen greys when the sky and sea merged sulkily some way out from the shore. We saw the water flat as a mirror, or rearing in green cascading mountains. We felt the earth tremble under its onslaught, but we were never afraid. We loved to walk by the sea, with old Berta sitting nearby or my mother walking alongside. One hot day we went paddling in the water, which thoroughly frightened the old nurse.

'It's fins you'll be wanting next! Perhaps you'd like to bath in the Ocean?'

'Why not?' cried Dahut, and threw off her shift, dancing naked into the waves.

'Come back, Princess! It was only a joke! I didn't mean anything by it.'

Dahut just laughed, and laughing I also followed her. The water was cool but the waves were small that day. That first bathe was the most exhilarating thing. Poor old Berta! She had never been in the sea in her life. She was frightened that the Sea God, or his infamous daughter, would come and snatch us. We two splashed around, jumped waves, threw water at her, but we would not come out. She, on the other hand, was too scared to come and get us. She was also scandalised at our nakedness. It was not so bad with children, of course, but it was not a Good Thing. It gave us a compelling sense of freedom to feel the salt water and the warm sun on our bodies. It was nothing but a new game.

My mother appeared, and Berta hobbled over to meet her, alarm and despondency in her voice. Mother laughed, and kicked off her sandals to paddle at the water's edge.

'No further than that, now,' she said. 'You aren't fish, you know.'

'Yes, Mamma! Why don't you join us. It's lovely!'

'I'll bet it is. You know, I just might!' She looked around to see that no one was near. Then she stripped off her shift as well, and waded cautiously out to us. Berta was nearly apoplectic by this time, and mercifully lost for words. Mother took our hands in hers, and we jumped the waves together, shrieking as the cold water splashed our bellies.

That night, tucked up in the bed which we shared in the villa, Dahut and I sleepily went over the day's events as usual.

'I love the sea,' said Dahut.

'Mm. So do I.'

'No. I mean really.'

'Really? How do you mean?'

'The Ocean isn't a thing, Keri. It's alive. It's like a person. I could hear it talk to me when we were out there today.'

'Don't be silly. The Ocean's just a lot of water.'

'Yes, but it's more than that, too. It's a home for many things. It moves. It gets angry and throws things. It makes a noise. It speaks.'

'You do come out with some fantastical things, Dahut. It's reading those poets that does it.'

'Oh, you don't know what I mean at all.'

'No. Go to sleep.'

After that we would always bathe when we got the chance. My mother would occasionally come with us, but mostly there was only old Berta, tutting away on the shore, crying out to us not to go too far, not to get too cold. Occasionally we would manage to sneak out from the villa unobserved, and bathe or wander without hindrance. We rarely saw a soul, but it was on one of these trips that we met Megan.

It was summer, and we had been bathing as usual. The sun was warm, and we lay down on the beach to dry out. The coast here was rocky and hostile, but there were sheltered coves with sandy beaches in them, and it was to one of these that we used to take ourselves on our clandestine outings. The cliffs behind were covered with bushes and deep grass, and there was little chance of being discovered there except by someone who found the route we used. This left the clifftop and wound down from one outcrop to another, although there was no real path as no one ever seemed to come this way.

So there we were, talking as we lay in the sun. Dahut was again expounding her view that the Ocean was a living thing, and I was half-agreeing, not wanting to quarrel. Then a shadow fell across us, and a woman's voice said: 'You are right, little lady, the Ocean is alive.'

We sat up with yelps of alarm, convinced the Sea God's daughter was here at last. But it was only a woman from the village, it seemed. She was dressed in a rough brown shift, and wore a motley collection of beads around her neck. Her skin was as brown as her dress, and she seemed very old to us, although I suppose she was only about thirty. Her hair was black, with grey streaks in it, and was very short for a woman's. It was clean, though, like the rest of her, cleaner than was the custom amongst the villagers. Her eyes were large and as dark as her hair. Her face was plain, and the short hair made her head seem very round, but when she spoke we saw a full row of white teeth. She was not beautiful, but well preserved, for women age quickly on the land or by the sea. Work and childbearing make sure of that. She did not look like a gentlewomen, but somehow not like a peasant either. She smiled at us.

'Did I startle you? I'm sorry. I didn't mean to.' She spoke kindly. Her voice had a softness and richness that was hard to define. She sounded very womanly, but somehow not motherly like most women of her age.

'I always think of this as my own beach,' she went on, 'but of course it isn't.'

'We didn't mean to disturb anyone,' I began.

'Good Mother, it was I that disturbed you! I don't own the beach; I'm just rarely blessed with company here. That's all.'

So saying she sat down next to us and put a woven basket in front of her. Lifting the cloth which covered it she began to unpack the contents – bread, dried fish, and fruit.

'I would be happy to share something with you,' she said, catching our hungry looks. 'There's more than I need. Here, have some.'

We needed no second bidding, but fell to with a will as children do. The bread was still warm from the oven, and the other things just as fresh. There is no better food in the world.

'What's your name?' I asked her at last, having thoroughly filled myself up on her food.

'Megan, I live up there above the cliff.' She pointed up to a spot behind us and to our left.

'Your cottage is a long way from the village, then - further than our villa.'

'Ah, so you are at the villa. I thought as much.' She turned to Dahut, still busy eating. 'And you are the King's daughter?'

'How did you know?'

'Ah, I know many things. But you will see that for yourselves.'

'What do you mean?'

She smiled – a warm, friendly smile. 'I mean that I think we will see each other again, and show each other many things. You will be here for some time, if you are waiting for the plague to die away.'

'How did you know that?'

We looked at her in open-mouthed astonishment.

'There's no magic in that. Even here we hear news of the outside world. We know the plague is in Kemper now.'

'My father said nothing about it in his letters.'

'And do you fear for his safety? He tries hard to protect you, I think. But ask the rider next time, and you will hear.'

We were a little disconcerted. Megan seemed friendly enough, but she seemed to know things about us that no stranger would know. I wondered if she were a witch; I wasn't sure if there were such things — my mother said not — but Megan was given me second thoughts.

'I'm not a witch, child.'

'Pardon? I didn't mean, that is —'

A far-away look came over her face. 'The thought was written on your face, little lady. Again, no magic, I'm afraid.'

'Do you have a husband?' asked Dahut suddenly.

'No, I have no husband, but I did have a child once. He died. He was struck with fever, and died so quickly that there was nothing to be done. I know of many medicines. They all take time to work. There was no time.'

'How terrible for you,' said Dahut softly.

'Yes.'

'Do you make medicines yourself?' I asked.

'Surely. There are many medicines growing in the wood and the hedgerow. I know them all. What I lack is someone to pass the knowledge on to. A daughter would be nice. There is little chance of that, though. I am not past childbearing yet, but I soon will be.'

There was nothing we could say to that. Presently Megan lifted up her shift and rolled it into a pillow for her head. Then she lay back in the sun and closed her eyes. The parts of her body which would normally be covered were just as brown as the rest of her, I noticed.

'Do you often just lie in the sun?'

'Yes. If it is like this I do. It is healthy.'

'Aren't you afraid of someone coming by?'

'No one comes here. Besides, I am not ashamed of my body. Neither should you be of yours. But you should look after it. I would say you have been out in the sun long enough for a beginning. If your skin is too white it will burn.'

'We should be going, anyway,' said Dahut.

We both got up and slipped our clothes back on.

'I'll see you here again,' said Megan. It did not sound like a question.

We climbed back up the cliff path. Just before we headed back through the bushes at the top we looked back. Megan was still lying out on the sand far below. As we watched she got up and strode towards the water. She did not falter as she reached it, but walked out until it was waist deep. Then she dived forward and began to swim. She even dived under the water, her legs flipping up like a tail.

'She's a sea-spirit!' I gasped.

'No,' said Dahut. 'What would a sea-spirit be doing with a cottage?'

And we rushed off home, aware of how late it was growing. With us went an unspoken agreement not to say anything about our new friend. No one would understand why we needed a thirty-year-old woman for a friend, especially as we didn't ourselves. So we just arrived back at the villa out of breath, but not nearly so hungry as usual.

It was several days before we saw Megan again. It was another bright day, but the occasional patch of cloud warned of showers. When we looked out from the villa we could see the showers move across the bay, each patch of cloud trailing its contents like a veil.

'Let's go for a walk,' said Dahut. 'I love it when there's just been rain – everything smells so beautiful and fresh.'

I needed no encouragement. My mother was in conference with this week's rider from the King; Berta was sewing in the nursery. We crept away down the garden and through the little door in the wall at the end. The old gardener used to go out here to dump the garden rubbish in the bushes, and the door was protected only by a bolt. Soon we were running free along the clifftop path, rejoicing in the sun and wind. Without thinking about it we headed in the direction of our secret cove.

'Hey, there! Where are two little ladies running off to in such a hurry?'

The voice appeared to come from out of the centre of a bush. We came to a startled halt and watched as Megan extricated herself from the thicket. She did this in the most precise manner, picking brambles off her shift with thumb and forefinger. The woven basket was in her other hand, but this time it had bunches of greenery in it.

'Megan! You made us jump!'

'You always do,' laughed Dahut. 'But what are you doing here?'

'Collecting herbs.'

'Collecting them? You should have said something. We grow them in our garden. I'd have brought you some.'

Megan smiled. 'It's a kind offer, Princess, but I doubt if you grow all the ones I need. Besides, I'd take your whole crop. It's not just a pinch of seasoning I need.' She crouched to examine a sprig of something near her feet.

'What then?' asked Dahut.

'I make medicines.'

'Oh. You're a wise-woman, then?'

She looked up at us strangely.

'Well, I prefer that name to some others. I make medicines. I heal people. They show their gratitude by giving me food, or cloth, things I need. That's how I live.'

'What are you looking for now?' I asked.

'I was about to look for comfrey. There's some hereabouts most years.'

'Can we help?'

'Do you know what it looks like?'

We shook our heads.

'Then look for a plant about two or three feet high, with fleshy, hairy leaves which come to a point. The flowers will be small and mauve-coloured, growing in rows on little curved stalks. The ground is marshy just here where the rainwater drains down towards the cliff. That's the kind of soil that comfrey likes.'

We set ourselves to the task, but it was not long before Megan herself announced that she had found some. We helped her to pick the leaves and select one or two fat roots for her collection. As we finished this we became aware of a pattering sound, and the sun was blotted out by a cloud. Within moments the rain was pelting down hard, breaking through the leaves and splashing in darkening spots on our clothes.

'Come on,' said Megan. 'It gets cold quickly enough when the sun is hidden. Let's run to my cottage. It isn't far.'

So we ran behind her through the bushes and trees until we came to a dense group of tall oaks. Half-hidden underneath them was a small cottage, built in brick. This itself was a surprise – most of the village hovels were of wattle and daub – but when the door was opened there was another. Tiles! Real Roman tiles, cracked with age, but still serviceable enough. Whatever the cottage might be now, it had been something grander once – a small temple, perhaps.

'Come on,' said Megan, shutting the door. 'Get those wet things off and sit by the fire.'

And indeed we were wet through. Outside the rain was rattling on the roof in spite of the overhanging oaks. Occasionally a drop would find its way down the chimney and sizzle in the fire. We could hear this but not see it, for as yet the fire was nowhere to be seen. The room in which we now stood appeared to be the main hall of the old temple. It was sturdily built, but not richly. The walls were of plain white plaster, crumbling in places. There was a window high on each side, one with real glass, the other with a translucent skin drawn tightly across it. On the wall opposite the door was a curtain, apparently concealing the entrance to Megan's living quarters, for this outer room was clearly where she did her work. Standing in front of the curtain was a stone table, perhaps the old altar. Now it was a workbench with knives and a pestle and mortar standing on it. Down the right-hand side was a row of cupboards and shelves. On these were upwards of a hundred earthenware jars, each with a painted name describing the contents – herbs and potions of all kinds. Bunches of drying herbs hung from hooks in the wall.

Megan went forward and lifted the curtain, revealing a doorway through to the inner room.

'Come in and warm yourselves. There's a good fire here.'

There was indeed, on the left as we went in. A couple of good logs were burning merrily, driving out the cold that seems all the sharper when preceded by bright sunshine. There was a proper fireplace and chimney, not the smoke hole that one finds in a peasant hut. The room was almost square, and simply furnished. There was a bed in the far right-hand corner, and a table in the centre of the room with two benches. A large cupboard in the wall which backed on the main hall seemed to be the only place for Megan to store everything she owned. She went to it now and took three large blankets from it.

'There. Wrap yourselves in these while your things dry in front of the fire. I'll brew us up something warming.'

And she busied herself with a kettle and water and other things while we looked around us with eyes used to Gradlon's palace.

'Is this all you have to live in?' asked Dahut in wonder.

'Indeed it is. And what more do I need? There are many who have less.'

There was no answer to that. The poverty of the peasants was something which had led to rebellions against Roman taxes several times in the last century. But we had only heard of these, and seen the poverty from a distance. Besides, Megan was not poor as other people are. That is, she was not oppressed by her surroundings, short of food, or desperate for money, which in any case she didn't use. She had chosen to live simply.

Soon we each had a cup of Megan's brew. It was hot and sweet, with a bitter trace in it.

'Good for warding off colds,' she said.

'It tastes good,' I told her. 'Do you have a brew for everything?'

'Many things, not all. Some secrets the gods keep for themselves, I think.'

'Can you tell us some of them?'

'Do you really want to know such things?'

'Oh, yes!'

'The study of herb lore is not something to be undertaken lightly. A little learning is not enough when mistakes can kill. I can teach you, but only if you promise not to try out the knowledge on your own. At least until I say.'

We promised. We were very aware of the honour which Megan did us by sharing her wisdom, so we felt very important. She began right away, telling us of the comfrey we had helped her gather. I still remember that first lesson.

'Comfrey is a remedy for all kinds of ailments of the chest and throat. They say also that it softens the skin if used in bathwater, but I have my doubts. Anyway, I bathe in the sea or the stream, so I can't swear to it. Perhaps you could try it at the villa, or the palace?'

And so it went on. After that first day we returned many times eager to learn more. Megan soon found that we were eager pupils, and we learned fast. She would always pass on the received wisdom, but garnish it with observations of her own.

'They say that garlic aids the digestion, but then they say that about almost anything. I'll settle for camomile myself. Garlic does nothing for the breath!'

She taught us to look afresh at all kinds of common plants – dandelion, elder, nettle, yarrow. And she introduced us to others which were less familiar – coriander for rheumatism and indigestion, plantain for pain and for purifying cuts, tarragon for poor appetite, valerian for colds and headaches. At first we just played around, helping Megan when she asked for it, watching her and picking up hints. Then Dahut decided to learn seriously. She would spend hours listening to Megan's recipes — all of them very old, and handed on from others. Megan was clearly much more than just the village wise-woman. She could actually read and write, though not without difficulty.

'I was brought up in the worship of the Mother Goddess,' she said once, 'It was thought I might be a priestess. That is why I had some schooling. And where I learned the herb lore. But now that's all gone.'

'What do you mean?' said Dahut.

'The priests came – the Christians. They converted the poor people with promises of rewards in Heaven. So they persuaded them to deny themselves on earth. The landowners like that, of course. It keeps the peasants in their place. Anyhow, I never finished my training. The priestesses left. Some were killed, some fled to Sena.'

'Sena?' I had not heard that name before.

'It is an island off the coast. Some of the priestesses still live there, or did when I last heard. They had great powers once, but now all that is fading. The common people still observe some of the rituals, though. Every springtime fires are lit in the sacred groves.'

'What else do they do?'

'Men and women lie there together.'

'Lie there? You mean they ...?'

'If the Goddess moves them they come together in Her name. It is not for their own desire but for Hers, you see. She loves life, and that which makes life.'

I was a little taken aback by this revelation. The Roman and Christian traditions with which I was familiar both valued monogamy and fidelity in marriage. But Megan explained it in a matter-of-fact way which made it seem natural.

'Do you go to these, er, fires yourself?'

'Oh yes. I told you, I still hope for a daughter.'

She sighed then and looked away, and I didn't like to pursue the matter. Perhaps I could be her daughter, I thought. As I had no father, couldn't I be allowed two mothers instead of one? I said nothing of this at the time, but carried on visiting Megan when the chance came. The time when the messenger arrived from Kemper was usually the best. Everyone else was so eager for news that they worried little about us. Then one day we broke the habit.

The messenger brought two guests with him. One was Meriadauc, up from the South on a rare visit. The other was a Christian priest.

Chapter Eight

Parts of my story concern things which I myself was unable to see. Still, they have a bearing on the events of which I tell, and so I have used the accounts of others to piece together what happened. Such an episode is the story of Keban, a strange affair which took place during the first summer we were at Ker-Is.

Gradlon had fallen back into the depression from which he habitually suffered, and for the first time there were rumblings of discontent amongst his subjects. The plague had hit Kemper shortly after our departure. Fortunately, most of its force seemed to be spent. There were deaths, it is true, but it was not the disaster which people had feared. Many people even survived an attack of the disease if they were young and fit. None the less, the King was observed to lie in his palace in lethargy, and it added to people's resentment. Not that he was to blame, but he was expected to get out amongst his people and at least show them some leadership. Instead, he wept and raved, and most of the decisions were taken by Tiernan. By all accounts the steward was making a handsome profit out of the situation, too. He was left to give judgement in disputes, and soon found that it paid well to decide in favour of the rich. Indeed, as Gradlon's condition worsened Tiernan became more corrupt. He began assuming new powers, and found that no one challenged them, and it went to his head a little. By midsummer he had effective control of the army and the situation was becoming dangerous. Now when poor people arrived asking for justice they were turned away. Tiernan found it easier to dispense with the hearing altogether, as he still got paid either way. It was into this situation that Keban fell when she arrived in Kemper, seeking redress for the murder of her child.

Keban was a peasant woman, the wife of a woodcutter called Marc. They lived in the Forest of Nevet, to the north-west of Kemper. Not far away there lived a hermit, a Christian ascetic who tried to find God in isolation from his fellows. Personally, I have never understood how a man can lead a good life in this way, since being good surely means doing good to others. Still, there is a strong tradition of it amongst the Christians, one which goes back hundreds of years. Jesus himself is said to have fasted in the desert.

At all events, Keban had taken against this hermit, who was called Ronan. He had something of a reputation, and one which was not altogether savoury. For a start he was Irish, and the Irish were feared by the Western British as much as the Saxons were by their Eastern brothers. Irish raids had laid waste many a Welsh hamlet, and some Irish had even settled in southern Wales. Indeed, fear of the Irish was now becoming as important as fear of the Saxons in deciding the British to come to Armorica. Ronan was therefore the butt of prejudice on this account alone. But there was more. When he had first crossed the sea Ronan had settled in the northern part of Armorica, in Leon. No one seems quite sure what happened there, but Ronan departed under a cloud, amid accusations of sorcery. I am not sure that I believe in sorcerers, but many do, especially the Celts. It is one of their failings that they are prone to believe in wonders of all kinds. Still, Ronan had been living peacefully enough in the forest until Keban accused him. She appeared in Kemper early one morning, a brown, wrinkled woman of surprisingly mature years, considering her daughter's infancy.

Keban presented herself at the palace gateway, demanding to see the King in person. The guards just laughed, of course, and refused to let her pass. Budic, who had just been made deputy guard commander, was unyielding.

'Be off with you! Do you think His Majesty has nothing better to do than listen to peasants?'

She spat at their feet. 'Time was that Gradlon listened to any of his subjects with a just complaint, high or low. Tell the King I will not go until justice is given me.'

'You impudent old slag! Get going before you get justice of a sort you don't like!' And they shooed her away.

Keban was a crafty woman, and not one to give up so easily. She hung around all day, just out of reach of the guards, who dared not leave their post to chase her. She yelled her case to anyone who passed by, and lamented the fact that justice was denied to her. Eventually word came to Tiernan. Keban was much too poor to be of interest to him, and so he ordered her whipped.

'Maybe a dozen lashes will teach her to hold her tongue. If not she can have another dozen tomorrow, and the next day. Tell her there's plenty more where that came from.'

It was done as he ordered. Keban was taken to the marketplace, stripped to the waist, and whipped as a public nuisance. One of the soldiers who was present told me it seemed not to affect her at all.

'She sniffed a bit, of course. The pain of it brought tears to my eyes, let alone hers, I can tell you. Her a woman, too. Well it doesn't seem right. That stripping business is not so bad for a man. But it does more to a woman. It's an insult to her pride, you see. Not to Keban's, though. She took her flogging with hardly a sound. When it was over she covered herself up decent, like. Then she turns to the whip-man and she says: "Tell your master I'll be back tomorrow." And bugger me — pardon me, *Domina* – bless me if she wasn't. Large as life she was, outside the gate. Well, she struck lucky at last. Gradlon himself had heard something of her by now. I should think her yelling had kept him awake nights. Anyway, he orders her brought to him, for her case to be heard. You should have seen her, *Domina*. In the gate she walks, proud as a peacock. Then she turns and spits at each of the guard in turn – taking care to miss, mind, I think she realised they'd had enough – and then up the steps she goes, chuckling to herself, a filthy, half-mad old peasant woman going to see the King.'

I refrained from pointing out that at the time the King was filthy and half-mad himself.

Keban was brought before King Gradlon in the great hall where I had first seen him. The shutters were closed again, a never-failing indicator of the King's state of mind.

'Blessing on Your Majesty for graciously admitting me to your presence,' declared Keban, to the King's apparent amusement.

'Yes, well, I thank you for your blessing, woman. What do you want of me?'

'Your Majesty, I crave justice. I have been grievously wronged by a man who lives near us, on the borders of your kingdom. His name is Ronan.'

'Ronan the hermit. Hm. Some word of him has come to us. In what way has he wronged you?'

'Your Majesty, he has devoured my daughter.'

There was some confusion amongst the assembled company at this. Was the woman speaking figuratively, or was her complaint of cannibalism? The King raised a hand for silence.

'Devoured her? Do you mean he has eaten her?'

'He is a monster, Your Majesty. He poses as holy man, but in reality he is a sorcerer. He has bewitched many people in our neighbourhood. He turns himself into a wolf and prowls the forest at night. Oh, Your Majesty, he has even put my husband under a spell. My Marc has left our cottage and lives with the hermit as his servant. And this despite what happened to our dear daughter.'

'What did happen?'

Keban wept as she told the tale. 'One evening we were waiting outside our cottage for my husband to return. It was a warm day, and we were preparing dinner in the open air, with no thought of danger. We had often done the same. My little one was playing at the edge of the forest. Suddenly I heard her scream, and when I looked up a great wolf was standing there. The brute had grabbed her in his jaws, and she was struggling to escape. I snatched a burning log from the cooking fire and made for him, but he went off with her. I followed through the forest, guided at first by her cries, and then only by the trail of blood.'

Here she broke down for a while. Everyone waited in silence while she recovered herself.

'Your Majesty, I tracked the accursed fiend to his lair under a rocky cliff. There was a shallow cave, and the trail of blood led directly to it. As I approached I saw him. I saw Ronan the sorcerer. He had something in his hand. When I got closer I saw what it was.'

There was another interlude of weeping.

'It was my little one's arm!'

There was a renewed hubbub at this, but Gradlon waved them all into silence.

'What did Ronan do?'

'He ran off. I attacked him with the firebrand, but he escaped. I followed as far as his hermitage but he was not there. There was an altar there of wood. I set fire to it. He did not come back, so I returned home.'

'And what did your husband do when you told him?'

'He went to see Ronan straight away to challenge him. But the fiend put a spell on him. Marc returned saying Ronan was a good man. Now he no longer even lives with me. He has rebuilt the altar and lives at Ronan's hermitage. I am abandoned.'

'But, woman, surely all your evidence is circumstantial? I grieve with you for your daughter – I too have a daughter – but might there not be simple explanations for all you have told us?'

'Your Majesty! Ronan holds evil rites at his altar in the forest. His followers meet there to eat human flesh.'

'What?'

'They eat flesh and drink human blood, Your Majesty. Ask anyone in the forest. We all know about it.'

'Why has no one complained of this before?'

Keban knelt before him with arms outstretched.

'I am complaining now, Your Majesty. I accuse Ronan of sorcery, cannibalism and murder! I demand the justice which is the right of your lowliest subject! I beg you to stop this demon and his foul rites!'

She pitched forward on to her face, and someone ran to help her. Gradlon called his advisers to him.

'What do you think, gentlemen?'

'The woman's crazy,' said Tiernan.

'Maybe with grief,' said another. 'That doesn't make her a liar. I think we should have this Ronan here to answer the charges.'

A third man agreed. 'Can we have it said that King Gradlon refused to investigate such serious complaints. I think Ronan should be brought, and the woman's husband should come as a witness.'

'See to it! Tiernan, we'll have a strong escort for this Ronan. If he resists let him be brought in chains, but he must come!'

Tiernan grumbled privately, no doubt, for there was no profit for him in this one. Still he had to obey. The escort was duly sent, while Keban was lodged in the servant's quarters of the palace. It took three days for the escort to find Ronan and bring him back – alone, for Keban's husband was nowhere to be found. By this time the servants and soldiers were beginning to have doubts about his accuser. She spun a fine tale, to be sure, but she enjoyed the attention a sight too much for someone who was supposed to be so distressed. But who could tell with such things? Perhaps she was only pleased at the thought of the villain getting his just deserts.

On the third day Ronan's trial began before the King. Perhaps it is a measure of how far the Roman ways had already slipped from favour, but this was no trial in the traditional Roman sense. There were no lawyers, no judges except Gradlon, and no rules of evidence. When Ronan was brought in to face the assembled company he did not have a friend in the place.

I am told he was an impressive figure. Dressed though he was in the coarse brown habit of a monk, and barefoot, yet he was a powerful man, tall and broad. His ascetic life did not seem to include a starvation diet. Of course, this only added to the dark mutterings among those present. His hair was long and wispy, and not very clean, for these hermits seem to think it unholy to wash. His features were sharply chiselled and almost handsome. ('He had a big nose,' said Menevia, 'Obviously a nobleman.') For whatever reason, Ronan impressed the onlookers with his physical appearance, and his expression of tolerant amusement.

'You are not afraid?' said Gradlon.

'Should I be, Your Majesty?' The voice was deep and resonant, the sort of voice a bard might wish for. 'I have been promised justice. Why then should I be afraid?'

Gradlon shifted uncomfortably. 'Quite so. You are aware of the charges against you?'

The man nodded. 'I am. At least in general terms. Sorcery, cannibalism, murder, things of that sort.'

'Damn it, man, do not make light of such things!'

'Your Majesty, I do not. Not when they have really occurred.'

'You deny the charges, then.'

'You could hardly expect me to admit them, even if they were true.'

This was not quite the way the accused was supposed to speak, and Gradlon was clearly uncomfortable. Ronan's attitude was not so much insolent as quietly superior. Gradlon indicated Keban, now standing fearfully to one side.

'You know this woman?'

'Indeed I do, poor soul. I pray for her every day. She is in the grip of a madness born of bereavement. I pray that the Lord may send her release.'

Some interpreted this as meaning that he prayed for her death, and there were more mutterings around the hall.

'Be that as it may, she accuses you of sorcery. She says you change into a wolf and prey on others in this form.'

Ronan smiled. 'Indeed? And why should I do that? I am not a small man, as you will observe. I can handle a sword and a spear, and a club. Why should I need to change into a wolf? I could prey on others as a man, if I had such a sinful intention. But our dear Lord urges us to serve others, not to harm them, even if they harm us.'

'Keban has told us that her daughter was carried off by a wolf, and that when she tracked it to its lair she found you, just returned to human form, carrying the child's remains.'

'Does she say I was carrying them in my teeth?'

'What? Of course not!'

'If I were a wolf ... but no matter. She certainly found me at the wolf's lair. I had seen the child and was trying to rescue it.'

'Were you holding the child's arm?'

'It was all I could find.'

A buzz went round the room. Keban screamed.

'He admits it! The monster admits it!'

'Why did you seek for the child's remains?'

'To give them a decent burial, Your Majesty. The lair of a wild animal is no fit resting place for one of God's innocents.'

The King fell silent for a few moments. Then he tried another tack.

'Where did you live before you came to the Forest of Nevet?'

'In the kingdom of Leon, Your Majesty, and before that in my native Ireland.'

'Why did you leave?'

'I left Ireland because God spoke to me. He told me that the Armorican British were straying from the paths of righteousness. Indeed, that many had never been Christian at all. It was my duty to spread the joyous news of Christ's coming.'

'And why did you leave Leon?'

'I am afraid the Lord's message is not always well received.'

'They threw you out. We have had some word of you, you know. You were accused of sorcery there, too.'

'Your Majesty, I was accused, but only by ignorant folk who did not understand the ways of our Church. I invoked the Lord to heal people. This was a misunderstanding by some.'

'You seem to make a habit of being misunderstood.' The King was hardening against the man. 'Listen, Ronan, I am not pleased with your answers. I find them evasive. I like a straight answer to a straight question.'

Tiernan then spoke up. He was obviously searching for a way to get the business over with quickly.

'Why not put the man to ordeal, Your Majesty? That would settle the case quickly enough.'

There were murmurs of assent around the room. In most people's minds the man was guilty, and it would provide a spectacle if he were done to death in some suitably barbarous way. Gradlon was not usually given to the practice, being intelligent enough to see its obvious pitfalls, but on this occasion he gave way. Perhaps he too had already decided.

'Very well. Take him to the field!'

A cheer went up, and the man was led outside the palace wall to the field in which executions were normally carried out. This featured a large oak tree, from which murderers were sometimes hanged. For Ronan, however, the King had something different in mind. He ordered that the hermit be tied to the trunk. Ronan seemed remarkably unperturbed, as if his life were put in jeopardy every day. He asked only that his hands should be left free, in order that he might hold a crucifix, and that he might be given a few minutes to pray before the ordeal began. Gradlon could see nothing against this, and agreed. Ronan knelt for a few minutes in an attitude of prayer, and then rose.

'I am ready.'

They took him to the tree, still clutching his crucifix. He was tied standing up with his back to the trunk. A rope was simply wound around several times and fastened on the other side of the tree. Thus his hands were left free, as he had asked, and he could hold his crucifix. This was a large item, considering it had been hanging around his neck. No doubt he would have denied that he felt the weight. The cross was of wood, and on it was the figure of Christ in a polished metal. The man kissed it, and then held it over his heart.

'Fetch the hounds!' ordered Gradlon. He owned two large hunting dogs, and these were to be the basis of Ronan's ordeal. They would tear a man to bits if Gradlon ordered it, and would be governed by no one else but their keeper. Even some of those who thought Ronan guilty shivered at the thought of those beasts tearing the flesh off a living man. Not that Gradlon was that inhumane.

No doubt, if the trial went against Ronan, a speedy despatch would be ordered. Still, as the dogs arrived on the field, straining at their leashes, the crowd fell silent. Gradlon petted the animals and then slipped their leashes. They sat quietly at his command, while the King addressed Ronan once more.

'For the last time, do you wish to change your plea? Are you guilty of the charges?'

'No, Your Majesty, and no. You are a fair-minded man, but as I have denied the charges I would seem to have little to gain by changing my plea now.' And the hermit smiled ruefully.

'Do you not fear death?'

'With the cross of my Lord Jesus in my hand, and the love of God in my heart? No. What is there to fear? I will not die unless God wills it, and if he does, who am I to gainsay him?'

One or two Christians in the crowd cried out at this evidence of piety. Some demanded Ronan's release, but were quickly shouted down. Even Gradlon appeared moved by the man's apparent sincerity, and was seen to shoot an evil glance at Keban, grinning obliviously nearby.

'Woman,' he said, 'You had better be right, or you may find yourself in his place.'

'Do but set the dogs on him, my Lord King, and we will see who is right!' Her eyes burned brightly, and her breath was short, as if the prospect of death excited her. Gradlon turned away towards the hounds, and the crowd fell silent once more. Not a bird twittered as the King gave the command.

'Attack! Kill!'

Instantly the animals leapt forward. They had perhaps fifty feet to travel, and would cover it in moments. Ronan held his cross forward and began a sonorous incantation in Latin. To the common people this was obviously a curse in some demonic tongue, and was proof of his guilt. But the educated people present knew what was being said.

'Stay, hounds! May the Lord stop your mouth for me as he did the mouths of the lions for Daniel! Lord, let not the blood of thy servant flow in the mouth of the beast!'

By now the first beast was nearly on him. Suddenly, Ronan leaned forward as far as he could, as if to meet it. With the cross before him he spoke again, in a voice deeper and more vibrant than ever.

'In the name of Christ, I command you. Stop!'

The animal stopped.

Whether it was the commanding voice, or the man's sheer fearlessness, or whether (as Tiernan later claimed) Ronan dazzled the beast by reflecting sunlight into its eyes with the crucifix, the hound stopped in its tracks. Perhaps the Christian god really does exist; no one knows. But the hound stopped. Snarling and drooling, to be sure, but it stopped. So did its companion. Ronan continued to talk to them, but in a lower voice, still holding the crucifix out before him. No one could hear the words, but the effect was clear enough. The dogs sat, and their fierceness ebbed away. Then one of them turned and trotted back to Gradlon, wagging its tail good-naturedly. The other approached Ronan gingerly, sniffed at his robe, moved around the tree, and then piddled against the bark. This incident, so absurdly commonplace in the midst of such high drama, broke the mood in a trice. The crowd laughed, and the laughter turned to cheering. They ran forward to congratulate the man whose blood they had been demanding only minutes before.

Gradlon too walked forward to the hermit. He untied the man with his own hands. Then he spoke.

'Ronan, I have wronged you. I crave your pardon. You have been wrongly accused, and I hereby declare that you are innocent, and free to go wherever you wish in my kingdom. My hounds never obeyed anyone but me or their keeper, not until now. We have seen a miracle today.'

'Indeed we have, Your Majesty, and you remind me that I must give thanks for it.' And the hermit knelt on the grass and raised his arms heavenward. In a voice heavy with emotion he praised his god, gave thanks for his deliverance, and pledged his continued unswerving devotion. Then he stood and addressed the crowd.

'Today you have all witnessed the power of the Lord, the One True God. I pray that you will all heed it, and come to know the Lord through his son, Jesus Christ.'

There were a few amens from the Christians in the crowd, and some nervous agreements from some who were not, but thought they had seen a miracle. Gradlon took the hermit by the arm, his face aglow with excitement.

'You must come back to the palace with me. I wish to learn more of this god of yours.' Then he turned and saw Keban, who had tried to slink off and been grabbed by the guards.

'And as for you, Keban, I do not know which is the unkindest death for you, but be sure I shall think of it. You have deliberately tried to bring about the death, not just of a man, but a man touched by the divine power.'

Keban wailed, but it was Ronan who protested.

'Your Majesty! I beg you not to harm this woman!'

'What, after all that she had done? She has perjured herself, tried to kill you.'

'But not with evil intent, Your Majesty. I told you that I believe her to have been driven mad by grief. Can we condemn her for maternal affection so strong that it unbalanced her judgement when her child was so cruelly lost?'

Gradlon stared in astonishment. 'And to think that you called *me* fair-minded just now.'

'The man is a saint!'

This was from a peasant who had stepped out from the crowd.

'And who are you?' demanded Gradlon.

The man knelt before him. 'Your Majesty, I am Marc of Nevet, woodcutter, and husband of Keban. I was away working in the forest when Ronan was arrested, but I came as soon as I heard the news.'

'I see. Well, your priest could have done with your support, but he seems to have managed all right on his own.'

'Not on my own. The Lord was with me.'

'We will talk of that. Meanwhile, what of Keban?'

Marc spoke up. 'Your Majesty, I beg you not to treat her harshly. She has suffered greatly over the loss of our daughter.'

'Have you not also suffered?'

'Yes, Your Majesty, but our faith tells us that she is not dead, but gone to Heaven to live for ever with Jesus. I know that when my time comes I will see her again. My wife does not share that faith, being still ensnared by the false gods of the pagans.'

'It seems to me today that you are the better off.' Gradlon ordered Keban brought to him. She hung her head and refused to meet his eye.

'Keban, I had half decided to have you burned at the stake. You deserve it for your treachery, if you are sane. But your priest and your husband have convinced me that you are mad with grief, and cannot be held responsible. Very well. But since your madness seems to have settled on Ronan as the cause of all your trouble, be aware that it is to him that you owe your life. His plea has saved you, and into his care I will commit you. Will you agree to be placed in his care, and be ruled by him and by your husband?'

There was a long pause, while Keban wept noisily. Then she nodded. 'I will agree.'

There was a loud cheer from those around. After all, at the end of the day no great harm had been done, and their sympathies had been swayed by Keban's weeping. Anyway, surely she couldn't be all bad if Ronan and Marc were prepared to plead for her like that?

Ronan went to the palace with Gradlon, and stayed there for several days, teaching the King about his 'one true God'. It is said that Gradlon offered to make him Bishop of Kemper, and to build a church for him, but that Ronan refused. Be that as it may, less than a week later the King announced his conversion to the new religion. He did not ask anyone else to conform for the time being, but he did ask Ronan to send for monks from the island seminary of Brehat, to come and preach to the local people.

By the time that Meriadauc arrived back in Kemper it was already half Christian, a good many people having seen the light in order to further their ambitions at court. Many of the common people had also been converted after the scenes at Ronan's trial, although most of them combined their Christian and pagan observances to be on the safe side. As usual, Meriadauc called to pay his respects to Gradlon, and learned from him where we were. Gradlon readily gave him permission to visit us, but insisted that he take a monk with him 'to bring us the good news', and to preach to the village people.

By 'good news' he meant not only his new religion, but also the fact that no new cases of plague had been reported since he had adopted it. The way would soon be clear for us to return to Kemper.

Chapter Nine

'The Huns are on the move again!'

The envoy from Aëtius stood squarely in front of Gradlon and looked him in the eye.

'Aëtius reminds you that your people are here as a federate tribe of the Empire, and that you are bound to support it in time of war.'

War! A ripple went around the assembled company. Gradlon ignored it.

'I do not need an ambassador to remind me of my obligations,' he said truculently. 'Least of all those I owe to the Empire. If war comes, I shall not be laggardly in providing Aëtius with soldiers. But will it really come to that? The Huns have ridden out before, the Lord knows, and we have never beaten them on the field. Only the Emperor's gold has kept them away. Until the next time.'

The envoy shifted uncomfortably. Gradlon's cynical point of view was fully justified, and it was shared by half the Western world.

'Times have changed, King Gradlon. At last there is a real Emperor in the East. He has refused the Hun any more tributes, and Valentinian has joined him in his stand.'

I understood the background to this well enough. It was several years now since my mother had begun teaching Dahut and me in that first summer at Ker-Is. Our education had continued on our return to Kemper, and Gradlon had given his approval. We still went to Ker-Is in summer, but now it was more of a holiday from school. Only Megan taught us much there, and her teaching was of a kind not be found in any schoolroom. It was my mother who taught us history.

It had been over fifty years since the Roman Empire had split into two halves, West and East, with an emperor in each part. There were not supposed to be separate entities, and the emperors were supposed to hold their authority jointly, but the differences were real and deep-seated. Even the language was different. The East favoured Greek instead of Latin. The East had also suffered less from the attacks of the barbarians, although there had been one or two spectacular defeats. The Eastern Emperor had bought peace with gold, and the West had followed suit.

This year the Eastern Emperor had died, after forty-two years on the throne. The new Emperor, Marcian, was much younger, and determined to put an end to the Empire's humiliation. He had boldly refused to pay any further tributes to the Huns. The weak and effeminate Valentinian, now in his twenty-fifth year of rule in the West, had joined with him in defying the barbarians. Perhaps he thought he could revive Roman power even at this stage. At all events, Attila of the Huns could not ignore this new development. Without Roman gold he could not pay his army.

'And so war is inevitable,' went on the envoy. 'At first we thought Attila might move against Constantinople, but reports from over the Rhine say that many thousands of horsemen are moving westwards.'

'Then Lord have mercy on the Gauls. Even here we have heard how the Huns treat their enemies.'

'Perhaps, but the Huns are kindly enough to those who throw in their lot with them. It is opposition they cannot bear. Half of their army consists of German tribes whom they have made subject to their rule – Gepids, Goths, and the like. Aëtius believes that this may be their undoing. The subject tribes are mainly Christians.'

'Christians!' Gradlon was scandalised.

'Of a kind. Arian heretics, mostly, but it must be repulsive for them to be subject to a pagan king. Aëtius believes that if we can damage Attila enough, the subject tribes will rise and finish the work for us. Arderic of the Gepids is known to be restless, for one.'

'God grant that Aëtius is right.'

'Amen to that. In the meantime I am directed to ask that you provide the greatest possible force to help defeat the Huns when they cross into Gaul.'

'You shall have it,' Gradlon assured him. 'And I shall lead the force myself. But how many I can spare may depend on you.'

The envoy looked nonplussed. 'What do you mean?'

'Some of my neighbours are not altogether to be trusted. I would only feel happy leaving Kemper unguarded if I knew that Vorganium and the Veneti were doing the same.'

'I understand, I will visit them also, and make it clear that Aëtius requires the same support from them as from you. Furthermore, should anyone take advantage of the situation, I can guarantee our support in return for yours.'

'Very well. When does Aëtius want my men?'

'We believe that the Huns will sit out the winter north of the Rhine, and cross it in the spring. Aëtius plans to be ready for them by the time they reach Gaul.'

'Very well. It is now October. He shall have my forces directly after Christmas. You may tell Aëtius that we shall not fail him. We are well aware that Rome is all that stands between Christendom and barbarism.'

The envoy seemed well pleased with the reply. In the months that followed he visited all Kemper's neighbours and extracted similar promises from them. He also sent word that all had sworn to forgo any local quarrels until the Huns menace was defeated. This assumed that the Romans' defence would be successful, of course, but no one dared think what would happen if it were not. The Huns' reputation had grown in the hundred years of their attacks. They were feared even more than the Saxons.

In the meantime Kemper became a garrison town as the army was gathered together from all over Gradlon's kingdom. The military camp itself was just outside the walls, and a secondary camp grew up around it to meet the demands of the large body of men. The tradesmen and innkeepers did a roaring trade, as did the pimps and whores.

In the day the whole town rang with the sound of hammers on metal, as the smiths forged weapons and armour. At night it rang with the sounds of drunken carousing, as the soldiers waited impatiently to be ordered away, and chased the local girls, and sometimes even their mothers. It became a joke that the men and the women of the town were both growing fat, but for different reasons.

All of this had little direct effect upon me. I was too young to receive the attentions of any of the men, even those of the officer class. Only Tiernan seemed to notice me, and then in such a sly and furtive way that it was only disturbing. Young as we were, we were beginning to suspect that his sidelong glances and maudlin air in our presence were evidence of desires which were not altogether wholesome. Dahut being older than I, her development was that much more advanced. She was now fourteen, and her beauty deepened as she grew. She was not only pretty now, but voluptuous, with the body of a young woman. I mean in every respect, for it demonstrated its maturity every month now as women's bodies do. By contrast I was physically almost a child still, with the merest suggestion of breasts and none of Dahut's curves at waist and hip. Gradlon was not unaware of his daughter's development, and had talked of arranging a marriage for her if a match could be found. Dahut herself had no enthusiasm for the subject, and welcomed the fact that he was not too busy with the army to think of such things. Until, that is, Riwal arrived to join the forces now massing at Kemper.

We first saw Riwal when my mother took us to see the military camp. We had repeatedly asked her if we could watch the soldiers drilling, for we were bursting with curiosity about the army, the noise of which rang over the city walls day and night. She was not eager to grant this request, saying that an army camp was no place for children, especially girls. However, in the end she agreed to ask the King if we might just visit the place. He agreed, and placed a wagon and driver at our disposal, together with a couple of palace guards. He did this deliberately, as their uniforms were eye-catching and distinctive.

'It may save anyone embarrassing themselves if it is clear that you come from the palace,' he said. I did not know what he meant at the time, but mother clearly did, and even Dahut smiled knowingly. The truth, of course, was that any unprotected woman was likely to be accosted at every step. There had been several cases of rape, and already two soldiers had been hanged. Even the merchants' enthusiasm for the army was beginning to wane. Soldiers might be good for business, but not if housewives were afraid to venture out and buy.

We set out in an open wagon, complete with our escort and full of excitement about our trip. As we passed through the market place on our way to the city gate the impact of the military was already visible. There were soldiers everywhere, buying and bidding, drinking and wenching. The regulars were well-behaved enough. They were career soldiers, used to discipline, and keeping their service records free from blemish in the hope of promotion. The problem was that there were hundreds of levy troops who had been working in the fields until a few weeks earlier. Indeed, many places had to delay the raising of their levy until the harvest was in. Each town had a levy to raise, the number of troops decided according to its size and character. Many of them were very young and had never been away from home before. Their high-spiritedness was hardly surprising, and they got into trouble everywhere. For many of them it was also the first time they had been able to feel of any kind of importance, and they were easily recognised in the market, with their ill-assorted items of uniform and their swaggering air.

Soon we were through the market and out of the city gate. Not far from the gate the road was flanked by two clumps of trees, and as we came through these the camp was suddenly revealed. We were, to say the least, astonished. I had seen small encampments of troops in Britain, at Uncle Lucian's estate. At Kemper there were always some soldiers, although they had a proper barracks to live in. But this new camp was on a scale that none of us had ever seen. On both sides of the road there were wide open plains, and as far as the eye could see there were tents – great long tents for the soldiers, with smaller ones dotted about for the officers. There were fenced paddocks for the horses, hundreds of them, and long lines of supply wagons. As well as dray horses there were many of a lighter, speedier breed – presumably for the cavalry which formed an increasing part of the army, now that we had seen what horses could do for the Huns.

A little further on, to our left, there was a large clear space, where soldiers in full battle order were drilling. As the officers bellowed orders, the columns wheeled and turned, seeming to miss each other by inches. The ground was damp, or there would have been a constant cloud of dust over everything. On the right a similar clear space was occupied by other soldiers, training with wooden practice weapons.

'Can we stop and watch for a while?' asked Dahut excitedly.

Mother smiled and agreed. It seemed we had come at an interesting time. One young soldier was obviously emerging as something of a champion. He had apparently beaten a number of others, some of whom were sitting around nursing their bruises and hoping to see their conqueror defeated in turn. The trainer was standing to one side, shouting at the contestants.

'That's it, Paulus, under the shield! No! Under it, you fool!' and to the champion: 'Well parried sir! Now watch that left side! You're exposed there! Hah, he nearly had you then, sir!'

I wondered why he was calling one of them 'sir' but not the other. The object of his respect looked about eighteen – too young to have a high military rank – but I supposed he must be from an important family. That would be enough to get him some position of authority. He looked noble enough, what we could see of him as he ducked and wheeled in the mock fight, his lips tight, his chin jutting determinedly forward. His hair was concealed under his helmet. The eyes were large and dark, and never left his adversary. His leather tunic covered his arms only to the elbow. Below that they rippled with muscles, as did the legs visible beneath the skirt of it.

'Isn't he beautiful?' Dahut breathed in my ear.

'Dahut! I felt awkward and rather shocked. Our age difference mattered in things of this sort. Dahut was amused.

'Keri, dear, you're such a little girl still, and yet such an old woman, too!'

She laughed her engaging laugh, and I saw the princely youth glance upward at the wagon, momentarily off guard.

His opponent saw it too, and in a flash he had knocked the champion's shield aside with his own, running his sword underneath the other's arm and into his side. He fell down and a cheer went up from the others.

'Well done,' said Mother, who then turned to start a conversation with one of our escort.

'That's it, sir!' said the trainer. 'Lucky it wasn't the real thing, eh?' And he went off into a lecture about the importance of concentration. It was lost on the fallen champion, who sat in the mud rubbing his side and looking at Dahut with a rueful grin. I turned to her, and saw an expression I had never seen before. Her eyes were wide and bright, and her cheeks flushed scarlet. She almost looked feverish. But it was only the first sign of a sickness which comes to most of us at one time or another.

The cause of her condition got up and wiped off some clods of earth which had stuck to his tunic. Then he unfastened the chinstrap of his helmet and took it off as he walked towards us. As he looked up I heard Dahut sigh quietly, a strange, wistful sort of sound, and well she might.

With his helmet on the man was merely handsome. With his face properly visible he was a god. There are hardly words to describe him. If I say his features were fine it makes him out to be girlish, when he was intensely male. If I say he had a strong face it makes him sound coarse-featured. To say that he was handsome falls far short of the truth. His eyes burned. That I remember well. His eyes held you; they seemed to look through you. When he looked at me I felt embarrassed, almost undressed, and yet it was the briefest of glances. Dahut was the one he had eyes for.

'I hope, I hope I didn't distract you,' she mumbled. She could hardly speak.

'I'm glad you did.' He bowed stiffly before our wagon. 'Allow me to present myself.'

My mother had turned back from her conversation with the guard. She quickly decided that the situation needed taking in hand.

'You are addressing the daughter of King Gradlon,' she announced.

'I assumed that,' he replied evenly. 'Few others would warrant an escort of palace guards. I am afraid my guards are not with me. I am Riwal, son of King Maglus of the Osismii.'

'Oh, Your Highness, I ...'

He waved her apologies aside. 'How could you know? And with a princess to chaperone ...'

He spoke only a few more words, exchanged pleasantries, and listened politely while Mother introduced us all formally. His eyes never left Dahut, nor hers him. Then he backed away and bowed again.

'I hope I shall soon have the pleasure of meeting you again.'

Dahut could only nod, and he turned on his heel and walked away. She stared after him until his figure was lost among the tents. During the rest of the ride she sat without speaking a word, but when we were in bed that night she had plenty to say.

'Keri, what did you think of Riwal?'

I felt a little uncomfortable. I was aware of what was happening to her, but too young to understand it myself.

'Think? Why, I'd almost forgotten about him.'

'You can't mean that. Wasn't he simply the most beautiful man you ever set eyes on?'

'Well, I suppose he was handsome enough,' I admitted grudgingly.

Dahut giggled. 'Handsome enough? Oh, Keri, what is the matter with you? The very sight of him sent shivers through me. Didn't you feel the same?'

'No! I didn't feel the same! And you shouldn't be saying such things. It's no way for a princess to talk.'

'Since when did we worry about how princesses are supposed to talk? We are friends, aren't we? Can't we talk like friends? If I can't share my feelings with you, who can I share them with?'

'Maybe you'd better try your prince.'

'I intend to.' She paused for a moment. 'Keri, are you jealous?'

I wasn't sure what to say. I didn't know what I felt, but it was something I had never felt before.

'I feel a bit afraid,' I managed at last. 'Riwal is a prince. You are unpromised. Your father would probably let you marry him, and then you would go away with him, and I'd never see you.'

'Oh, Keri, do you think I could go away without my only friend? Anyone who takes me will have to take my principal companion too. After all, I'll have to have ladies-in-waiting, and you shall be the first. I'm not having some old dragon who only lives off the royal family because she couldn't get herself a man.'

'What did you mean when you said "I intend to"?'

She turned away from me. 'I don't know. I wasn't really thinking.'

And there it starts, I thought. She is already keeping things from me. I too turned away, and found that there were tears in my eyes. The first time a man made me cry, and he wasn't even mine.

It was not long before Dahut and Riwal met again. It seems that my mother had mentioned him to Gradlon, who found time to consider Dahut's future in between all the preparations for war. Indeed, he seemed to have time to consider everything. He ascribed his new-found energy to the power of his new god, and everyone agreed that his conversion had lifted a weight from him. But it was at least partly the war itself. Perhaps it gave him a sense of purpose. Perhaps he dreamed of future glories like those of his past, when he had found his flaxen northern queen. People certainly admired him as he rode through the town in clothes that befitted a king.

'Ah,' they would say. 'That's the old Gradlon again. It's many a year since he looked so fine, such a real man.'

He was aware of their approval, but he was intelligent enough not to let it go to his head. The battles were still to be fought. Let them see how they felt later when he returned – if he returned – and broke the news to those who had lost their menfolk. And his faith was not all in his god. He trained as hard as anyone, lest he should be amongst those who did not return.

His restored efficiency extended to domestic matters also, and when he heard about his ally's fine son, he invited them both to a banquet at the palace.

The excuse for celebration was that the preliminary training was now complete, but Dahut was convinced that it was all to do with Riwal. She walked on air, sure that her father would approve of the boy, and would negotiate a marriage agreement with old Maglus. I tried to reason with her, my jealousy unabated.

'What if he doesn't like him?' I would say.

'Who?'

'Your father. What if he doesn't like Riwal?'

'How could he not?' She was blind where Riwal was concerned.

'Maybe he has someone else in mind for you, someone of higher rank.'

'Higher than a prince?'

'Higher than a tribal chief's son, maybe. Perhaps he wants to make an alliance with someone. They often do that with a marriage, Mamma's taught us that.'

'He doesn't. I know. When I was betrothed before it was with that in mind, but the boy died, and there were no other unbetrothed sons. Father would have said if he had thought of someone else.'

The truth was that I was hoping for something else to happen. I suppose I knew that princesses marry, and often young, often for political reasons, but I didn't want it to be yet. I was not old enough for marriage myself, and I didn't want to lose my friend just because she was. Whatever she said, I couldn't see a husband putting up with his bride's childhood friend, and why should he? Relatives have to be tolerated, but why tolerate any other outside influences? There are enough separate ambitions at any court as it is.

The banquet did nothing to calm my fears, but it also marked the first step towards my acceptance of the inevitable. It was held in that same hall that Dahut and I used to spy on from our secret passageway. From my seat, to the left of the top table, I could just make out the missing bricks where we used to peep through. At the top table itself sat Gradlon and his principal commanders, including Maglus of the Osismii. Dahut was by Gradlon's side, and Riwal by Maglus's. It was clear that Dahut and Riwal still had eyes only for each other. Indeed, at times they got the chance to talk for a moment, and both would blush deeply, to the intense amusement of those around them.

And at times I saw Dahut look at him when his attention was elsewhere. Then she looked less like a passionate girl than a predatory animal. The look on her face was tense and unattractive – a kind of greed. Then he would look at her again. Her face would melt into a smile of warmth and affection, and I would think I had imagined it all.

My mother was next to me, and was as aware as anyone of what was going on. She seemed amused, too, but I thought she was also a little concerned. She spoke to me about it at one point.

'I do hope Dahut isn't too carried away, especially now that Maglus and his son are actually staying in the palace.'

'Whatever do you mean, Mamma?'

'I mean that love is a hard master. Any young couple as desperate for each other as those two should be married as soon as possible.'

I had only a vague understanding of this, but it made me think. Perhaps I was being selfish. Perhaps I should be glad if my friend had so much happiness in view. When I thought of my own behaviour, I felt a little ashamed. Dahut would not desert me. She would still need a friend, even when she was married. Other royal brides did. They had lots of relatives, whereas Dahut had only me. I would attend her, she had said so. She would not let me down. Which was why, when Gradlon rose and announced the betrothal of his daughter to Maglus's son, I was able to cheer and applaud as loudly as anyone, and mean it.

'A king has many duties,' began Gradlon. 'But not so many that he should forget his duties as a father. As you all know, my daughter Dahut is nearly fifteen years old, and thus of marriageable age. I must confess that I had given this little thought recently, because of the pressures of organising our fighting force. I know my daughter will forgive me for that.' He chuckled and added: 'Especially since she was anxious about the choice I might make.' There was polite laughter at this. 'Naturally, the choice of a husband for one's daughter is a weighty decision, especially so for a royal family. The candidates are a little restricted, shall we say.' Again there was polite laughter. 'However, recently I was reminded that there is amongst us now a most suitable young man. Not only is he of an appropriate rank in society, but he is also a brave man, skilled in arms as befits a king, and skilled in letters also, as befits a head of state. I believe that he will prove a good husband for my daughter and a good king when the time comes. To cut a long story short, I have discussed the idea with the lad's father, and we have agreed that the betrothal should be announced tonight. Therefore, I want you all now to drink a toast to my daughter Dahut, and her future husband, Riwal, son of Maglus, King of the Osismii.'

A roar of approval went up at this, and voices and goblets were raised all around the table. The objects of this attention looked down at their plates and blushed scarlet.

'What's more,' Gradlon went on, 'I understand that the young couple are very happy with the arrangement, because they had noticed each other before we did!' There were more cheers, and a few bawdy remarks, at this. 'So, my kingly and fatherly duties have been made a pleasure also, knowing that this marriage will be made in Heaven as well as at the negotiating table.'

Several of the pagan guests developed a great interest in the planks of the table at this point. They knew that Riwal's family had been Christian for generations, and that this sealed the future of Kemper as a Christian kingdom.

Maglus rose to speak. 'My friends, I thank you for your good wishes towards my son and his betrothed bride. Naturally, I could not be more pleased myself at this betrothal, and I am sure that God will bless this union of two people and two royal houses, as he will bless the military adventure which brought it about. And now my son wishes to present a small gift to his bride-to-be.'

Again blushing to the roots of his hair, Riwal rose and approached Dahut, who stood up also. He was carrying a small cloth bag, of the sort that travellers carry money in.

'I must leave when the army leaves,' he said in a clear voice, sounding suddenly earnest and rather young. 'I will pray for my safe return, and for your safekeeping while I am away. As a token I would like you to accept this small gift.'

From out of the bag he took a small object which flashed gold in the flickering torchlight. It was a brooch, fashioned in the Celtic style, with jewels set in it in the form of a cross. Everyone gasped, admiring the beauty of the thing, and there were one or two more sideways glances from pagan guests. Dahut pinned the brooch to her dress, and thanked Riwal shyly. Then he leaned forward and kissed her cheek, to applause from the assembled company. Old Maglus was heard to mutter that there would be 'plenty of time for that sort of thing later', but he meant it good-naturedly. Then everyone resumed their places.

Caught up in the mood of the occasion I applauded with everyone else, my feelings of jealousy apparently laid to rest. As the guests fell to talking amongst themselves again, I looked at Dahut. She seemed flushed and excited, radiating happiness and goodwill. In fact she was a little too giggly, and I thought she had probably drunk too much.

But when her eyes caught mine, and she smiled that knowing smile I knew so well, I realised that we still shared something no one else could destroy.

Chapter Ten

The next day Dahut showed clearly the effects of the night before. She looked pale and her eyes had bags under them. Old Berta chuckled at the sight.

'Well, my Princess, if you've drunk unwatered wine, then you must expect the gods' disapproval. Your father only allows you to drink it watered, and then only a little, and you know it's a sin to disobey him.'

But she was good-humoured about it.

'I'll obey him in future,' groaned Dahut. 'My head is splitting.'

'Good fresh fruit and honey is what you need,' pronounced Berta. 'We'll see what the cook has in.'

Only I knew that Dahut's condition was not all due to wine. I had heard her tossing and turning half the night. And later, when she thought I was asleep, I had felt the rhythm of the bed as she relieved her frustrated passion.

It was a couple of nights later that I first became aware of Dahut's nightly absences. Looking back on it I suppose it was inevitable that, given the feelings she and Riwal had for each other, they would find their way into each other's arms before too long. My mother had hinted as much at the banquet. She was not really disapproving but she was a practical woman, and realised the possibilities for scandal that existed, especially in a household which was gradually turning Christian.

When I awoke in the night and found Dahut gone I blearily assumed that she had got out of bed for the chamber pot. Then I realised that she was nowhere in the room, and began to wonder where she was. The connecting door to Berta's room was shut, and the old woman's snoring indicated that Dahut had not gone to her for anything. My next thought was that Dahut had gone to our secret passageway to listen in on the adults' dinnertime conversation, but I quickly realised that this too was the product of a mind still fuddled with sleep. We usually joined the adults for dinner these days, and in any case dinner was long since over. It was very quiet, and somehow it felt late. I lay in the dark for a while and waited, but I could not sleep again while she was gone.

At last I slipped out of bed and went out into the corridor to look for her. There was no one to be seen in either direction, so I made for our secret passage, as I could not think where else she might have gone. We kept a jug of water in our room, so she would not have gone to get a drink. Perhaps she had been hungry, but it had never led to this before. I would try our hiding place and then the kitchen. Perhaps she was not well? But then she would have woken Berta ... I was still going over such things in my mind when I reached the cupboard which hid our passageway from view. I paused at the crawl space under the cupboard shelf. It was surprisingly warm in the passage, and there was a dim light. A faint tang of lamp-oil hung in the air, along with the dampness of fresh human perspiration, and underlying that an unfamiliar odour, something like warm bread dough.

They were lying in the middle of the passageway, where they had put down blankets and the little rush lamp. They had not heard me, and unless I came closer they would not see me in the shadows. Riwal naked was even more splendid than Riwal clothed. He reminded me of the statues one could still see on the older Roman buildings, inspired by an ideal of physical beauty rather than the corpulent reality. He lay propped on his right arm, looking down at Dahut who was lying on her back next to him. I could not hear what they were saying, but the tone of tenderness was unmistakable, and I guessed they had made love already. From time to time Riwal stroked her body gently with his free hand, and sometimes she would raise her face to be kissed. After a few minutes his hand moved to her breast and began to caress more purposefully. His returning physical excitement was evident, and Dahut was clearly as eager as he was. She raised her arms, pulling him down to her, fixing her lips upon his.

I should not have watched. I knew that it was not 'nice' to watch anyone when they thought they were private, and what could be more private that this? But the last time I had witnessed human sex was when I had seen my mother raped. It had frightened me badly, I was on the brink of womanhood now, and I needed to know it could be different. When at the climactic moment Dahut cried out, and held her lover to her, and smothered him with kisses and words of love and gratitude, I knew it could be. As I crept away my face was wet with tears, although whether of joy for Dahut or pity for my mother I cannot say.

My mind was racing as I went back to bed. What should I say to Dahut? Should I even admit that I had noticed her absence? Part of me wanted to raise the subject, if only to see if she would lie. Was I still worthy of her confidence? It struck me suddenly that her comment of the other day – 'I intend to' meant that she had already decided to sleep with him then. At the time she had turned my question aside with an evasion. Why should things be different now? I dozed fitfully, full of anxiety for our friendship and for my friend herself. At last I awoke fully to find that Dahut was returning to bed.

'Dahut!'

'Yes, it's me, silly. Who did you think it was?'

'It's all right, I've not been properly asleep for a while. You've been a long time. Where were you?'

There was a long pause, while she obviously debated whether to tell me.

'I've been with Riwal,' she said quietly.

'Dahut!' My elation must have got across to her, for she was startled.

'Quiet, Keri. You'll wake old Berta.'

'Never. She'd snore through an earthquake. What do you mean, you've been with Riwal?'

'Why do men and women usually meet secretly at night?'

So she would tell me after all!

She giggled salaciously. 'If you'd seen us you'd know the answer to that. Oh, we know what to do, all right.'

I was glad it was dark. My face must have been crimson with embarrassment. 'If you'd seen us' indeed!

'I'm sure you know what to do, Dahut. Every creature knows that, from an ant to an elephant. That's not what I mean. If an ant or an elephant is pregnant no one minds. But a princess, Dahut?'

'Don't worry, my dear. You should have guessed that I would have seen to that. Megan's teaching is being put to good use.'

It was true that Megan had taught us a great deal. Much of her teaching was about the bodily functioning of women, and how to influence it. There were herbal methods to control fertility, but they were less than perfect. I did not think I would have entrusted myself to them if I had been in her position.

'Riwal is a brave warrior, and yet the gentlest lover. I love him so much. Do you blame me, Keri?'

'No, of course not.'

'I thought ...Well, I wasn't going to say anything. I thought that after what happened to your mother you might have strange ideas about it – about love, I mean.'

'Yes, I did, but I've got over that.'

And if I had, it was all thanks to Dahut, who could spare a thought for her friend's feelings even in the grip of deepest emotion. Oh, Dahut, devourer of men, whatever happened to the girl who burned with that first sweet innocent passion?

After that she was absent most nights, for at least part of the time. Our shared secret seemed to bring us closer together, if anything, driving away my earlier fears that our friendship might fade as love burned brighter. Dahut was happier than I had ever seen her, despite the clouds of war which were gathering. I saw little of Riwal myself. He was training with the army during the day and only returned to the palace with his father at night, not always in time for dinner, which was when we most often met. Sometimes they were away for a few days at a time, seeing to some business or other. Riwal, of course, was not only training to be a warrior, but also a king. When his father had kingly duties to attend to on their tribal land he often took Riwal with him, so that the son might learn from the father's example. I did see Riwal alone once, when we met by chance one day in a palace corridor.

'It is good to see you, Keri. We meet so seldom.'

'That's true, but then you are so busy. And when you are free I can hardly expect you to seek me out.'

He grinned boyishly at this. But then, he was little more than a boy.

'It's true there is a rival attraction,' he said. 'But I'm glad to see you all the same, because I have something to say to you. I want to thank you for keeping our secret.'

'Thank me? Why, what else could I do? I can't betray my friend.' I was surprised he had even mentioned it. I had expected him to keep a discreet silence. He hesitated for a minute, as if the real purpose of this conversation was something else, and he found it difficult to broach.

'You know,' he said, 'it will be Christmas in a matter of days.'

'Yes, I suppose it will.' With a pagan mother I had not given it much thought.

'After Christmas we will be moving north to join Aëtius and the main army.'

'Yes, I know. I wish you the best luck there may be.'

'I have no fear. God will protect me.'

'Ah.'

He had expected a more pious rejoinder.

'Of course,' he said. 'You are not of the faith. I forgot. Actually, I think my father intends to give God a helping hand. He will put himself where the fighting is worst, I know. He wants me to come back to rule after him. Between the one and the other, my safe return is certain, I should say.'

Then his face clouded, and he went on: 'But, just in case, I want you to promise me that if I do not return you will look after Dahut for me. Help her through her grief.'

I stared at him in amazement.

'Ye gods! Riwal, I thought you were different from other men, but you are all alike!'

He seemed genuinely puzzled. 'I don't understand.'

'No, I don't suppose so. I am Dahut's friend. We are more than friends. She is my sister, as near as can be. Do you think I would not help her all I could if she were bereaved?'

He just looked embarrassed, and coloured a little.

'Listen, Riwal, you knew what my answer would be, so why ask me?'

'I just thought ...' he began.

'You just thought! You just wanted to feel better about leaving her. You just realised that she has bound herself to you, and if you die a part of her will die too. Now you want to share the burden. Well, you can't. I love Dahut, but I cannot be a lover for her, nor a husband. If you want to unload your guilt why not go to your priest and confess.'

The boyish grin returned. 'Ah, but Keri, if I do that he will tell me to stop!'

Suddenly we were children again, and I laughed along with him, seeing how I must have looked through his eyes.

'Oh, Riwal, I am sorry. How pompous of me.'

'Don't be sorry. It is because you love her too. I am grateful for that. It sets my mind at rest.'

'I shall pray to any gods there may be for your safe return.'

'There is only one god, and his people grow daily. You know that Gradlon will be celebrating Christmas this year?'

'Yes, I know, and he wants Dahut to be instructed in the Christian faith.'

'I want it, too. We will be married according to Christian rites. Soon this whole kingdom will be Christian.'

'Perhaps.' I thought briefly of the Saxon with his crucifixes, and shuddered.

Christmas was, of course, a pagan festival – under another name – before the Christians arrived. I think every tribe used to celebrate the passing of the year's shortest day. After that the days grew longer, and the world began to come to life again. In ancient Greece they told the legend of the sky god who married the Earth Mother for a year and then died, only to rise again from the dead in the spring. The Saxons also believe some such nonsense. Even the Christians have a god who died and rose again, which they celebrate in the spring. My mother would have said they copied it from the pagans.

She refused to attend any of the Christian rites. The King would not order her to, but he did try to persuade her. She remained adamant, and neither she nor I set foot inside the church which had been established inside the palace grounds. The King had had it converted from an old Mithraic temple which had fallen into disuse. The priest was delighted at this. The Christians hated Mithraism more than most pagan cults. For they thought its rites were a mockery of their own. The acquisition of the temple was not only a victory for them, but an omen.

Gradlon's tolerance over religious dissent did not extend to his daughter. Dahut had no strong religious views, but she had been influenced, as I had, by my mother's cynicism and Megan's paganism. She felt, however, that she owed her father something.

'You know,' she said to me,' he could have looked for a better match, better from the political point of view. But he realised that I loved Riwal, and that was enough. That is one thing about the Christians, they do revere love before all else.'

I thought of Budic burning that altar in the forest, and of Megan's tales of murdered pagans, and held my peace.

'I think I should at least listen to what the priest has to say. Father wants me to be instructed in the faith, and so does Riwal. He is a Christian too, you know.'

'Yes, I know.'

She laughed. 'Of course! You must be tired of hearing about him!'

'No. I'm happy for you.'

'Dear Keri! What a true friend you are. You know, we must find you a husband one of these days.'

'Not yet!' I protested. 'I'm far too young. Besides, I'm not sure I want to marry.'

'Oh, you'll change,' she said, in that knowing way that adults often use. In some ways she was rather like an adult these days.

'I don't know,' I said. 'My mother was married once. I don't think she was all that happy. She doesn't seem eager to do it again and Megan has managed all right without. Besides, I'm not beautiful and I'm not rich, and I'm not a princess. What have I got to offer?'

She looked at me for a minute.

'That sounds so bitter, Keri. It's not like you.'

'I'm not bitter. It's life, that's all. I may as well face facts.'

'Very well, but also face the fact that you are a good, sweet person. Riwal and I are not marrying for politics or wealth, and neither will you. It will happen, though. You'll see.'

I noticed she did not mention beauty.

The middle of winter came and went. People on both sides of the religious divide celebrated it in their own ways. Mother and I did not celebrate it at all, except that we decorated our rooms with the branches of some woodland shrubs – a custom older than Christianity. We also gave each other small presents, which the Christians do. It seems a pleasant enough custom. Mother tactfully maintained her refusal to engage in Christian services, despite Gradlon's assurances that his life had changed since he had discovered the One True God. He was obviously right in some ways. His dark depressions no longer visited him with such force. He had resumed the duties of a king, gradually pushing Tiernan back into the role of adviser and assistant. He no longer threw rages at dinner when someone said the wrong thing. He would rebuke gently but firmly, as became a king.

'His self-confidence has come back,' said Mother. 'He has decided that whatever happens now is God's will, and that lightens the burden of responsibility upon him. Maybe his conversion has done some good after all.'

With Christmas over the dreaded day came when the army must march forth. We rode out in a wagon to see them go. Dahut was filled with anxiety, but also a kind of pride, as she watched Riwal march out at the head of his legion. He was entitled to ride a horse, but he said that Julius Caesar had won the respect of his men by marching with a full pack as they did, and so would he. Besides, no officer should ask a man to do that which he was not prepared to do himself. He was still only nineteen, but what a man he was!

The camp had been struck. All over the plain there were the charred patches where cooking fires had been. There were yellow rectangles on the grass where the tents had stood, and rows of turned earth marked the site of the latrines. In a few months the grass and bushes would have reclaimed the land, and nothing would survive to show where the hundreds of men had trained and lived and prepared to die.

Unit by unit they marched forward to the roadway, and turned away from the city. Gradlon himself led out the first cavalry troop. Maglus led the infantry, but he no longer had his son's strength, and led from horseback. We watched, along with many other townsfolk, and waved until the columns disappeared in the distance. Many of the women were weeping. Dahut looked pale, and her eyes were red, but she did not weep. She had done plenty of that the night before, I guessed. There was a lump in my own throat, as I thought of the fine young men who set out, some of whom would not come back.

'That is a sight to remember,' said my mother softly. 'But remember this, too. We British provide the best auxiliaries in the Empire. The main reason for that is that we train hard. You will have seen that for yourselves. I would guess that we will lose a smaller proportion of men than any of the other federates.'

She was right about our fighting quality, but wrong about our losses.

There now began a time of feverish preparation for Dahut. She threw herself wholeheartedly into plans for her future life with Riwal. I think it was really a way of keeping herself busy so as not to think of the war. As the winter retreated and the armies advanced, she made preparations for the wedding. I helped her to decide who should be invited. We had talks with my mother about who would have to come for political reasons. She knew enough of the politics of Kemper to help us make a provisional list. Then there was Dahut's dress to consider, and her trousseau, and her dowry. We spent days in excited planning of this and that, then tearing up the plans and starting again. What a game it was! How young we were!

Riwal was never far from Dahut's mind. Sometimes at night I would wake up and find her crying.

'Oh, Keri, I'm so afraid for him! He's brave. He'll be where the fighting is worst, I know it. He'll not hold back and have it said that he let others bear the brunt.'

'Hush, Dahut. He'll obey his orders like the good soldier he is. He'll do what his father tells him to do. Maglus won't risk him. He wants Riwal to reign after him. He'd sooner put himself in the front line than endanger Riwal.'

She would snuggle up to me in the dark, cold as ice, her tears wet on my shoulder.

'Do you think so? Oh, I hope you're right.'

The worry never left her.

I had not realised before how obsessional her love for Riwal was, nor how dangerous it might be. Now that he was gone it had turned into an anxiety, equally obsessive, which would only be cured by his safe return. God only knew what it would do to her if he did not, and it was to God that she turned now in an effort to influence events.

Gradlon had taken his personal chaplain with him, but another monk-priest had arrived from Ronan. The hermit had a thriving community now, and it was being reinforced from across the water. The Irish were constantly raiding the southern coasts of Wales at that time. Many Welsh monks were fleeing to Lesser Britain, where the Roman Empire still held sway, at least in name, and there seemed a better prospect of peace. The new arrival's name was Emrys, and he was to give Dahut her Christian instruction. I learned to hate him.

Emrys was a thickset man, not much taller than Dahut herself. His hair and eyes were dark, his nose a hook from which more dark tufts protruded. He never smiled, or at least never in mirth. Like so many other monks he was not over-scrupulous about keeping clean. I have never discovered why so many Christian monks think dirt brings them closer to God. Perhaps they equate cleanliness with vanity, or perhaps washing is a distraction from higher things. On the other hand, perhaps it is just an affectation. Emrys was a full member of the brotherhood in this respect.

Another thing I disliked was his apparent feeling that he had to convert not only Dahut but me as well. When he arrived in our room to teach her, he would insist that I stay to hear the glad tidings. This smouldering jubilation of those who already believe themselves at the gate of Heaven is something I have never been able to stomach. It is so smug, I suppose. Brother Emrys had this also in full measure. As he told tales of the Christian god and his prophets his eyes would light up and his voice would rise in pitch until he seemed about to burst with enthusiasm.

And Dahut believed it. He saw to it that she did. He saw her weakness and played upon it. She loved Riwal, she loved him fiercely. Yet she feared for him. She feared for his life, and for her father's. Emrys taught her to pray. He taught her that faith could move mountains, and win wars. Had not the great Constantine himself seen the Holy Cross in the sky on the eve of battle? With Christ's protection all things were possible.

I was much less vulnerable. I did not fear for anyone the way Dahut did. I loved only my mother and Dahut, and they were both with me, and in no danger. At least, no physical danger. When I saw how eagerly Dahut fell upon the monk's reassuring dogmas I argued, not from any malicious intent but from a desire to clarify things and to approach the truth. Emrys soon found that my participation in his lessons was not necessary. Perhaps my soul was not worth saving.

This did not stop me talking to Dahut. I remember once entering our room just after Emrys had left it, to find Dahut kneeling in the corner, head bowed.

'Dahut, whatever are you doing?' Actually, I knew perfectly well. I was feeling off-colour that day, and not as considerate of my friend's feelings as I might have been. I thought she was behaving stupidly, and today I was in no mood to disguise the fact.

She got up awkwardly, embarrassed. 'I was praying.'

'Oh.'

'I was praying for Riwal. Brother Emrys says –'

'Brother Emrys says a great deal. He knows what you want most.'

'Oh, Keri, how can you say that? Emrys is a devout man. You only have to look at him when he talks of God to see how truly he believes.'

I had to concede that. 'I never said he didn't believe. I just think he'll tell you anything to get you to believe, too.'

There, it was out. Dahut was scandalised.

'You're jealous, Keri. You were before, when I first met Riwal. Now you don't want me to have this, either. You're always jealous when I do something which doesn't include you.'

'That's not true! I don't want to be included!'

'Well, then, don't interfere! Both Riwal and my father want me to accept the faith. Surely there's no harm finding out more about it?'

'Dahut, I don't care what you worship. There are plenty of religions, and probably some truth in all of them. I don't know. But I don't like Emrys, and I don't think he is being fair to you.'

'Fair! What do you mean?'

'He is using your love for Riwal, bending it to his own purpose. You are afraid for him. Emrys tells you that prayer will protect him. I suppose he's told you to pray for your father too?'

She nodded. 'Of course. Keri, I have to believe in something.' She turned and began to pace the room in her agitation. 'I have to do something. I'd have ridden with him if it were possible. I'd have fought at my man's side as the Scythian women used to. Oh, I know you said his father won't risk him. He wants Riwal to rule after him, I know all that, but in the heat of battle who knows what may happen? Who knows which way the battle lines may shift? Who can decide a man's fate in the midst of such chaos? Oh, Christ preserve him. Bring him back to me. That's what I pray, Keri.'

Tears began to run down her cheeks. I had never seen her so openly miserable. And after all, what right had I to take away her one crumb of comfort? I found myself crying too, as we fell into each other's arms.

'Dahut, I'm so sorry. I didn't mean to make you unhappy. I'm sorry. I won't bring it up again, really I won't. Pray all day if you want to. I don't care. I won't say a word.'

Old Berta tottered in at that moment.

'What's this? Tears?'

'It's nothing, Berta, really,' said Dahut. 'Just a silly quarrel, but we've made it up, haven't we, Keri?'

I smiled through my tears. 'Yes, of course we have.'

The old woman stood and looked at us both for a moment. Then she turned away, chuckling.

'Girls, girls. All the same at your age. Falling out and making it up again. And all over nothing, I suppose. The sooner your young man comes back the better, my Princess. Marriage soon settles a girl, you mark my words.'

Not long after this we had our first message from Gradlon. He sent a courier to bring us the sensational news that the Huns had already suffered their first setback.

The imperial army, a collection of Romans, federates and auxiliaries, had finally been brought together on the banks of the Liger. Aëtius had moved up from Arelate in the south, which was the capital of the Prefecture of Gaul. High-sounding titles they seem these days, but then the Prefecture included all of Spain, and all of what is now the Kingdom of the Franks. Aëtius was well pleased with his army, and especially the Armorican British, the best federates in the Empire. As the army mustered, the news came that Attila had already penetrated as far as Cenabum. Orleans, the Franks call it now; gods, what an age this is for changing the names of places! The Huns had cut a swathe across northern Gaul, burning, looting and killing. They seemed to have no idea of preserving things. Perhaps as wanderers from the great plains to the east they only knew about hunting. At any rate they laid waste farms and stores with no thought for the next season. Cenabum stood in their path, and quailed before the advancing horde. According to Gradlon, the townspeople had been persuaded by their Bishop, Ananius, to hold on. The city walls were strong and the garrison well manned. The saintly Bishop urged the populace to pray for help from the Christian god, and most of them did. The city held. So did the Bishop's authority.

Aëtius, meanwhile, had heard of the siege and set out with his forces to relieve the city, which was only a few miles away. Within a day they reached their objective, to find that the Huns had withdrawn to the north-east. There were a few warriors still left to harass the imperial army and slow it down, but there had been little fighting. Riwal, Maglus and all of the other leaders were safe. For the moment we could sleep easy. The big battle was still to come, and probably not for some weeks yet.

Chapter Eleven

As the drays dragged on Dahut became more and more convinced by Emrys and his preaching. I think this was mainly because of her increasing desperation. I cannot say it made her any happier. Indeed her sleep was more disturbed than ever. She was prone to nightmares, and often woke up crying. During the day she was sunk in a depression reminiscent of those which had plagued her father not so long ago. Emrys told her that prayer and fasting were the only cures for maladies of the soul, and she did as he advised, bringing herself only more misery. I felt helpless, and soon found that old Berta agreed with me.

'What does a monk know of young girls?' she asked me in exasperation. 'All this starving herself – it's not healthy. She needs to feed herself up, to get herself fit and buxom for that young ram of hers when he returns.' She chuckled coarsely, and I looked at her in alarm, wondering if she was quite as senile as we thought her. But there was nothing to show that her remarks were anything but casual.

In Gradlon's absence Easter went uncelebrated. Tiernan was no Christian when the King's eye was not on him. The church held its services, and those attended who felt the need. Outside the town on the hills and in the woods the spring was celebrated in a fashion older than Christianity. On Beltane night we saw the fires in the sacred groves of the old religion. With most of the army's Christians away the peasants went about their traditional devotions with an enthusiasm unhindered by fear of ambush. Seeing the distant flickering one night my mother remarked that by midsummer most of the peasant girls would soon be as productive as the cattle they drove. Again, I did not feel that she disapproved altogether. She observed no religion in particular, and cared not what others might believe or practise, so long as they kept it to themselves. Like me, she was deeply distrustful of the wily Emrys, and resumed teaching me herself rather than let him near me.

Another object of our distrust was Tiernan. Now Gradlon's regent, he was busy again trying to build up his support amongst the people. This was pretty fruitless, as the most influential people were away with the King, as was most of the army. Still, his little schemes rankled, and added to the divisions in the palace. He obviously recognised our dislike of him, and returned it equally. Dahut and I had asked if we might go to the villa at Ker-Is, but Tiernan had refused us leave, saying that he had no orders from the King on the matter. Soon His Majesty would be back, and he would decide. Dahut's prayers redoubled their fervour. The distance between us widened.

I first heard of the arrival of the King's courier while in my bath, of all places. The servant, Menevia, had filled the bath for me and left me to soak in it, a habit which I had developed as I grew. Always fond of water, I loved to spend at least an hour in the bath, sometimes calling for more hot water. If we could not have the full joys of the old Roman baths, now in ruins, at least we could enjoy them on a smaller scale.

'My lady! Mistress Keri! He's here! He's come!'

I returned sleepily from some distant dream or other, having dozed off in the warm water. 'What? Who's here?'

'It's the courier, *Domina*. The King's courier is here. They say he has the most tremendous news!'

'Pull yourself together, Menevia. Of course they say that. But you know as well as I that, whatever the news is, the courier will not breathe a word of it until he has informed the Regent. Now, get me towels and fetch me that plain shift. The gods know what colour I should wear, so I'll wear something colourless.'

And indeed, until the news was out none of us knew what to wear. Were we mourning a king, or celebrating a great victory, or even both? For the first and only time I envied the monks. At least they always wore exactly the same thing. But then, so did the poor, so perhaps there was not much to envy.

The great hall was full of people when I finally arrived, hair still wet and clothes sticking to my hastily dried body. I was not the only latecomer. Tiernan had been outside the town when the messenger had arrived, and had been sent for in haste. He arrived slightly after me, and ascended to the throne at once. Dahut, as the King's only immediate relative there, sat at the regent's right hand. Her face was pale, her excitement and tension showing only in the form of two bright pink patches on her cheeks. Her eyes were wide, like those of a child who sees a strange animal for the first time, and knows not whether to pet it or shy away in fear.

Tiernan came straight to the point, and beckoned one of the palace servants.

'Let us have silence, and have the courier brought in at one.'

The doors at the end of the hall were thrown open even before the footman reached them. The courier had been waiting for the word, and strode in at a pace that was hardly decent. He knelt before Tiernan and handed him the wax tablets from the King. Tiernan studied them for a few minutes, while the entire room held its breath. For a moment he appeared to be struggling with himself. Then he put down the tablets and stood up.

'These tablets can only tell the bare bones of the story. I will announce more when I have spoken at length with our courier, who will have seen and heard more than a scribe can write. But let it be announced at every street corner that King Gradlon is returning in triumph! The King and his allies have prevailed. Attila the cur has been sent back to the barbarian lands with his tail between his legs! He has suffered his greatest defeat, while the Empire has won its greatest victory! The Huns have been destroyed!'

The rest of his announcement was drowned in a mighty cheer, and the news was passed from person to person, out of the doors and into the town faster than any official could bring it. By the time the criers went out later to broadcast the news their audience already knew it. Indeed, they had gone further. Half of them had it that Attila was dead, and that Gradlon himself had cut the barbarian's head from his shoulders. Tiernan had to send out the criers again the next day to quell the rumours which had sprung up.

Meanwhile everyone wanted details. Dahut leaned forward to the courier, trying to attract his attention beneath the hubbub.

'The Prince Riwal?' she was saying. 'Is he safe?'

I could see the man's face. He stiffened. He had heard, but pretended not to. And he would not let her catch his eye. It was left to Tiernan to break the tension.

'Alas, this great victory has been won at a terrible price. Many brave men have perished. Most notable among these is King Maglus of the Osismii.'

Dahut leaned forward, her knuckles whitening where they gripped the throne.

'Princess, you have my deepest sympathy. Prince Riwal has also fallen, defending his father.'

Silence fell abruptly over the hall. All eyes went to Dahut. She rose unsteadily to her feet, the two bright patches of her cheeks standing out in starker contrast to the deathly pallor of her face. She lurched and looked down. For a moment I thought she would faint and I hurried over to her. But she drew herself up straight. Without a word she turned, taking my hand in a crushing grip. I squeezed back hard and together we walked slowly from the hall. Hurried snatches of condolence came from those we passed, but Dahut heard nothing, saw nothing.

I supported her up the stairs to our room. Tears ran down her face, but still she said nothing. Berta scuttled after us, having heard the news already. She took one look at Dahut.

'Bed!' she said decisively. 'Let the poor lamb rest, and keep her warm.'

Indeed, Dahut was shivering violently, although there was a warm fire crackling in the hearth. We undressed her and put her to bed. Then I sat by her and held her hand. She was asleep within seconds.

Old Berta didn't like it.

'Too quiet,' she muttered. 'A bit of screaming wouldn't have come amiss, not from a maid in her place. She's too quiet altogether. There'll be screaming yet, you mark my words.'

'What a battle it was, Your Excellency. I have been at some local skirmishes, but this was a battle fit for the history books.'

The courier paused for another sip of his wine. He was a plain and pleasant little man, very conscious of the honour done to him by the invitation to dine at the Regent's table.

'The great Aëtius – now there is a man, sir, a truly great general – well, Aëtius had heard from his scouts that the host of the Huns had camped on an open plain called the Catalaunian Fields, by the Sequana River. He resolved to meet them there without delay. You should have seen the army, sir. Not only our own brave men, sir, banners flying, and King Gradlon himself at the head. There were Roman legionaries, crack troops in the smartest fighting gear I've ever seen. Then there were the other federates, especially the Franks and the Visigoths. Well, sir, they were a sight. Ragged enough, some of them, and not exactly marching in military style, but the light of battle was in their eyes. The Franks are all tall blond Germanic types, wearing furs and with long beards. The Goths are a more mixed lot, sir, with more decorative gear –'

Tiernan was impatient. 'Yes, yes. I don't want a tailor's description, man.'

There was a ripple of laughter around the table, and the poor man blushed at his own enthusiasm for his tale.

'Begging your pardon, sir. Well, we came upon them at first light. Aëtius had had the ground spied out well enough. The enemy's strength was in his horses, you see.'

'Those Huns are wild men, but they can't fight worth puppies' piss once they're on foot, er, pardon my language. Funny short fellows, they are, bandy-legged from so much horse-riding. Fierce, though. They drug themselves up on some barbarian brew and it drives all fear and pain away. Some of them bled to death before they noticed they were wounded, I tell you.'

He took another sip of wine while his audience considered the inhuman nature of the enemy.

'Well, Aëtius had the advantage that he knew the ground, having been in the area before. Besides, all the local people were loyal, and his scouts filled in any gaps in his knowledge. So he chose his place carefully, and approached

Attila's army at a place where the Huns would be tempted into marshy ground, a bad place for horsemen. He knew the Huns well. They don't plan a battle properly like civilised folk. They just make mad dashes against their enemy with no real pattern to them. They lost a lot of men that way before the fight was really started. Then they drew back, and Aëtius reckoned that they were having a reconsider – that's Attila and his subject chiefs. Arderic and his Gepids made a sally against the left wing of our army, but they were Roman regulars and soon turned them back. Before they could recover Aëtius sent in Theoderic and his Goths to smash them completely. There was a terrible fight, and Theoderic was killed.'

Some of the older listeners sighed at this, their minds doubtless harking back to other tales of heroic kings lost in valiant combat.

'Theoderic's son, Thorismund, saved the attack from failing. He galloped up, seized his father's standard as he fell, and rallied the Goths with a fearsome war-cry. Their spirits were raised so much they all began to yell like demons, and took a terrible revenge on the enemy for the loss of their king.'

'Maybe Attila was dismayed by this and lost his nerve. Or maybe he hoped to win the day by one bold stroke. Who knows? Anyway, suddenly he threw all he had against the centre line of our army – not just Huns, there were Ostrogoths, Alans, Slavs, all manner of barbarian scum. There was the most terrible slaughter imaginable. Men fell in heaps, and their comrades fought around them and fell in their turn, so that mounds of the dead piled up. I saw it clearly. Our own people were there, in the centre. Aëtius said we were the best, and he put us there on purpose. "The shield boss at the heart of Gaul" he called us. By God, he was right. I was doing courier duty in the field, you see. On my way from Aëtius, who was on high ground where he could see it all, to King Gradlon. I couldn't get through. The fighting was too thick, and I had to fight off two attacks myself. Both runty barbarians, tired from the battle. They were easy. Then I saw I could never get through. It was too late, anyway. There was no way to organise the battle now. It was all hand-to-hand, every man for himself. I saw our men stand firm as a rock, while the barbarians swirled around them like a raging tide. And just as the tide carries off little pieces of the rock, I saw men swept away and swallowed up. And still the rock held.'

There was total silence in the hall, as the man faltered. He put one elbow on the table and rested his forehead on his hand. His face was mostly hidden, but we saw the tears fall to the table. After a few moments he went on, his voice hoarse from the memory of the carnage.

'I saw the King fall from his horse. At first I thought he had been killed, but later I saw him fighting on foot. His head was bloodied, but that was all. I saw Old Maglus of the Osismii. He looked like a young man again, the way he threw himself into the fight, laying men low all around. But there were too many, you see, too many. He fell at last, dragged down by at least three of the scum. They fight like animals – no honour, no single combat. I saw Prince Riwal. He fought his way to his father's side. He killed I don't know how many. I didn't see him fall, but I lost sight of him in the rush of men and horses. I saw many of our men go down. They sold their lives dearly, but they're gone just the same. Budic of the palace guard went down, but I saw him later, only wounded. Old Benoic is gone, so is Marc of Condevincum, and all his three sons. Sweet Jesus, what a massacre!

'Aëtius tried to save the worst of it. He did what he could – counter-attacked with his Franks and Visigoths. But the Armorican British saw the worst of it, and they held. Immovable they were. The shield boss held. Attila's gamble failed. The attack spent its force on us, and then the Franks and the Visigoths closed in. I suppose we should be glad they were on our side, but they're as bad barbarians as the Huns, that lot! They left a trail of severed Hunnish heads across the plain, I don't mind telling you!'

Tiernan was moved to interrupt at this point. 'And Attila?'

The courier snorted. 'Got away, as well he might! We could have had him. We could have had the whole Hun army for good and all.'

'What do you mean?'

'Aëtius called off the pursuit. Once he saw the Huns running away he gave orders for the Visigoths to be recalled. Young Thorismund was running them down, but he had to stop. Aëtius let the murdering bastards get away!'

There was astonishment at this revelation.

'And what did you do then?'

'We counted the dead, God rest them. And God preserve us from another victory like that one. I don't reckon more than half of them that marched out will march back again.'

We had had news of individual casualties earlier that evening, and there were many heads that shook sadly as the courier spoke.

'But Attila?' persisted Tiernan. 'Why did Aëtius let him go?'

The courier shrugged. 'Who can say? The Lord knows the answer to that. Only, I did hear someone say that Aëtius wanted the Huns beaten but not destroyed. He's used them as mercenaries often enough before, and might need them again. The Visigoths and the Franks were with us this time, but it might not always be so.'

Tiernan nodded slowly. That kind of intrigue was something he understood well. He took from his sash a couple of gold coins and gave them to the courier, who looked suitably grateful.

'I think I shall retire now,' said Tiernan. 'We have kept this loyal messenger up long enough.'

There were murmurs of assent, and one or two other coins passed the courier's way. He acknowledged them with a bow and a grin. Then I saw several heads turn towards the small end door which led to the living quarters of the palace. I also turned, to see what had attracted their attention.

Dahut was standing there, a dark blue cloak flung over her nightdress. She stayed for a moment at the door, looking down the length of the great hall, with its guttering torches. The torchlight shone on her hair and seemed to feed the light in her eyes. She was in a state of high emotion, yet holding it in check with great effort. She strode stiff and straight, holding her cloak around her, until she came to the middle of the top table next to Tiernan. Everyone gradually fell silent, wondering what was going on.

'Well, Tiernan, don't I get a seat and some wine like the other guests?'

Tiernan was disconcerted, the first time I had really seen him so. 'Ah, Your Highness, we were, ah, just about to retire.' But he made room for her and she sat down next to him.

'Retire, then,' she said, 'but leave the flagon.'

I thought my heart would burst for her then. She looked more miserable than I have ever seen anyone. As if all the fears of the last few months had been visited upon her at once – which I suppose they had. I started to speak, but she waved me into silence.

'You are my one true friend, Keri, but don't try to stop me tonight.'

She took a flagon which stood on the table and reached around for a cup. A servant brought one, after Tiernan had nodded to him silently. She poured herself a cup, drank it down, and poured another. For a moment she tilted her head on one side, like a bird looking at a worm. In that instant she was the image of her father. I had never before noticed the strength of the resemblance. Nor the weakness inherent in it. She was on her third cup of wine in as many minutes.

Around us the conversation began again in that faltering way it does after an embarrassing incident. Emrys, sitting a little way down the table opposite me, was obviously perplexed and annoyed. He felt it was his moral duty to speak out, of course, but the Regent had said nothing and he was Dahut's guardian for the time being. Even so, as she started on her fourth cup he rose from his place and made his way towards the top table. Tiernan noted the movement but did nothing. Dahut watched the monk approach with eyes of steel. He reached her side, and bent to say something. Both that and the reply were inaudible, but it was clear from Dahut's upturned and defiant face that he was not getting very far. She turned back to the table, and he laid his hand on her arm – a serious error. She froze, and then turned her head slowly to look at his hand. Her lip curled with distaste and her rebuke was more than audible.

'Take your hand off me! This is a princess you are touching!'

'Indeed it is,' he said, leaving his hand where it was. 'And a princess should know how to behave in her father's court.'

For answer she threw the contents of her cup in his face. He withdrew his hand, and another embarrassed silence fell on the assembled company as they waited to see what would happen now. Tiernan, I noticed, was smiling silently. He would have smiled as he strangled you, that one. Emrys wiped the wine from his face with the back of his hand.

'My Princess,' he said, 'is this any way to grieve for your loss? All here share your grief. We would help you bear it if we could.' To give the man his due, I think he meant it kindly, but he was already lost.

'You can help me bear it.' She paused deliberately for effect, and then bellowed at him. 'You can get out!' She rose to face him. 'Get out! Out of this room! Out of this palace! Out of this kingdom!'

Emrys turned beseechingly towards Tiernan, but the Regent seemed to have developed a sudden interest in the dregs of his wine-cup. Meanwhile Dahut turned towards the company.

'Don't go to the priests! False comfort is all they have to offer! Pray! God will protect! It is all God's will! Faith can move mountains!'

Her speech was already slurring from the wine, and she swayed as she turned to face me.

'You tried to tell me, Keri.' My ears burned as the whole hall turned to stare at me. Emrys looked as if he would happily kill me. 'My friend, my only friend. You told me what he was up to. You told me he would say anything to get me to follow his god, and you were right.'

Out of the corner of my eye I saw Tiernan whisper to one of the servants, who departed in the direction of the living quarters. It looked as if he'd decided enough was enough, and sent for Berta. Dahut was now haranguing the room in general.

'She told me! This monk-priest was telling me everything, anything, to make me believe. He knew I had a weakness. A fear. He used it, like the priests use everyone. Just do God's will. Of course, we'll decide what God's will happens to be. Well, I had a weakness. I had a love. Emrys here will tell you that God is love. But Emrys knows bugger all about it. Emrys has forsworn love.'

'Only unchaste love!' interrupted the monk, but she ignored him.

'I used to feel what you were talking about. When I saw his face in the crowd I would fill with love, a love that spread out to encircle the whole world. I thought that's what you meant. I thought you knew what you were talking about. But you're a cold calculating bastard, Emrys. You don't love the world. You can't even love one person. There isn't even enough love in you for that.'

I saw her hand groping about on the table, and leapt up as I realised what she doing. The knife was halfway to Emrys's throat when I screamed.

'Dahut! No!'

She wavered and swayed back. As I ran to her side she dropped the knife on the floor. I took her arm and looked at her beautiful face. She was smiling foolishly, but her pupils were like pinpricks.

'Oh, Christ,' she said. 'I think I'm going to –'

She swung away from me and completed Emrys's humiliation by vomiting down the front of his habit. I heard a rich chuckle beside me.

'Heh, now he'll have to wash it at last!' cackled Berta.

The next day dawned bright and clear. I leaned on the window ledge of our room and looked out across the palace garden. Dahut slept peacefully in our bed, having virtually passed out on her return from the great hall. Berta had managed to make her drink vast quantities of water, which she assured us was a good prophylactic measure against illness the next day.

'The poor lamb,' she said. 'Still, a maid's got to learn how to drink wine before she's a woman. And how not to. Not that you can blame her, after what she's been through.'

Privately I had an idea that the worst was yet to come, but I was not going to say anything to Berta. Anyway, this morning was enough to cheer a person a little, even if they bore a great sadness. Down in the garden I saw Emrys, wearing a grey habit instead of his usual brown, and I could not suppress a smile. Unfortunately, he looked up and saw me, and glowered furiously. This only made me giggle, which was worse. He walked angrily on his way. I decided to go on mine, since Dahut was still dead to the world.

I dressed quickly in an old white tunic and went to the great hall to see if my mother was down to breakfast yet. I found her sitting at the table in earnest conversation with a man who looked strangely familiar. When he turned I recognised him at once, in spite of the full beard he had grown since our last meeting.

'Meriadauc! You're back!'

He jumped up and kissed me on both cheeks.. 'Let's look at you! My, you've grown a foot since I last saw you! Ho, Olivia, your daughter's almost a woman!'

My mother gave a tight-lipped smile. She was none too pleased at the thought of being old enough for that. But I hardly noticed at the time.

Meriadauc had just returned from Italy, and I wanted to hear about the Emperor's court.

'Court?' said Meriadauc. 'Well, I'm not sure you'd think much of it as a court. It's more formal than this place, but not half so homely. And the household! Phew! Our Gradlon has his moments, as the gods know, but he can't hold a candle to Valentinian.'

'The Emperor? Why, what do you mean?'

He shook his head gravely. 'I wouldn't repeat this just anywhere but, strictly between us, Valentinian is crazy! He is plagued by rages and jealousies, and sees plots all around him. The trouble is, half the time he's right. What's more, he's feeble. And his mother, Galla Placidia, she's worse. I suppose she was Regent for so long when Valentinian was a lad that she can't get out of the habit of intrigue. For his part, he's a real mother's boy.' Here he exchanged a meaningful glance with my mother. It was years before I understood what that meant. 'The military commanders are all vying for power, and plotting, and murdering each other. It's a madhouse!'

I didn't want to hear about politics. 'I suppose the Emperor's palace is magnificent, though!'

'Oh, Keri, I'm sorry to disappoint you. The old palace in Rome was, I expect, but Ravenna's more of a fortress than a palace. It's surrounded by marshes, which are riddled with mosquitoes and fever. The fortress itself is a solemn, brooding sort of place. It's cut off from the real world, and so are the idiots inside it. Do you know, Galla Placidia – the world's most powerful woman, probably – spends half her time designing her own mausoleum? She's as mad as the rest, but with her it's a religious madness. She's so bound up with thoughts of the next world that she can't spare the time for this one. And while these lunatics act out their intrigues and fancies, the world is falling to pieces.'

He shook his head sadly.

'Maybe it's not all falling to pieces,' I said. 'You'll have heard about the Huns?'

'Yes, your mother told me the news. And that this is still not the end of Attila, that Aëtius allowed him to escape. Still, that's it, you see. He probably felt he'd need him again. Aëtius knows the Huns. He lived amongst them as a boy, when he was taken as a hostage. When he first came to govern Gaul he brought sixty thousand of them with him.'

'Could the Huns ever soldier for him after this?' I cried. 'Surely not!'

'Oh, they might. Especially if Attila died.'

Incredibly, Meriadauc was right. Years later some of the Huns did fight for Rome again, but only after Aëtius and Attila were both dead.

Mother, tired of being in the background, interrupted at this point. 'Well, now we've settled the ills of the world, why don't you tell her your own news, Meriadauc?'

'Yes, of course. Well, Keri, I've done some thinking since I saw how things were in Ravenna. This place seems like an island of sanity by comparison, and I've decided to cease my wanderings and settle down. Right here in Kemper.'

'Settle down? But how will you live?'

He laughed loudly. 'Oh, Keri. What a practical girl you are, and no mistake! But since you ask, let me tell you that I am no longer Meriadauc the sea captain. You see before you Meriadauc the merchant. I've got enough money together at last. I can even buy a little house. From now on others can sail for me, while for most of the time I stay on shore and handle the business side of things. One thing, at least I should be a hard man to cheat. I know all the tricks by now! Anyway, Snorebeard will be my captain, so there'll be no worries on that score. I'm afraid it means you won't be seeing much of him, though.

I was sad at that news, I must confess. I liked Snorebeard, and so did my mother. Still, we liked Meriadauc, too. Indeed, I still harboured hopes that they might marry. Besides, I knew Meriadauc would be a friend to us, maybe a protector if need be. I kissed him on the cheek.

'Well, Meriadauc, I'm glad you'll be with us from now on. It means Mother can stop pining away.'

He guffawed loudly at this. Mother turned crimson with embarrassment and threw a piece of bread at me.

'Be off with you, child! What a thing to say!' But she was laughing as I scuttled out of the door and into the garden.

I ran down the garden path which followed the side of the palace. Turning the corner of the building I ran slap into Emrys, who stood blocking the path, his face like thunder. He gripped my arms tight and shook me.

'Evil child! Spawn of Satan!'

I was terrified, as much by the suddenness of the encounter as its ferocity. I tried to talk, but nothing coherent came out.

'Do you think I am blind? Do you think I am deaf? Did I not hear what was said last night? It is you who have undone my work here. You who have turned the Princess against our Lord!'

So that was it! Dahut had unwittingly pointed the finger at me with her drunken speech the night before. My grinning face at the window this morning must have confirmed his darkest suspicions.

'But I didn't, I mean, I'm not, I only said –'

'Silence! You are a wicked child! Wicked! Some demon is in you! You and your mother both have defied me, and the Lord's purpose! Beware. The wages of sin is death!'

I knew no better. I thought he meant to kill me. With a terrified shriek I pulled away with all my might. He held one arm still, but the other came free and I swung backwards, overbalancing the pair of us. He fell on top of me, driving the breath from my body. His wild eyes stared straight into my own. His dragon's breath was in my face. His yellow teeth were bared, as he still called down divine retribution. All might have been well, if the crucifix which he always wore had not fallen forward out of the neck of his robe and landed on my chest.

All at once I was reliving the terrors of that night years ago in Uncle Lucian's house. He was not Emrys the priest, but the Saxon who collected crucifixes. Again I saw him inflict some half-understood hurt upon my mother, and cringed in the corner, sure I was next. Far away I heard someone screaming uncontrollably.

I wish she'd stop it, I thought mechanically.

Then the weight was gone from me. Through a fog I saw Emrys kneeling by my side. He gripped my arms, shook me, spoke. I could hear nothing because of the screams. Then, aware of the ambiguity of his position, he put his hand over my mouth to shut me up. It was only then I realised the screams were mine. Still burbling in utter panic, I dimly heard him speak.

'Quiet, child! I have done nothing!'

Then he turned aside and spoke to someone else.

'I have not touched her!'

He backed away, his arm gripped by another, I saw Meriadauc's fist smash into his face, and saw Emrys fall back on the grass. My mother was suddenly there, shouting abuse at the monk while she held me to her. I clung like a babe, my weeping slowly subsiding.

'Did he hurt you, Keri? Did he —?'

'I did nothing to her, only took her by the arm. We fell. It was an accident.'

'Keri, is that true?' I think Mother was ready to kill Emrys if it wasn't.

I managed to nod.

'Then what is that?' asked Meriadauc grimly, pointing to my clothes, the lower half of which were stained with fresh blood.

I cannot say why, but the sight of it had a strangely calming effect on me, and I found my voice again at last.

'He did not do it. We fell, as he said. I think I have become a woman. That is all.'

My mother helped me up and brushed off some of the mud which had stuck to me. Then she put her arm round me and helped me back to my room.

'I think I would like a bath, Mamma.'

'Yes, of course. I'll call Menevia.'

Later, while I had my customary long soak, Mother gave me one of those long mother-to-daughter talks. I knew the basic facts already, of course, for she had told me what to expect. But, like many other mothers, she went over it all again in case I had missed something. Then, when she was sure I was all right, she left.

No sooner was she out of the door that Dahut came in, looking only a little the worse for wear. She pulled up a stool and sat on it.

'So,' she said, 'I hear you've been wrestling with Emrys while I was asleep?'

'Yes. Meriadauc thought it was rape, and hit him in the face!'

She chuckled. 'Oh, I wish I'd seen it! And your mother tells me you're a woman now.'

I nodded sheepishly. 'It started this morning, maybe as I was wrestling, as you called it!'

She was suddenly serious. 'Ah, well, then that's two ways in which you're luckier than me this morning.'

'Whatever do you mean, Dahut?'

'I haven't had the sign for three months now, Keri. I'm pregnant.'

Chapter Twelve

Seated once more on his throne in the great hall King Gradlon eyed his daughter more sternly than I had ever seen before.

'Daughter, what is it that I have heard? I cannot believe that you would behave in such a way. Your grief is shared by us all. You know that. But it cannot excuse the blasphemies I am told you have uttered. What has led you to this?'

Dahut looked straight back at him, and deliberately held her head up high.

'I think, Father, that sanity led me to it. During the previous months I was mad. This monk of yours made me mad.'

'Brother Emrys? He is a devout man, full of the Lord's praises. What can you mean?'

Dahut tried to explain. It did no good. Gradlon had found his own salvation, and now he could see no blemish in it. The very fact that this interview was taking place in public, with the court looking on, was an indication of how seriously he took the affair. It was one of the first matters he had attended to since his return the day before, at the head of an advance party of cavalry. He had already heard from the adults involved. He listened to his daughter, and then he turned to me.

'Come forward, Keri.'

Despite the trembling of my limbs I managed to hobble a couple of paces. The King's manner was kind enough, but I felt very conspicuous.

'Now, child, Brother Emrys tells me that you have persuaded my daughter away from the faith. I know, of course, that you have not yet come to God, although I pray that you will. But surely you have not presumed to try to thwart my will in this matter?'

My jaws seemed to be stuck together. I felt that the King himself was almost accusing me of treason. My mother stepped forward and began to speak, but Gradlon silenced her with a peremptory wave of his hand. I noticed Budic of the palace guard staring fixedly at me, knowing our anti-Christian views. Then I saw Emrys smirking behind his hand, and anger gave me the courage to speak.

'Your Majesty, I would never do such a thing. The Princess has sometimes asked me what I think, and I have told her. After all, Your Majesty, to tell lies is sinful, is it not?'

A smile appeared briefly on his face. 'Olivia Galeria, your daughter is as sharp as you are! Well then, child, tell me one more thing. Certain things have been said, and I must put them to you. Has your mother ever asked you to influence the Princess in her beliefs?'

This too was dangerous ground. My mother, accused of court intrigue!

'No, Your Majesty, she never has.'

He held my eyes with his own for a time, and then nodded. 'Very well, my child, I believe you. Now tell me, why do you dislike our Brother Emrys so much? Surely he has never harmed you?'

I did not know what to say. The jealousies which lay at the root of my hatred for Emrys were not for repetition here.

'Your Majesty, Brother Emrys frightens me.'

There were a few guffaws from the assembled company, but Gradlon's frown silenced them.

'Frightens you? I don't understand. How does he frighten you?'

Again, what could I say? Could I tell this Christian King that I was terrified of the crucifix? What would he think?

'He, he is very stern, Your Majesty. He always seems angry.'

'Does he, now?' The King looked around at the monk, who was sitting away to one side. 'And did he frighten you in the garden that day, the day that Meriadauc hit him?

'Oh, yes, Your Majesty. He said terrible things.'

'What things?'

'He said I was wicked. He said I was the, the spawn of Satan. He took hold of me too, and shook me till my teeth rattled.'

There were some angry mutterings in the crowd at this, but whom they were aimed against I could not tell.

'And, Your Majesty, he said that I was sinful, and the reward for sin was death, or something like that. I'm sorry I lost my head and screamed, but I really thought he meant to kill me. I think that is why Meriadauc hit him, Your Majesty. He thought Brother Emrys was harming me, because I screamed.'

'And did he harm you, child? Did he do anything to warrant your screaming?'

I hesitated. There was silence in the room, and I sensed that a great deal hung on my answer. For a moment I was sorely tempted to lie, to land Emrys in the trouble he so richly deserved. But it was not my nature to be so devious, and I had probably lost friends enough as it was.

'No, Your Majesty. I was only frightened. He did nothing that was, well, he didn't do what Meriadauc feared.'

'Very well, child. I believe you have answered truthfully.'

'Yes, Your Majesty.' I crept back to my mother's side, exhausted with the proceedings. The King pondered for a few moments, while the crowd exchanged looks and muttered comments. One or two people patted me on the shoulder or the head, so I knew we had some sympathisers. At last Gradlon spoke.

'I have now heard from all of those involved in these incidents, and my first conclusion is that I can see why the good Lord made kings. People left to fend for themselves without guidance do not fare particularly well.' He was smiling as he spoke, and a ripple of dutiful laughter broke out.

'However,' he went on, 'I find that no crime has occurred here. It seems to me that tempers have frayed, and that misunderstandings have arisen. But I believe those involved were acting in good faith. Meriadauc believed himself to be acting in defence of the honour of an innocent virgin. This being so, what could he have honourably done, other than what he did? Indeed, if he had been less restrained he might have used his dagger rather than his fist. In the past he has done this kingdom many services, not all of which can be told here. He has always kept our laws, and has now asked my permission to stay and live here in Kemper. I find no fault with him, and I shall grant his request.'

Meriadauc being a popular character, there was applause at this. For my part, I was wondering what secret services he had done the kingdom. But I supposed that a sea captain would be a useful source of information because of his travelling. The King went on.

'Next, Olivia Galeria. She is my kinswoman, albeit a distant one, but this would not save her from banishment if she were trying to sow dissension in the royal household itself. I am satisfied that she has not done so. Indeed, her presence here has often been of great value to my family. My daughter lacks a mother, and has benefitted from the presence here of a mature person of her own sex and of a suitable social station. But Olivia Galeria has not yet come to know the Lord, and this disturbs me, for a child's faith will surely grow the better if she is surrounded by suitable examples. I have therefore decided that the guidance of my daughter shall be placed in the hands of a mature Christian woman. Although free to live in my kingdom wherever she pleases, Olivia Galeria will leave my household.'

There was some hubbub at this. For the first time I was aware that some had thought my mother to be the King's mistress. There were other mutterings, to the effect that war had sharpened the King's decisiveness, and he was making a clean sweep of the pagans, and maybe Tiernan was next. But he wasn't.

'Now to Brother Emrys. I know him for a man of piety, and it grieves me to have to criticise a man of God. But it seems to me that he has been over-zealous, and sometimes unfeeling. The incident in the garden was ill-considered. If he had cause to complain of the child's behaviour his proper course would have been to take up the matter with her mother. His angry approach to the child provoked another man to violence, and the result might have been worse. Brother Emrys's piety and good intentions are not in doubt, but I feel he has something to learn about how to handle people. He will return to the community from which he came, and I will ask for other brothers to come and preach God's word in Kemper.'

There was some applause at this, too, but Gradlon frowned severely and it soon died down. The King gave a deep sigh.

'Lastly, I come to my daughter, but what am I to say? Her grief is, of course, public knowledge. The loss of her betrothed, a fine man whom she knew and loved, is a loss to us all. But how can it excuse her behaviour? Many of you have also lost loved ones, but you did not vent your feelings on all and sundry in this unseemly manner. Nor did you threaten your religious advisers with knives, or blame your loss on them. I do not know what to say, except that the behaviour of a princess should be above reproach. Grieving is a matter of private concern, not public display, though perhaps it ill behoves me to say so. Yet my own failings in the past, before I knew God, are not an excuse for my daughter's now. I have decided that she shall leave the court for a time, and go with an appropriate person to my villa at Ker-Is. I hope that the seclusion and instruction which she receives there will restore to her a proper appreciation of the faith, and of the duties of a royal daughter. That is all.'

Without more ado he rose and left the room. Dahut stood there still, unable to speak. Tears coursed down her face. I realised that she had been humiliated publicly, but when she found her voice at last it was not to complain of this.

'Keri,' she wailed. 'Don't you see what it means? He wants to separate us for good!'

That evening we stayed in our room and talked about the situation in which we found ourselves. To say that we had become as sisters was an understatement. Sisters I have observed were never as close as we were. They fight and squabble over little possessions, and vie with each other for their parents' attention. In short, they compete in everything. Dahut and I did not. Only one thing had really threatened to come between us, and Dahut had now spurned it. We were closer than sisters. I do not mean that in a bad sense. The gods know, we shared a bed for years, and had ample opportunity if we had been that way inclined. But neither of us was of a Sapphic persuasion. Our love was not the kind that brings men and women together. It was of a kind that cannot exist between men and women, I think. For them, the issue becomes clouded by their natural desires.

Whatever name you give it, the strength of our feeling meant that we had to find a way to stay together. Neither of us had another young friend, and we both remembered the loneliness of the time before we met. Besides, there was the question of Dahut's pregnancy. Whatever solution we might try, it would have to involve Dahut's absence from court for the rest of the summer. We knew that Megan would help, and in that way a banishment to Ker-Is was a relief father than a punishment, but a way had to be found for me to go too. We were still talking through the problem when there was a knock at the door. After a moment's delay it opened, and the King himself appeared. We immediately jumped to our feet, preparing to curtsey, but he waved us down again.

'I'm here as your father, not as the King' he said gruffly to Dahut.

We sat down again gingerly, and he grabbed a chair and flopped into it. This was the first time I had seen him close up since his return, and I was shocked to see how careworn he looked.

'Shall I leave you, Your Majesty?' I asked, thinking he might want to talk privately with his daughter.

He grinned that boyish grin of his. 'I don't suppose you two have any secrets. You might as well stay, and spare Dahut the effort of repeating it all to you later.'

This promptly cut through the tension in the air, and set us both giggling. He smiled briefly, but then came to the point.

'Dahut, my daughter, you know you are more precious to me than anything or anyone in the world. It grieves me to send you away, but it must be done. I must be seen to chastise behaviour such as yours.'

Dahut lowered her eyes and nodded dumbly.

'As I said in the hall, I accept that you were deeply grieved by Riwal's loss. Your marriage would, I know, have been the joining of two hearts as well as two great families. What I cannot accept is the public denial of god. There are greater things at stake here than you realise.'

He leaned forward in his chair as he warmed to the subject.

'You are both very young, but you must be aware of great events going on. The Empire is threatened on all sides. Attila's attack is only one such. The Franks were on our side this time, but there have been threats from that quarter before, and will be again. Likewise the Goths.

'While I was with the army I spent some time talking with Aëtius. Now there is a man who understands. He believes the barbarians do not want to destroy the Empire. On the contrary, many of them have become federates and fought hard to defend it, and preserve its customs. The Vandals are different, of course, but they have isolated themselves across the sea in Africa. The rest of the Empire can be saved. All it needs is a unifying force, a shared way of looking at things. I believe that is why god has sent his word among us at this time. That is the unifying force. If we accept Christ now, we will be invincible. The Empire will not only survive, it will be transformed into the Kingdom of Heaven on Earth!'

I thought of Galla Placidia, the emperor's mother, expending herself on plans for a mausoleum in the middle of the Ravenna marshes. The Kingdom of Heaven on Earth seemed a long way off, and Valentinian seemed poorly cast as the king of it. But the flames of zeal burned bright in Gradlon's eyes.

'You see,' he went on. 'That is why I will not have the faith abused in public, and why I shall do my utmost to establish it permanently in this kingdom.'

He sat back and waited for Dahut to speak. She carried on looking at the floor for a moment. Then she rose, walked over to him, and knelt at his feet.

'Father, you know I would do nothing to go against you. I know I did wrong in behaving as I did. Some time away from court at Ker-Is will give me time to think and perhaps to change.' Tears came into her eyes. 'Only, Father, do not take away my friend. Keri is the one friend I have. Without her, I truly believe that my behaviour would have been worse, much worse. She has counselled me daily to restrain my feelings, and to accept your will, and I have tried. Please don't part us now. Who else will help me? Berta is no more than a nurse, a slave. I have no mother. You said yourself that Aunt Olivia had served us well. Please do not separate us. I will do anything you say!'

She rested her head on his knee and, and began to shake with heavy sobs. The King put his hand out and stroked her hair lightly. I think I saw the gleam of tears in his own eyes, but he blinked them away quickly.

'Dahut,' he said hoarsely, and then cleared his throat. 'Listen to me. I will do one thing. I will let Olivia and Keri go to Ker-Is with you.'

'Oh thank you, Father!' She looked up, her tear-stained face suddenly beaming. He held up a hand.

'Listen to me. They can stay in the household until the autumn. But by the time you return to Kemper I shall have chosen some proper attendants for you, mature ladies of a sound Christian disposition. Then you will have proper Christian examples to follow, and all will see that I meant what I said today.'

He got up then, and kissed her forehead.

'I must go. Goodnight to you both.'

As the door shut behind him Dahut turned to me with a mischievous grin.

'Marvellous what a few tears can do, isn't it?' she said.

The weather was brilliant the day we set out for Ker-Is. I could not help remembering the first time we had made the journey, the roads a quagmire and the country veiled in rain. This time the horses found an easy footing, and the wheels of our wagon rattled and jolted over the sun-baked earth. Whatever the sadnesses of the war, it was as if Nature had declared peace from today. Dahut, pleading tiredness, lay on the wagon floor on a mass of cushions. I suspected that the pregnancy was causing her discomfort, but she said nothing. I rode my own pony behind the wagon, listened to the birds greet the summer, and breathed in the scents of grass and woodland.

Mother rode next to me for a time, and we watched the birds wheeling above the trees, disturbed by the rumble of wagons and hooves.

'It's getting warmer quite quickly,' she said. 'Summer's coming early this year.'

'I hope so, Mother. Perhaps it will take everyone's minds off the war.'

'Not much chance of that, I fear, with so many widows and orphans left behind it. How is Dahut these days?'

'She misses him still. I suppose you're right. It is still too fresh in people's minds.'

'I remember saying that a passion like theirs had dangers. I must admit I wasn't thinking of this one.'

'No, Mother. Oh, look at that!' I had seen a hawk swoop down on something in the trees, and seized upon it as an excuse to change the subject. We watched for a few moments, as we travelled by. Then we saw the hawk rise again, with a tattered object fluttering weakly in its talons. I watched it out of sight, hoping the wounded prey might regain the strength to escape, but it did not. I saw an omen in this, as young girls are wont to do. But I hoped Dahut would fare better.

We stopped at last for a midday meal. Dahut and I went off into the bushes to relieve our bladders, neither horse riding nor pregnancy being very helpful in that department. As we squatted companionably we speculated on who might be appointed to 'guide' Dahut in the autumn.

'I hope it isn't Brica,' she said, referring to the pious and humourless widow of one of the captains.

'No,' I agreed. 'She just looks like she's got piles.'

Dahut giggled. 'Don't make me laugh. I've just peed on my ankle.' Then she gave a grunt of surprise.

'What is it, Dahut?'

'Keri, there's blood!' The anxiety in her voice was palpable.

'Wait here. I'll get a cloth from the wagon.'

She had gone white. 'Oh, gods above and below, don't let anything happen to the baby.'

Personally, I thought it might well be the solution to the problem, but we had talked about it and Dahut was adamant. The child was all she had to remind her of Riwal. It was a part of Riwal still with her, and she would cherish it on that account. What would happen when it was born was another question, and one for which there was as yet no answer.

'What's the matter?' called my mother, seeing me run back to the wagon.

'Oh, nothing,' I lied glibly. 'It's Dahut's time of the month. She's just started.'

'Oh. Can you manage?'

'Yes, of course. There's no problem.'

I felt myself blushing furiously as I went back to Dahut. I hated lying to anyone, but to my mother most of all. Besides, it was by no means certain that there was 'no problem'. If Dahut miscarried wouldn't it be obvious at this stage what had happened?

In the event there was no miscarriage. Dahut remained in the wagon until we arrived at the villa, and then she went straight to bed. The next day the bleeding stopped. We managed to pass the whole thing off to my mother as a heavy period, and she seemed to accept this. Dahut was jubilant, and I felt a little ashamed of my thoughts on the road. But what were we going to do?

'Don't worry,' said Dahut. 'We'll go to Megan. She'll know what to do. She always does. And anyway, there's the whole summer to spend here at Ker-Is, and there's no better place on earth!'

Chapter Thirteen

On the second day after our arrival at Ker-Is we went out to meet Megan. We thought she might be at her little beach, but she was not.

'The water's probably too cold at this time of year,' said Dahut, and we made our way back up the cliff at a gentle pace.

At the top we struck off through the woods to the place where Megan's house stood. As we approached it we could see she was at home, for there was a trail of smoke rising from the chimney and the smell of wood smoke on the air. I ran ahead, Dahut not wanting to overtax herself at the moment, and banged on the door.

Megan was there in a moment.

'Come in, the pair of you! Delighted I am to see you! I heard the villa was occupied, so I guessed you'd be here sooner or later. In fact, I had hoped to see you yesterday.'

'Ah, well,' I said. 'Dahut wasn't quite well, but she's all right now.'

Soon we were settled in her little living room, enjoying the fire and drinking a hot herbal tea she had made for us. She had been mixing some medicine when we arrived, and carried on grinding up dried herbs with her pestle and mortar while we talked. She had only heard a little about the war, and we had much more to tell her. Then we came to the subject of Riwal. Megan listened intently while Dahut regaled her with enthusiastic tales of her lover. And while she wept over him.

'Oh, Megan, I miss him so much. I long for him. For weeks I hoped that it was a mistake, and he would appear at the palace gate one day. Silly thoughts. I know he won't; he was seen by the men of his tribe afterwards.'

Megan put her arm around Dahut's shoulders, and then let it slip down to her waist as she cuddled her close. She gave me a sharp look suddenly, but said nothing until Dahut's sobs had quietened, and she could talk again.

'And tell me, little lady, how long have you been with child?'

'Megan! How did you know?'

'Your waist has thickened. And I could tell there was something you were still holding back. Well, how long?'

Dahut sniffed. 'About four months, I think.'

'I see. And you thought I might help?'

'Yes, Megan. You will, won't you?' Dahut's voice was pleading.

'I will if I can. But, tell me, were you thinking of getting rid of the child?'

'Getting rid? You mean abort it? Oh, no, Megan, I couldn't do that.'

'No, well, it's probably too late. It could be dangerous now. I'd not advise it. Have you thought it out? What's Keri's mother like? Would she help?'

I thought about that. 'I think she would. She won't be concerned about the chastity of a good Christian woman, and all that sort of thing. She's much more practical. She'll want to know how we intend to look after the child.'

'That's easy,' said Megan. 'I will look after it. If you agree, of course.'

'Oh, Megan!' cried Dahut. 'Agree? I'd be delighted! There's no one I'd rather have do it. But are you sure?'

'Indeed I am. I'd like a child, I told you that, and the Mother has not seen fit to grant me one of my own, in spite of my going to the fires at Beltane. Perhaps this is why. Perhaps She intended me for this.'

'One other thing,' I said. 'I don't think my mother will want to tell the King.'

'What would the King do if he knew?' asked Megan. Dahut jumped at the very mention of the idea.

'Oh, Megan, I shudder to think! He gets more pious by the day. He'd shut me up in a nunnery for life, probably, while the good sisters prayed for my soul. No, whatever happens we must keep it from him.'

'He might send for you before the baby is born,' said Megan.

Dahut shook her head. 'There's not much chance of that, I think.' And she went on to explain to Megan how she had disgraced herself at court. The older woman chuckled in places, especially when we described Dahut's being sick over Brother Emrys. But she was serious too.

'Don't drink so much again, my Princess, if you want to have the child. Too much wine could harm it.'

'I won't. I've learned my lesson. Once is enough!'

We all laughed at that.

'Now, my little ones,' Megan went on. 'We must think and plan. First of all I must meet your mother, Keri. She must be let into the secret.'

Dahut was nervous at that prospect, but Megan persuaded her.

'It is the season for wearing loose clothes,' she said. 'But in spite of that you must soon begin to show. Keri's mother cannot be kept in the dark then. And when the baby comes, what will you do then? It may be the middle of the night. Will you be climbing out of the bedroom window to come to me? No, the preparations must be made, and Olivia Galeria must be involved.'

'Very well,' said Dahut. 'Tomorrow is Sunday, and we will be going to the church in the village.' She grimaced apologetically to Megan. 'My father insisted. After the church we were talking about going for a walk by the sea. Perhaps you will meet us there?'

Each week we were to accompany the Christians of the household down to the little thatched church which now stood in the village. Mother would not, but Dahut and I went as we had promised the King. The villagers were distinctly wary of us, and bowed and scraped before us as we passed through the congregation. What they said behind our backs I do not know. As members of the King's household we always went to the front of the church, and had wooden seats provided. The rest of the congregation had to stand, or kneel on the beaten-earth floor. We therefore had the closest view of Father Johannes at the altar, but I can scarcely remember a thing. They say the mind can bury memories somewhere within itself, if they are painful. I think my church attendance was not so much painful as soporific. Once or twice I actually did fall asleep. At all events, if anything of interest happened it passed me by. I found the whole idea of worshipping gods inside dusty shacks quite distasteful. It seemed to me that the peasants had it right. The Creator of the world should be worshipped outside, in the fresh air and green woods that He (or She, according to Megan) created. In the old days this was always the way it was done, even in Rome. It was the mystery religions of the East which hid their practices from the uninitiated – Mithraism, Judaism, and Christianity.

Mind you, I was only dimly aware of such things then, if at all. I just felt suffocated, and Dahut felt the same. Still, we went through the motions of worship. Father Johannes had gained some converts in the village and outlying farms, which had all been totally pagan when we had first started coming to Ker-Is. Nonetheless his congregation was small, and heavily outnumbered. The worship of the Mother was still prevalent then, and Teutates and others of the old gods. Indeed, even today it must survive, or why would the bishops condemn it regularly, as they do? The bigotry has not changed.

Not that Johannes was all that bad at first. He used to ask for prayers for members of the congregation if they were sick. He would also bring cases of hardship to people's attention, and ask volunteers to help. He was not above rolling up his sleeves and helping out himself, if there was a job to be done. For those reasons he had won respect from people, even if they disagreed with him. He was a less fearsome figure than Brother Emrys had been, he was slimmer and only about average height. His face was thin, and his eyes occasionally twinkled in a display of humour which Emrys had never shown. Like so many of the Christian churchmen he displayed a fervour which was often alarming. His sermons sometimes reached levels of emotion which would have seemed ridiculous to any educated person, but there were none among his flock except for us, and we were still too young to realise it.

'All around the servants of Satan are in arms against us!' he thundered on one occasion. 'Yet, do not imagine that we face them only on the field of battle, in the form of the Hun or the Saxon. Even in times of peace the servants of the Evil Once are ready to tempt us when we least expect it, and our guard is down. There are those who still follow the evil practices of demon-worship, at Beltane, at Samhain, at every season of the year. Some of them even come in turn to this church, as if Christ were only one lord among many. The Lord is merciful. Again and again he will forgive our transgressions, for he knows well our weaknesses. But this I tell you – any hour may be our last, and woe to the miserable sinner who dies with the stain of demon-worship still upon him.'

He drew himself up to his full height, such as it was. The worst of his condemnation was yet to come.

'He who worships in the hedgerows and the groves of oak endangers his own soul. But worse than this is the one who entices others away from the worship of the One True God. *He* imperils the souls of others. He has set himself up against God, he has joined the ranks of Satan, and his reward will be the eternal fires of Hell!'

At this point his excitement overcame him, and he relapsed into a fit of nervous coughing which rather spoiled the effect.

Johannes also had the responsibility for teaching Dahut and me. Since he knew nothing about anything except the Church he was not very effective, but he undertook to bring us to God. If our souls were saved presumably that was all that mattered. We soon realised Johannes was not actually very bright. We teased him with innocent-seeming questions as I had done with Emrys, but unlike Emrys he failed to realise what we were up to. Mother had told me a good deal about the history of the church in the Empire, and we used this knowledge to worry him. I once asked him why the Christians had changed their Sabbath from the old Jewish Saturday to the holy day of the sun, as they did under the Emperor Constantine. I also asked him why the Christians revered Constantine's memory so much when he had remained a priest of the cult of the Unconquered Sun all his life, and only been baptised a Christian on his deathbed. The priest's confusion was almost embarrassing; it was obvious that he had not known either of these things before. Baiting Johannes livened up our instruction somewhat, but I wish now that we had not done it. It caused us to underestimate the man, and the gods know we paid for it later.

After that first Sunday service we went down to the beach with Mother, as we had arranged with Megan. She was still not there when we arrived, so Dahut and I decided to go for a paddle at the water's edge. The day was warm, although the water was a bit of a shock when we stepped into it. The sea needs a good summer to warm it up. Bathing in a cold autumn is often warmer than in a fair spring, when the winter has not yet released its grip.

Once we had got used to the water Dahut suddenly lifted her loose shift over her head and handed it to me.

'Take this, will you? I don't want to turn around, or your mother will notice my belly. I'd rather she spoke to Megan first.'

'But Megan – '

' – is coming down the cliff path.'

I turned and took the garment back up to where my mother was sitting. Megan was indeed approaching from the cliff. Dahut was now waist deep in the water, and splashing at the gentle waves which were rippling in from the calm ocean. Mother didn't hear Megan because of their noise, until she flopped down next to us with her ever-present basket.

'Good day to you, Olivia Galeria,' said Megan.

Mother narrowed her eyes – she did not know Megan from the Emperor's chambermaid. Her attitude showed in the disdainful look she gave to this presumptuous peasant woman. It was strange that I had never noticed her snobbishness before, but now that I had, it seemed it had always been there. Perhaps I was growing up.

'You have the advantage of me,' said Mother stiffly.

'Mother,' I broke in. 'This is Megan. She lives near here. We are old friends.'

Mother turned to me and raised an eyebrow. 'Indeed? You have never seen fit to mention the fact.'

'Ah, no, that's true. We thought, that is, I thought, that it was best not to say anything.'

'To your own mother?'

'*Domina*,' said Megan. 'I am not a gentlewoman, as you can plainly see. I think your daughter and the Princess were not sure how such a friendship would be viewed.'

Mother nodded. 'And why do you make it known now? There must be a reason.'

For answer, Megan turned towards the sea, where the ripening figure of Dahut swayed amid the waves.

'She is a beautiful creature,' said Megan. 'The Mother creates such beauty for a purpose. The Princess is fulfilling that purpose this summer.'

Mother stared for a long time, the colour draining from her face.

'She's pregnant?' It was a whisper.

'Yes, *Domina*. She carries the child of Prince Riwal.'

Mother was recovering with amazing speed. 'And you? You are the midwife?'

'I am a midwife, amongst other things.'

'Mother,' I said. 'Megan will foster the child when it is born. We can stay here until after the birth, and go back to Kemper for the winter with no one the wiser. But we can only do it if you will help!'

She sprang up, suddenly angry.

'Help you? Do you think I am mad. You come to me with a crazy scheme like this! Do you know what is involved? Think, child! That baby will be the heir to two royal houses! Two! There are many who would kill all of us to prevent it coming of age.'

'*Domina*,' put in Megan gently. 'First of all they would have to know about it! Besides, as an illegitimate child what rights would it have? Under the old law maybe it would fare better. But it seems the law of the Christian will soon hold sway here. A royal bastard will not count for much with the priest and the bishops.'

Mother hesitated. 'I must think!' And she strode off across the beach, arms folded angrily in front of her. I made as if to go after her, but Megan took my hand suddenly.

'Let her go, Keri. She has a right to her thoughts. Meantime, let us fetch that Princess back before she freezes.'

We called Dahut in, and Megan produced a cloak from her basket to rub her down.

'You are cold, my Princess. You stayed out there too long.'

'I love it,' mumbled Dahut between shivers. 'The sea is alive. I feel no cold out there. It is like the caress of a lover's hands.' The irony of what she had just said suddenly struck her, and she burst into tears. As Dahut's body shook with her sobbing, Megan rubbed her back to warm her.

'Aye,' she said soothingly. 'Well, this lover's hands are like to freeze you to death!'

'And if it weren't for my baby I would welcome him with open arms!' cried Dahut bitterly.

I looked up and saw Mother pacing back towards us. Her face looked grim and determined, and I rose and went to meet her.

'I must be as crazy as the rest of you,' she muttered as I approached. 'But to let this become public would be disastrous. Equally, to tell Gradlon – who really has a right to know – would be folly. There's no telling how he might react. I can see no way out but to help as you ask.'

'Oh, thank you, Mother, thank you.' I put my arms around her, but she felt stiff and unyielding.

'It's incredible,' she said. 'Incredible, that a young woman in her position ...'

'Don't judge her harshly,' I said. 'She and Riwal were passionately in love.'

'Love? What do you know of love? You're a child! Love, indeed! I pulled away from her, surprised at her bitterness.

'Not so ignorant of love that I can't see the obvious!' Now it was my turn to stamp off in a huff, but she followed me.

'And just what do you mean by that?'

I swung to face her. 'Do you think I don't know what it means when you look at Meriadauc the way you do? When you go all girlish as he approaches? When you feast your eyes on his bum as he leans across the table –'

Her open hand hit me on the side of the face. I was caught off balance and went full length on the sand. She was beside me in a trice.

'Keri, I'm sorry! I didn't mean it!'

I rubbed the side of my face, a little dazed, and blinked away tears. 'I'm glad of that. I'd hate to be around when you do.'

We both giggled stupidly at that.

'I wasn't criticising you,' I said gently. 'I want you to be happy. And if you want to marry him, there's no one I'd rather have as a stepfather. And if you don't, there's no one I'd rather have as my mother's lover. I'd gladly help you smuggle in and out of the house at night, if you're worried about what the neighbours will think.'

She blushed, and giggled again, although there were tears on her cheeks. 'I wish it were so simple, Keri. I really do.'

'It is, Mother. You have a right to your happiness. It's as simple as that.'

She shook her head. 'No, there are still things you don't understand. But let me worry about them. For the moment, we'll concentrate on your friend.'

As we got to our feet, she suddenly put both hands on my shoulders and looked me straight in the eye.

'I'm sorry, Keri. I've been thinking of you as a child still. I can see I'll have to stop doing that.'

We linked arms and walked back to the others, who had been staring open-mouthed at our behaviour. It was the first time I had ever seen Megan at a loss for words.

'Everything all right, then?' she said at last.

'Yes,' I replied. 'In fact, everything's a lot better than it was.'

We soon settled into a routine which in some ways was even better than it had been on our previous visits. We had no need to sneak out now when we wanted to visit Megan. My mother was happy to come with us. Indeed, after Megan had helped her over one or two minor ailments, Mother developed a considerable respect for her.

'She is certainly wise in herb lore,' she said to me one day. 'And she knows a great many things for one from such a humble background. Even the Christian monks use the same sorts of preparations when they try to heal the sick. When others do, of course, they accuse them of witchcraft.'

'How ridiculous,' I said. 'How could anyone think Megan was a witch?' And yet that was exactly what Dahut and I had thought at first.

We paid regular visits to Megan at this time, because of Dahut's pregnancy. The direct route from the villa to Megan's house was fairly short, and more or less on the level. Dahut was physically quite fit, and kept that way by walking and swimming. Megan had also advised some exercises, but I think these were mainly to do with making the birth easier. Whenever we visited for one of these examinations Megan would lie Dahut down on the bed and listen to her stomach. She would ask her a few questions, and sometimes examine her more closely, and pronounce herself satisfied.

It was obviously desirable that our regular presence at her house should not become public knowledge, and Megan always asked us at a time when she expected to be alone. None the less, there were times when we would arrive just as someone else was leaving, or pass them on the path. They would always greet us with the shy respect that any peasant shows to the family of the King, but sometimes I would turn and look behind. There they would be, staring after us in puzzlement, wondering where we were off to. Since no one else lived along this path the answer was self-evident. How foolish we were to imagine we could keep such a thing secret! But there was no alternative, so we had to believe it possible. There must have been talk in the village because Father Johannes raised the subject on one of his visits to the villa.

Mother was out of the way, as was her wont when the good Father visited. This time she was supervising the cook. On other days it would be something else. The priest sat with us in the villa's main hall, and held his hands before the fire. As usual, we waited for him to speak first.

'Ah, it's cold it is today.'

We said something harmless in agreement.

'Yes. It's a time when many of our people catch cold, the weather being warm and cold by turns, and often wet. Many of the fishermen have a touch of the cold right now.'

We sympathised with the poor fishermen, but I was not altogether happy, as it was clear he was leading up to something, and it wasn't fish.

'Then of course, you'll have seen them yourselves.'

'What do you mean?' asked Dahut.

'Well, I mean, on your visits to the wise-woman. Morgan, isn't it?'

'Megan,' I corrected him.

'Ah, yes, well I see you know her better than I.'

Perhaps he was not so stupid after all.

'We do know her, yes. She helps a lot of the people around here when they are not well. There is no doctor nearer than Kemper.'

'Ah, yes. You know, you should really send word if you are not well. I would gladly ask the congregation for prayers. Perhaps I could even pray here with you.'

'You are very thoughtful,' Dahut said. 'We would hate to bother you over trivial matters.'

'It's no bother. Ah, trivial, you say? Yes, I was thinking you'd never mentioned being unwell. And, of course, you both look the picture of health.'

This was getting to be less of a conversation and more of a cross-examination. I decided that embarrassing him was probably the only way to end it.

'There are, of course, some complaints that a woman does not like to discuss openly,' I said. 'Especially with a man. Even a man of God.'

He coloured noticeably. 'Ah, yes, forgive me, I had no wish to pry.'

'The very idea!' put in Dahut, smirking.

'Megan is well versed in the workings of the female body.' I went on relentlessly. 'You know, irregular periods, that kind of thing.'

He was scarlet now. 'Quite, quite.'

'Of course,' said Dahut innocently, 'we need not explain. You are a man of the world.'

There was an awkward silence. A 'man of the world' was exactly what he was not.

'Dahut,' I said, 'you have embarrassed the good Father. You can hardly expect him to be so familiar with female problems. After all, priests are not allowed to marry.'

'I know that, of course,' she said, and then turned to Johannes directly. 'But didn't I hear that some priest and monks actually do?'

'In the further-flung reaches of Christendom – Ireland and Cornwall, mainly – there are some married priests. I have heard so, at any rate,' he said stiffly. 'It is a practice forbidden by the Bishop of Rome. There are some who do not fully accept his authority, but they will, in time. The Emperor has ordered it so.'

'How convenient,' murmured Dahut.

'I beg your pardon?'

'Well,' she said, 'it practically means that to disobey the Bishop of Rome is to disobey the Emperor, which is treason. I should think that's very convenient for both of them.'

'I think,' said the priest hurriedly, 'I think I should perhaps tell you something about the Bishopric of Rome, for it was founded by Saint Peter himself, and is the source of all the Church's authority.'

As the summer wore on – not a very good summer, at that – we fell into a routine. We were too old for lessons now, but Mother would pass on information when we asked. She knew a good deal about the history of the Empire, and numbered some of the great histories of it among her books. She sent for a number of these by the regular messenger to Kemper, and Meriadauc sent her some he had managed to buy. We continued to be instructed by Father Johannes, and to attend his church, but it was clear that he wanted me to be baptised. I did not want to go through with that, and Dahut supported me.

'It's a mistake,' she said. 'No matter what your secret feelings are you are seen to be joining the Church. I wish now that I had never done it. Of course, it made Riwal happier, so I supposed it was worth it.'

I noticed a gradual change in her when she spoke of Riwal. Whether it was something to do with the pregnancy I was not sure, but, while she still mourned him, there was also a slightly resentful tone to some of the things she said.

'I don't know why I should weep for him,' she confided one day. 'He's beyond all the troubles of this world now, but he certainly left me with some!' And she patted her swelling front with a rueful grin.

Regular visits by Megan were also part of the routine now. She would advise Dahut about what to eat, as well as examine her.

'A summer pregnancy is less comfortable, because of the heat,' she said once. 'But it makes better babies. There is plenty of everything, you see. If you need fruit, or greens, well, there is someone who has them.

As near as she could judge, the baby was due in mid-September, and she was well satisfied with Dahut's progress, unlike Dahut herself. Every pregnant woman I have ever known reaches a stage where she gets tired of looking like a wine barrel and feeling as heavy. Dahut, being less patient than many, reached that stage by about the middle of June. Suddenly, she was no longer able to climb down the cliff path, however gently. Swimming was therefore out of the question. The walk to Megan's cottage also began to tax her unduly. Besides, she was beginning to look obviously pregnant, and there was a risk of being seen on the way. Both Mother and I took to wearing roomy summer smocks so that Dahut might not look so large by comparison, but there is a limit to what you can achieve by this kind of illusion! We reached this limit about six weeks before the baby was due, and all agreed that Dahut would just have to stay in the house.

The most difficult part of this was in explaining her absence from church. We thought of hiding her, and giving out that she had gone back to Kemper for a while, but this would have been easily disproved. In the end the simplest solution was to pretend that she was ill. I saw Father Johannes and hinted darkly at unthinkable female complaints. The poor man, easily embarrassed as he was, would not pry. When he came to the villa Dahut was in bed, 'resting'. He saw her there, and we all three prayed together for her recovery.

Meanwhile, Megan was making plans of a more practical nature. It was obvious that we could hardly conceal a labour and birth from anyone in the villa, so Dahut would have to be moved to Megan's house when it started. The wise-woman was owed favours by many people in the area whom she had helped. Two stout and reliable men agreed to come at her call and carry a friend who might be too ill to walk. They were pagans, and could be trusted, especially when told that the priest would forbid it if he knew. The other arrangement was more problematic – the provision of a wet-nurse – but Megan kept her eyes and ears open for news of stillbirths locally. The rate of deaths among infants being what it was, there was a good chance. Of course, by the same token it was possible that no wet-nurse might be needed.

There was nothing else to do now but settle down for a long wait.

Chapter Fourteen

I have said before that the Celtic mind harbours a love of mystery. Let any incident occur, and within days it will be elaborated with all kinds of details which escaped the notice of those who were actually there. Within weeks the tale will have acquired a magician, two spirits of the air, and the transmigrated soul of a king. Within years the original characters will be gone completely, and the whole story will be about some hero and his confrontation with the gods.

The gods may be changing, but the love of mystery seems to be the same. There are several versions of the story of Gradlon's first meeting with Corentin, although the truth, as always, is much more mundane than many of them. I was not there. I was still at Ker-Is awaiting the birth of Dahut's child. But I had the story from those who were there – from the court regulars, and the servants. People underestimate servants and slaves. In fact they are often good witnesses. They spend long periods with nothing to do except observe what is going on, for they are seldom a part of it.

People will tell you that Corentin miraculously fed all of Gradlon's party when they chanced upon him in the forest. They even say that he kept a fish in a pool, and that he could cut off the fish's back half and it would always grow back again at once. If you ask me, someone mixed up the story with the Christian tale of the feeding of the five thousand! The only true part is that Gradlon really did meet Corentin in the forest west of Kemper while out hunting. Since his conversion to the new religion, and the lifting of his black moods, he had resumed some of those kingly pursuits which the court expected, and he had always enjoyed. Boar-hunting was one of them. Of course, as any educated person would know, a hunt is planned to last all day, so there is always a wagon with food, and servants to prepare it. The hunting party meets them at a pre-arranged time and place, and the food is ready. No miracles.

On this day the hunt had been unlucky. They had started one boar, but it had killed two of the dogs and made off, leaving a trail of blood and broken branches. The hunt had tried to follow, but without success. The boar had found a way through the dense undergrowth that the horses could not follow. The dogs were recalled, and Gradlon suggested that everyone should go to the wagon for the midday meal. Following what they thought was a shortcut, the party lost its way and came to a clearing in the forest. In the centre of the clearing was a great stone and sitting upon it was a man in monk's clothing. He stood up as the party emerged from the trees, revealing himself to be very tall, but thin. Excessive fasting had made him skinny, and rather bent, so that at thirty-seven he could not stand up entirely straight.

'Good day, Your Majesty!' called the man. Some take this as magical foreknowledge, for no one had yet introduced the King, but it was not so.

'How did you know who I am?' asked Gradlon, ready to believe in a miracle. The man just shrugged.

'Your men bear the royal symbols on their shields,' he answered. 'How many kings are there in Kemper?'

Gradlon laughed. 'Just the one, my friend, in spite of anything you may have heard to the contrary! Tell me, do you know these woods well?'

'Tolerably well, Your Majesty. How may I help you?'

'You could find us a boar,' suggested Gradlon, and the hunting party laughed. 'But first you may be able to put us on our way. We are due to meet our kitchen party where the Vorganium and Darioritum roads meet. We have gone astray in the woods, I fear.'

The monk smiled. 'Many have lost their way, but those will find it again who turn to the Lord.'

'Those are true words indeed,' answered Gradlon. 'Can a man of the Lord set us on the right path this morning?'

'It will be my pleasure to do so,' said Corentin. 'I am in fact heading in the same direction, returning to my little community at Pluguffan.'

'In that case you must ride with us!' declared Gradlon, and beckoned one of his escort. 'Here, give this holy man a helping hand. He will ride behind you until we reach the kitchen party. And he can eat with us there.'

'I thank you for the ride, Your Majesty,' said the monk. 'But I do not eat at midday. I fast from dawn till dusk, except for a little water.'

The chosen soldier wrinkled his nose at the holy man, but helped him up on to the horse. They rode alongside the King, who wanted to talk with the monk as they went. There is no doubt that Corentin made a great impression upon Gradlon. When they came to the crossroads where the kitchen wagon stood, Corentin allowed himself to be persuaded to stay a while, and to continue the discussions he had started with the King. Others were there who joined in from time to time, especially Tiernan. He was always wary of any influence the monks might bring to bear upon the King. Well, he was not alone in that! It must have been the only point on which he and Dahut and I agreed. Tiernan interrupted at one point to try to direct Gradlon's attention elsewhere.

'Your Majesty. Forgive me, but is it not time to resume the hunt?'

'It's all right, Tiernan. As far as I am concerned we can manage without wild pork for once. By all means lead the hunt yourself, though, if you want; I have no wish to spoil the day for everyone else. But I think I shall stay a while with the excellent Corentin here. He has a novel way of looking at some things, and a Christian king must concern himself with such matters. By all means go if you wish.'

There was little for Tiernan to say to that, so he sighed and went to call the others together. Meanwhile, attended by a few servants, the King and the monk talked, occasionally stretching their legs by taking a walk on the edges of the forest. So far as anyone knows, from the snatches of their conversation which were overheard, the main subject for discussion was the faith and its propagation. Gradlon was essentially a fair-minded man. He loved the new faith, but he was reluctant to enforce it. Ideally he would have liked to win people over to it voluntarily. He had a great faith in the power of the Word. Surely all it took was a missionary of sufficient faith and skill? He had thought that Ronan might be that man, but the monk had refused to take on the task.

Corentin was different. He had none of Ronan's zest for living, nor his forgiveness. Ronan had pleaded for Keban's life; Corentin would have condemned her to the flames as an agent of the Devil. For him, the issue was simple. The Church must triumph. The Emperor had identified the Church with the Empire, and the fate of one was bound up with that of the other. As Dahut and I had said to Father Johannes, this was very convenient for them both. Treason to one was treason to the other. Treason was punishable by death. What a powerful argument to use on those who were reluctant to convert!

Not that Gradlon was willing to go quite that far yet. He argued with Corentin that the way to build a strong church was to win over men's hearts. Once could force compliance upon them, but not belief. Corentin replied to the effect that if paganism were stamped out there would be only one way for the heart to decide. Successive church councils had agreed, and called upon temporal leaders to stamp out the observation of pagan rites. So had successive emperors since Theodosius. Perhaps the barbarian threat now was god's punishment for our failure to do this. Corentin was a great believer in punishment, and so was his god. Gradlon was not entirely convinced, but he was convinced enough to ask Corentin to come to Kemper to lead the Christians there as Bishop.

'But I can hardly do that,' protested Corentin. 'I have my community to lead. The flock needs its shepherd, does it not?'

Gradlon smiled. This was the same objection that Ronan had made, but this time he had an answer.

'Corentin, what is the quality of your flock's pasture right now? If you come to Kemper you can bring your flock with you. I can give you good land, and I can lend you men to clear it, and to build your community's house too. Is there any law which says you cannot be both abbot and bishop?'

'None that I know of, Your Majesty. Indeed, there are many such.'

'Very well. Let it be done. Come to Kemper.'

'Your Majesty, I thank God for your generosity. I see now that you are his instrument in all this. Why else did we meet today, as if by chance? Why else did you lose your way, in a forest which you know well, if not to bring that meeting about?'

Gradlon nodded gravely. Some people, of course, see the supernatural in everything. And it is not only the pagan Celts who love mystery.

Within a matter of weeks Corentin's fledgling monastery was being built at Kemper. Gradlon donated them a site outside the town, on the flat land where the army had trained before marching off to meet Attila. He put the army to work for them – it was one of the ironies of the times that he had to keep a standing army but seldom had anything for it to do – and the land was cleared in a remarkably short time. There were plenty of builders in Kemper willing to work for the Church if the King was paying, and the first buildings had begun to rise on the site by midsummer.

One might be pardoned for wondering where the money came from for all this. Gradlon was certainly not poor, and he avoided spending money on court paraphernalia and similarly frivolous things, but some say that he was well paid by Aëtius for his help in defeating the Huns. They also say that the Huns were carrying a great deal of gold with them, and that Aëtius managed to get the lion's share for himself and those he favoured. Young Thorismund of the Goths, whose father had been killed in the battle, was supposedly tricked into going home empty-handed. Whatever the truth of it, the fact remains that over the next few years Gradlon appeared to have plenty of money available for public works. It was this mundane fact, more than anything else, which brought about the eventual rise of Ker-Is.

Corentin was formally declared Bishop of Kemper in July, and charged by the King with the spiritual welfare of all his subjects. From then on he was never far from Gradlon's side. He functioned as the King's personal chaplain and confessor. He advised him on religious matters, whether private or public, and increasingly he took it upon himself to try to influence personal behaviour at court and elsewhere. He appeared to be especially interested in sexual misconduct, and adulterers or unmarried lovers were publicly denounced. After some persuasion, Gradlon also took to fining them and donating the fines to the Church. In vain the victims protested that they were not Christians and therefore could not be expected to keep to Christian rules.

'This is a Christian kingdom,' was Gradlon's reply to one supplicant. 'My laws will be based on the laws of God and all will keep them, no matter what false gods they follow.'

Some news of this reached us at Ker-Is, by way of the regular messengers. Needless to say, it strengthened our resolve to keep Dahut's condition secret at all costs. Her father's attitudes were obviously hardening. Perhaps he really would have sent her to a nunnery.

With the church now firmly established as a force in the kingdom, and especially in the town of Kemper itself, certain changes began to come about in everyday life. Corentin's monks were busy for much of the time supervising operations at his monastery, but it was too late for planting crops, and the ground needed a winter's frosts to help break it down. They had previously grown their own food, but now they lived out of Gradlon's purse until the new season. They therefore had more time on their hands than they were used to. Some of them took to wandering about the town, looking for sinners to denounce. ('Looking for mischief', as Mother put it.)

Kemper was a port. Ships called there from all over the Empire, and everyone knows what sailors are. Sometimes they would whistle and jeer after the monks as they went about their self-appointed task of guarding Kemper's morals More often they would flaunt their 'sins' in the monks' faces – especially their consorting with prostitutes, of whom there were a good many. I suppose everyone has their own attitude to this oldest of professions, but I think I heard the most practical one from one of its members, a woman I came to know some years later. She was a high-class courtesan rather than a common whore, but as she herself put it, the difference is mainly in the tariff.

'So a sailor or a soldier finds himself miles from home, with money in his purse and loneliness in his heart. Is it so wrong for him to take a little comfort where he can? What harm to his wife or his woman, even if she's not straying herself while he's away? Let's face it, there are far worse things a man can be reduced to if he's away from home for weeks and thrown together with other men day and night.'

And then, of course, there were those regular customers who were not away from home, but simply had no woman of their own.

'In a lot of ways they're the best,' she said. 'It's regular satisfaction for them, and regular money for me. I prefer a mature man, mind you. The young ones are apt to get silly and start asking you to marry them. The older ones just get to be friendly and a little confidential. Sometimes I've even been paid just to listen to their troubles. Thank the gods I've never been that lonely.'

Corentin's monks were not so tolerant. Like their leader, they seemed to take a particular pleasure in seeking out sexual licence in others. My mother's view was typical.

'They're not getting any such comforts, so they can't see why anyone else should,' was her comment. 'I think they'd stop it between married couples if they could, but even their holy books don't go that far.'

Outside marriage, though, sex was a sin. Perhaps Dahut had been right, on the night when she had got drunk and accused Emrys of not being capable of love. Certainly these monks talked a lot of loving one's neighbour, in a general sort of way, but there was nothing personal in it. They did charitable work, it is true, but in a detached sort of way, as if it were their job. Or perhaps, after a time, that is all it was. Corentin's monks took their cue from him. Wrongdoing was their chief interest, along with its punishment.

Some of the punishments meted out were severe by Gradlon's standards. One sailor who had got fed up with being abused in public punched the monk responsible and knocked him down. For this he was whipped in the marketplace. The jailor who carried out the sentence was a loving Christian, and stripped the man's back to the spine. On the other hand, a monk who lost his temper and struck one of the smaller sailors was dealt with by Corentin himself. He had to do penance, which I think meant saying some prayers.

In such ways it soon became clear that there were now two classes of citizen in Kemper. The Christians could hardly be expected to complain. They were the privileged class. Besides, many of the people saw the way the wind was blowing and decided to join the faith. So, whether by accident or design, the behaviour of Corentin's monks drew more and more people into the fold. By the time we returned to Kemper in the autumn there were already three new churches, and another one was being built. Christianity, which had first been persecuted, and then tolerated, was fast on the way to being compulsory.

Gradlon himself was largely ignorant of what was happening. He only saw the results, and the full churches were a joy to him, as well as confirmation that he was right in his beliefs. As the pace of change gathered momentum his spirits rose even further. Nothing would turn him aside from his new faith now, nor from his desire to see it spread the length and breadth of his kingdom.

Not that it was spreading entirely unchecked. The dissemination of any new faith requires a lot of hard work on the part of many priests. The Christian priesthood is all male, which bars half the population from the work. Personally, I think that to be successful there would have to be a priest in every village in the Empire, and I don't suppose that will ever be. At all events, there were few enough at that time. There were several monasteries and nunneries, and some mixed religious communities which were the subject of much prurient gossip. Kemper was the only really large town in the kingdom, and directly under the eye of the King, but in the country it was a different matter. Christianity might have been the official religion of the Empire for two generations, but it had never been strongly observed by the peasants. How could it be? The men and women who work on the land are close to the forces of Nature. They sow, tend and reap. Their lives are governed by the cycle of the seasons. The worship of the Mother comes naturally to them. They can see for themselves how the womb of the earth is fertilised by the sky and grows fruitful, in the same way as all living things. What appeal can they see in the image of a man from a far-away country broken on an instrument of death? The Church will have to do better than that if it is to win over the peasants of Armorica.

Thus the situation arose that in the country, where the authority of the King and his bishop was weaker, the old ways hung on. There were Christians there, in scattered groups, and there were some priests, as at Ker-Is. But when it was Beltane, or Samhain, or any of the old festival times, out the people would come, to light their fires, worship in their groves of oak, and make offerings at their sacred streams. The old priesthood, banned by the Romans for generations past, had withered away. There were isolated religious groups – it is not just the Christians who have their monks – but these had to keep themselves secret. The old ways were hard pressed, but not yet beaten. Indeed there were those who hoped for a revival, and the rolling back of Christian and imperial power, which were one and the same.

But all of this was happening miles away, that summer when we waited out Dahut's pregnancy and prayed that no one would discover it. I actually did pray. Whether the influence of my friend's condition was responsible I cannot say. Still, it seemed then that we could feel the presence of the Mother all around. We felt sure that all would be well, that we were somehow protected. Our secret was kept till the last, shared (said Dahut) only with the Ocean. I laughed when she said such things, but there was a Sea God in times of old, and Dahut felt his presence as I felt that of the Mother Goddess.

Adolescent fancies! Everyone finds their secret beliefs for a while at that age. It is a way of testing and rebelling, I think. Perhaps we would have been different if we had had more friends, but we only had each other. There was no one to test these ideas out with, no one to broaden our view of things. When I tried to talk to my mother about them she just changed the subject. Whatever her views were, she kept them to herself, but it was clear that the worship of the old gods was no more a part of them than that of the new.

In fact, it was difficult to speak to Mother at all at the moment. She seemed preoccupied. At the time I wondered if it was anxiety over Dahut. She had once asked me what I thought would happen if Dahut died in childbirth. What would Gradlon think then? It would certainly be impossible to keep the truth from him. I had no answer. On the whole, though, I did not think that this was the problem on Mother's mind. I felt it was more to do with Meriadauc, and our future status in Kemper. The King had said that she would have to leave the royal household in the autumn, and the time was drawing nearer when she would have to decide what to do. I guessed that Meriadauc had asked her to marry him, but that she was not certain. She had once told me that a woman had to give up much on marriage. That stormy scene on the beach had told me that the whole subject was a difficult one for her, but I could only guess.

And then, suddenly, more practical considerations intervened. On the first day of September, in the middle of a night gripped by the severest early frost I had ever known, Dahut went into labour.

Chapter Fifteen

Dahut lay on the rug on Megan's floor and groaned for the thousandth time. Megan was quite unperturbed.
'Do not worry, my Princess. All is well.'
Dahut grimaced. 'Well, is it? I'm glad things are not going badly!'
She managed a sickly grin for me, and was then seized by another spasm.
'The pains are coming often now,' said Megan. 'I'd say it won't be long.'
'Is she really all right?' I asked anxiously. With no experience of such things it seemed to me that there was a lot of pain and noise.
'Yes, yes. Birth is always a time of toil, you know, especially a first.'
It had been some toil bringing her here, too. As soon as we had realised what was happening we had sent a servant for Megan. He was told only that Dahut was ill, and the wise-woman was needed. A local man, he knew all about Megan and her healing, so he accepted the story readily enough. Megan arrived in no time, with two stout men and a litter. She supervised the loading of the litter, with Dahut on her side and covered with thick blankets so that no one might see her condition. Then Megan was away to her house, flitting nimbly along the slippery woodland paths as if they were bright as day. The litter, my mother and myself followed more gently, for the ground was surprisingly frosty. Once one of the men slipped and nearly dropped the litter, which caused us all some alarm, but he recovered his balance and we went on, past the black trees and prematurely fallen leaves.

Now Dahut was comfortable in front of the fire in Megan's house, and the labour was well advanced. Megan had told us to try to sleep, as it would take several hours. Mother had managed to sleep, but I had dozed fitfully, waking each time I heard Dahut groan. Megan's various potions had eased her pains, but they could not stop them altogether. I wondered why the Mother Goddess, who so loved life, had made the giving of it such a difficult business. And now that it would be long, I wondered idly what sex the child would be. Mother had said it would be the heir to two kingdoms. I hoped it would be strong enough to cope. Lost in such thoughts, I dozed off again.

'Keri!'
I leapt into wakefulness. 'What is it?'
The weak light of early dawn was filtering in through the windows, but the candles were still lit. Megan was kneeling in front of me, where I sat propped in the corner of the room.'
'It's time! The baby is nearly here. You will be needed.' And she turned back to her patient.

I stood up groggily. Dahut was half-sitting, legs apart, so that Megan could examine her.

'The child's gateway to the world is well open,' she said. 'Look.'

I looked, and stopped breathing for a moment. The top of the baby's head was visible now, moving slightly. Suddenly the whole process of being born seemed to take on a significance beyond the paltry concerns of this world, as Dahut's child hesitated on the brink of entering it. I gasped with the strength of the realisation, causing Megan to look at me sharply.

'What is it?'

'It is Her,' I said. 'Can't you feel it, too? She is here.'

Megan smiled, and nodded briefly. 'When there is a birth, She is always at hand. But we must keep our feet on the ground if we are to do Her work.'

She gave Dahut some brisk instructions. 'Now, too much pain is a sign that something is wrong, so get into as comfortable a position as you can. Women are not all the same. Some stand, some kneel, some go on all fours. It doesn't matter; the baby's on the way and nothing will stop it now. Just keep your head and do as I say.'

Dahut groaned, 'I want to push.'

'Not yet. It's too soon. Don't use up your strength before you need it.'

'I want to stand.'

'Then you must stand. Olivia Galeria, would you please help the Princess? Take one arm and hold her up. Keri, take the other.'

Megan knelt on the floor in front of Dahut. Mother roused herself and we each took an arm. Megan had adopted a brisk, no-nonsense tone, and we just naturally fell in with it. I noticed Mother looking at the wise-woman as if she were seeing her in a new light. We were both quite ignorant when it came to midwifery. Without Megan I do not know what we would have done. Mother was conscious of her social position, but she always had respect for those who could do things that she could not. So, her demeanour towards Megan now was one almost of deference. At least, I had never seen her take orders before as she took them now.

'I want to push!' Dahut's face was red with the effort of holding back.

'Not yet! Wait for my word.'

Dahut's swollen belly seemed to be pulsing with a life of its own – which it was, in a way. She had carried this extra load for months. Now her body seemed desperate to expel it with a haste which was almost indecent.

'Now, my Princess! Now you can push!'

Dahut was redder than ever. 'No!'

Megan started. 'No? What do you mean, "No"? One way or another it has to come now.'

'I can't,' gabbled Dahut. 'I need to use the chamber pot!'

Megan looked up at her with a half-smile. 'Chamber pot? In the middle of all this? We can't send the child back to await your modesty. Keri, reach over that pot. Place it where it may do some good. Princess, push when I say. I don't care if you turn my floor into a privy. It will clean up. Now, Princess, PUSH!'

Dahut let out a great yell.

'The head is here! Push again!'

Liquid splashed on the tiles. Dahut yelled again. While I performed one of life's humbler offices for my friend, she pursued life's greater purpose as women have since time began. The heir to two kingdoms was born like other babies, swimming on a tide of water, blood and bodily wastes. There was a mess on the floor. My feet were wet. I hardly noticed. My eyes were fixed in rapt attention on Megan's hands. She was showered in blood to the elbows, but cupped in her hands was a perfect, tiny human being, its feet still issuing from its mother's body. Deftly, Megan held the child up by the heels with one hand, while she cleared some material from its mouth with her finger. She did not smack the child, but patted it gently on the back.

'Come on, my beauty,' she crooned. 'Cough for Auntie Megan.'

The child spluttered briefly, and began to cry – a tremulous, high pitched bleating like a lamb. Megan turned her – for it was a girl – the right way up and smiled at us all.

'There! Princess, you have a daughter, and she is perfect. Well, sit down. You've done the hard work!'

We all smiled, even Dahut, and we lowered her down to a clean part of the floor, with blankets folded beneath and around her.

'We must wait for the afterbirth and cut the cord,' said Megan. 'Then you may clean up and rest. Olivia Galeria would you please start to fill that big bowl with hot water and put more on the fire to heat?'

And my mother, meek as a servant, did as she was asked.

Later, when everything was done, and Dahut was put to bed, I went over to her. Her eyes were closed, and her hair was still damp in places from her exertions, but there was no mistaking that indefinable beauty. It had faded somewhat during the pregnancy, especially as hiding indoors for so much of it had made her pasty-faced. But it had returned all of a sudden. The features were as fine as ever, and the skin as fair. I bent and kissed her forehead. Her eyes opened sleepily.

'You were wonderful,' I told her, knowing it should have been Riwal who said it.

She smiled. 'And you are my soul's sister.' And then she slept.

Megan approached me. She nodded towards a bowl which she held in her hands.

'In the old days we always gave the afterbirth back to the Mother. As an offering.'

'Yes,' I said. 'I know Dahut would like that. And I felt Her presence here; I told you.'

'Yes. Bring the child also. She will be all right wrapped in her blankets.'

We made a strange little procession, Megan, my mother, and myself carrying the baby, round to the back of the little house. Here there was a simple altar, built of rough stones and with a little stone fire-bowl upon it. The charcoal was already glowing red.

'I knew what your answer would be,' explained Megan. She took some twigs from a box next to the altar, and added them to the fire. Then, when the flames were strong, she tipped the contents of the bowl on to them. The fire sizzled and spat. Megan stepped back and knelt on the ground, bending forward to kiss it.

'We pray to all the gods. To the gods of the air, to the gods below, to the gods of the tribes. But most of all we pray to You, Mother of the World. We ask You to accept our offering. These things have done what You have laid down for them to do. Now we return them to You. We ask Your blessing for this new mother. Let her not suffer the fever, but grow in strength to serve You again. We ask Your blessing for this new child. Let her grow strong also, so that she may grow to her womanhood and fulfil its purpose. Let them both keep Your ways, now and for ever. Let it be so.'

'Let it be so,' we echoed.

After a pause, Megan stood up and turned to look at the child again.

'Isn't she pretty? If she has half her mother's looks she may be fulfilling woman's purpose sooner than any of us think.'

I felt warmth on my cheek. The early morning mist was clearing, and the sun was breaking through between the hills.

'Look,' I said. 'A new dawn, and a new life.'

'May that be an omen,' said Megan.

'Let it be so,' we echoed again.

Mother and I returned to the villa later in the morning. We called for food, and told the servants that the Princess was recovering from her illness. Megan had advised us to leave Dahut with her for a couple of days, we said, truthfully enough. I felt a weight had been lifted from me, and babbled on childishly to Mother as we ate some breakfast. She was quiet and pensive by contrast, as if her mind was elsewhere. It took me some time to notice, I was so caught up in the excitement of the events around me. Dahut's child born, the secret kept, the birth free of complications. And a girl for Megan to pass on her wisdom to. Finally it penetrated that my breakfast companion was rather preoccupied.

'What is it, Mother? Are you tired?'

She smiled. 'Yes. Aren't you?'

'I suppose I should be, but I'm just wonderfully pleased at everything.'

'Yes. Well, I'm tired, and pleased too, but I was also thinking about things.' She paused for a few moments. 'Megan is very capable, isn't she?'

'Yes, I told you she would be.'

'Yes, Keri, you did. She is very wise in the ways of women. She seems to have passed on some of her knowledge, too.'

And she looked at me in a calculating fashion.

'Some things. How did you know?'

'Just the way she speaks to you. She assumes you know a great deal, so I suppose you must do.'

'What is it you need, Mother?'

She hesitated again, unsure of how to put things, I think. 'Your Megan, does she know much about, well, about love? I mean physical love?'

I think I was rather less embarrassed by the question than she was herself. Megan had introduced us to so many things in a matter-of-fact way, and we had no contact with other young people to learn the adolescent's usual smutty prudery. I considered my answer carefully.

'I'm not sure,' I said at last. 'I know she once had a child, but she was never married, and I know she plays a full part in the Beltane festival. She was hoping for a child; now she will have one. But is that what you mean? I don't think she has a regular lover or anything, or ever has had. She seems too, well, self-sufficient.'

'I was wondering whether to ask for her help.'

'Oh, I see.' But I didn't. I could hardly see my mother asking for a love potion to slip in Meriadauc's wine. Besides, I would have bet that there was no need for one.

'Did you mean what you said on the beach that day? About welcoming Meriadauc as a stepfather?'

'Yes. Or as your lover.'

'Indeed. I remember. That's where my problem lies, I'm afraid.'

For a moment I still didn't understand. Then it came to me, all in a flash.

'It's that cursed crucifix collector, isn't it?'

'Who? Oh, I see. Yes, it is to do with that. How did you guess?'

'No need of guessing. I was there. I saw what he did to you. Small wonder if it's left you with a problem. Mother, I'm sorry for the things I said on the beach. They must have hurt you.'

I saw tears come into her eyes, but she shook her head.

'No, it's all past. You couldn't know, anyway. But you see why I am so unsure. I would marry Meriadauc, I think, but how can I marry a man when I cannot love him? Except in my heart.' She grinned. 'He's still a young man. I can't ask him to be satisfied with that, can I?'

I found myself smiling, too, at the thought of my mother consulting her virgin daughter about such a matter.

'Go to Megan,' I said. 'If there is an answer, I would guess that she knows it.'

Suddenly I felt very tired indeed.

Dahut made a very quick recovery. The next day she was on her feet, despite Megan's warnings that she should not overtax herself.

'Don't fuss, Megan,' was all she said. 'You don't know everything.'

The look she got in reply suggested that Megan disagreed, but was not prepared to have an argument about it. Meanwhile, she busied herself preparing for her new role as a foster mother. She had managed to find a wet-nurse. A girl from one of the farms had had a stillborn child.

'At least,' said Megan, 'that's what they told me. I'm not sure, but I think they killed it.'

Dahut was horrified. 'And you'd let her near my child?'

'Would you rather your child died for lack of nourishment? You must return to Kemper soon. Who will feed her then, my Princess? Besides, the babe is in no danger. Lea will not harm her.'

'Why do you think they killed Lea's baby?' I asked.

'Because of who its father was. I think it was Lea's own father.'

If anything, we were more shocked by this thought than by the suspicion that the baby had been murdered. But Megan interrupted our protestations.

'Listen to me, both of you. Your shock is understandable. Such things do not happen in the circles that you come from. But they happen quite often in the houses of peasants and farmers. If a man's wife is unresponsive, or has died, as in this case, then it is easy for such things to happen. We are not talking of fine palaces, and stone rooms, but hovels of wattle and daub with all sharing one room. Even this place is a palace compared to some of the peasant cottages. Building costs money, and these people have none.'

We felt chastened after this speech, which was a long one by Megan's standards. She made us realise that we were of a privileged class, and had no right to judge. But she went on.

'Having said all that, I must admit that Lea is not quite all there. You can see how it happened. But she will be safe here with me, and so will our little one. The only thing is, Lea's father wants money for her.'

'Money?' echoed Dahut. 'You mean he wants to sell her?'

'He has agreed to sell her to me for five silver sesterces. As a slave, she isn't worth half of that, but as a free woman in milk she is worth all of that to us and more. I will not keep her as a slave.'

'Then that is settled,' said Dahut. 'We can get the money. Olivia Galeria has money from the King to run the household at the villa.'

'I thought that, so I agreed.'

We went on to talk about naming the child. Dahut wanted to call her Riwalia, after her father, but Megan was set against it.

'Riwal is a common enough name, but if her mother becomes known it will be clear who her father was.'

'Why should it become known?' demanded Dahut sulkily.

'Who can say? But you have already been noticed coming here. An alert watcher could make guesses. There is no reason to make it easy. If she is supposed to be a peasant's child, there is no point in giving her one of your Romanised names. A good Celtic peasant name is what we need. Brica, perhaps.'

Dahut and I burst out laughing. 'Not Brica! The only Brica we know is a dried-up old widow at court! No, spare us that!'

Megan smiled. 'Well, if she is to be passed off as my child, perhaps a name something like my own would be better. Not the same, of course, but a bit like it.'

We thought for a minute, and then Dahut suddenly said: 'Morgan!'

'Ah,' said Megan. 'The girl from the sea. Well, that's a good name for one who lives by it. Of course, they will say the Sea God was the father.'

'But that's perfect!' Dahut exclaimed. 'It just fits the ideas they have of you round here. Yes, let it be Morgan.'

Looking back on it, how easy it is to hammer nails into someone's coffin, and not even know.

Later that day we had our first meeting with Lea. She was a fat, cow-like sort of girl, which was appropriate enough. She took to Morgan at once, and with Megan's help she was soon feeding the child as if she had always done it. Dahut was a little jealous, I think. She stared at what was happening with a peculiar expression. But, even if the child had been legitimate, it was not the custom for a princess to tend her own child. No doubt the treatment Morgan would have had in the palace would have been much the same. In her own infancy Dahut had Berta, after all. Lea's father had accompanied her to Megan's house, but he was obviously ill at ease there. I think he thought we were a witches' coven or something. A short, thickset dark man, he growled out his demands for money, and bit the coins when they were given to him. He nodded curtly to his daughter by way of farewell, and hurried off again through the woods, glancing back over his shoulder in case we were following him, and making the sign against the evil eye. We laughed about it, and turned back to the child. She was already a beautiful baby, as any child of Dahut and Riwal would surely have to be. Her skin had lost the redness of birth, and was as soft as down. Her eyes were the deepest blue-grey, and her hair as fair as a Saxon's. Dahut's mother, the northern queen, had been fair.

'It means nothing,' said Megan. 'The child may grow darker; they often do.'

We only had another couple of weeks at Ker-Is before returning to Kemper. It was not long, but long enough to be sure that the baby's hold on life was secure. Megan seemed certain that the child would thrive and be strong, and she was usually right.

The King's messenger arrived on one of his routine visits, and brought a letter telling Dahut that her exile was over. She was free to return to court whenever she wished. Of course, that was the courtly way of issuing an order. In effect, she was commanded to return as soon as was reasonable. With baggage to pack, and the house to be closed up against the winter, this meant leaving within a few days. We were even sadder than usual to go, but it was all the more important to maintain the semblance of normality. No one must suspect that Dahut's exile had been as conveniently timed as it had. A life might depend upon it.

As our little group of horses and one baggage wagon pulled away from the villa, Dahut, who was riding at my side this time, turned to me. 'I will come back here every summer, and see Morgan as much as I may. Then, when I am Queen, I am going to build a palace here and bring her out of hiding and deck her in jewels. She will be Queen too, in her turn, and all of Europe will marvel at the kingdom on the edge of the world – the kingdom of Ker-Is.'

Chapter Sixteen

World events moved fast. As if to prove he was not beaten yet, Attila crossed into Italy the following spring and laid siege to Rome itself. The Pope, as they like to call the Bishop of Rome, went out before the city gates and parleyed with the Huns. No one knows what he told them, but the result was clear enough. Attila packed up and went home without a fight. This not only brought a sigh of relief throughout the Empire, but increased the Christian Church's standing immeasurably. Many waverers saw the hand of the Christian God in this episode, but some people will believe anything. The fact is that Pope Leo knew – and probably told Attila – that a large army was approaching from the Eastern Empire. The Emperor Marcian, whose refusal to pay the Huns more gold had sparked off Attila's latest attacks, obviously intended to stand by his western brothers. In the face of such united opposition Attila could do nothing, especially since the Eastern Romans had a large army of Goths to help them. The Goths hated the Huns more than we did.

In Kemper the power of the Church was maintained, and Corentin strengthened his hold upon the people. His followers preached on every street corner, and continued to harass all those whose way of life displeased them. The churches increased in number as the original few became overcrowded each Sunday. Old pagan temples were adopted, the images of their former occupants smashed and defiled. Corentin himself would conduct rites which were supposed to purge the buildings of their associations with the old gods, which like Johannes, he termed 'demons'. Gradlon overlooked the excesses of the monks, and welcomed the growing strength of Corentin's Church. Corentin himself was not often seen at the palace. He came on Sundays to take services in the little church there, but during the week he was generally at his monastery, supervising the building and the missionary work with equal zeal.

Tiernan, who had been less than enthusiastic about Corentin, soon saw which way the wind was blowing. If being a Christian was the way to power in Kemper then he would embrace the new faith cheerfully. Privately, I don't believe Tiernan ever worshipped anyone except himself, but in public he made the right noises.

Mother, in accordance with the King's instructions, had left the palace and bought a little house in the town. He kept his word, and gave her a grant with which to buy it. He also provided soldiers to carry our baggage to it, and sent her a German slave woman, Gisla, to help her to keep it. Thereafter he had precious little to do with her, which was not difficult for her to bear. My own position was more ambiguous. Naturally, Dahut and I would not contemplate being parted. Gradlon disapproved in principle, but he gave in to his daughter's entreaties, as always. I was to be allowed to stay in the palace as the Princess's companion, but I had to be absent on the Lord's day, Sunday, as the presence of a pagan would not be fitting on that day. I was well pleased with this arrangement, for I had no wish to be forced to attend Corentin's cosy little services in the royal chapel. Dahut, who had no greater liking for them than I, had to attend for the sake of appearance. It was clear that Corentin had no notion of her real beliefs. Every Saturday, as I prepared to leave the palace, Dahut would grumble, and pull faces at me as I departed.

'Rat!' she would say jokingly. 'Are you deserting this sinking ship yet again?'

'It may look like it,' I said, 'but it will be up again on Monday, buoyant as ever!'

We would both laugh. Sometimes, in secret, we would cry together too. Dahut was made miserable by having to leave Morgan behind at Ker-Is. I had thought that she might find it easier to bear when we had been away a while. Her attitude to Riwal had certainly changed. Now she remembered him with affection, but not with the overpowering grief which had gone before. She seemed a good deal older as the result of reaching motherhood. She was a true woman now. She also experienced a woman's longings.

'If only things were different,' she said to me one night as we lay in bed. 'I don't understand why we are given these feelings if we do not have the means to fulfil them.'

'What feelings?' I asked sleepily.

'The need for a man,' she said simply, which made me wake up in an instant.

'Dahut! What about Riwal?'

'Riwal is dead.'

'Don't you miss him?'

'I miss what we had,' she said. 'But I cannot live on memories. I need to try to find it again with someone else. While I was pregnant I didn't think about it, but since then I think about it more and more. I think, once these feelings are awakened, they can't be turned aside for long.'

'I suppose so,' I said, irritated by my lack of knowledge. 'But, honestly, what's all the fuss about?'

She giggled in the dark. 'I'm sorry, Keri. I really am. I don't mean to make fun of you. The fuss, as you call it, can't be explained unless you've experienced it.'

I found this a most unsatisfactory answer. Between my friend and my mother, I felt that I was being asked to share too many worries about something I couldn't understand. Not that I was totally without experience, at least of the feelings. I had seen handsome young men at court, and my heart still fluttered when some of them came near, but that was all rather pure and girlish. Since they were all Christians it looked likely to stay that way. Riwal was an exception, it seemed. Most of the young Christian men were unwilling to risk the reputations of the girls they cared for. They therefore gave their hearts to them, but their bodies to slaves and servants who had no reputation to lose. It seemed all wrong to me. Since I had felt the presence of the Mother at Morgan's birth, I believed in Her implicitly, and knew She hated this hypocrisy. Men and women were made for each other, but not to split their emotions apart and spread them around where it would cause least offence to the monks. The children conceived by slaves and servants were not produced at the will of the Mother, but for the convenience of men. The women generally found it very *in*convenient, but the priest made it clear that women's feelings were inherently sinful anyway. Did not their holy book say that it was a woman who had brought sin into the world? Of course, by sin they meant sex, but I suppose that is to be expected of a celibate priesthood.

Actually, not all of Corentin's people were able to maintain their celibacy. Even in those early days there were cases of monks who were unable to withstand the temptations of the flesh. There were even stories that some of the town prostitutes had deliberately seduced monks as a means of attacking the Church's – that is to say Corentin's – authority. There were other stories that they had been paid to do so by those who would not be sorry to see the Church undermined. Corentin retaliated by physical attacks upon the brothels, his men entering them and smashing them up, sometimes surprising the most unlikely people amongst the clientele. In the end, Gradlon ordered the brothels closed 'in the interests of public order'. The task fell to Budic, so the monks got what they wanted.

Gradually it seemed that Kemper was becoming a more sober place. Because the monks frowned upon outward displays of wealth Gradlon began to discourage them at court. People left off wearing jewellery and bright clothes. Crucifixes and plain simple garments became the rule. Dahut and I had to conform, although it was easier for me – I had no rich clothes! I would not wear the crucifix, of course.

What with spending weekdays in the palace and Sundays at my mother's house, my life became split in two. I found that I enjoyed it in many ways. It was a relief to be able to leave the palace sometimes, not only because of the intrigue and gossip, which were always there, but now also because it was a dull place to be. Mother's house, the Villa Rosea was a haven of peace by comparison.

The house was some way out of the town centre, on the road to the coast. It was a quiet stretch of road, and there were several such houses along it. Mother had laughed at the name – 'the house of roses' – for it was such a cliché. Almost every retired imperial servant called his house by some such name. Still, the name was already set into the gatepost in pieces of mosaic tile, and it was accurate. There were fine roses in the little walled garden. At the back, reached by a narrow alley between the Villa Rosea and the next house, there was a small stable with some other sheds. A gardener came in regularly to see to the roses and the vegetables. It was smaller than the King's villa at Ker-Is, but it was comfortable. There were only four rooms upstairs, and a similar number below, but there was an extensive single-storey wing at the back, housing the kitchen, bath house and stores. It also had a real asset – a working Roman-style hypocaust. Warm feet at last, even in the winter! Life was comfortable there for my mother. She had money of her own, having sold some of her jewellery before Gradlon's new dress rules had caused a glut on the market. The house was away from the worst parts of the town, but close enough to be convenient for the market. And for other things, as I soon found out.

One lovely Saturday morning in the spring after Morgan was born I decided to walk over to the Villa Rosea. I usually went later in the day, but Corentin was coming to the palace and it was better that I was out of sight. I had been up at dawn, and the walk of two miles or so to the villa would give me an appetite for breakfast. There was no danger in walking out alone. The road was always busy at this time, as people came into Kemper for the market. For three generations past they had not been allowed a Sunday market – first in honour of the Unconquered Sun, and then in honour of his successor. Besides, most of the route lay within the city walls.

It took me well under an hour to cover the distance, despite stopping to watch the odd item of interest. The villa was still shuttered and quiet as I approached, and I wondered if my mother and Gisla, the German slave, were up yet. As it happened, the girl answered my gentle knock almost at once.

'Is my mother up yet, Gisla?'

'Er, no, mistress.' The girl looked very shifty, but I was in too happy a mood to wonder about it.

'Not mistress yet,' I laughed, and made for the staircase. 'Fine! I'll surprise her.'

The girl shrugged helplessly, her long blonde hair bobbing on her shoulders. 'Aye, that you will.' The significance of this remark failed to sink in until I had come to my mother's bedroom door and opened it.

The room was still very dim because the shutters were closed. None the less, I could see Mother's bed, and the two figures lying asleep in it. I could not recognise the man in the dark, but I did recognise Meriadauc's studded belt and British-style boots on the floor. I felt a twinge of shock, and for a moment I just stood there. It seemed always to be my fate to intrude upon things that were not meant for me to see. As I turned back to the door Mother spoke.

'Ye gods above! Is that you, Keri? How late is it?'

'It's me, Mother, and it's very early still.' My voice was hindered by a lump in my throat.

'Oh, dear. I'm sorry, child. I wasn't expecting you till this afternoon.'

'No.'

Meriadauc slept on as she removed his arm from across her chest and got out of bed. Then she was suddenly aware of being naked, and she who never normally worried about such things felt the need to cover herself with a robe.

'Just a moment, Keri. Wait for me downstairs. I'll be down right away.'

I wandered down the staircase, passing a worried and fidgety Gisla on the way.

'Er, can I do anything, *Domina*? May I fetch you something?'

I shook my head, and drifted into the main living room. She withdrew in the direction of the kitchen, leaving me to my whirling thoughts. I had told my mother that day on the beach that I would have smuggled Meriadauc to her bed if it would make her happy. As so often, the saying of a thing was easier than the doing. I was not exactly shocked – I had seen too much to be so prim – but I was certainly surprised. I wondered how long it had been going on, and what difference it would make to me, and if they would get married.

'Keri.'

Mother had thrown on a robe of bright scarlet. How appropriate Corentin would have thought it! She came into the room and went to open the shutters, still speaking.

'I'm sorry, Keri. I didn't know what to tell you, so I told you nothing. I should have done.'

That was it. I felt that I had been treated like a child again.

'Well, I know now. Did you ask Megan's advice, then?'

Bright light flooded the room. Her face was almost as red as her dress.

'Ah, yes.' She smiled nervously.

'Was it good advice?'

She nodded. 'Your feelings are hurt. I'm sorry.'

'No, it's nothing, really. But I wish you had told me. I felt a fool walking in like that. Even Gisla knew. She tried to stop me going upstairs.'

'Well, she could hardly not know.'

'I suppose not.'

There was an awkward silence. It was a strange thing, I thought. I had lied about my feelings not being hurt. It seemed to be the same every time someone dear to me formed an attachment to someone else. I denied it because I could not justify it. I knew I was being unfair, but I couldn't help it anyway. It was not the pleasantest thing to find out about myself.

Old Berta died that year. Dahut was very upset at the time. The old woman may have been a slave, but she had had the care of Dahut since she was born. She had done many of the things a mother would normally do, and had never stopped working till the last year of her life, when she became too infirm. It was inevitable that Dahut's free affections should have been extended to include the old woman.

The King set about choosing a new companion for his daughter. Dahut was too old for a nurse, but still a little young for ladies-in-waiting. If anyone filled that role it was me. He had in mind a mature woman – a Christian, of course – and one fit to act as a guide for a princess. She had to be from a good family, used to the ways of court society, and preferably either a widow or a confirmed spinster. Married women were too likely to let their own families distract them from the King's. He chose Brica, a war widow of about forty, and the last person Dahut would have chosen for herself. She was the one we had laughed about when Megan had suggested the name for Dahut's baby.

Brica was a thin, angular person who dressed and acted like a woman much older. She wore dark, sober colours, and followed every detail of Corentin's edicts on dress and display. The crucifix was her only item of adornment, and she even covered her hair most of the time. What little crept around the edge of her shawl was as thin and wispy as the woman herself. Her features were thin, too, and if her piety and rectitude brought her joy it was seldom reflected in a smile from those thin pallid lips. We felt sorry for her, but we also disliked her intensely.

She had not long been appointed to her new position when Dahut asked if we could go to Ker-Is again. The King was hesitant at first. It was still early in the year, although it was now a firmly established custom that we went there for the summer. Eventually, though, he relented under the pressure from Dahut, and we were allowed to make the journey. Mother, of course, could not come, as she was no longer part of the King's household, but she was too realistic to expect me to stay with her.

'Only be careful,' she said to me as I took my leave of her. 'Don't get into any trouble. I know that the Princess will always try to shield you, but remember also that she is older than you... What is right for her is not necessarily right for you.'

As if changing the subject, I asked her about Meriadauc.

'What are you two going to do?'

'Do? Oh, well, I think we are just going on quietly as we are for the moment.'

'Then you should be careful as well. This town is full of Christians now, and none of them want to see you getting something when they can't'

'Keri!'

'Well, it's true, Mother. You are a grown woman, and should be able to do as you like, but don't count on it. At Ker-Is I shall be safer than you. The country is still mostly pagan, they say.'

Ker-Is was as rugged and beautiful as ever. Our hearts lifted as we drew near, and could hear the waves and smell the salt air. Our hearts needed lifting. Brica was in charge of us now. Her company was tedious, and so was her piety. I have always distrusted people who wear their piety like a robe. In its way it is just as much of a display as the rich clothes which Corentin hated so much.

Brica called upon her god at every opportunity, not fervently but as it were in passing. 'Please God', she would say, or 'God willing', when expressing almost any intention. When we stopped near the place where Budic had burned down the altar several summers ago, she was horrified to see it had been rebuilt. She prayed loudly to her god to strike it down with fire, and when he failed to oblige she started to do the job herself. A few well-aimed stones came from the surrounding wood, and our guards judged it best to move on quickly. Dahut and I chortled with glee; clearly the local pagans had seen us coming and decided to fight back this time.

'I really can't understand,' said Dahut as we rode on, 'why so many Christians have this obsession with burning and destroying. You would think that they would treat others better, after the persecution they suffered themselves in the old days.'

'Now, Princess,' said Brica. 'You really must not talk like that. I know you only do it to annoy me, and I shall not rise to it. You know very well that that was different. When the Romans persecuted Christians they were trying to stamp out the worship of the One True God. We are merely trying to stamp out the worship of demons and false gods.'

'The people who threw those stones didn't think their gods were false,' I commented.

'You are a pagan,' retorted Brica, as if that were answer enough. For her, of course, it was. She clearly disapproved of my presence, but could hardly tell the King what to allow in his own household. 'I pray that you will see the light,' she added.

'I can see well enough without it, thanks,' I said to her, but she just smiled in a way which contrived to be knowing and pitying all at once.

Now that we were within sight of the Ocean we could look forward to spending more time away from her. Sundays would still be a problem, but I was resolved that this time I would not be attending Father Johannes's services. We should be able to give Brica the slip when we wanted and go off to see Megan and the child.

The day after our arrival we made our way to Megan's house as in times gone by. Dahut was in a state of high excitement. It would be her first sight of her daughter for nearly six months. I had some misgivings. It was ever a failing of Dahut's to go at things like an attacking fury, when sometimes they needed the stealthy approach of the deer hunter.

'Go carefully!' I protested. 'I'll get a sprained ankle at this pace, even if you don't. And remember, the child will not know you.'

She laughed and hurried on, but I think something of my warning penetrated. When we reached the clearing where Megan's house was, Dahut suddenly pulled up and stood for a moment, smoothing back her hair and obviously composing herself.

'Well,' she said at last, 'Here we go.'

Megan was at the door before we reached it, and greeted us as if we had just popped out for something a minute before.

'Hello. Did you have a good journey?'

'No,' we chorused.

'Remember the awful Brica we mentioned?' I said to her. 'The one we didn't want Morgan to be named after? She is in charge of us now.'

'Oh dear,' Megan replied. 'I think you'd better come in and sit down, and meet your daughter. Lea is in there with her.'

We entered the cottage, and found that things had changed. The outer room was now Lea's bedroom as well as a store and workroom. There was also a cot for Morgan. The cow-like Lea was sitting on a rug next to her bed and playing with the baby. As we came in they both turned towards us. Lea smiled.

'Hello,' she said. 'You've come to see Morgan.'

'Of course we have,' said Dahut, who was always a little impatient towards the girl. 'And how's my baby, then?'

The child was sitting up and grinning. I had an awful shock. For the face was like a miniature of Riwal. I could see that Dahut was also taken aback, and her voice faltered. The likeness was incredibly strong, apart from the surprisingly thick blonde hair. Her eyes were a more intense colour than ever, and inescapably reminiscent of Riwal. Dahut stared for a minute. Then she turned away and burst into tears, her head on my shoulder. The baby was still a little wobbly, and in her surprise she fell over. She whimpered, and Lea picked her up at once, making the soothing sounds one makes to babies, and smiling half apologetically at Dahut.

We approached more closely, and Morgan buried her face in Lea's copious bosom. She associated us with her fall, now, and would not face us. From the folds of Lea's ample figure came a muffled yell.

'Oh, Keri,' said Dahut in sudden anxiety. 'What can I do?'

'Sit down, Princess,' said Megan from behind us. 'Let things come in their own good time.'

She was right, as always. Once Dahut's feelings were soothed and Morgan was used to our presence she soon lost her strangeness and wanted to investigate these newcomers. She was a bright little thing, and cheerful, and wanted to examine everything. Within half an hour she was happily sitting on our laps and allowing herself to be fed and played with. Meanwhile Megan told us her history. How well she could crawl, the fact that she had four teeth, the childhood ailments she had already had but thrown off easily.

'She's a pleasure,' concluded Megan. 'She's a bright child, and strong, too. And she will be beautiful, mark my words. She is herself a princess in the making.'

At this the princess-in-the-making emitted a loud flatulent sound, and we all laughed.

That summer at Ker-Is was the last of the carefree summers of childhood. Blissfully, I was unaware of it at the time, although Dahut may have felt it more. We gave Brica the slip at every opportunity, and would go to see Morgan or visit the beach or the forest as the fancy took us. Dahut was happy to see how well her child was growing, and I think she was secretly relieved not to have the daily responsibility of her. She needed to feel free for a little longer, for she realised that a king's daughter must either marry or become queen in her own right. In either case an illegitimate child would be something of an impediment.

Brica was the bane of our lives. Quite apart from her twittering piety, she never left us alone if she could help it. This meant that we had to deceive her shamelessly in order to get time away by ourselves. Often we would slip out through the garden door, but eventually she realised what was happening and had the gardener nail it shut. Then we took to climbing the wall by means of one of the gardener's ladders, which he always left lying in his little shed. After climbing down on the outside we used to hide the ladder in the grass, ready for our return journey. Things came to a head one day when it was spotted by a workman who had come to inspect the wall itself. The find was reported to

Brica, who waited for us and caught us red-handed as we climbed back into the garden. She was, quite simply, furious.

'What is the meaning of this?' she thundered, or would have thundered if she had been that impressive a person.

We looked at her in silence for a moment, rebelliousness vying for expression with our sheepishness at being caught out.

'Well?' she continued. 'I'm waiting for an answer!'

Dahut's feelings boiled over.

'Sit down!' she ordered.

'What?'

'Sit down! You've got a chair there. Prepared for a long wait, were you?'

'Really, Princess, I –'

'Princess indeed!' snapped Dahut, her eyes flashing in a way which frightened even me. 'Princess it is, and remember it in future. You ask what this means. I'll tell you what it means. It means that the heiress to the Royal House of Gradlon cannot enter or leave her father's villa without interference or harassment. It means that a princess who is for all practical purposes a grown woman cannot go here or there without a dried-up old husk of a busybody poking her nose in at every turn.'

She advanced upon Brica so threateningly that the woman stepped back and actually fell into the chair she had been ordered to sit in.

'That's better,' said Dahut, bending over her so that she could not stand up if she wanted. 'Brica, I have had enough. Enough of hiding, enough of lying, enough of you. Starting tomorrow I shall go in or out of the front door of this house as I please. You will come with me only when I require it.'

'But your father engaged me to…'

'Yes. He engaged you. Thank you for reminding me that you are only my father's servant.'

'Oh, Princess…'

'A high class of servant, I grant you, but a servant none the less. As we all are. I will obey my father, Brica, because it is his right as King and as my father. But I will not take orders from you. You are here to advise and assist me, not to command me.'

And with that she strode away in to the house. I was as dumbfounded as Brica, I think. Again I was reminded that Dahut was a little older than me, but what an important little it was. Brica began to cry, and now looked so pathetic that I felt sorry for her.

'Don't cry, Brica,' I said, as soothingly as I could manage. 'She has a point. You must admit, it is a bit silly when she has to climb the wall just to see a friend.'

'I only want to see she is protected.'

I decided not to enter that argument, and said nothing. Then my last sentence must have sunk in.

'Friend? What friend?'

'Well, even a princess has friends, you know. When we were here before we used to, er, play with other people we met here. Now we are older we still see them.'

'What sort of people?'

'Friendly people. Brica, this is just the sort of prying Dahut was complaining of.'

'But a princess must guard her reputation. That is part of my responsibility. If these friends are so harmless why can I not meet them?'

'You must ask the Princess that,' I improvised, thinking that I had let too much slip already.'

'Oh, dear,' she sniffed. 'I don't feel that I have handled things at all well. I have not gained the Princess's confidence.'

I could only gape at her. Brica was a devout Christian. I realised now that between Dahut and such a person there could at best be an uneasy truce. At best.

Chapter Seventeen

The gods know how small we are in their scheme of things – if there is indeed a plan. Sometimes I have wondered if there are gods at all, the way that so much evil seems to happen for so little cause. The year after Attila was turned back from Rome he died. His sudden and unexpected death at the height of his power threw the Hunnish horde into confusion. Their subject-allies rebelled. Caught between the Ostrogoths of the East and the Gepids of the West, the Huns were torn to pieces and the remnants dispersed. In the course of one bloody season they vanished from the stage of history. It would be pleasing to record that they left the Empire in peace, but it seems we were quite capable of creating discord for ourselves.

Dahut matured speedily. She was less in my company now. Gradlon knew that she had a shrewd mind, and he would often have her at his side when he attended meetings of his counsellors, or met foreign envoys. She encouraged him to give her more responsibility, and he was as responsive as ever to her entreaties. Still, she insisted on her long trip to Ker-Is every summer, leaving as soon as the roads were passable. I always accompanied her, of course.

Morgan grew strong and healthy. Megan was as good a foster mother as we had hoped. The peasant girl, Lea, was no longer needed, and she had married a man from the village and lived not far away. She had a child of her own now, and seemed as happy as any villager might be. Dahut always gave her money when we saw her, so that she might be a little happier than some. The arrangements had all worked out very well, or so we thought.

In the summer of Morgan's fourth year the omens all became bad at once. World events set the tone. The great Aëtius was summoned to a council at Ravenna by the Emperor. Valentinian's persecution mania was worse than ever, and he accused Aëtius of plotting against him. An argument ensued, and the Emperor drew his dagger and murdered Aëtius in the council chamber itself. The army in Gaul threw its support behind Aegidius, the chief lieutenant of Aëtius, and so the province still refused to come to heel. In fact, Gaul was now for all practical purposes an independent kingdom. A few months later, at a military parade, Valentinian was himself assassinated by an old comrade of Aëtius. The situation was thrown into confusion. Whatever Valentinian's many faults he had ruled over the Western Empire for three decades, and his going was bound to be felt from one end of it to the other. Within the next year there were three emperors in succession. The real power in Italy was now Ricimer, the commander of the army, and his henchmen. Being German they could not claim the throne themselves, but they could make emperors and break them again if they did not do as they were told.

Dahut was not completely dismayed by this turn of events. 'Rome is finished,' she said to me. 'The future lies in our own hands once more. All the subject nations can now go their own way. Kemper is a small kingdom, but it is strong enough. We shall make it stronger.'

'What does your father say?' I asked.

She smiled. 'He laments the breaking up of the Empire, because he thinks it means the breaking up of the Church. I am sorry he is distressed, but I can't see it his way.'

'Don't you think the Church will break up as the Empire does?'

'Oh, yes, Keri. At least, I hope so. But I need hardly tell you how little distress the prospect causes me.' And she laughed aloud.

I was not so sure. When thrones fall they crush ordinary folk beneath them. And even churchmen become desperate when they see power slipping through their fingers.

Our trip to Ker-Is began earlier than usual that year. Dahut was determined to get there for the onset of summer, and the Beltane festival. She was convinced that the time was ripe for a revival of the old ways. So, it seemed, were others. Dahut had tried to persuade her father to let us travel free of court ladies, but he had insisted that the proprieties must be observed, at least until Dahut came of age the following year. The unwelcome company of Brica was therefore forced upon us yet again, as it had been for three summers past.

Strange as it may seem, this had one unexpected advantage. As soon as we were settled at the villa, Brica always made a call upon Father Johannes, while we would go to see Megan and Morgan. On this occasion our arrival was only three days before Beltane, and when we had all returned to the villa Brica told us that the Christian priest also had plans for the festival. We were sitting in the main room at the villa, drinking a little wine before dinner while she told us of events in the village. Most of her chatter passed us by, for we were still feeling the joyful after-effects of renewing our acquaintance with Megan, and the kingdom's fairest child. Then Brica mentioned Beltane, and we were suddenly alert.

'Father Johannes says that these dreadful pagan practices must be stamped out,' she twittered. 'The Church Council at Arelate has again called for action to stop the lighting of fires, and the worship of trees and demons.'

Dahut's lip curled disdainfully. We knew no one who worshipped demons, although there were groves of oak which were claimed to be sacred.

'And how does the good Father propose to carry this out?' asked Dahut.

'He says that he will lead a band of good Christians to the Beltane fires and denounce the wrongdoings that go on there. He will exorcise the demons with a prayer.'

'Well,' said Dahut slowly. 'I would not have seen Father Johannes as a man of action.'

'Ah,' said Brica. 'It is the Holy Spirit which moves him.'

'Of course,' said Dahut. 'That must be it.'

If Brica noticed the sarcasm she gave no sign.

'He also says that he must break the power of the witch.'

'Witch?' A chill touched my heart.

'Yes. Surely you must have heard tell of her? She lives not far away, in a deserted temple dedicated to some demon or other.'

'You don't mean Megan?' I asked, as casually as I could.

'Yes, that was the name, I think. Father Johannes says she leads the pagans hereabouts, and consorts with demons. She even has a child which was conceived out of wedlock – some say the child of a sea-demon.'

'Father Johannes is very prone to see demons everywhere,' Dahut said angrily. 'How can Megan be a witch? She does nothing but heal people and do good. Didn't Christ himself heal the sick?'

'Certainly he did, but not by magic, which is the work of de – of evil spirits. He healed by invoking the Holy Spirit, which is the only true healing.'

There was no arguing with the woman. The only thing to do was to see that Megan was warned. We went out to do that the next morning, two days before Beltane.

As we went through the woods I had the strangest feeling that we were being watched. I could not see or hear anything amiss, but I still felt eyes upon us. Dahut was chattering away, and noticed nothing. Megan's door was open, and she was standing there apparently bidding goodbye to someone. He was a lad of about twenty, with curly fair hair that fell forward to his eyebrows, and a cheeky captivating grin. They both turned to us as we came up. Megan, however, was not grinning.

'Come in, both of you,' she said worriedly, and to the lad: 'Stay a little longer, and tell these ladies what you told me.'

We all went into the little room where Megan lived. Morgan was playing on the floor, and looked up with a smile as we entered.'

'Hello, Aunties!' We were always 'aunties' to her. It saved explanations.

'This is Cynan. He lives at the other side of the village. He holds no love for the Christians, and he has often helped me in the past. Cynan, these ladies are Dahut and Keri. They visit me from Kemper.'

He started, and his blue eyes widened. 'Kemper? Dahut? Pardon me, *Domina*. You are not the Princess?'

Dahut smiled. 'Yes.'

He fell on one knee. 'Forgive me, Your Highness, I did not know who you were.'

She was pleased at the respect he showed her, but impatient to hear his news.

'Please get up. Your news is more important than your obeisance. If Megan vouches for you then I know you can be trusted. What have you to tell us?'

We all sat down, and Cynan began to talk. I was a little puzzled, for he was obviously an educated person, and yet I could not see how he fitted in to Ker-Is. His accent was unfamiliar, and not local. Still, no doubt I would learn more in good time.

'A man has been asking about Megan in the village. He is a stranger, and well-dressed. They say he is from Kemper, but no one knows for certain. I have not seen him myself. He is especially interested in Morgan.'

'Morgan?' There was anxiety in Dahut's voice. 'What does he want to know about her?'

'Everything, it seems. He was very interested to know exactly when she was born. Then he asked about the father, but of course no one knew.' Here he glanced sheepishly at Megan. He must have heard the tale about the sea-demon like everyone else. 'Anyway, he has also been asking about the royal villa, and who the Princess visits when she comes, and if she knows Megan.'

I felt a sickness in the pit of my stomach. Anyone who was asking this much must have a good idea of the answers already. One glance at Dahut's face told me she had come to the same conclusion.

'I don't know what this all means,' said Cynan, 'but I see it alarms you. If I can be of any service you need only to ask.'

Dahut looked at him levelly. 'Can you handle a sword?'

He nodded. 'I am a good swordsman, though I say it myself, but my sword is at my father's house beyond Ker-Is.'

'Will you fetch it? And any other men you can trust?'

He nodded. Then he stood up.

'I will be back as soon as I can, tomorrow noon at the latest. I wanted to be here for Beltane anyway.' Again the sheepish grin. I guessed he had intended to celebrate Beltane in the fullest possible manner. Something stirred within me at the thought. As he turned to leave his gaze rested on me for a moment, and there was a twinkle in his eye. My heart turned a somersault. He winked, and went grinning on his way. Moments later we heard him ride off through the wood.

'A nice lad,' commented Megan. I shot her a quick glance, and she smiled warmly back. She missed nothing. 'He will be back for Beltane.'

Was there a special meaning in that? If so, there was no time to consider it now. We told Megan what Brica had said.

'I do not fear the priest,' she commented when we had finished. 'He is a weak man, and not very clever. Some of his followers are unpleasant types, but Christianity does teach that violence is wrong.'

Dahut laughed bitterly. 'Tell that to the citizens of Kemper! The monks there have been violent enough when it suited their purpose. And there are plenty of Christian soldiers like Budic to help them!'

'Perhaps,' said Megan. 'But there has been nothing of that sort here. Besides, I know these people. I have brought a lot of the younger ones into the world. No, they won't hurt us. It's this stranger I don't like the sound of. Whoever he is he is probably from Kemper and he knows too much. Or guesses, which may be as bad.'

'How could any word have got to Kemper?' I asked. 'My mother would never have breathed a word, I know. Apart from anything else, it would put her in danger herself.'

Dahut nodded. 'No, Aunt Olivia can be trusted. It must be someone else, and it must be something we have not considered. Perhaps talk has got back via the servants or slaves. It happens everywhere. And we thought we were being so clever! We should have known it would be obvious what condition I was in. Anyone might have guessed. Still, so long as he does not see my child he cannot actually know. We must keep Morgan hidden. One glance, and anyone who knew Riwal would know the father at once.'

'We must take her back to the villa,' I said. 'If anyone looks for her it will be here. This man already knows where she is.'

'But what could we tell Brica?' demanded Dahut. 'And Megan would have to come too. How would we explain her presence? Brica thinks she's a witch.'

Megan herself broke in. 'I will go to Lea's. She and her husband will take us in. They are good people, and they are both fond of Morgan, although they have a child of their own.'

We talked it over for a little longer, but it did seem the best plan. Megan packed some things at once, and set off with us. We decided to walk with her to Lea's, partly to help carry her bundles, but mainly to see her safely there. As we went through the wood I kept looking all around, but if there were eyes upon us I could not see them.

The next day was the eve of Beltane. Megan had things to do, so she was up at dawn and away by the time Dahut and I called at Lea's cottage to see her. It was a round house in the old Celtic style, but clean and well kept. There was a fine drizzle, but the cottage had a sound thatch, and inside it was warm and dry. Morgan was playing with Lea's little boy, who was two. She greeted us as cheerfully as always, oblivious of our anxieties. We were about to leave and look for Megan when she arrived back herself, with Cynan and two of his friends. They were armed with swords, but Megan looked cheerful enough.

'The stranger has gone,' she announced 'He told a couple of the villagers yesterday that he was returning to Kemper.'

'Aha!' said Dahut. 'So he was from Kemper.'

'It seems so,' put in Cynan. 'But he has certainly gone. He was seen to ride away this morning.'

'Where did he stay?' I asked. 'There is no inn at Ker-Is. Did one of the villagers give him lodging?'

'It was the damned priest,' replied Cynan. 'Father Johannes.'

'Strange,' muttered Dahut. 'If he was one of Corentin's men, why was he not dressed as a monk?'

'Yes,' said Megan. 'And why was he so secretive? The priest's style is usually to make pronouncements during Sunday's service. If he wanted information he only had to ask his precious flock.'

'Never mind,' said Dahut. 'I for one am greatly relieved that he has gone.'

'And I am greatly puzzled,' said Cynan, the impish grin on his face again. 'Why should anyone come here asking questions about Morgan? She is an innocent child, surely, and sweet as honey. What is the mystery?'

We all hesitated. Then Dahut spoke.

'Her father is dead now,' she said. 'But it is possible that he had enemies who would make use of the child for their own purposes. More than this we cannot say.'

He nodded, his face suddenly serious. 'Very well. If the stranger comes back we shall be ready.'

'You are good friends,' said Dahut. 'One day I hope I can reward you as you deserve.' And she looked him straight in the eyes in a way which constituted an immoral suggestion in itself.

He grinned again, and I felt a pang of jealousy when he treated her so reverently.

'Virtue is supposed to be its own reward,' I said acidly.

'So it is,' said Cynan, and winked at me. 'Oh, by the way, I've heard a sort of description of the stranger. Do any of you know a red-haired man who rides a chestnut mare, and wears a grey tunic with a brown riding cloak?

The description meant nothing to us.

'If he has gone away,' said Megan, 'then it should be safe to go back to my house.'

We agreed that it probably was, and Megan and Morgan returned along the cliffs with Cynan and his friends. Dahut and I went back to the villa, where we had agreed to join Brica for lunch. She seemed agitated when we arrived, but that was nothing unusual with her.

'Will you be going out again today?' she twittered. Was it my imagination, or was there a special slyness in the look she gave Dahut? Surely not. Brica was not capable of anything sinister.

'We will be,' Dahut replied. 'We have only just arrived, you know, and there are people we have not seen for half a year..'

'Oh, of course, of course.' Brica was unnaturally tolerant; there must be something. 'I too have much to do – the household to provision properly, and so on. Please don't worry about me. I shall be much too busy to come out.'

She went out of the room, and Dahut and I looked at each other in puzzlement.

'She's finally gone mad,' said Dahut, and we both laughed.

We were both in high spirits as we approached Megan's house later that afternoon. We were free of Brica yet again, and without any unpleasantness. We were free of the stranger. Tomorrow we would welcome in the summer at Beltane. We were both going to attend the festival, although we were not clear how fully we would partake of the proceedings.

'You know,' said Dahut as we tramped along, 'that Cynan lad has his eye on you.'

'On me? Oh, Dahut, don't be silly. Anyone could see how taken with you he was.'

'I'm a princess,' she said simply. 'Men are often taken with me. It means nothing, and certainly not that I am taken with them.'

'Didn't you like Cynan, then?'

'Oh, yes.' He's a handsome enough lad, and strong. He has character, too. But I didn't like him enough to – well, enough for what you're thinking.'

'Oh. Dahut, what exactly are you saying?'

'I'm saying that you are eighteen, and sensible enough to cope with having a man. If you want one. If you want Cynan I should say you're halfway there already.'

I could feel myself going red. Dahut glanced at me and giggled.

'For all the gods' sakes, Keri, it's nothing unusual. And Beltane would be the time, wouldn't it? If the Mother demands it of you. It is a kind of worship.'

'Yes, I suppose it is. And you're sure you don't want Cynan?'

'Well,' she said, with a twinkle in her eye, 'if you don't I daresay I might change my mind. Of course, we could always share him.'

'Dahut!'

'Aha! I've shocked you at last! Well, who knows what the Mother may desire of us? We've shared everything else!'

We finally embarrassed ourselves into fits of giggles, just as we came in sight of Megan's house. The door was standing open, and there was a horse tethered to a tree nearby. It was the chestnut mare.

We ran the last few yards and burst into the living room together. Megan was sitting on the bed, cuddling Morgan on her lap. Cynan was sitting on a stool by the fire, his sword unsheathed and laid across his knees. His face was like thunder. In the biggest chair sat a man with red hair, a grey tunic and a brown riding cloak. He greeted us with a satisfied smile.

'Good day, Princess,' said Tiernan. 'I've been admiring your fine daughter. Prince Riwal would have been proud of her.'

Tiernan and Dahut were walking outside, while he put some plan or other to her. It was clear he felt he held all the cards, and wanted to use his knowledge of Morgan to blackmail Dahut in some way.

'I knew he must be the stranger we'd heard of,' said Megan. 'But the King's steward? Who would have thought it? These humble walls are seeing some high-class visitors.'

'What did he tell you?' I asked.

'He told us who he was, first off. Cynan's friends had gone, but Cynan had his sword in his hands as soon as Tiernan knocked at the door. He wanted to make sure he wasn't run through before he could speak.'

'I'd still do it if the Princess asked it,' growled Cynan. He was humiliated because he felt he had not protected us after all. I gave him the warmest smile I could.

'You are not to blame,' I said. 'You could hardly murder the King's steward.'

He smiled back gratefully, and in spite of the tension my heart flipped over again.

'He said he knew who Morgan was,' Megan went on. 'He promised he would do no harm. He just wanted to talk to the Princess when she arrived.'

'I'd love to know what they're talking about,' Cynan said through gritted teeth.

We found out soon enough. The door was thrown back with a crash as Dahut stamped in. Tiernan was hot on her heels.

'Think again!' he was saying in a warning tone. 'It will go hard with you if you refuse me!'

'It's treason to threaten the Princess!' yelled Cynan, starting up.

'Wait,' said Dahut quietly. 'He only means he will tell my father. There's no treason in that.'

'Is that all the answer I will get from you then, Princess? Will you not think it over?' His quiet tone was more menacing than any amount of shouting.

She turned to Tiernan, her eyes ablaze.

'Tiernan. Get out of here. Never come back. Never come within my sight again. Tell my father what you wish. I do not care any more. He may send me to a nunnery, but take care he doesn't send you to the gallows when he finds out how you have wronged me! I may not be of age yet, but I am Princess in Kemper and the only heir to the throne.'

She raised her arm and pointed at his face. 'Get out! If ever I see your face again it will be on your way to the hanging tree!'

He backed away into the doorway. Then he turned and stamped out. Before he rode away we heard him yell out. 'I curse you! All of you! I curse you, Dahut, and your child. You will regret this day!'

Cynan leapt up, sword in hand. '*That's* treason!' he shouted triumphantly, and ran to the door. But Tiernan's horse was already galloping away.

Dahut sat down with a sigh. I looked at her. She seemed calm enough, although two red patches on her cheeks spoke of suppressed nervousness.

'What did he want?' asked Megan gently.

Dahut paused for a moment, and then her anger returned.

'Can you believe it? That ... that disgusting, selfish old man and the daughter of Gradlon?'

She shook her head in disbelief.

'He wanted nothing less than to marry me!'

Brica had been the informer, unwittingly at first. Tiernan had befriended her, he told Dahut. She thought they might be lovers, but I laughed at the thought of the saintly Brica in bed with Tiernan, who was anything but pious. None the less, it was she who had told him of Dahut's behaviour at Ker-Is and her secretiveness about her friends there. He had then questioned the servants from the villa, and found out about Dahut's visits to Megan, which were apparently common knowledge. So much for all our precautions! Enquiring about Megan, he had heard of her child, who had been born just at the time when Dahut had been taken from the villa at night with stomach pains. He was no fool. It was enough. 'He said he had loved me since I was a child!' exploded Dahut. 'He said if I married him we would rule together in Kemper. I think he believed we could raise troops and depose my father. Gods above and below, what a prospect.'

'Did he *say* that?' Cynan was still looking for treason.

'Virtually. Usually he says nothing he can't explain away later if need be, but I think he's grown desperate!'

'He's always been trying to build up his power,' I pointed out. 'I suppose he's seen the power of the Church increasing, and his life slipping away with nothing achieved. He's over fifty, you know. It's his last chance of supreme power, and he has thrown caution to the winds.'

'He must be mad!' Dahut exclaimed.

'We always said he had an unhealthy sort of interest in you,' I reminded her. 'I think we knew that even before we were old enough to understand what it meant.'

She nodded. 'Love, indeed! He is a perverted, lustful man, and I told him so. I can't have been more than eight when he first started looking at me in that way.' She shuddered. 'I fear him, though. He may be dangerous. He has risked all in speaking to me, and gained nothing.'

'Don't worry, Dahut,' said Megan. 'You are among friends. We will all be safe here.'

Chapter Eighteen

Beltane fires are lit on hilltops, so as to be nearer to the gods. Megan had organised a troop of wood-gatherers, as she did every year, and they had built a mighty pile on the summit of the hill which rose behind her house. In the old days the Romans had killed the Druids who had tended the grove of sacred oaks there. The conquerors abhorred the practice of human sacrifice, which was widely used then, and other customs of the Celtic priesthood. But it was the rites the Romans stamped out, not the belief. In time, the Celtic gods became identified with Roman ones, so that Teutates was thought to be Mars, and so on, but the identification was never certain. The worship of the Mother had wavered, but returned again later when the Persian religion of the Great Mother Cybele arrived in Rome itself. Surely one name was as good as another, they were all the same Great Mother Goddess.

In the dusk we trudged up the hill. All of us were there – Dahut, Megan, even little Morgan. Most of the village would be there, including many who went to the Christian church on Sundays, just hedging their bets. They were uncertain times, and men thought it best to placate any gods there might be. The atmosphere was not fearful, though. It was a festive occasion. People had brought food and drink with them, for the custom was to stay out and see the first summer sunrise. A muffled drumbeat sounded from the hilltop.

'That is the call,' said Megan cheerfully. 'The Christian has his bell, we have our drum. We muffle it now, but one day it will drown out his bell for ever.'

There were murmurs of assent. The church bell, endowed by Gradlon the previous year, had disturbed many a Sunday's rest. Little Morgan giggled, delighted to be up way past her normal bedtime. She trailed along a little rag doll with one clay eye. Earlier she had got me to pin a tiny bunch of blue speedwell to its dress in honour of the occasion. She might not know what the ceremony meant, but she would know it was a time for fun and celebration.

We made our way through the undergrowth and between the trees, the light of torches in front of us. As we got to the top, panting now with the effort, I saw that there was a considerable crowd already assembled. It was good to see so many. I felt that I was at last among my own people, for it was impossible to feel really at home now in Kemper. I looked across the clearing in which the bonfire – still unlit – had been built and saw the drummer. It was Cynan. He was sitting cross-legged on the ground, with a one-sided drum balanced on his knee. His other hand held the bone, with which he struck the drum skin at regular monotonous intervals. About his shoulders there was a cloak of thick fur, although I could not tell what kind. It looked inviting. He saw me and grinned cheerfully, and that tremor went through me again. He saw that I was looking at his cloak, and gave me a quizzical look. I found myself blushing and turned away.

Megan had disappeared with some women I did not know. Morgan and Dahut were wandering about, greeting people and talking. There was a hubbub of conversation, as if the occasion was a family outing, which indeed it was. Some of the children asked their parents for food and drink but they were refused. We were to fast until after the prayers, which would be soon. The drumbeat stopped. People raised their torches high.

Megan reappeared from the surrounding trees, but this was a Megan I had never seen before. She was dressed from head to toe in white. Her feet, visible at fleeting moments under her hem, were bare. The gown had sleeves which covered her arms to the wrist, although they were loose and flapped around her. Her face was half hidden by a veil of white, but what we could see was covered in painted symbols – stars, half-moons, and suns. The crowd parted for her as she approached, and she walked right up to the edge of the fire. Then she lifted up her arms, and as the sleeves slipped back I saw snakes painted up the length of them. Then I looked closer and saw that they were not painted, but actually spiral amulets of copper which glinted in the torchlight.

'It is the time of Beltane!' she called. 'Let us welcome the summer, season of ripeness and fruitfulness. Let us thank the gods for our deliverance from the icy wilderness of winter. Let us also pray for the indulgence of the gods, that all our seeds may root and grow, that our cattle may grow fat, and our fishermen's nets heavy with fish, so that we may face the next winter with equal strength. Then let us show the gods that we know how to use their gifts, and celebrate their bounty.'

There was a chorus of assent, and the ceremony began. First the torchbearers threw their torches on to the fire. It caught easily, and was soon ablaze. There were prayers to all the gods, of course, except the one whose church stood in the village. But mostly the devotions were to the Mother, for the summer is Her season, when She brings forth the harvest from the womb of the earth as women bring forth children. I did not know the prayers, but many there did, for they had often been to the Beltane fire before. How different it was from those dry services in the Christian church, hidden away from public view as if in shame. Here we were at one with the earth, with the natural gifts for which we were here to thank the giver. I didn't need to know the prayers. I knew the feelings; it was enough.

After the devotions, the atmosphere became like that of a family party. People brought out their food and drink, and shared it around. The children, so easily restored by a little food, were soon playing and laughing. I sat with Dahut on a blanket and nibbled some oatcakes, and we might have been anybody. After the formality of court life it was like being set free for a while. People greeted us, introduced their friends and relatives, and asked Dahut's blessing for their babies.

'Are you enjoying your first Beltane, Keri?'

I jumped at the sudden voice next to me. It was Cynan. He sat down beside me and rested his arms on his upraised knees.

'Yes. It's not quite what I expected.' I could hardly speak, my heart was beating so fast.

'What did you expect?' He seemed amused.

'Well, something more ... more formal, I suppose. More like the services Father Johannes holds.'

'Ah, Johannes. Yes, he's the village priest, isn't he?'

'Didn't you know? I thought you were from the village.'

That grin turned to a laugh, and I found myself blushing as if I'd said something silly.

'I've only been in Armorica a year,' he told me. 'Couldn't you tell that from my speech?'

'I didn't know the accent,' I said. 'And it seemed rude to ask, even if there'd been time to talk.'

He nodded. 'Yes, we have been busy, haven't we? No, I'm not from here, I'm from Devet, in Wales.'

'Wales? Whatever are you doing here?'

'Have you not heard of the Scots?'

'I think so. Aren't they the people from Ireland?'

'They are indeed, and they're a ferocious breed of men. For the last hundred years or more they've been raiding us from across the sea. It's only a short voyage, much shorter than the journey to Armorica; it takes only a few hours if the wind is fair. Anyway, now they seem to be invading in earnest, and my father felt the time had come to move away. We thought about going to the east of Britain, but the High King still has his hands full there with the Saxons. More of them every year, it seems.'

'These are terrible times. There seems to be war everywhere. It is an age of death.'

He put his hand on my arm, which increased my heart rate to a dangerous level, and said; 'Then it is all the more important to celebrate life, is it not?' And then he kissed me quickly on the lips, and my heart seemed to stop altogether for a moment.

'I've never heard that one before,' said Megan's voice at his elbow. 'And I thought I'd heard most.'

Now it was Cynan's turn to be embarrassed, and he looked away from me. Megan handed us a cup of a warm drink, heated at the fire.

'Here. Share this. It's a brew of my own. It's very warming.' And she moved on.

I sniffed at the brew. There was alcohol there, but much else besides. I thought I could smell cinnamon, which was a rarity. It tasted delightful, and it was certainly warming. It flowed through my body to the tips of my fingers and toes, and made me feel calmer. My heart returned to normal, and I knew now what I wanted to do.

'Will you come for a walk with me?' asked Cynan.

I looked at his eager face, and guessed that walking was not foremost in his mind. I couldn't help giggling, and he smiled uncertainly.

'Later I will, Cynan. But not yet. After midnight.'

He looked even more puzzled, but just shrugged. 'I'll wait,' he said, and wandered off amongst the crowd.

Someone started to play a harp. I looked around, and saw Megan sitting with a man who was dressed in a robe as white as hers. He was sitting on a rock, and she was at his feet, leaning against him in an attitude of familiarity. She saw me and beckoned me over.

'This is Coel. He usually comes here for Beltane. He is the finest harper in Armorica.'

The man chuckled, and left off plucking the little harp. 'Is that all? He said in a voice that rasped like gravel. 'Faint praise, considering how few harpers there are in the whole province. I am glad to meet you, Keri. Megan has told me a little of you.'

He had a face which was weathered and lined. He looked about forty-five, but his face was kind, and the lines were mostly laughter lines. I could see that Megan and he shared something, but what it was I could not tell.

'She has told me nothing of you,' I replied evenly.

He laughed. 'Aha! There is nothing to tell, you see! But we are old friends.'

'More than that,' Megan said in a tone of soft reproof.

He looked down at her and smiled. 'Aye, more than that.'

'Are you going to play for us?' I asked.

'I think so, unless they yell at me to stop! I must think of something suitable.'

He started playing after a few moments' thought. He sang also; that voice which was so rough when speaking acquired a deep resonance when he sang which sent shivers through me. And most of the other women, I reckoned.

They sat to listen, but they would probably have been hard put to it to stand with their knees so weak. The voice seemed to have a life of its own. It departed from the singer, and floated around the crowd, each hearing it differently. He sang epic tales of the hero kings of the past. He sang songs of longing, and tales of magic. I think he worked magic himself that evening.

It seemed a long time later that he stopped singing. I awoke as if from a dream, wondering vaguely how late it was.

'It is nearly midnight,' said Megan beside me.

'How strange,' I said. 'I was just wondering about the time.'

'I'll bet you were.'

'You *are* a witch, Megan!'

She chuckled. 'I know a thing or two about young girls, that's all. Especially on Beltane night. Here, you must come and jump the fire.'

The bonfire had burned low now, and it was the custom to leap over the glowing embers and make a wish. A queue of people was forming now to take their turn, and I joined it. The fire, when it was my turn, was surprisingly hot. I had thought it would be merely warm, but a blast of heat went up my skirts as I jumped.

'Oh!' I said to Dahut, who was at the other side to help steady me. 'I felt all the hairs on my legs shrivel in the heat.'

She laughed coarsely. 'It's a good thing it didn't reach any higher then, isn't it.'

'Dahut!' But she laughed again, incorrigible as ever. She did not ask what I had wished for.

Cynan came to me not long after. Without a word he took my hand in his, and we walked away from the crowd and down the hillside.

'Let's walk down to the beach,' I said.

'Yes, if you like.'

'Dahut and I spend a lot of time there when we're at Ker-Is.'

'Do you come here every summer?'

'Yes. We love it here. Half our childhood was spent along this shore. Dahut loves it especially. I don't know what she'd do if she couldn't come here.'

We walked along in silence for a minute. Then Cynan spoke again.

'Is Morgan really the Princess's child?'

I hesitated. I felt I could trust him, but I had given my word to Dahut. He sensed my discomfort.

'No need to answer,' he said. 'Your hesitation is answer enough. Anyway, I never believed all that nonsense about Megan mating with the Sea-God. If it had been Coel now ...'

'Have you met Coel before?'

'He visited us in Wales a couple of years ago. He travels the world, that man.'

'I admire his courage,' I said. 'These are dangerous times to travel in.'

'Coel says no one ever harms a bard. Even the barbarians think he is touched by some god, you see, so they let well alone. Anyway, he's no threat to them. He never carries a weapon. Oh, and don't be put off by his modesty. He's the finest singer and harper on either side of the Narrow Sea.'

We talked of these and other inconsequential things, making conversation in order to stop ourselves thinking. My heart was racing again, and in spite of the season I felt a warmth only partly due to my woollen shawl and Megan's brew. As we threaded our way through the undergrowth an occasional giggle or sigh told us that others were celebrating Beltane in the traditional way. Once a sharp cry of ecstasy in the dark nearby set us both giggling like children, and we ran down the next fifty yards.

Soon we came to the clifftop, and made our way down the path to the beach. There was a bright moon now, and we could see our way clearly. If there had been any others near we could not have heard them. The restless ocean's roar covered all other sounds in the night. The sea was calm enough, but there is never any silence on that coast, where the breakers come rushing in from the world's edge to spend themselves on the land. We sat in the lee of a rocky outcrop. Cynan drew his furry cloak around us both for warmth, and we watched the waves break on the shore.

'Why would you not come with me till after midnight?'

'Because I don't want a child,' I said. 'Not yet.'

'I don't understand. I thought you women had ways of controlling these things.'

'We do, to some extent. But a child conceived at Beltane cannot be interfered with. To do that is to go against the Great Mother Herself.'

'Yes. I see.'

And since that said it all we spoke no more, but let the Mother's will guide us. I thought once of Dahut, laughing at my lack of knowledge. Now I knew, and yet somehow I had always known. Wrapped in Cynan's cloak, Cynan's arms, I was borne on a wave which burst through the gates of childhood and left me truly a woman at last.

We lay on the beach for some time, still wrapped up in Cynan's cloak, and savouring the joy of being close to each other. Now we found ourselves able to talk properly. Cynan told me a great deal about his past life on the Welsh coast, a constant prey to raiders from Ireland. I told him about our own reasons for emigrating. Not about my mother, but the rest. His father was from a powerful family, and his mother had died years before. Their home sounded rather bleak, without the softening touch of any female presence. He had no sisters, only an older brother who had been killed by the Scots.

'All my father's ambitions rest on me now,' he finished, sadly, I thought.

'Does that make you unhappy?'

He thought before answering. 'Not unhappy, exactly. I respect my father, though. He's a hard man in many ways, but he's fair, and he doesn't really ask much of life. I'd like to be able to give him what he does ask.'

I sat up, gently pulling down the cloak. The night air was cold, but I had known worse. The sea looked as if it were waiting for something to happen. It was even calmer now.

'Do you swim?' I asked Cynan.

'Swim? I should say not. Swimming is for fish.'

I stood up, and slipped my dress right off.

'Keri! You're never going in the water now! You'll freeze!'

'Not at all. I'm made of sterner stuff than you!' I said teasingly.

Still sitting, he caught my hands in his and turned me so that he could look at my body. 'You really are beautiful,' he said.

I laughed. 'Oh, Cynan, you don't have to flatter me. I know what I look like. Presentable, yes, but not beautiful.'

He would not let go, 'You aren't beautiful as the Princess is beautiful. But her beauty is skin deep. When she is old it will have faded altogether. Yours will never fade, because it comes from within.' He stood up and pulled me to him and kissed me. 'Now, go and swim, but not for long. I'll rub you dry with my cloak when you come out.'

I had a quick splash in the water. It was bitterly cold, and I soon regretted the impulse. Still, it was refreshing, and Cynan did rub me dry when I came out. His closeness and his firm caress were leading my thoughts towards further pleasure when suddenly he stopped.

'What is it?'

'Look at the hilltop.' Then the note of puzzlement in his voice changed to alarm. 'The fire – why is it suddenly so large?'

Looking back I saw that it had indeed grown hugely. It must be out of hand, perhaps destroying the old sacred grove. We dressed as rapidly as we could, raced up the beach and clambered up the cliff path. At the top we paused for breath.

'Listen!' said Cynan, panting. There were sounds, shouts and clashing steel.

'Oh, Mother, it's the Christians!'

Heedless of bramble thorns we rushed towards the noise. Dahut, Megan, our friends – what was happening to them? We heard a cheer of victory, but whose?

My heart was pounding as we reached the clearing. My chest hurt with the effort. Then we saw it. The Beltane fire had been built up to the height of a man. The hilltop was shrouded in smoke. Gasping, I fell to my knees. Cynan too was bent double and panting for breath.

'Wait,' Cynan gasped. 'We would need our breath back to do any good.'

Grey shapes appeared. Shapes which gripped us with strong hands. I shuddered. The victory cheer had not been from our side. Still breathless, we were roughly dragged into the clearing. Another shape loomed, then became clear. My heart lurched in my breast.

'Well, well,' said Tiernan. 'The big fish is gone, but we've got some minnows.'

'Where is Dahut?' I managed, but he only shook his head and sneered.

'Keri!' Megan's voice, taut with fear, came from across the clearing.

Tiernan smiled in his twisted way, his eyes bright with excitement.

'We were just debating the best way to deal with a witch,' he said.

There was a chorus of guffaws. All knew the penalty for sorcery.

'Megan is no witch!' I cried. 'She cures half the ills in the village.'

'But with what power?' Johannes voice interrupted me as he stepped into view.

I was ready to appeal to anyone, even him.

'Father!' I cried. 'Stop this madness. You preach love and mercy. Please!'

There was another cry from Megan. I saw her by the fire. Two men with swords were driving her back. Already the flames seemed to lick at her feet. She weaved as if to get by, but one of them tripped her up. Tiernan and another ran forward and seized her. Cynan broke free from his captors, but a club instantly brought him down.

'Filthy scum!' I screamed. 'Murdering bastards!'

I was half-choked by an arm around my neck. But Tiernan had been distracted and Megan seized her chance. She grasped a flaming log and brought it down on his shoulder. He roared, but even as Megan ran another man felled her with a sword-slash to the calf.

I saw them pick her up, one at her hands and another at her feet. They swung her back and then forward. I caught one last anguished glimpse of her face, contorted with fear.

A flurry of sparks rose as she crashed on to the incandescent heap. It collapsed under her weight, plunging her into the burning heart of the huge fire.

I screamed. Oh, how I screamed. Mother help me, it was the only way to drown out the dreadful sounds of Megan's dying. Then a tiny bundle of terror flew to my side, clinging and sobbing.

'Auntie Keri! Auntie Keri! Stop them!'

Johannes turned; his eye lit on Morgan.

'No, Johannes! No, not the child. She is innocent! I beg you not the child!'

It seemed a moment of infinite length. Morgan clung to my skirts as he reached towards her. I have an image of him before the fire, cradling her like a father. He was actually praying over her. I closed my eyes, then heard the scream as she followed her foster mother into the flames. Tiernan stared for a moment, and then he lunged with his sword into the heart of the fire. There was a sudden silence, but for the sizzling and crackling. Tiernan turned slowly away, as if the enormity of what they had done had touched even his cruel heart.

For a moment he watched the others edging me closer to the flames, his face contorted with indecision. Then he made up his mind.

The rest is confusion. Tiernan gruffly telling them to let me go. Johannes muttering false comforts about the purifying flames. They let me fall and then they went away.

Time passed. Then lights and voices. Coel's face, and Dahut's. Dahut, shaking me in distraction, demanding to know the fates of her child and her friend. I pointed at the fire. Within the embers, charred horrors told their own story. Dahut wailing, screaming vengeance, swearing to burn every church and hang every priest in the land, madness in her eyes and in her voice. A clear image of Coel's tortured, tear-stained face.

Then sweet oblivion.

Chapter Nineteen

I do not know how Dahut and Coel contrived to get Cynan and myself down the mountain. I only know that I awoke in the villa, in my own bed, and it was morning.

Coel had brought me some bread and herbal tea. Tears came to my eyes when I saw it, for our herbal recipes had all been learned from Megan. I could eat nothing. I drank the tea, but it might as well have been water. Coel hesitated for a while, then told me that Dahut had gone.

'She told me nothing, just asked me to make sure you and Cynan were comfortable. Her mood was ... unnatural. I have never seen anyone so strangely calm. She was pale as a ghost.'

He crossed over to the window, still fastened against the night air, and opened the shutters. As the light streamed in he gave a grunt of surprise.

'There's a fire in the village. I can't see exactly where – the trees are in the way – but there's a lot of smoke.'

I looked at him blankly.

'Coel, I would like to get up now. I must see Cynan.'

'What? Oh, yes, of course. We put him in the woman's room – Brica, is it? I'll be downstairs. Call if you need me.'

I had a grey cloak in my box, and put it around me while I crossed the landing to Brica's room. Cynan was still asleep, but his breathing seemed normal and his heartbeat strong. I sighed with relief. There was a lump on his temple like a hen's egg, and the skin was broken and caked in dried blood.

'Cynan!' He stirred, but that was all. A pang went through me, and the sudden anxiety brought a surge of energy. 'Cynan! Wake up, it's Keri! Wake up now!'

He turned his head towards me and opened one eye, then the other.

'Keri?' He turned his head quickly to look at the room, and winced with the effort.

I took a deep breath, and began the story. He had received his blow before Megan's death, and knew nothing of the events of the night. My tears returned, and he put his arms up to me. I lay in them, my head on his chest, while I told the tale. When I had finished he held me silently until I could stop sobbing.

'I'm sorry, Keri.'

'Sorry? What have you got to be sorry for?'

'I wasn't much use to you, was I? All I did was get myself knocked down, and as for Megan ...'

'Listen to me, Cynan! Don't you go filling yourself with any silly male ideas about how you are a failure because you didn't get killed! There were far too many of them for any of us to do anything useful. What use would you be to me dead? What use would you be to your father, who has already lost one son? We are all to blame, even Megan, may her soul find peace. We all underestimated the priest. We thought him harmless. We thought he would talk and sing, and go away. We did not know that he could preach peace and love, and then commit foul murder. Now we do know, and we will not make the same mistake again.'

He sighed. 'I suppose you're right. It's just that women have a right to expect their men to protect them.'

'If you want to torture yourself then do it, but don't try to make it respectable by dressing it up in such talk!'

He chuckled suddenly. 'I'm not allowed to feel sorry for myself, then?'

'Definitely not. I want you whole again as soon as possible, in your mind as well as your dear body.'

There was silence for a minute. Then he said; 'Is my body really dear to you?'

'Can you doubt it, after last night? I don't have anything else to compare you with, but I can tell you this: if I live to be a hundred I will never forget last night – the first part as well as the second.'

He sighed again. When I sneaked a look at his face his eyes were closed. I left him to sleep and went downstairs to Coel.

'If Cynan has Brica's room, where did she sleep?'

'A good question.' Coel turned a frowning face towards me. 'She has not returned all night.'

And when I went over to our two guards' outbuilding, they were missing too.

It was early afternoon before we heard anything. Then it was not the sound of hoofbeats, but a sort of tired shuffling. I had busied myself looking after Cynan, washing and bandaging his wound and persuading him to take some food. Once again he was asleep and I had left him to rest, when I heard the slow dragging steps of someone entering the courtyard. The kitchen door banged, and I ran downstairs to find Brica, travel-stained and footsore, sitting at the table. Her arms were resting on it, her face hidden in them. Her hair was dirty and tangled and her cloak was torn.

'How dare you come back here! Have you no idea what your prattling to Tiernan has cost us?'

'What?' She raised her head, and I saw that her face was bruised, and stained with tears as well as travel.

'Gods above and below! What have you been doing to yourself?'

She ignored the pagan oath and sniffed.

'I didn't do it,' she said, and began to cry. 'He's abandoned me, Keri. He said cruel things to me – that he'd no use for me now, that I had served my purpose. And worse. When his horse went lame he pushed me down and took mine. I begged him to let me ride with him, but he wouldn't listen. I didn't even know why he was running away.'

'I presume you mean Tiernan?'

'The Princess and her party met me on the road. They told me ...'

She burst into a fit of sobbing. In spite of everything I began to feel sorry for her. She was stupid rather than evil, and had been cruelly used. Besides, Tiernan could probably have taken the servants gossip and put two and two together without her help.

'Go and clean yourself up,' I said wearily. 'I'll make you something to eat.'

Dahut was dirty and windswept, and the two soldiers were worse. She would say nothing at first, but asked after Coel and Cynan. Then she sat in the kitchen with the soldiers and ate some food, while she told us what had happened.

'I'm grateful to these two. Once I told them the story they realised what they had to do. It is, after all, a matter of murder, and that is a breach of the King's laws, whatever the circumstances.

'What *did* you do?' I asked.

'We went down to the village to look for Tiernan and that murdering priest. There was no one at the church, so we began to call at the houses, especially those we thought would be friendly. Lea was distraught when she heard the news, and raised a band of men from around the village, pagans all. One of them said his brother had been with the priest last night, and we dragged the brother from his bed. He was terrified, but he swore he hadn't known what was going to happen. I believed him, but I told him he must prove his good faith by helping us, and he did. The priest had announced his intention of desecrating other pagan shrines in the district, and had left the village by the north road to go to the sacred well. We followed them, and met the crowd on the road.'

'And?'

'There wasn't much they could do. They weren't armed, the fools. Our two soldiers positioned themselves by the priest, and I told him he was under arrest for murder. He began to rave about demonic plots and heresy, but he admitted the killings, right there in front of everyone. Nothing could have suited me better. I ordered him taken to the village. His friends made as if to free him, but I warned them that we would execute him on the spot if they did. Eventually we got him away, still ranting and praying like a madman. We took him to his living quarters at the back of the church. Then we tied him to his mattress and set the place on fire.'

'What?'

Dahut looked at me calmly. I felt Coel shudder.

'And Tiernan?' I asked.

'Gone. They say he was seen with the priest's mob not long before they left for the well, but he didn't go with them. I was determined to find him. We owed him a lot more than we gave the priest. We thought he had probably gone the opposite way, knowing the way his mind worked. Towards Vorganium, that is, and that's how it turned out.

'Many of the men had swords. We're not the only ones to feel unsafe today. So we took all the horses we could find and followed the north-east road out of the village, if you can call that overgrown cart track a road. Con the hunter was there. He certainly knows how to follow a trail! A few broken twigs, and the occasional hoofprint, and he could say that two horses had passed that way since the rain the night before.

'I was surprised there were two, but he was adamant. The hooves were different sizes or something. Well, two or one, we were enough to take them, I thought, so on we went.

'We had not been an hour on the road when we found Brica. She was sitting at the roadside, looking like she'd been dragged through a hedge backwards, weeping and wailing and calling on her god. Tiernan's horse was nearby. It had stumbled and gone lame, so the vicious bastard had taken hers.

'I might have killed her, but the others talked me out of it. She had been used by Tiernan, they said, and meant no harm. I suppose that's true, though she did help him. Anyway, we soon got out of her that Tiernan was not far ahead, and riding her little lady's pony, which was far too small for him. She went off into fits of wailing again when we said why we were after him – he hadn't told her a thing – and we left her to it.'

'I know,' I put in. 'She arrived back here a couple of hours ago.'

Dahut rolled her eyes and continued her story.

'We saw him soon after. The road goes over a hill, and there are trees on both sides. We saw him on the skyline as he went through the gap between, but when we reached the place he had vanished.

'He must have seen us and taken cover in the trees. We reined the horses in for a moment. Then an arrow came from nowhere. It passed clean through my cloak and lodged in Con's leg.

'When we realised he had a bow we dismounted and scattered. I took cover in the thicket on the right-hand side of the road, shouting to distract him, while Gaius here crept forward.

'Then I saw him. He was leading the pony between the bushes on my right. He had obviously decided to ride off across country. There was no one to stop him but me. I picked up a rock and threw it, and then another and another. I missed him, but hit the pony. It reared and bolted, just as he was mounting, and his foot caught in the reins. The more he screamed the faster the animal went, dragging him through the undergrowth and over the stones, flinging him this way and that, battering him to pulp!'

'Dahut!'

She was standing now, her voice getting louder and louder, her eyes flashing in an echo of the madness of the previous night.

She paused as if in surprise, then sighed and sat down heavily.

'We found the pony a mile down the road. Tiernan was dead, a bloody mess. We brought him back to show him in the village. Today he'll be left on display. Tomorrow he'll be burned.'

She leaned back, exhausted.

'You two should go now,' she said to the soldiers. 'You have done more than enough. Your loyalty and bravery will figure in my report to His Majesty.'

She dismissed them with a flutter of her fingers. Then wearily, she began to cry.

'He cheated me, Keri! If I had got my hands on him he wouldn't have had such an easy death. I had such plans. He would have begged to die...'

'Dahut, stop it! Hasn't there been torture and killing enough? If we don't stop somewhere what do we become? Monsters!'

'Maybe that's what it takes to fight them! What kind of monster is it who murders a sweet, innocent, child?' And again she relapsed into weeping.

Before I had time to comfort her, Gaius burst into the room again. Brica had hanged herself from the gatepost.

After the bodies were buried Dahut wrote a long account of what happened, together with statements from witnesses. She did not tell everything – Morgan's true parentage, for example. She described Megan as a harmless peasant woman, who scratched a living from her herbal cures. She described fully the misdeeds of Johannes, and of Tiernan. The latter's death was described honestly – he had not only committed murder and treason, but had gone on to injure one of the arresting party, so there was nothing to hide. About Johannes, however, she was less open. She wrote that he had been detained in the church pending removal to Kemper to be tried before the King. The fire, she said, must have started when he upset a lamp while trying to escape. At all events, the door had been barred from the outside, and by the time the alarm was raised it was too late. Dahut concluded with praise of the two soldiers, and a reminder that the King's people were no longer free to practise their chosen religion without fear of ambush. This she sent to the King, with a letter asking him to approve her actions, taken because there was no time to consult him, and saying that we would return to Kemper as soon as possible.

Gradlon was appalled at Dahut's story. He praised her quick thinking and decisive action, but he was horrified by the dangers to which she had been exposed. He summoned Corentin, and told him in no uncertain terms that he could try to win the pagans over by persuasion and preaching, but not by force.

'The Lord's word will surely win out in the end,' he declared. 'In the meantime, I will not have this kingdom split apart by sectarian strife. The Church can and must be a force for unity.'

Dahut rejoined her father in the business of the palace, and it was tacitly accepted that I was her companion. There were no moves to rid the royal household of its last pagan, perhaps because of the disloyalty of some of its first Christians. The King accused no one directly, but former friends of Tiernan found themselves sent on suitable tasks abroad, or in the more remote parts of the kingdom. One or two entered the Church, and so Corentin gained yet more monks by the back door.

Dahut was still prone to strong black moods, which descended on her in the evenings when there was nothing much to do. Her hatred of the Church was total, and I worried lest it bring her further confrontations with Corentin and her father. She worked long and hard on state business – to stop herself brooding, I suppose. The post of steward was unfilled and Dahut came more and more to carry out its functions. She rode out to inspect the King's lands, and reported on the condition of the harbours and roads. She even received envoys and judged disputes from time to time. When busy and involved, she could be buoyant and sharp, entertaining the court with her wit and intelligence. She liked to try to thwart the desires of the monks and could be lively and alert at times. But the darkness of depression was often just around the corner, waiting to appear.

When she could, she would make judgements in such a way as to curb the powers of the Church and foster the traditions of paganism. It was an uphill struggle, but it was the beginning of her revenge. Corentin's monastery was now an important local landowner. Disputes about boundaries and the like were serious, for land is food to peasant people. A tendency soon developed for the monks to complain only when Gradlon was in the judgement seat, and for others only when Dahut was. She favoured the smallholders over the monastery even if they too were Christians, hoping thereby to drive a wedge between Corentin and his own congregation. Sometimes she succeeded, and several important converts lapsed into paganism. Corentin was furious, and complained to the King in front of the full court.

'Your Majesty,' said Corentin, 'I have been patient. I have bided my time, hoping that maturity would guide your daughter's hand more wisely, but it has been in vain.'

Gradlon listened with mixed feelings, to judge by his expression. He shifted uncomfortably in his seat, and glanced at Dahut from time to time. She sat by his side, her stern gaze fixed firmly on Corentin's face.

'Of what am I accused?' she demanded.

Gradlon sat up straight at the word.

'We shall not talk of accusations,' he said gruffly. 'Bishop Corentin wishes to advise us; that is his right.'

'Indeed so, Your Majesty,' the bishop replied. 'The problem is simply that the Church has been involved in several disputes recently. They are not important ones – minor disagreements over field boundaries, that sort of thing – and Your Majesty has not always been able to attend to them personally. No doubt because of their minor nature, these matters have been judged by the Princess Dahut.'

'And?'

'Your Majesty, I assure you that no criticism of the Princess is intended, but in all cases these judgements have gone against the Church. Can this be fair? Naturally, interpretations may differ, and perhaps two judges would not always make the same decision, but is such a one-sided result reasonable?'

The King turned to his daughter. 'Dahut?'

'Father, what the good Bishop says is true. The Church has lost a lot of cases recently. However, I should point out that in each case the complaint was brought against the Church by others of your subjects – good Christians mostly – who felt that the monastery had taken too much upon itself. Too much land, usually.'

There was laughter at this, and Gradlon glared at the assembly until silence was restored. 'I see no cause for amusement,' he said. Budic, the royal guard, nodded sagely.

'Father,' Dahut went on, 'it seems that the monks, excellent and pious fellows though they may be, are not well versed in mathematics.'

'What has mathematics got to do with it?'

'They have difficulty measuring, Father, and counting. They erect walls on other people's land, sometimes even buildings. They also have trouble finding their way, which causes them to graze cattle on other people's ground. It seems their cattle have increased, too, sometimes bearing other people's brand marks. Miraculously, no doubt.'

There were loud guffaws from one or two people, but Gradlon ignored them.

'This surely cannot be true, Bishop?' he said to Corentin.

'I do not graze the animals personally,' said the Bishop stiffly. 'Still, I would have thought that a simple misunderstanding or two could have been cleared up without recourse to royal judgment.'

'You may not graze the animals personally,' said Dahut, 'but you are in charge of the monastery, are you not?'

'Of course.'

'And it is to you that complaints are made in the first place, is it not?'

The Bishop nodded. 'It is.'

'Then perhaps you should exercise more tolerance at that stage, and be more willing to reach a compromise when a complaint is made. Then, as you say, there would be no need for such trivial matters to waste the King's time.'

The Bishop was furious. 'Your Majesty, must I be spoken to in this way?'

'Father,' said Dahut evenly, determined to seem reasonable. 'It has been clear to me that some of these disputes could indeed have been settled between the parties concerned. The problem has always been intransigence on the part of the monastic authorities. It seems they will never agree to anything except total surrender by the other side. The other side is usually a poor peasant or small farmer. The land is their livelihood. They cannot be expected to allow its gradual ... acquisition by another.'

The King sighed. 'Let us all be honest with one another. Is there not an antagonism between you which is nothing to do with disputes over land?'

The Bishop leapt in a once. 'Your Majesty, the Princess opposes the Church at every turn. She has even been heard openly to scoff at the servants of the Lord as they go about his business.'

Gradlon turned to his daughter. 'Dahut, is this true?'

'Oh, Father, there are a few priests who attract the humorous attention of the community. Even you have laughed at some of the antics of Brother Constantius.' There were giggles among the company at this. She was referring to an enormously fat monk, who was a well-known visitor to any kitchen with a fire lit. Even Gradlon smiled.

'You see, Corentin, it is unwise to place too much credence in a rumour.'

'It is indeed!' snapped the Bishop. 'And it is also unwise to allow a father's love to blind him to all the faults of his offspring!'

'Enough!' shouted Gradlon. 'More than enough! I command you both, as your King I command you, to settle your differences! I will not have this court the scene of unruly quarrels over policy!'

He leapt to his feet. 'Now, get out of here, all of you, and leave me in peace!'

Dahut's fist crashed down on the arms of the throne. Her face was purple. 'That damnable Bishop!' she cried. 'He will not be satisfied until our lives are one long funeral!'

'Out!' bellowed Gradlon. 'Enough, I tell you!'

Dahut picked up her skirts and swept out. I scuttled close behind.

That evening the King came to our quarters, still deeply troubled by the earlier exchanges. He seemed oblivious to my presence, so I sat in the corner and listened.

'Dahut, my dear, it is clear that you and the Bishop do not see eye to eye. But please try to see that he has only our best interests at heart. His concern is not for this fleeting existence, but for the welfare of our souls in the eternal life to come.'

Dahut rounded on him.

'Oh, Father, you must try to see some things too! Do you not remember Kemper as it was? There was gaiety then, and brightness. These monks are taking away everything of worth. We cannot amuse ourselves in any harmless way – wearing nice clothes or jewellery, or singing, unless it is a hymn.'

'And what is wrong with hymns?'

'Nothing, Father, in their proper place. But we should be allowed to sing other things too. We should be allowed to dress well if we want. We do not all have to be monks. Besides, look at the monks. They don't dress well, the Lord knows, but they have more than their share of rich things. And we are constantly urged to give them more, for the glorification of their churches.'

'Do not criticise the churches, Dahut. The churches are the houses of God.'

Dahut turned away from him, tears of frustration beginning to run down her face. I put my hand out to her, and she took it for just a moment.

'What can I give you that will make you happy?' he entreated her earnestly.

For a moment she just sobbed quietly. Then she said: 'A city.'

'What?'

'Give me a place of my own. I am almost of age. You say I am a great help in affairs of state. You even said that since I took over Tiernan's work you need no other steward. Give me a city of my own to rule. Under you, of course, but in my own right.'

The King stared at her for a moment. Then decided it was some sort of joke, he threw back his head and roared with laughter.

Over the next few weeks Dahut became as depressed as I had ever seen her. She was restless in the quiet sober court and frustratedly aware of Corentin's growing power over the King. Her father noticed her gloom. One evening he found me in our rooms alone, his daughter having been persuaded to join some of the other palace women downstairs.

'What is wrong with Dahut?' he asked me, sitting himself down on one of our wooden chests. 'She seems so unhappy at the moment. Does she make any complaints about me? Is there anything she wants? Is she unwell?'

'She is perfectly well, Your Majesty. No, her unease is of the spirit, not the body.'

'Ah! Then she is pining. The poor chid. First her betrothed, and then this terrible business with Tiernan.'

'Perhaps. But I know she has felt greatly honoured to be able to assist you with matters of state. The work has been good for her, too. I think that is why she has thrown herself into it so completely. But it means staying here, and her heart is elsewhere.'

'At Ker-Is?'

'Yes, Your Majesty. If you could arrange for Kemper to be moved to Ker-Is I think it might solve the problem.'

He chuckled.

'I fear I cannot do that. Faith may move mountains, but the scriptures don't mention moving cities.'

He got up from his seat on top of the blanket box and then paused.

'And you think she would flourish better by the ocean?'

'I'm sure of it Your Majesty.'

'Hmm. Well, I must consider the matter. And I shall pray. Goodnight, Keri, you have given me food for thought.'

I didn't think the visit was worth mentioning to Dahut on her return. She came in looking as downhearted as ever, and we went to bed in silence.

I had told my mother as much as I could of the Beltane incident, glossing over the details of my relationship with Cynan. She had rejoiced to hear of Tiernan's death, and spoke disparagingly of the feeble Brica.

Meriadauc was away in Namnetum. He rarely sailed now, but he had to go to see other merchants, and sometimes to sort out problems with the authorities – harbour fees, taxes and the like. Mother still would not marry him, and it put a strain on their relationship. Meriadauc wanted children of his own. She was in her late thirties now, and not likely to provide him with any if she left it much longer.

She told me all these things one evening as we sat by the fire at the Villa Rosea. Then she returned to the subject of Cynan.

'When will I see this Cynan?'

I was thrown by the question. I had no idea that she realised his importance.

'Well, er, what makes you ask?'

She smiled. 'Come, my daughter, you blush whenever you mention his name.'

'Do I?' I said inanely. 'Ah.'

'Keri, I don't want to pry. You are a woman now, and must make your own life. But you will find that life is quite simply easier if you don't have to conceal too much.'

I grinned. 'That makes sense.'

'I know you went to the Beltane fires with Cynan and the others.'

'Yes.' I took a deep breath. 'You want to know if Cynan and I ... celebrated Beltane together.'

'I suppose so.'

'Well, what can I say? We went down to the beach, and he rolled me in his cloak, and we gave ourselves up to the Goddess.' I turned to her. 'Are you ashamed of me?'

She looked startled. 'Ashamed? Why, no. I am a little envious, perhaps. I wish I had had the courage at your age.'

'You grew up in a Christian household,' I said. 'That's the difference.'

'You're not pregnant, are you?'

'No, no. I can be sure of that.'

'Good. One adjustment at a time is enough.'

We both turned to look at the flickering logs. For a host of reasons, pregnancy was a difficult subject right now.

Cynan came to Kemper near Christmas. His friend Hoel had come with him and they stayed for a week while Cynan saw various people on his father's behalf. Mother thought he was lovely, which was a relief. I didn't want her seizing him with embarrassing questions about his intentions towards me. We both stayed at the Villa Rosea, and she tactfully turned a deaf ear on Cynan's nightly visits to my room. After such a long separation we made the most of those nights together!

I soon realised that both men were keeping some sort of secret. They would exchange glances now and then, or one would interrupt the other to prevent him giving something away. I tackled Cynan about it one night.

'Oh,' he said airily. 'I suppose you could call it a secret. Things happen outside Kemper, you know, even in little places like Ker-Is.'

'What sort of things?'

'Never mind. You'll know soon enough, I promise you.'

'When?'

'In the spring.'

Oh, you're impossible!'

It was on this visit that Cynan first asked me to marry him. I had been half expecting it, from the way that he'd been talking. He was involved in managing his father's estate, and selling its produce, and was going to be a busy and fairly well-off young man. He would have a position in society, and he would need a wife to help him keep it.

'Oh, Cynan,' I said to him. 'I don't know. I don't feel ready for marriage. Sometimes I'm not sure if I ever will be. It's a big step, and it can take a lot away from a woman.'

I think he was a little hurt as he departed, but he accepted that, for the moment, things would have to go on as they were. Why not, after all? My mother had done the same with Meriadauc for years now. Not that *that* was plain sailing.

'I can't see why you don't marry him,' I said on one occasion. 'He would be good to you. And he's not poor, the gods know. Why don't you marry him?'

'Oh, I don't know. Meriaduc is a good man. I don't doubt him, just the idea of marriage.'

'It is possible to divorce.'

'Not under the law of the Church, which is the only law that counts now.' She sighed. 'Perhaps I had better talk with Meriadauc. It doesn't seem fair on him, does it?'

'Is it the idea of children?'

My mother gave me a sidelong look.

'No,' she said at last. 'Why?'

'Oh, I just thought it might be. After all, you haven't even got me off your hands yet, and I'm full-grown!'

She chuckled. 'Did you really think you were so much trouble?'

'Sometimes. When I was small.'

'No. You never were. And I'd gladly have more now. Motherhood came upon me uninvited at an early age. For a long time I didn't want to think of it again. But I would now.'

'Then do it, Mother. Time waits for no one.'

Whether my advice was responsible I don't know, but my mother married Meriadauc within the month, and announced her pregnancy within another. The couple had to go to Namnetum, where a civil marriage was still possible – only Christian marriages were performed in Kemper now, and neither wanted that. Snorebeard was in Kemper, and they sailed with him in the *Boreas*. I did not go with them, but we had a great celebration on their return. Snorebeard had brought a sealed jar of Arabian perfume as a wedding gift. It must have cost him a fortune.

'I've been keeping it for your wedding day, Olivia Galeria,' he said, the usual twinkle in his eye. 'It's had to wait so long, I hope it hasn't gone off!'

And then, almost before we knew it, spring was upon us again, and with it the bitter-sweet memories of Ker-Is in other springtimes.

'This is the year,' said Dahut. 'This is the year things change!'

Chapter Twenty

We came at last to the hill above the Bay of Ker-Is, from which we usually gained our first view of the village, and stopped, thunderstruck.

There are some memories which fade almost as we try to recall them, like a sudden cry in a storm wind. There are others which spring afresh into the mind's eye each time we reach for them, bright and clear, and unsullied by the dust of the years. Such is the memory of my first sight of the new city that spring morning.

It was a clear day, cool but fine and sunny. We could see right across the bay. But, on this side of the water, and slightly to our right, a miracle had taken place. Gone was the village of Ker-Is, gone the pathetic hovels of the villagers. In their place stood a town, a complete, living town. There were people in the streets going about their business. There were builders and masons still at work. Most of the buildings were of wood, but there was one great house of stone – obviously the palace of a prince. Or a princess. To the left by the sea's edge a natural outcrop of rock had been shaped into a quayside, and extended further to form a breakwater to shelter the little boats which now nestled on the landward side of it. On the shore a similar process had levelled a long stretch of land, and a line of buildings had arisen right under the cliff edge. There were houses, and an inn, and merchants' stores.

The coastline here curved sharply, like a horseshoe, and the town lay in it snugly, the streets all converging upon the square which lay before the palace in the centre of the curve. An earthwork stretched from the cliffs on one side to the rocky outcrop which formed the harbour on the other. Topped by a wooden palisade, it created a formidable defensive wall across the landward approaches to the town. Our road lay directly towards the wall, which was broken in the middle by a gate topped by a guard tower. As we came in sight of the tower, still gaping in disbelief, we heard shouts as our arrival was noted.

Then we came upon a board fixed to a post. On it, in Latin, was the explanation of a king: 'HIC YS URBS STAT. INEAT NEMO NISI IN PACE – Here stands the city of Ys. Let no one enter save in peace.' Whoever had painted the sign had changed the spelling, but that was the least important detail. Beneath such a proclamation one usually finds the sign or device of the authority which issues it, but on this one there was only a blank space. The sign of the local ruler was still awaited. At last I understood the secret which Hoel and Cynan had been keeping. And Gradlon. Gradlon above all, who had striven in secret to realise Dahut's dream of a city at the Ocean's edge, to present it to her at her coming of age.

I took a sidelong glance at her as we kicked our horses on again. She was flushed, her eyes bright and wide. She knew what the city was, but dared not believe it yet. Unable to contain herself any longer she kicked the horse into a gallop and shouted for joy as she sped down the sloping road to the city gate. I followed at a more sedate pace, a grin forming itself on my face whether I liked it or not. I had just realised that we could now stay permanently in Ker-Is.

Before Dahut had reached the gate a group of riders galloped out through it. I could see Gradlon clearly, for he was in the lead. Behind him were several young men, and some royal guards. Dahut and Gradlon reined in their horses as they met, and I could hear shouts of laughter borne on the wind as they dismounted and hugged each other. As I reached the group Dahut looked up at me, tears of joy streaming down her face.

'It is,' she said. 'It really is. It's my city at the edge of the world.'

I dismounted and curtsied to the King, who took my hand and kissed my cheek in welcome.

'Ah, Keri, I tell you we've had some trouble keeping this little project a secret. Oh, the arms I've had to twist! Here, both of you can come with me now and take some refreshment. Then we shall have a tour of this new city of yours.'

He smiled dotingly at Dahut, and patted her shoulder. Then we all mounted our horses again and rode in through the city gate.

The palace which was to be Dahut's own was hardly the match of that at Kemper, but it was roomy and well-proportioned, with windows of real glass. It was one of the few stone buildings, and although it could not match the old Roman buildings of the capital it was clearly designed for a ruler. It had an audience room with a carved wooden throne, and a dining hall with long tables like those in the King's own palace. Behind these long tables were others in which the administrative business of the city might be carried out. There was a large kitchen wing, and a walled garden. The old gardener from the King's villa had been transplanted, as he put it, and he was delighted to have such a project – a complete garden to design and build up from scratch.

'I only hope I'll live long enough to see it through,' he said, and went off cackling to himself.

The private quarters upstairs were certainly fit for a princess. Dahut's bedroom had a large window that looked out over the bay. From it we saw that a channel left the harbour and ran right up to the palace. Under Dahut's window there was a small quay, and on the left a boathouse.

'My own private harbour,' she said proudly. 'Keri, this is wonderful! I can't believe it!'

'No,' I agreed. 'It doesn't seem possible, does it? Well, that's what comes of having a devoted father.'

'And a rich one!'

'Yes. That helps.' I went to the window and looked out. Beyond the stone harbour wall the sea was choppy, but the harbour itself was calm. I hoped it would always be like that – an oasis of calm on the world's edge – and I wished I could see what the future held in store. Perhaps it is just as well that we are blind in that respect.

After we had eaten and washed, the King and a couple of his attendants took us on foot through the town. It was the strangest thing to walk round the incomplete site. I have seen towns before, but never one which had the appearance of Ys. Of course, as always with the Celts, the legend has grown since those days. The Franks, who now claim the area, are little better. There are those who will tell you that the streets of Ys were paved with gold leaf. Others, less extravagantly, will say that it was the richest city on earth, full of palaces decked with marble, full of people decked with jewels and fine silks. Well, it was not. I was there, and I know. However, it was certainly the most elegant town I ever saw. Most towns are an awful mixture. Someone arrives from the county, builds himself a shack, and if he prospers he moves on to a house. His shack is then adopted by someone else, and so it goes on. Perhaps a new arrival will build a house of wood, or brick, or stone, according to his means. At all events, the result is a hotchpotch of warring styles, a spoil heap for people to live in.

The new Ker-Is was built all in one piece. Gradlon had brought in architects from the Mediterranean, and they knew a thing or two about style. The buildings all had the same character, enlivened here and there by little individual touches to make each one different from its neighbours, but harmonising with them just the same. The impression was not so much one of riches as of refined taste. This reflects wealth only in the sense that it takes wealth to buy such taste. So, Ys was not the richest city in the world, as some would have you believe, and it was certainly not the largest, but it was the finest I ever saw. Dahut loved it.

'I can't believe it!' she kept saying. 'I really can't! And all in less than a year!'

Gradlon smiled. 'Time is no obstacle when money is no object. Aëtius's gold – God rest his soul – has done more than he ever imagined.'

This is the only time I ever heard him admit the source of so much of his wealth. He usually piously attributed his good fortune to the generosity of his god.

'I sent for the best,' he went on. 'And the best are still found in the Empire, or what's left of it. I believe that out on the fringes – like Britain, for example – they're back to building mud huts. But one day this place may be the capital of my kingdom.' – he smiled at Dahut – 'well, your kingdom, at least. It needs to be a place fit for that.'

Dahut scolded him. 'Father, you mustn't talk of such things. You are not an old man yet!'

He chuckled. 'Perhaps not, but that is no guarantee of anything. You were right when you told me you needed the experience of governing somewhere yourself. These days, who knows when another war might take me, or another plague, or any one of the Devil's other scourges?'

Dahut looked uncomfortable. 'Well, Father, I love this place already. I will try to rule it wisely in your name. It is the best thing you could have done for me, and I really do appreciate the effort is has cost you, and all those whom you have employed here. I will thank them all personally.'

'And thank the Lord.'

'Oh, of course, Father, of course.'

We exchanged a look as Gradlon turned to lead us onward.

That night we sat in front of the fire in Dahut's room and talked of the day's events. We had sent down for some mulled wine, and were warming ourselves before going to bed. As usual, we were to share the one in Dahut's room. Dahut stared into the fire. Her dark eyes were wide, and her cheeks flushed, but whether with emotion or from the fire I could not tell.

'This is going to be such a place, Keri,' she said. 'It really is. My own city at last, to rule as I please.'

'In your father's name,' I reminded her, and she giggled.

'And why not? It's come in handy before! No, but Keri, can you not see what it means? Here we can be the guardians of our own ways, the ways of the Mother and the old gods, the ways of the people, until I am Queen in Kemper as well as Ys.'

'That is not all it means,' I warned her. 'You are only to be Princess here, not Queen. Your father is still the King, and his laws will still run here. And the Church will not let you stray too far from their chosen path.'

'The Church can go hang. I will not let them spoil Ys the way they have spoiled Kemper. In any case, when I am Queen their days will be numbered.'

'Do you think they don't know that? Don't underestimate Corentin. We underestimated Father Johannes once, and it cost us dear.'

She nodded slowly. 'Yes, dear Keri, you are right, as always. You know, you are my dearest friend, and my best counsellor. The gods know where I'd be without you.'

'Happier probably, without this old harridan nagging you.'

She laughed at me. 'Harridan, indeed! You make yourself sound like an old woman, and you're younger than me!'

'I beg your pardon, Your Highness. I did not intend to imply that you were old.'

'Be careful, now, or I may have you locked up for, well, something or other.'

We shrieked with laughter and turned towards the bed. As we shuttered the window, which had been open a crack, I paused to look out over the town. It was mostly sleeping now, for it was late, but here and there was a noise or a light to show that someone was still active. I let my gaze wander down to the harbour, a mass of gloom with darker shapes where the boats were, and the black rectangle of the harbour wall. I was about to turn away when another light caught my eye. It seemed to be far out on the sea. It was not a ship, I thought, for who sails these coasts at night? No, it must surely be land.

'What is it?' asked Dahut from the bed.

'Just a light. Way out to sea.'

'A ship? How strange.'

'I don't think it's a ship. There must be land out there.'

'Land? Well, there's Sena, of course.'

'Ah, yes, the island of the priestesses. Megan spoke of it once.'

'We'll go to the island some day and see if there really is anyone there.'

'Yes, we must do that.'

She yawned. 'Come to bed. We need our sleep. There's going to be a lot to do.'

There was indeed much to do. Over the next couple of weeks I hardly saw Dahut. She was closeted with the King, and with his advisers and assistants. They had to hand over all the running of the city to her, and the area of countryside around it. There were leases and sales of land, for Gradlon was not giving his houses away free; they were to be a source of income for his daughter. There were matters of taxation, for the city had to support itself. There were trading arrangements and fishing rights, obligations to provide military training, public works still in progress – all the administrative concerns of a kingdom in miniature. Dahut threw herself into all of these with a will, and soon her father felt able to return to Kemper for a while, leaving her in charge. She did not ask me to help much. There were secretaries and scribes enough for that. Besides, I think she knew my heart would not be in it. Whatever the future held for me, it was not to be a female Tiernan.

One day I rode out alone, and took the clifftop path to the south. It was not the easiest of paths for a horse, and I had to go slowly, but that suited me well enough. Dahut's mind was well occupied, but my own was free to ponder over things, and a slow pace would be conducive to thought. There was much to think about. It was almost a year since our last Beltane, the Beltane at which Megan and Morgan had died horribly, and Dahut had hunted down their killers. A year since Cynan had brought me to real womanhood. I thought of us again, rolling on the beach, the power of the Goddess coursing through us, and smiled to myself. What a year can bring!

I passed by the King's old villa, wondering idly what would become of it now – he would hardly need it, with a whole city to stay in. I rode on, past the spot where Megan had once picked comfrey with us, in that first lesson in her lore. I passed the path down to the beach, where we had mistaken her for the Sea God's daughter. Soon the little clearing came in view, and the house which had once been a temple. I almost expected to smell the woodsmoke and see the door standing half open as it used to, but that was an idle fancy. The dead may return in dreams, for sleep is close to death, but I have never encountered them in daylight.

And yet, there was something of Megan in the air. I do not believe she was in any sense present, but to a friend who had loved her there was still something in the place that spoke of her. The little altar was still there behind the house. Further away was a little plot where she had grown vegetables – overgrown as it was, it still bore the unmistakable marks of cultivation. The little house itself was undamaged – either by the storms of winter or the storms of religion – and that would always be Megan's house to me. I tried the door, but it would not budge. There was no lock, of course, but it had jammed with damp or something. I put my shoulder to it, and it suddenly gave, spilling me inside in a heap.

As the shaft of daylight split the gloom two rats ran away squealing their disgust. I picked myself up off the tiles and looked about at the outer room, brushing my cloak down with my hand only making it worse. The room was the same as ever, apart from the dust, and there was plenty of that. My arrival had stirred it up, too, so that now there were golden glints floating in the light beam from the door. There was an unhealthy smell in the air, partly from the dust, but partly from damp and lack of ventilation, and something else. I pushed the door as wide as it would go – to let in the fresh air as much as the light – and turned back to the room. The light now showed up the large stone table that we thought had once been an altar. Earthenware jars which had been left on it were now smashed – by the rats, no doubt – and their rotten contents had added their contribution to the atmosphere. I went across to the far wall behind the altar, and opened the door to Megan's old room.

It opened easily, discharging a stench of rottenness such as I had never smelt before. Gagging, I pulled back and covered my face with my cloak. The room was in darkness, because the window opposite had been left shuttered. I stepped quickly over to it, ignoring the rat droppings and the scuffling sounds in the corners, and managed to get it to open. Instantly the pale sunshine flooded in, and the place began to look more familiar again. The source of the stench was not difficult to find. There were two hams hanging from hooks in the ceiling, where the rats could not get them. They will keep for a long time like this, but not indefinitely. I stood up on a stool and unhooked them. They were wrapped in muslin, so I was spared the necessity of handling them directly. With a shudder, I threw them both out of the window, and the air began to seem clearer almost at once. I got down from the stool, wiping my hands reflexively on my cloak, and looked around again.

It needed cleaning up, all right, but it would do. For what I had in mind, it would do very well!

That evening I broached the subject with Dahut. We were at the dinner table, and already the future was foreshadowed. There were new faces there, people I had never seen before. Dahut's entourage had had to grow, as she found more to do. There was a man called Nodens, whom I disliked for his arrogant manner. There was another named Martinus, a quiet and unassuming fellow. Hoel was there, so was Cynan, sometimes. There were no women. Dahut never surrounded herself with others of her sex. I was the exception, and she always had time for me, work permitting.

On this occasion I waited until the eating was over, and the last of the wine was being passed around. There had been much talk of official matters at dinner, and I had found it rather tedious. Having finally disposed of the day's business, Dahut turned to me.

'And what have you been doing today?' she asked cheerily.
'I took a ride,' I said. 'I went along the coast to see Megan's old house.'
A shadow crossed her face. 'Yes, poor Megan. Why did you go?'
'I don't know, really. I felt I had to. I wanted to see if it was still there.'
'Still there? Why shouldn't it be?'
'Well, you know how things have been. It isn't everyone who loved her.'
'No. Well, was it there?
'Yes. It's bit dirty, but it's still habitable.'
'Habitable? We have a city here to live in. Why do we need another house down the coast?'
'I was thinking of myself.'
'You?' She laughed. 'You don't need a ruin like that. Your place is here with me.' And she made as if to change the subject.
'Dahut!'
'What's the matter, Keri?'

'Dahut, I have no place here. Oh, I like the town, it's beautiful. I enjoy being a member of your household. It is an easy thing to enjoy. But I have no position here. You never needed a lady-in-waiting, and anyway I am not sure how good a one I'd be. I am not the person you need for a steward. What am I, then? I am on holiday here, at your expense.'

She looked incredulous. 'But you know you can do whatever you want.'

'Then let me make my own contribution in my own way. Megan taught me most of what she knew. Her materials are still at the house. From here we can send for whatever else is needed. Let me take up her work.'

She looked at me in silence for some time, digesting the arguments.

'It is the work of the Goddess,' I added.

She nodded slowly. 'Very well. I must admit I can't see you as a civil servant, either. See Plotinus the Mason in the morning. Tell him it is my wish to refurbish Megan's house. It will be my gift.'

My spirits soared instantly. 'Thank you, Dahut, thank you!'

'Yes, well, see you are not too far away. I might need a wise-woman from time to time.' She gave me a far-away smile.

'I don't know about "wise-woman", but I will always be here when I am needed.'

'Promise?'

'Yes. Always.'

Chapter Twenty-one

Plotinus the mason was not quite what I was expecting. For one thing he was an Italian, one of those whom Gradlon had imported to build the city. This meant that he spoke Latin, although with an unfamiliar accent. For another, he was not in the least servile. He was not a workman but a skilled artisan, a leading officer of his guild, and a man of some substance. He was about forty-five, and regarded me as a girl who knew nothing. He eyed Megan's house with disdain, his rounded face tilted upwards to see the eaves, and his brown forehead wrinkled against the sun.

'It'll take some work,' he said at last.

'I assumed that,' I told him evenly.

He thought for a bit longer, his practised eyes flicking over the building from one point to another. He walked round to the back of the house, prodding the mortar here and there.

'There'll be some repointing to do. Otherwise you'll get damp coming in.'

We went inside, the lingering stench of rottenness still there, albeit in muted form.

'Hmm. I'd suggest a complete redecoration here. Those tiles are good quality, *Domina*. What was this building?'

'I don't know. I thought it might have been a temple of some sort. To Mithras, maybe.'

'Heathens,' he said contemptuously. Like most city Italians he was a Christian. 'Well, it hasn't been a temple for a while, I'll be bound.'

'No, not for a while. It was a house.'

'Ah.' He continued on his round of the place. He was disgusted at the living quarters – not only because of their condition, but also because of their cramped layout, which he compared unfavourably with a rabbit hutch.

'I could build on,' he said. 'The place is close to running water. I could make a proper water tank, proper privy. There are plumbers in the town.'

'Whatever you think best,' I said. 'I'm sure you know your job much better than I do.'

He preened himself a little at that, and carried on with his survey. Then he went off to plan his work schedule. Within another fortnight work had begun.

It was almost Beltane. I was still living with Dahut while the work went ahead on my house, and we had plenty of opportunities to talk about the festival. Her father, of course, had little idea of her true feelings, and she was reluctant to come out in the open about them.

'Still,' she said. 'I'm not expecting him to visit again for a while. I think we should be free to do as we please.'

'Will there be anything official?' I asked.

'No, not this year. It's too soon. I can't do anything to offend the priests until my hold here is secure beyond doubt. But the day will come. You mark my words.'

Strangely, I did not feel much comfort at this. The King was weak in some ways, but I had known him for many years, and I liked him. He was kindly by nature, and I did not want to see him hurt by his daughter's eventual rebellion. Still, perhaps he would realise in the end that his new faith was not the only path to happiness. Or perhaps he would die happy, before things came out in the open. As he himself had said, there was no security in these troubled times.

I would ride out every couple of days to see how things were progressing at Megan's house. Plotinus, who regarded my visits with great suspicion, would give monosyllabic answers to my questions, and made it clear that he was a skilled man who did not have to be spied upon. He was right. The little house was taking on a new appearance. A new door had appeared in the end wall of the living room. This gave on to a small hall with doors which led to a new bedroom, a kitchen with a proper storeroom beyond, and a back door. Outside the back door, overhanging the little stream which ran by, was a purpose-built privy. This was quite a luxury after the previous, rather public, arrangement! Plotinus, in spite of his gruff ways, took my comfort seriously. He had even called in a gardener to tidy up the kitchen garden. Planting was already under way. I felt very lucky in Dahut's choice of artisan, and more certain than ever of my own choice of residence. This was my place, near the people who needed the help of the Goddess. Hers were the gifts of nature and Hers the power to heal, to give life.

I was lost in such thoughts as these one day when I heard a horse approaching, picking its way gently through the undergrowth. I turned to see Cynan riding across the clearing. He was smartly dressed in a brown tunic, with a deep blue cloak around his shoulders. Quite the aristocratic landowner's son. He dismounted and approached briskly, I went to kiss him, but he stood aloof from me.

'I thought I would find you here.' His tone was almost accusing.

'And so you have. Would you like to see the work I am having done?' And I took his hand and led him around the house, pointing out everything, and explaining the jobs which were not yet finished. He gazed at them all wordlessly, while I prattled on to cover his silence. At last we came out to the bank of the stream, and sat on a large flat rock.

'Don't you like it?' I asked nervously.

'It's all very well – for a peasant woman,' he said stiffly.

'Peasant woman? Cynan, how many peasants live in stone houses with tiled floors? How many have proper fireplaces with chimneys, instead of a thatched roof with a smoke-hole?'

He waved my protest aside. 'You know what I mean. It's tiny.'

'It's big enough for me.'

'Yes,' he said bitterly. 'I suppose it is.'

'Cynan, what is it?'

'You know what it is, Keri. I want you to marry me. Leave all this foolishness and come to live with me. You will have a grand villa, servants. My father's business is doing well. We will want for nothing.'

Want for nothing! 'Nothing,' I said, 'except the forest and the sea, and the Goddess.'

He looked at me blankly. 'What are you talking about?'

'Cynan, if I marry you I shall live the life of a grand lady, no doubt. But I was never cut out for that. If that was what I wanted I could have stayed at the Princess's court. You are asking me to be a society matron, to run a household, entertain your friends. I would be ... I would be your personal civil servant. That is not my place in life.'

'You would rather live in a hovel?'

'I have already answered that,' I said primly. 'It's enough for my needs. And one of my needs is privacy. Not all the time, but when I choose it.'

He glowered sullenly at me. 'You've changed.'

'And so have you. You have come a long way since the night we honoured the Goddess together.'

He looked uncomfortable at that, and turned away to walk back to his horse. I went with him.

'I'm sorry if you are upset, Cynan. I really didn't want you to be hurt.'

'I'll get over it,' he said stiffly.

'Yes.'

He reached the horse and prepared to mount. He turned his head to me. His eyes were sad, I thought, but he betrayed his emotions in no other way. My own were in turmoil, as at the prospect of healing surgery. Once knows the knife must cut, but fears the pain which comes before the cure. I felt tears stinging in my eyes.

'I won't ask again.'

'I know.'

He swung himself up into the saddle and spoke once more. 'You realise that I must now consider myself free?'

'Of course. I could hardly expect anything else.'

He nodded. 'Well, that's clear, then. Goodbye.'

'Goodbye.'

I watched him until he had disappeared in the trees and the sound of hooves had died away. Then I walked along the clifftop path, tears rolling down my cheeks. I had made my choice, but the Mother was a hard mistress.

Of course, it was unthinkable that I should stay away from the Beltane festival, although I had mixed feelings about it. For one thing, I thought Cynan was sure to be there, and I was half afraid my resolve might weaken if I saw him again. In any case, it would mark the anniversary of the death of Megan and Morgan. What pleasure could I take in that? And who was to organise the proceedings now that Megan was gone?

I had reckoned without the persistence of tradition among the people of the land. One day, after visiting the house, which was now nearly complete, I decided to walk up the hill to the grove of sacred trees. I felt it was a necessary journey. I had ghosts to exorcise, perhaps.

It was a fine day, but blustery, and I had wrapped a woollen shawl around myself against the wind. As I climbed the hill I could see fluffy clouds scudding along over the blue sea, and gulls wheeling in the air currents. Every so often one of them would fold its wings and plummet like a stone into the water, rising a second or two later with a fish in its beak. Somewhere far away someone was cutting wood with an axe, and the sharp sounds were borne to me on the breeze. As I climbed higher I could see Ys around the bay. It shone in the strong sunlight, surely the cleanest and fairest of all cities.

Suddenly I could go no higher. The slope evened out at a sort of shoulder, so that the ground ahead was almost flat. Immediately I saw blackened patches where the ground was still scorched from the year before, when Johannes's mob had tried to fire the whole hillside. There were fallen trees, too, some lying in the charred patches. There was one symbol of hope, though. One tall tree had survived the fire, and sprouted new green shoots on all its branches. Perhaps in time others would rise. It was then that I heard the sounds of men, coming up the hill from the other side.

I went forward, pushing through some bushes until I reached the clearing where the Beltane fire had been the previous year. I stopped, amazed. Someone was already preparing for this year's festival. A great pile of logs was being constructed, obviously intended as a bonfire. Even as I watched, two young men emerged from the bushes on the other side, dragging another large log between them. This was quite an effort, even thought they were both big strapping fellows, dressed in the peasant style and obviously used to work.

They had almost reached the bonfire when they saw me and stopped, one nudging the other and nodding in my direction.

I decided to meet the situation head on, before they decided I was spying on their preparations. Pulling the shawl tight around me, for it was cool in the shade, I strode forward and put on my most commanding voice.

'Good day to you!'

They mumbled a greeting in return, exchanging dubious glances. I addressed the one who seemed to be in charge. He was the younger of the two, slim, with freckles and a shock of red hair, unlike his companion, who was dark and very Welsh-looking.

'I see you are preparing for the Beltane fire,' I said. 'I am glad to see that someone is. I was a good friend of Megan, who used to live in the old temple. I am going to live there now.'

One of them nodded. 'We saw the work going on there, *Domina*. Will you be taking on old Megan's healing work, too?'

'Megan taught me much of what she knew,' I said. 'I will be doing what I can.'

The other spoke up. 'That'll be good news, that will. Megan was kind. She cured my poisoned finger, she did. Cured it all better.'

'Don't pay no attention to that one, *Domina*,' chipped in the other. 'He's a half-wit.'

I thought he was probably right, but it was brutal to say so in front of the poor creature. Not that he seemed to notice.

'We wondered who you were,' the red-haired one went on. 'We heard about the working at the house. No one'd go near Megan's house, dead or not. They say she was a witch.'

He shrugged. 'It's all the same to me – and to her now, I daresay. Will you be coming to the Beltane fire? There are those who say it should all be stopped now.'

'I will come,' I said. 'I am not a Christian.'

He nodded, and turned back to his half-witted companion. 'Let's get on.' And they heaved the log on top of the others.

'Wait a minute!' I called, as they turned to go. 'You haven't answered my question.'

'Question?'

'Who is organising the festival? Who asked you to build the fire?'

The red-haired man shrugged again. 'It was time, that's all. Does a sparrow need to be told when to build a nest?'

And they walked off, leaving me feeling foolish, but glad in my restored faith. I had always known that the Goddess was close to the land, and the people who lived by it. She was the personification of Nature, and the seasons were Her moods. The red-haired man's last comment seemed to me the confirmation of my choice. I would be able to face Cynan after all.

I took up residence a week before Beltane. Dahut fretted and worried about my going, but I reminded her of my promise; I would always be ready when she needed me. She had to be content with that. For my part, I felt as excited as a new bride, which was ironic after what had passed between Cynan and myself. Yet perhaps it was for the best. I did feel that I was called, and that the Goddess planned a role for me which was not that of a rich landowner's wife. When I had been younger, I had despaired of my lack of beauty, fearful of one day being left on the shelf. Now I realised it was not important, and I no longer had the feeling that I must marry or be a failure. The Mother provided other means for a woman to fulfil Her purposes.

Early on the moving-in day I went up to the house with Dahut, who had taken time off from the cares of governing. We went on horseback, and after us rode a detachment of soldiers. Gradlon had given his daughter her own palace guard, and they went with her everywhere now. Another of the burdens of office. Along with them came a wagon with my belongings, which I had sent for from Kemper. My mother had sent a letter-tablet with them, in which she told me that all was well with her. Her pregnancy was going well, and Meriadauc was delighted – 'as if he had done something clever', she said. I was pleased for her. She had had a hard enough life, and she deserved some happiness now.

We reached the house without mishap, although the wagoner said he had had some awkward moments. Not only was his cart heavily laden, but the furniture which had been made for me was piled unsteadily on it. It was considered bad luck to break anything moving into a new home, and he had not wanted to be blamed. Fortunately nothing happened to blame anyone for.

'Look,' said Dahut. 'Someone's left a welcome.'

On the doorstep there were some flowers, freshly picked, and next to them a loaf of freshly baked bread and a bundle of logs. It was to wish me health, plenty to eat, and warmth in my new home.

'I wonder who can have done it!' I exclaimed, thinking of Cynan.

'Ah,' said Dahut, knowingly. 'I hear the word is abroad that the wise-woman's house is to be occupied again. The peasants like to make it clear that they welcome those with power. Life is safer that way.'

'Power? Me?' I was amazed.

'They think so. It is known that Megan taught you much.'

'I must put them right about that,' I said earnestly, but Dahut disagreed.

'Don't disillusion them. If they believe in you, your medicines will work better. Then they will believe in you more, and the medicines will work better still.'

And so I have often found it. Through means we can only guess at, the mind sometimes has the most amazing influence on the body. So I took Dahut's advice, and never did anything to disabuse people about my supposed powers. If it comes to it, to be called by a goddess is to be granted a little power.

My things were moved in by midday, and I spent some time with Dahut arranging them the way I wanted. Then we packed the labourers off and stopped for something to eat. The guards sat outside and ate food which they had brought, and drank their appalling watered vinegar, a legacy of the Romans.

'Do you know?' said Dahut suddenly. 'I haven't had a swim since last year. Let's go down to the beach afterwards and say hello to the Ocean.'

'Dahut, don't you have official business to see to?'

'No. Not today. I told them I would be busy all day. Besides, what is so urgent that it can't wait until tomorrow? No, let's spend a little time together. We don't often get the chance.'

And so after the meal we went down the cliff path, leaving the guards back in the trees.

'Are you sure they'll stay there?' I asked Dahut.

'I think so. Anyway, if not it'll give them a treat! Did you see that nice young officer with them? Maybe he'll come down and give us both a treat!'

'Dahut!'

She laughed at me. 'I forgot you were already fully occupied in that quarter. It's different for a princess, you know. Everyone's available, but no one dares make the first move.'

'Actually,' I said, 'I haven't seen you in private to tell you, but I'm not occupied at all now.' And I told her the story of Cynan's visit.

'Ah, well, that explains why he's spending so much time at Ys.'

'Cynan?'

'Yes. He's often there these days. I wondered why, since he's supposed to be so busy with his father's estate, but now it's clear. I suppose he's looking for a society wife.'

'I suppose so.'

She looked at me sidelong. 'Well, I'm sorry, but you've made your choice, haven't you, just as I've made mine?'

'You?'

'Oh, yes. Ys is my city. Mine alone. I couldn't hand it over to anyone now, no matter how good a husband. It's my work, and I must carry it through.'

We were at the foot of the cliff now. We went down to the water's edge. We could see Ys around the headland on our right.

'It's like a dream,' said Dahut. 'It shimmers there like a mirage, but when you approach it doesn't fade.'

We took our clothes off and stepped into the water.

'Gods above and below!' Dahut yelled. 'It's freezing!'

I had another visitor the day before Beltane. I had been out gathering plants for my medicines. It was too early in the year yet for many of them, but there is something in every season. As I made my way back to the house I saw a white horse tethered to one of the trees at the edge of the clearing. I was expecting no one. Even the peasants were not coming to visit me yet, and they didn't have horses anyway. I knew no one with a white horse, so it was with some nervousness that I pushed open the front door and walked quietly in.

There was a figure standing just inside, wrapped in a pale grey robe with a hood. As I pushed the door open the figure turned, and shrank back with a gasp. It took my eyes a moment or two to adjust to the dimness.

'Coel!'

He pulled the hood down.

'I'm sorry,' he stammered. 'Just for a moment then ... With the light behind you I couldn't see clearly...'

'No, Coel, I'm sorry. It's only me. When I first came back I felt as if she was still here, too. But the dead do not return, I think.'

He nodded, and turned away towards the living quarters. I followed.

'You have come for Beltane?'

'Yes. I always used to. I nearly didn't this year, but there was nowhere else I wanted to go, so in the end I gave in to habit. Besides, I needed to see it all at least once more'

'I know. One does. But here, let me give you some food and drink. Come into the new kitchen, and see the alterations Dahut has had done for me.'

'I saw some of her other alterations, down the coast there.'

'Ah, yes. At last she has her city by the sea. Isn't it wonderful? All our dreams coming true.'

He smiled. 'Perhaps.'

'Have you come far today?'

'I rode from Kemper yesterday. The roads were good, and I stayed the night in a village along the route. In the past year though I have been all over Western Europe. The news is not good. Barbarians on the move everywhere.'

'Do you think we may escape the worst here?'

'You may, but I do not think anywhere will be left entirely unscathed. Strangely enough, I hear the Britons are rallying, under this High King, Uther. He has a son, too, who is said to be a great military commander in the making. Arthur, they call him.'

It was thus that I heard of Arthur for the first time, as I cut bread and poured beer for Coel. 'And the news in Kemper?'

'All seems well. The King is said to be very pleased with his new city, and with his daughter's abilities. The Bishop was not so happy, it seems. There was some public discussion about it the day before I left.'

'What's the matter with Corentin this time?'

'Churches, or rather one church in particular. The one in the town square at Ys.'

'But there isn't one.'

'The Bishop's point exactly.'

'Oh, gods above and below, does this mean more trouble?'

He nodded. 'I expect it does. The Princess is still subject to her father, and she cannot do much about it if he commands a church to be built.'

Coel looked straight at me, and raised one eyebrow quizzically.

I offered Coel the hospitality of my house for the night, and he was glad enough to accept. It saved him the additional journey into Ys, although he wanted to see the town the next day. We talked over old times, and inevitably touched on the violent events of the previous Beltane.

'It's not really the religion that's to blame,' said Coel. 'I've done some studying of it since last year, you know, read some of their holy scriptures, spoken to some of their priests. This Jesus person never hurt anyone in his life. Peace, love of one's fellows, self-sacrifice, generosity to those in need – these are the things he preached. Fine things. It's those who came after who corrupted the message to serve their own ends. It's not Jesus who's to blame, it's the Church, people like Corentin, and that murderous fellow here – Johannes. Romans, all of them.'

'Romans? Surely they're Celts.'

'Romans in spirit. You know, there is a battle going on within the Church itself, a battle for power. The Bishop of Rome demands to be recognised as the head of the Church, as head over all the bishops. Some of them won't agree, and there is every possibility that the Celtic clergy may break away and found their own church.'

'King Gradlon said he thought the Church was a force for unity.'

The harper smiled. 'Yes, so it might be. But only if the clergy all accept the authority of Rome.' He paused for a moment. 'You know, the noble families of Rome can't get good jobs for their sons any more. The army is a rabble of German mercenaries, hardly the career for a gentleman these days. The civil service is in chaos because the central authority has collapsed absolutely since the death of Valentinian. Do you know where the sons are going these days for a secure career? They're all joining the Church. It's the one opening for hundreds of educated young gentlemen.' He shook his head in wonderment. 'The Church will not save the Empire. The Church will *be* the Empire. My guess is that they'll still be burning us hundreds of years from now. Us and other heretics yet undreamed of.' He sighed, and looked into the dying embers of the fire.

Beltane night itself was like the old ones. I wore a plain white robe like the one Megan had worn. It was not that I sought to take her place. It just seemed that plainness and purity were in order at a religious festival. Coel agreed, and he knew much more about the old beliefs than I did. He too wore white, and carried his harp with him up the hill. I felt a tingle go through me as I caught the first beats of the drum, but the drummer was not Cynan. A youth whom I did not know was squatting, almost in the same place, calling the assembly together in the time-honoured way.

There were fewer people than in the previous year, but we were not dismayed. It was only to be expected that some would stay away. There would be time enough. Dahut would rule here, and the Goddess would be respected, and Her followers would grow as time went on. Coel's words about the lack of a church in Ys came to mind, but I banished them firmly. This was a time for optimism.

Suddenly there was talking and happy laughter. A new group of people approached from the other side of the hill. They were richly dressed, and clustered around their leader, a woman who looked like the princess she was. Her eyes flashed in the light of the burning torches. Her lips were full and red. She too was wearing a white robe, but on her breast hung a solid gold disc with engraved flames radiating from the centre. As she came forward she raised her hands, and someone put a torch to the fire, which kindled in a sudden burst of flame. The fire glittered and flashed on the gold and the white cloth. Dahut entered the hilltop clearing like the sun coming out in the middle of the night.

Chapter Twenty-Two

Dahut wanted all her friends to come and break their fast at the palace, where she had arranged for a huge quantity of food to be prepared. Coel pleaded tiredness and went back to my cottage, but I stayed with the party. We came down from the mountain as the sun's first rays were breaking through the clouds to the east. The light threw long shadows, and the contrast between light and dark made it more difficult to see in some places than when it was night. We could not see Ys at all, because the cliffs threw a cloak of darkness over the coast, and anyone who was not with us was in bed, so there were no lights. Thus it was that we could not see what had happened until we were entering the city gate and found ourselves paddling ankle-deep in salt water.

There was consternation among our company. Many of the people had homes in the town, and feared for their belongings. If it was ankle-deep here, how bad was it by the sea front?

'We have offended the Sea-God,' wailed one woman.

'Perhaps he is jealous of our devotion to the Mother,' suggested someone else.

'Superstitious nonsense!' cried Dahut, although she was ready enough to see the gods at work when it suited her. 'No, the explanation is simple. The Sea-god has been hearing how beautiful our city is, and he's coming to see for himself!'

There was some nervous laughter at this, but it helped to restore calm. Meanwhile Dahut exhibited the decisiveness for which her father had praised her.

''Listen, I have work for some of you! Nennius, go to the harbourmaster and find out when the tide is due to go down. Ban, you can go and get Plotinus out of bed. Tell him I want to collect all the masons together to discuss the strengthening of the sea defences. That will be straight after breakfast. Then you, Rivelin...'

And so it went on. She deliberately picked out the most nervous, so that action would calm their fears. The worst thing is for people to feel that they are powerless. Dahut knew this, and that is why she steered the talk away from gods to high tides, and from divine jealousy to practical matters like sea walls. Men cannot fight gods, but they can certainly build walls. When she had given the orders she wanted we carried on paddling towards the palace as if we always approached it like this, our feet sloshing through the water, and sending ripples running to the walls of the houses. When we were at the steps Dahut turned to me with a smile.

'It's a good thing we're too close to the sea to have cellars. Just imagine what would happen to the wine!'

I laughed dutifully, but in truth I was very anxious. I didn't believe in the jealousy of the Sea-god, but I did believe in the possibility that the masons had got something seriously wrong. Still, we were soon breakfasting at Dahut's long table, and it's wonderful what a difference a full stomach can make to one's spirits.

'I'll consult with the masons afterwards,' Dahut said. 'We'll soon see to what needs doing. If it's higher walls, we'll build higher walls. You'll see. Nothing is too good for my city.'

'But Princess,' said one of her new advisers, 'can the royal coffers be opened yet again? Ys has cost the King plenty already.'

She smiled knowingly. 'You leave my father to me. The cost of better sea defences will be small compared with what has already gone. Besides, what can we do? We can't let the city be flooded too often, or the houses will fall down.'

I remember the logic of this seemed irrefutable at the time.

We were interrupted by Nennius, the young man who had been sent to the harbourmaster.

'My Princess,' he said bowing. 'The harbourmaster says that such tides as this are known to happen rarely. He says that the next tide will be dangerous, and the one after, but that we can expect lower tides thereafter.'

'And did he mention the sea walls?'

'Begging your pardon, Princess, the sea walls are plenty high enough. The water is

still several feet below the top. But there has to be a gap for the ships. That is the problem. The harbourmaster says there must be a sea gate.'

'A sea gate?'

'So he says, Your Highness. A gate which will close to keep the sea out.'

She turned to the rest of us. 'A gate to keep out the sea!'

We all laughed as we were supposed to.

'I will enquire,' she said. 'I will find out if such a thing can be built. I will send to Rome if necessary.'

'Small point in that,' I suggested. 'There are no tides in the Mediterranean.'

'No tides?'

'No, I doubt if you will find your expertise there.'

She pondered that one for a moment. 'No matter. We shall find it somewhere. Now, let us eat and drink, and dry our feet! Nennius, join us.'

And the young man sat next to her, preening himself at the honour, and giving her intense looks every time she glanced in his direction. The poor man was clearly besotted. In fact, as I looked around the table I thought I recognised the condition in several others. I supposed it was inevitable if you were as beautiful as she was, and I saw no harm in it. When, later, Dahut and Nennius slipped away together I hardly noticed.

Before dark a messenger was already on his way to Kemper to tell the King about the need for a sea gate, and to ask for finance. Dahut's city was not yet self-supporting by any means.

I went back to my cottage, collecting some herbs on the way. It was late afternoon, and the sun was low. I picked some young comfrey leaves, and that reminded me, as it always did, of our first lesson in herb lore from Megan. Once again, I suddenly felt as if she were present, somehow. I found myself on my knees, praying aloud.

'Mother, whatever it is you want from me, I will give it, only let my friend's spirit rest.'

It may have been nonsense, I only know I felt compelled to say it. I felt as if my mind were being prised open like an oyster. A sudden gust of wind blew through the wood, sending last year's fallen leaves flurrying through the undergrowth. I felt ...entered! And as the wind died down I seemed to hear a distant voice, singing a mournful song.

I came to myself suddenly, and shook my head. The singing was still there. A man was singing, and there were the tones of a harp. Of course, it was Coel, at the cottage. I picked myself up unsteadily, and plodded homeward, listening intently. It was a lament for a friend. He had composed it about Megan, I knew that at once. His soul was in that song.

He was sitting alone by the fire. As I entered the room he stopped, and turned towards me, putting the harp down. I crossed the room and pulled his head to my breast. He looked up and opened his mouth, but I stopped it with my own. To this day I do not know if I was possessed by the Goddess, or Megan, or my own nature, but I did not want to hear any conventional protests.

Later, as we lay in the dark, he spoke.
'You know, I never thought of us – well, like this.'
'Nor I.'
'I would never have made the first move.'
'I know. But of course, it's all your fault really.'
I was smiling, but he seemed genuinely alarmed.
'What do you mean?'
'It's your singing, you wicked man. I think you put some magic in it to charm away a woman's resistance.'

He chuckled at that. 'Now that really would be magic. Oh, if only I'd really had it, what a life I might have led.'

'What sort of life have you led?'

'Oh, a wandering, poor sort of life, compared to many. A bard's life is like that.'

'Have you never stayed in one place?'

'Not for long. I stay if people ask me to, sometimes. A bard needs work like any other man. But I'm always afraid of being forgotten if I don't keep visiting the same old haunts. Besides, you'd be surprised how easily people tire of you if you're there the whole time. They don't want the same songs all the time, sung in the same way. No, no, I soon move on. I try to leave them still wanting more, so that I'm always welcome again. It's a delicate business.'

'And women? Do you like to leave them the same way?'

He chuckled. 'Oh, there haven't been so many as you might think. Everyone knows a bard travels alone. He will never be anybody, not as the world sees it – no land, no houses. Most women want a home, a family, stability. So do most men, however much they pretend they enjoy the single life. I don't have much to offer most women.'

'And Megan?'

'Ah, Megan. I thought you might ask.' He sighed, and paused a moment longer. 'Megan was not like most women. She had her own way to go. She knew I had mine. She knew there would be other women along the way, as I knew there would be other men. It was not important. But we loved each other, in a way not like the love of most men and women. We shared much over the years, but we felt no desire to ... to merge our lives. Can you understand what I mean?'

'Yes, I can understand that. Cynan could not, nor even Dahut, I think.'

'Cynan is a young man. He will learn.'

'I'm young too,' I protested.

'And don't I know it!' He was smiling in the dark, I could tell. 'But you know a great deal that he does not. That means your soul is older.'

'Oh, stop. It's too late at night for metaphysics.'

'Then what would you suggest?'

I playfully nibbled the nearest part of him, which happened to be his shoulder. 'Let me show you.'

He made a mock protest. 'Oh, no. Take care, I'm an old man. I am feeble! Send for the wise-woman!'

'She's here,' I murmured. 'And she has just the medicine you need.'

Dahut's messenger returned from Kemper in a few days, but the message he brought was not the one she was looking for. We were in her private chambers at the time, supervising some of the final arrangements she was making there, new furnishings having recently arrived by sea from Italy. A servant brought the news that the messenger was in the great hall.

'I will come at once,' she said, and swept out of the room after the departing man.

'Let's hope it's the answer you want,' I said, remembering Coel's words about Corentin, and his efforts to increase his power.

The great hall was empty except for the messenger who knelt as soon as we entered.

'Rise, rise,' said Dahut impatiently. 'What word have you from my father?'

'His Majesty expresses his most devoted fatherly affection ...'

'Yes, yes. Cut out all the ceremonial stuff. I just want the message.'

'Well, Your Highness.'

Dahut was thoroughly exasperated by now. 'Get to the point. Will he grant my request to finance the building of a sea gate?'

The messenger looked helplessly at me, but all I could do was shrug.

'I am sorry, Your Highness, to bear bad news. His Majesty has refused.'

'What? Refused?' She looked thunderstruck. 'Impossible!' She wheeled on the unfortunate messenger. 'You're lying! Why do you lie to me?'

'No, Your Highness, I swear. Why would I lie?'

I decided to intervene, as she was pushing the man in her anger.

'My Princess! It's not the man's fault!' She turned towards me, shaking with fury, and I put both hands on her shoulders. 'He is only bringing the King's answer, as you told him to. He is not responsible for its nature.'

She gradually brought her breathing under control, and looked at the man again.

'Did you not tell the King that our citizens are begging for help to save their homes?'

'I did, Your Highness. He says: "Why should these people, for whom he has already done so much, complain about their misfortunes when the remedy is in their own hands?" He says: "Perhaps God would not have deserted them if they had invited him into their city, where God has no house at all."'

'"No house?" God has no...' Dahut almost choked on the words in her outrage. She gripped the arms of her throne and with a visible effort regained her self-control.

'So that's it! He wants me to build a church!'

'Yes, Your Highness. His Majesty commands that a church be built in the main square.'

'But that's a market square. Or will be, when the town is fully populated.'

'The King says a market can meet anywhere. God's house, he says, must be at the centre of things, as is your own palace.'

Dahut turned to me. 'Well, I suppose we can always lay the foundations. It's not my fault if constructional problems hold things up.'

The messenger spoke. 'With respect, Your Highness, there is more. The King says he expects the church to be built by the end of the summer. He will visit Ys then, and says he expects to be able to give thanks at the Lord's altar. It is a royal command, he says, and disobedience is ... is not to be thought of.'

'I don't believe this,' breathed Dahut furiously. 'What if it rains all summer? Men can't build in the rain!'

'His Majesty did not say. He did say, though, that you may put the matter of the sea gate to him again when the church is complete.'

'I see,' she murmured grimly. 'I am a donkey, to be driven with the stick, but rewarded with a choice morsel if I'm good.'

'We are all the King's subjects,' I reminded her. 'His word is law.'

'I know, but he's my father too. I thought ... well, I didn't expect to be given orders like any captain in the army. He said I could rule here.'

'It's his religion, 'I said. 'It's the one thing he won't give up on. Let the church be built, and see how many attend it.'

She nodded, and dismissed the messenger with a wave of her hand. We walked slowly back to her private chambers, where she threw herself down on the bed and wept tears of anger.

'It's that crafty bishop! Damn Corentin, I'd give anything to be rid of him! We used to laugh in Kemper, we used to enjoy life. Then Corentin turned the song of life into a dirge! Well, I won't let him do the same here. Ys will be a city of joy and laughter, of music and dancing. Then, when I am Queen, the whole country will be the same.'

I sat next to her and put my arms around her, paying little heed to what she said. I knew that much of it was the product of her immediate feelings and these would change with time. Still, as I rocked her gently in my arms, I could not suppress my own anxiety. The city was scarcely finished, and Dahut and her father were already divided.

The church was started immediately the danger of flooding had receded. Dahut, spurred on by the hope that her father might finance the sea gate, got the builders to work at top speed. The church was a wooden hall, unlike the brick and stone temples of Roman days, and it was much quicker to build. Even so, it was all the men could do to complete it in the stated time. But by midsummer it was done, only the decorative details left to be finished. Dahut sent word to the King that all would be ready for him when he came to Ys, and he replied formally, thanking her for her devotion and telling her that he would be bringing a priest with him when he came. There would be a service to consecrate the new church at the end of August.

'Consecrate the new church, indeed!' said Dahut in disgust. 'Oh, what are we to do?'

She had come to see me in my cottage, which was proving to be a refuge for her sometimes. She herself was glad to point this out, and to laugh at her own early misgivings.

'It is Corentin who is the problem,' I said. 'He is always there to whisper in your father's ear, and we are a long way off. If it was the other way round his influence would be much less.'

She sat up suddenly, as if struck by sudden pain. 'That's it! Keri, you are a prophetess, I swear it!'

'What are you talking about?'

'When my father comes this summer I shall persuade him to stay permanently.'

She got up and began to pace the room.

'Yes, that's it! Corentin's had things all his own way because he's always been at the centre of power. Well, two can play at that game. As soon as he arrives I'll get to work on my father. I'll get him to make Ys the capital and rule the kingdom from there! Then we shall see who can whisper in the King's ear!'

Privately I thought this an unlikely idea, but I knew better than to argue. These days, Dahut took such enthusiastic flights of fancy as often as she flew into rages. Indeed, it was often the collapse of the one which caused the other, and the unhealthy cycle worried me. I watched her go that day with mixed feelings – part foreboding, and actually part relief. The house might be her refuge, but it was also my place of work, and her presence did tend to inhibit people from coming.

They came frequently these days. As far as the local people were concerned I seemed to have taken over from Megan. The people of the town came also, although their tradition was different. Some of these I knew from my visits to the palace, but they behaved very differently when they were on my ground. I was also visited by the midwife, who thought I was trying to steal her livelihood, and was very relieved to find that I wanted to learn from her instead. The peasants paid me in kind, of course. Sometimes they had nothing, but I would treat them anyway. Then one day, maybe weeks later, I would find a gift left on the doorstep, usually some vegetable which was now in season, or a share in an animal which had been killed. They paid their debts, those people.

It was a matter of pride. It was probably also the fear of a spell if they failed to show their appreciation! In spite of all my protestations, they still thought I was at least half witch.

The city people were less superstitious, and they paid in gold. I had little use for this in the ordinary way, but I kept some hidden and used some in the market. In terms of riches, I suppose the townspeople were my best customers, but I preferred the manner of the peasant folk. They were shy, but they treated me as someone with a skill to practise. The rich treat everyone like servants.

I was glad now for all the time I had spent learning Megan's ways, and notes I had made of her treatments. I would never have remembered it all. Her spirit no longer seemed to inhabit the place, but her influence would last as long as I did.

Coel had to move on before midsummer. He usually went to a festival in Gaul at this time. There was still some trade, still some wealth, and still some employment for a bard. He kissed me many times, then mounted his white horse and rode slowly away through the forest. We both shed some tears, but we both knew he had to go, as I had to stay.

It was now some months since I had left Kemper, and in all that time I had heard little of my mother and Meriadauc. She, being pregnant, was not fit for a long journey on horseback, and Meriadauc's business kept him occupied. Still, I had hoped for more than the one letter she had sent. Then, I reasoned, the whole process of sending and receiving letters was a haphazard affair. One had to find a friend or trustworthy traveller who was going in the right direction, and even then there was no certainty that the letter – or even the traveller – would reach the other end of the road. There were robbers in places, treacherous paths in others, and people might simply change their minds for some reason and go somewhere else. Dahut had spoken of arranging a regular letter service by ship to Kemper, but that was still to be organised. Therefore, although keen to hear about my mother, I was not unduly anxious.

A few days after Coel's departure I went out to gather yarrow. This did not grow near the cottage, but away inland near the sides of the Kemper road, and it was mid-morning before I reached the place. It was a fine day, and I thought I would probably catch a good deal of sun before I was through. I had been at my work for about twenty minutes when I heard the lone horseman, and straightened up to have a look. I could not see much yet. The road curved away between bushes and trees, and the horse was not yet in view, and travelling slowly. As I watched, it rounded the bend, only walking, and with its rider hunched forward as if he was very tired. I was so unsuspecting that the man had approached to within a few yards before I recognised my stepfather, and a cold chill settled on my heart.

'Meriadauc!'

I knew at once why he had come. There could be only one reason for his long and lonely journey. If I had had any doubts, the sight of Meriadauc's lined and haggard face, a sickly white in spite of the sun, would have told me. I sat down on a rock, and he dismounted and sat on another opposite. I spoke again, although the lump rising into my throat made it difficult.

'What ... how did it happen?'

He looked sharply at me. 'You know?'

'How could I not?' He looked alarmed at that.

'Oh, Meriadauc, don't be silly! It's not witchcraft! Why else would you be here?' Strange that I found myself denying being a witch, just as Megan had done. 'Tell me what happened.'

'It was childbed fever.'

'Childbed? But she wasn't due for another three months yet!' My voice had taken on a high-pitched and wavering tone.

'She had a miscarriage, a bad one. The fever came. In three days she was gone.'

He blamed himself, poor man.

'You mustn't think what you're thinking.'

He looked startled. 'What's that?'

'You're thinking it was your fault – that she'd be alive if you hadn't insisted on marriage and children.'

He nodded dumbly.

'Well, you shouldn't. She wanted it more than anything, you know. I urged her to it, too. You gave her more happiness than she'd ever had in her life. We should be grateful she had that much before she died.'

He looked at me in amazement. 'You're a very remarkable young woman.'

'Yes,' I said, my eyes brimming over. 'I have a great capacity for weeping.'

He took my hands in his, and we sat in the sun and cried like children.

If this seems to have become a sombre narrative, then all I can say is that this was a sombre time in my life. It was also a time of great change. In a short space of time I had lost my mother, lost Cynan, and been parted from Coel. I had also drifted somewhat away from Dahut, although this was not as difficult to bear as it would once have been. Her violent and unpredictable swings of emotion worried me, but they made her an uncomfortable person to be with. Oh, I saw her often enough, but I was no longer part of her daily life in the way I had been. On the other hand I too seemed to have started on a new path, serving the Goddess in the tradition of Megan, and earning my own living by doing so. It was as if the Goddess were removing all traces of my past life so as to leave me free for the new. That, at least, is how I comforted myself at the time. I suppose it was a variation on the theme of 'Never mind, it's all for the best.'

Whatever the truth of it, the fact is that I had a great need to be busy, and suddenly found a great demand for my services. There was an outbreak of a kind of influenza that summer. I never caught it, but many were very sick, and some old people died. Consequently, people's anxieties were high, and they would send for me at the first signs. Megan's recipes were put to the test, and seemed to help. At least, the ones who died had not been treated by me, so the idea went around that all might have died but for my intervention. The logic might be imperfect, but it kept me busy, and that did me good. At the beginning I had encountered some prejudice on account of my age, especially among the older people, but this quickly dwindled as the outbreak went on. Even when it was over I remained busy, for they now brought me many smaller problems which they had kept to themselves before. In return they gave me food, did work for me if I needed it, and offered a loyalty which was worth more than all of these in the end.

Meriadauc did not go back to Kemper immediately. He wanted to see Ys again, and to investigate the possibility of doing more business there. Dahut encouraged him. Ys had to be self-supporting, and trade was wealth. He did not stay at the cottage, apparently out of some sense of propriety, but Dahut insisted that he should stay at the palace. In any case, it was more convenient for business purposes to be in the city itself. He too seemed to need to be busy. He gave me some jewellery of my mother's which she had wanted me to have. In vain I protested that I had little use for it.

'Keep it,' he said. 'Even if you don't wear it, you never know when you may need its value. These are difficult times, and the value of money is not certain. The British have largely abandoned the Roman coinage, you know, and others may follow. But gold is always valuable, the more so when times are hard. Keep it by you.'

He came to see me often, and I think it was partly because my mother's death had quite shattered him. His manner was totally changed. He still looked haggard and pale, and he never seemed to laugh any more. I think seeing me reminded him of her, and he found some strange comfort in that. Strange, because such things usually work in the opposite way.

Then, before I knew it, the summer was almost over, the influenza died away, and the King came to Ys to view his new church.

Chapter Twenty-Three

Dahut held a banquet to welcome her father to the city, and I was asked to attend as a favour to her.

'I'll need all the support my friends can give me,' she said. 'He's written to say he's bringing that accursed cleric with him.'

By this she meant Corentin, of course. He was Bishop of Kemper, and Ys fell within his 'diocese', as he called it – a Roman word for an administrative district. It was inevitable that he should attend the consecration of a new church in his own area. We had still not heard who was to be the new priest.

'Just so long as it isn't Emrys,' I said to Dahut. 'I think I really would turn to witchcraft if he came.'

I did not see Gradlon's arrival, but came into Ys later that evening for the banquet. I must have been the only guest who was walking, to judge by the horse droppings which littered the streets. One has to be very careful in sandals!

We sat in the great hall of Dahut's palace. The royal guests were still in her private quarters, but when it was certain the rest had all arrived word was sent to her, and she and her father entered to a burst of applause and cheering. The people of the city and its surrounding area held Gradlon in the highest esteem. His faith in the place, as they saw it, had given it the chance to develop and grow rich. Why, that very day three ships had arrived from various foreign parts bringing goods to trade. The fishing fleet was already growing, the demand for food was encouraging the clearance of more farmland, and all the signs were better than one might have hoped. So, they thought of their wealth and cheered. Again, I thought that Dahut had better go carefully if she wanted to defy her father.

I looked anxiously around as we took our places, but it seemed Cynan was not there. There was a fine-looking young woman almost opposite. She had long black hair, elaborately curled and arranged, and wore a good deal of gold and silk about her person. Her features were fine and aristocratic, her eyes black as her hair, her fingers long and delicate. I could imagine them sewing a fine seam, or fluttering lightly across the strings of a harp. I saw her lean across to the person next to her, obviously asking who I was. When she was told, I saw the eyebrows rise in acknowledgment, but she did not speak to me. As I could see no reason why she should have any interest in me, I put her out of my mind.

I had been placed near Dahut; both she and the King addressed occasional remarks to me. He was as friendly and courteous to me as ever. Corentin sat opposite me, near the elegant young lady. He was cool but formally polite. He nodded approvingly when I told him that I no longer lived at Dahut's court.

Clearly, he felt that I was one pagan less to fight. I did not tell him why I had gone, and he did not think to ask.

The evening was reminiscent of the old times at Kemper, but it was in many ways a more cheerful affair. Everyone except Corentin drank too much, but Gradlon became good-humoured instead of melancholic, and told a number of genuinely funny stories. Dahut was full of the news about Ys, how everything was really getting organised, and how bright the future looked. There was the little matter of the sea gate, of course, but then the King had agreed to consider this anew when the church was built. Tomorrow he could inspect it and see how he felt. Gradlon nodded and hiccupped cheerily. He seemed quite changed – relaxed, even a little sleepy, and refusing to worry about anything. The evening passed off well, although it was rather subdued by Dahut's normal standards. More and more these days, her parties had a reputation for a certain wildness. Fortunately, Corentin did not yet seem to have discovered this, but he would if he stayed long enough.

I was staying in the palace that night, in a room not far from Dahut's own. It was a small room, intended for a servant, I think, but it was enough for me. Dahut saw me off to bed in the corridor. She was rather drunk, and propped herself upright with the aid of a servant girl, who was highly amused at the whole scene.

'G'night, then,' Dahut said, swaying. 'Sorry the room isn't up to standard, but things are pretty crowded here tonight.'

She had said all this earlier. 'Go to bed,' I told her. 'You need to sleep it off.'

She persisted, as drunks do. 'No, you must understand why it is. I don't want you thinking I don't value you – value you more than this other crowd, eh?'

'It's all right. I do understand.'

'Right. That's all right, then.'

'Yes. Go to bed.'

A thought struck her, and she giggled. 'You know, we could have saved space by making the guests share beds. That would've been interesting. Who could we have put in with Corentin, eh?' She chuckled lewdly. 'I'll bet he likes boys. Could we have found him a boy, d'you think?'

I found myself entering into the drunken fantasy. 'Corentin's a typical monk. He probably has cold baths and flagellates himself to drive out the devils.'

'Well, at least he does bath.' Dahut giggled stupidly. 'And what about you?' She shot a sideways glance at the servant girl, who smiled conspiratorially.

'Me?'

'Who could we put in with you? Who would you fancy? Nennius, perhaps, or Hoel, or Con?'

'No, thank you,' I said pompously. 'If I want a man I'm quite capable of choosing my own.'

She giggled again, and turned away, still leaning on the servant. They went into her room, and as the door shut I heard a peal of laughter from both of them. I knew Dahut thought me mad to have slept with Coel, and I wished I had never told her. She was convinced that I had only done it out of pity, or because I could get nothing better – by which she meant younger. As for her, she did not take me into her confidence as she used to. Dahut needed a person to be there the whole time. I was only beginning to realise how dependent on others she was, and the influences to which this weakness left her exposed. Sometimes I felt I should have stayed at Ys after all. Then I would think that if the Princess couldn't look after her own interests there was little chance that I could do it for her. No, she had made her bed and now she must lie on it. The fact that she seldom lay on it alone was only a further cause for anxiety. Quite apart from the risks there might be to her health, lovers were almost certain to become involved in court intrigue. I worried whether she knew what she was doing.

On our first confident night at Ys I had wished for the power to see the future. Now I was glad it was hidden from my eyes.

The next morning I was woken by the servant girl who had put Dahut to bed the night before. She brought me a bowl of water and some perfumed oil and a towel. She had left me to sleep late, and after the night's revels I was glad to do so. Still, when I enquired after the rest of the guests the girl told me they were already up, and attending the service of consecration in the new church.

'Her Highness said that you did not want to attend, you being a follower of the Mother Goddess.'

'Her Highness was right. What's more, I don't think Corentin would have me in his church. Tell me, what is your name?'

'Tilda, *Domina*.'

'Tilda? What sort of a name is that? German?'

'Oh, no, *Domina*. I am Frankish.'

The Franks were a German tribe as far as I was concerned, but I let it pass.

'Well, tell me, Tilda, how did you come to be here? The Franks live to the north of Gaul, don't they?'

'Indeed they do, but my mother followed my father when he came to fight for the great Aëtius. When my father died we were left without anything, but Aëtius gave my mother a grant, because of my father's service to him. She used it to come to Kemper and settle, far from the wars, she said.'

'Where is your mother?'

'She died also. Last year. Her Highness took me into her service, and now I wait on her personally.'

There was a note of pride in her voice, and why not? She had done well for the daughter of a mercenary soldier.

'But you are not at church?'

Tilda laughed out loud as she left the room. 'Not me, *Domina*! Nor Her Highness, if she could have her own way. She'll soon have her sea gate, I reckon!'

So the Frankish servant was in the Princess's confidence. I was mildly surprised, but Dahut was always one to speak openly when she could. A person's station in life made little difference to her.

After washing I dressed and went to the window. It was a fine day, and a light breeze off the sea brought the tang of salt. Seagulls wheeled and cried over the bay, while the town lay quiet in the foreground. Many people were at the church service. Dahut had pressed her friends into supplying a convincing congregation for the Bishop, and the normal business of the town had been suspended. There was a gentle knock at the door. I assumed it was the servant again, and spoke rather crossly when I bade her enter.

It was not the girl. It was the beautiful dark woman I had noticed at last night's banquet. She looked superb, as though her appearance had demanded much work on the part of a maid. She was clearly the sort of well-off young lady who would have one. She wore a rich dark blue gown, cut very modestly, with a gold crucifix on a chain around her neck. I had not noticed one the night before. When she spoke her voice betrayed a soft Welsh lilt.

'I hope I am not disturbing you.'

'No, not at all, but I fear this is no place to receive a guest, even if the bed had been made and the bowl cleared.'

'It is private. That is what matters.'

I gestured towards the crucifix. 'Why are you not at the service?'

'I go to the mass on Sundays. Other services are not essential, and I needed to see you privately on a matter of urgency.'

I was puzzled. 'But I don't even know you. Do you want to consult me about a health problem?'

'Not exactly.' She hesitated. 'My name is Gwladys, daughter of Aneirin.'

The name meant nothing to me. 'I am sorry, I still don't know you.'

She hesitated again. 'I, well, I don't know quite how to say this.'

She was fingering the crucifix nervously, and kept glancing towards the door, as if to make sure that escape was still possible. It dawned on me suddenly that she was actually afraid of me.

'Please,' I said. 'Sit down, and tell me what troubles you. I will help if I can.'

She sat on the bed, and her face began to colour. 'It concerns someone we both know. Well, someone you knew well. Very well.' She looked at me helplessly, and the truth hit me at once.

'Cynan!'

She started, and her face suddenly lost its colour again. 'You know!'

'I know nothing, and unless you tell me I don't look like finding anything out! What is it? Is he your lover?'

She looked away in embarrassment. 'Not that. Well, not as you mean it.' She turned back to face me, and spoke with some difficulty. 'He has asked my father for my hand.'

'Ah! I see.'

'I know, that is, I have heard, that you and he ...' She tailed off awkwardly. 'What I mean is, what do you think about it?'

'What do I think? What does it matter what I think? It's not my business.'

'I thought you might be angry ...'

'Oh dear, Gwladys. Were you afraid the dreaded witch might put a curse on you?'

She began to protest, but a look at her face told me that was exactly what she had feared. I threw my head back and laughed. She smiled nervously.

'You mean you don't mind?'

I shook my head. 'No. In fact, I wish you both well. Cynan and I were never destined to marry, I think.'

'Did he never ask you?'

I decided a lie would be the kindest thing. 'The question never arose. It's strange.'

'What is?'

'You coming here to see if I minded your marriage. I might as well ask if you minded the fact that Cynan and I were once ... what we were.'

She suddenly became very earnest. 'Oh, no. His past life doesn't matter now.'

'You are very generous.'

She shook her head. 'You don't understand. Cynan's past sins have been washed away. He has been born again in Christ.'

That hit me very much harder than the news of the marriage. Of course, I should have known that a Christian lady would never marry a pagan. In any case, her Christian father would never have permitted it.

'That surprises me greatly,' I managed at last. 'So that is why de did not come to the Beltane fire?'

'Yes. And will not again.'

'Well, then, even less reason why I should bear you ill will. A Christian man would be no good to me, a follower of the Mother Goddess. I'm sorry he has gone over, though. And after what we have seen. Our friend Megan was murdered by Christians. So was her child.'

'Yes, I know. Please don't judge us all by that. Christ urges us all to be kind to children.'

'I do not judge, I just observe that the actions do not fit the words, except when it is convenient. It starts with Jesus preaching' – I tried to remember Coel's words – 'peace, love and concern for others. It finishes with a dear friend screaming her last breath in the flames. And she was not the first. The Christians' campaign of murder and persecution started with the Emperor Constantine.'

She coloured again, and rose to her feet. 'I'm sorry that you feel like that. I shall pray for you.'

'Save your breath. But rest assured you have nothing to fear from me. You will make him a better wife than I ever could. A good Christian wife, a society wife. It's what he wanted.'

She went to the door, and then turned. 'Well, thank you. I can see now that you are not what they say. I shall pray that you see the light.' And she went out.

I wondered what exactly it was 'they' said.

The palace had a long balcony along the south side at first-floor level. I was sitting there when Dahut came back from the service, her face like thunder.

'I will kill someone before this is over!'

Without breaking stride she picked up a plant pot. Turning round she flung it the length of the balcony. It hit the wall in a flurry of shattering earthenware, soil and flowers.

'Dahut, whatever is the matter?'

She sat down heavily next to me. 'It's that damned cleric!'

'Corentin?'

'Who else? He finished the mumbo-jumbo he came for and then began to lecture us all on the Christian life. It's obvious my father is completely under his thumb again. He just sat there nodding sagely, while that dried-up old bugger warned us all of the dangers of hell fire. He said that the City of Ys had got off to a bad start by not building the church before all else. He complained about the dress of the people, their supposed immorality. He must have spies here, he knows too much. And what he doesn't know he makes up. He didn't mention me by name, but he did go on and on about the duty of those in authority to set an example of righteousness, instead of dissipating themselves in revelry and pleasure. Gods above and below, I wish I led half the life he thinks I do! I'd be half dead with pleasure!'

Having heard a thing or two about Dahut's revelries I kept silent on that score, but there was something else I wanted to ask.

'Do we know who the new priest is to be, when Corentin goes back to Kemper?'

'Oh, some cadaverous-looking monk called Fracanus. Another dried-up eunuch! I'd say he's not too dangerous.'

'We thought that about Johannes,' I said thoughtfully. If Corentin had put someone weak in place here it was a miscalculation, and not typical of the man.

'Maybe, but I'd still say we're safe with this one. It's that thrice-accursed Corentin! He's the one behind it all.'

'When is your father going back to Kemper?'

'It's not certain. He's going to stay for a few days. Personally, I'd like him to stay here permanently where I can keep his ear, but I don't know if it's possible. The business of the kingdom has always been conducted from Kemper.'

'You could probably persuade him,' I offered. 'You always used to be able to.'

She nodded slowly, her eyes narrowing. 'Yes, I always could, couldn't I?'

I saw the gleam in her eyes, and a pang went through me.

'Careful, Dahut.'

She shook her head slightly, and that familiar far-away look appeared. I wondered what she was planning this time, and why she wouldn't tell me.

Corentin went back to Kemper that same week, but the King announced that he was going to stay for a while, and view this edge of his kingdom while based at Ys. I gave little more thought to this at the time, beyond assuming that Dahut's filial charm had prevailed again. I was busy with my work. The local people were now firmly in the habit of consulting me about a variety of problems, and there were plenty of ills to plague them. I resolutely turned away all those who wanted me to practise witchcraft, and there were many who did. At times I had to be firm in pointing out that I served the Mother, which meant using Her natural gifts to help others. Curses and spells were not a part of that, and nor were love potions. I reasoned that if the Goddess wanted to effect the union of a man and a woman She had already arranged a very fine way of achieving it.

I often looked out across the Bay of Ys, as it was called these days, and saw ships on their way to the port. They looked tiny, like a child's toys. As the autumn brought the first of the bad weather they came less often, and I heard that trade was suddenly bad again. Still, the wealth of the city was not in danger. Yet.

Dahut got her sea gate. The King, it was said, stayed indoors much of the time. He was rumoured to be ill, and leaving much of the business of state to his daughter. She imported the best coastal builders to be found, and they erected a great barrier of earth across the entrance to the harbour, so as to keep the sea back. Inside the entrance a great wooden gate was built. A sill was cut into the bedrock beneath it, and great stone jambs erected at each side of the entrance. When the gate was finally hung it was the most impressive construction anyone had seen. The outer face was covered in bronze plates, and studded with bolts. The top, twenty feet above the harbour bottom, was broad enough for a man to walk along it. When it was closed it would be strong enough to withstand the pounding of even a heavy sea.

The gate was designed to open outwards, so that if it was closed before high water the increasing pressure of the sea would hold it shut. Once the sea receded, however, the water in the harbour would push it open and find its way out. Thus, the sea would do most of the harbourmaster's work for him.

On the day that the gate was ready, Dahut announced a holiday and a celebration of the great event. Removal of the barrier of earth was begun as soon as the tide began to go down, so that as much time as possible would be available. The tide here runs right away from the cliffs at its lowest, leaving harbours dry. This meant that at low tide the workers – most of the able-bodied men of the surrounding countryside – could attack the barrier from both sides. By the time the tide was approaching the harbour entrance again, its path was completely cleared. The harbour walls were lined with people of all classes, waiting to see if the new gate would live up to expectations. The priest Fracanus was there, slightly disapproving. He seemed to feel that the architects were tempting Providence. Still, as the waters rose, even he had to admit that the city would benefit from the new gate.

We had a long wait. The builders had warned that the gate might not withstand the entire pressure of the sea if it was closed at low water. They seemed confident that it could cope with a difference in water levels of a few feet on either side, and that was all that was needed. By the time high water came, it was obvious that they had got their calculations right. The level outside the gate was a good four feet above the level inside, and the gate showed no signs of strain. Admittedly the sea was calm, but a cheer went up when the builders pronounced themselves satisfied, and Dahut announced an ox-roast in the market square. The King was there too, nodding amiably at everyone, but with his mind seemingly elsewhere. When I approached him to pay my respects it seemed as if he hardly knew me.

'Ah, yes, Keri, of course. And how is your dear mother?'

A chill passed over my heart.

'She... she died some months ago, Your Majesty.'

He looked around him in puzzlement, as if he had just woken up in the wrong house. 'Oh, of course, yes. Forgive me. I've not been myself of late.' And he was led off by a manservant, as if he needed a keeper these days. It was a far cry from the Gradlon who had ridden out to the defeat of Attila.

I saw Dahut later. She was holding court amongst the crowd which had gathered around the roasting ox, surrounded by a group of admirers, young men who hung on her every word and vied with each other for her attention. It was a measure of the gap between us now that I hardly knew most of them. She waved to me, and called me to come and get some food. One or two heads turned as I approached, but they quickly turned back again to the centre of attraction. One of the palace slaves gave me some food, and I found a bench to sit on at the edge of the crowd. The smell of burning fat and the greasy smoke were too much for me. After a few minutes I was joined by a fair-haired young lad in the red and white tunic of the court servants. His name was Sylvanus, and I knew him slightly from Dahut's entourage.

'*Domina*,' he began, 'may I sit with you a while?'

'If you wish, but don't expect fine table manners. It is impossible to eat this way with any elegance.'

He gave a wan smile. Oh, dear, I thought, someone else bringing their problems. The boy was about fifteen, good-looking in a boyish unfinished way. I guessed that he would break some hearts later on, though. Right now it seemed to be his own that concerned him.

'*Domina*, may I say something?'

'Of course.'

'Will you promise not to tell? I don't know what would happen if you did.'

'Hmm. Are you about to confess a murder?' I asked in mock seriousness.

He was instantly scandalised. 'Oh, no, nothing like that! It's only, well, it's a friend of mine, really, he has a problem.'

I tried to contain my amusement. A friend, indeed! That is one of the oldest approaches there is, and therefore the least believable. As if realising how feeble it sounded, Sylvanus lowered his eyes and muttered incomprehensibly at the ground.

'What sort of problem? In my experience, all young boys have a problem, and the only solution is a young girl.'

He looked up at me in alarm. How easy it was for people to convince themselves you could read their minds, when they wore the contents on their faces in full view!

'It is not a young girl he pines for, *Domina*. It is a lady of position.'

'Then he is an unfortunate young man. If the lady is married –'

'Oh, no, she isn't. Nothing like that.'

'Then she will want to be one day, but not to a poor boy, I think. Your friend's love is doomed to be unrequited.'

'You think so?'

'I do. Ask yourself, what use has a woman of high station for a servant boy? She wants him to run errands. She does not even think of him in the way that you – your friend, that is – would like. Who is the lady, anyway?'

'It is his mistress.'

Mother, the poor lad was in love with Dahut! Well, he would have some fierce competition, and from older and better men. I felt sorry for him, for the pains of unrequited love are that much sharper in youth, but I could not take his problem very seriously.

'Your friend should put aside all thought of her. Perhaps he should ask leave to go away for a while, maybe to see his family.'

'He has none.'

'A change of duties, then. Something to give him other things to think about, and to take him into the company of others. Soon he will see the problem in perspective, and find other girls, more accessible ones.'

He shook his head sadly. 'He wants no one else.'

'Then he has decided he would rather keep the problem, and so there is no solution anyway. Now, come and eat something, you look starved.'

He muttered something and went off into the crowd. Later I saw him hanging around Dahut's little group. Well, if he was determined to torture himself there was little that I or anyone else could do about it. Of course, in thinking this I forgot that there was one person.

I was almost ready to go to bed when I heard a commotion in the crowd. People were shouting and laughing, and gathering in a tight knot around something that was going on. As I tried to get nearer I realised that two men were fighting. I could hear the thud of fists on flesh, and the hoarse cries of abuse. Seeing who I was, the crowd let me through, and soon I could see what was happening.

I did not know the men, although I had seen them both in Dahut's company of admirers. Both had been well dressed, but were now the worse for wear, their clothes torn and dirty. One had a cut lip, and the other some swelling bruises on his face. As I watched they were on each other again, punching and gasping and pulling hair. They were probably both drunk, and I was alarmed at the damage they might do before they realised it. The crowd were taking sides, as crowds do, and shouting encouragement to one or the other. No one seemed anxious to stop it. Then I caught sight of a palace guardsman in the throng.

'Can't you stop this?' I called to him.

He shrugged. 'I reckon not, *Domina*. Her Highness says it's only high spirits, and to let them be.' He shrugged again, and looked on disapprovingly, leaning on his spear.

I could not be content with that, and pushed through the couple of rows in front of me until I was in the circle with the two men. They were both on their knees, facing each other, panting from their exertions.

'Stop it!' I did not yell, but spoke firmly, as if I expected naturally to be obeyed. Both of them hesitated and looked up at me. Then, the one with the cut lip stood up shakily, turned around, and began to limp away. His opponent called after him.

'Dog! We shall see who wins her!'

With that the other turned and spat. With a cry of rage the kneeling man leapt up. I saw the flash of a knife as he half-staggered on to his enemy, who was drawing his own from his belt. They stood there for a moment, while the crowd held its breath, wondering which one was hurt. Then they tottered apart, and both fell separately to the cobbles. I ran up and knelt between them, but there was little I could do. One had a dagger still protruding from his chest. The other had been stabbed in the belly and the cobbles around him were running red. As I leaned over him he shuddered and lay still. The other was already dead, blood welling up from between his lips as he lay staring blindly at the night sky. I became aware of someone standing next to me, someone with leather boots and a velvet cloak.

'Are they both dead?' asked Dahut.

'Yes.'

She looked the muscular young bodies up and down.

'What a waste. What was it about?'

'A woman, it seems.' And I looked her straight in the eye.

She snorted loudly. 'Men are such idiots! Now they have lost everything. And all for the sake of something they might have shared!'

She laughed that wild laugh of hers and turned away. The crowd parted wordlessly for her as she walked to the palace. I think it was partly out of fear.

Chapter Twenty-Four

We went to Sena in the autumn, on one of the last days fit for sailing. Dahut had been saying for years that she would go and see if the priestesses of the old religion were still there. Meriadauc had sailed into Ys to arrange some trade, and he agreed to take us over on the *Boreas*. To our delight Snorebeard came with him. The Armorican giant was the same as always – only a few greying hairs betrayed the advance of age. Otherwise, he was as rotund as ever in body. In spirit he was outgoing and cheerful as the day I had first met him.

Indeed, it was just like my first-ever sea voyage all over again. The waves were not large, but not insignificant either. Dahut felt a little green for a few minutes, but nothing could dampen the euphoric mood she was in.

'I've looked forward to this for so long,' she said. 'First my city and now Sena. Great things will come of this, you'll see. I will ask the priestesses to found a new temple at Ys. They will take in new novitiates and train them in their time-honoured ways. When the time is ripe, we will have enough to lead a whole army of converts back to the ways of the Mother!'

'Don't let your imagination run away with you,' I warned. 'We don't know what we're going to find yet.'

'Oh, don't be such a killjoy, Keri. Everything is going to be wonderful. I feel it in my bones.'

She turned to the wind, and let it blow her hair back in a black stream. She was aglow with anticipation, like a child embarking on a special treat. I smiled and shook my head. In this sort of mood no one could take her seriously. Even herself.

Dahut had brought her Frankish servant girl with her, and Sylvanus, and a couple of guards. I hoped Sylvanus would strike up a friendship with the girl, but it was clear that she had no time for him. Meriadauc was in his element. He looked older, but his manner was still the same – boyish and yet commanding. It suddenly struck me what a pity it was that he had no son.

As we left the comparative shelter of the bay the wind hit us strongly, and the ship began to race along, swaying and creaking. Waves broke against the sides, and salt spray dampened us thoroughly. We could have gone below, but I found it exhilarating and Dahut was determined to see everything.

It was only a short voyage, compared with our journey from Britain all those years ago, but the time made no difference. For a while I too felt like a child again, looking forward to a new life of safety, and freedom from the dreaded Saxon. Since then I had found that there were other sources of fear in the world.

Meriadauc pointed, 'There it is.'

Through the spray the island appeared as a greyish blur, but soon we closed on it, and the blur took on distinct features. Even so, it did not look a very welcoming place. The crew headed the ship toward a rocky outcrop, in the lee of which we might get some shelter. There was no sign of any true harbour.

'We can get in fairly close, I think,' said Meriadauc. 'One of the men at Ys reckoned he'd been here. There's no proper harbour, so we'll have to anchor and go ashore in the small boat.'

Within a few minutes, it seemed, we had passed into the lee of the headland, and suddenly everything was much quieter, the wind lighter, and the ship steadier. Meriadauc had the crew drop anchor about a hundred yards from the beach, and the small boat, which would only take six people, was lowered into the water. Our clumsy descent into the boat by rope ladder gave the crew cause for laughter, but we could hardly blame them. I managed to spin the ladder around and twist it about my legs, but in the end we got there. Meriadauc and Snorebeard took the oars and rowed us to the beach. I was at the bow ready, so I was the first to jump out into the shallow water and help pull the boat ashore.

The place seemed deserted. The island was low-lying, and the wind blew across it with hardly an interruption. We walked up the shingle and climbed the rocky outcrop behind. There was a stretch of flat land here, and the first signs of human habitation – the land was cultivated. The cries of a couple of goats were borne on the wind, and we turned towards them,

'Look at that,' said Meriadauc, and pointed.

Perhaps half a mile away there was an ancient stone structure. Not a building, but one of those stone circles built by our ancestors for some sacred purpose unknown to us. It was not a large example, but it was of interest to us because of the three houses which stood in a row alongside it. They were of the traditional Celtic type – round houses with thatched roofs. None looked as if it would house more than a small family. It was the custom to build on to these houses by adding larger circular walls outside the originals and roofing over the gap, so that the house grew in a series of concentric circles. These, however, seemed never to have been extended. Either they were very new, or they had been abandoned, or perhaps the population was static. As we drew nearer we could see that they were not new. In fact, they were in some need of repair, so that ruled out one possibility. For some reason there was a strong smell of woodsmoke in the air.

Outside the first house an old woman was sitting, dressed in black with a woollen shawl around her shoulders. She was sitting on a large stone, with her back against the doorpost, and apparently engrossed in grinding something with a small pestle and mortar which she held on her knee. She did not look up, but when we had approached to within a few yards she suddenly spoke in the Celtic tongue, in a voice like a crow.

'Who disturbs our peace?'

It was not much of a welcome, but we had no idea what to expect anyway. Dahut stepped up to the old woman, who was still grinding away at whatever was in her mortar.

'I am Dahut, daughter of Gradlon, King of Kemper.'

'Ah, she who has built the city.'

'You know about me?'

'How could we not? What do you want here?'

'I have come to see the priestesses.'

The old woman paused. 'Ah. Many there are who would like to see the priestesses. Many indeed, there are.' And she carried on grinding.

'Are the priestesses here still?' persisted Dahut.

The old woman nodded slowly, and finally stopped her grinding. She raised her face so that we could see for the first time her leathery lined features, and her sightless white eyes. 'Aye, they are here. All of them are here, but none will ever leave.' Sightless the eyes might be, but they could still produce tears, and two wet trails ran down the old crone's weatherbeaten face. We were wondering what to ask next when Meriadauc gave a cry. He had wandered to the end of the line of houses, and stood there, pointing at the ground. We soon saw what had excited him. Beyond the line of houses stretched a line of scorched circles in the ground. There must have been other houses here once, but they had all been burned down, leaving only their shapes baked into the earth. On closer inspection, the nearest one was obviously still warm, and covered with white ash, a handful of which floated away with every gust of the wind.

'What on earth is going on here?' muttered Meriadauc to me, but I had no more idea than he had. The old woman was no help. She seemed to speak only in riddles.

'Is it possible she's the only one here?' asked Dahut.

'No,' I said. 'The old woman said "we" knew about Ys, whoever "we" means.'

'Maybe, but she's more than half mad anyway, if you ask me.'

'True.'

The voice caught us completely by surprise. It was soft and feminine, and yet strong enough to carry above the rushing breeze.

'How can we help you?'

We wheeled around, the banal shopkeeper's phrase more startling than a challenge. Two more women were now standing next to the old crone. They both wore long white robes which stretched to their feet, and white veils which covered their hair. They were younger than the woman in black, but not young. The nearest figure, a woman with strong elegant features and greying hair, stepped forward and fixed us with an icy stare from pale blue eyes.

'We have come to see the priestesses, Mother,' I said, and knelt down in the dust. The woman came forward and took my hand.

'Rise,' she said. 'You need not kneel to us. If you come seeking the gods then come with your heads held high and joy in your hearts. The gods are little enough to be seen these days, so do not seek them like timid children.'

'Who are you?' I asked. 'Where are the others?'

She looked at her companion and then back at me. 'There are no others; not now.'

The significance of the funeral white now struck me. They had just buried – or maybe cremated – one of their number. The priestess seemed to read my thoughts.

'Her funeral pyre was on the plain. You must have smelt the smoke as you walked here.'

'Yes, Mother, but we did not know its meaning.'

She nodded, and turned to Dahut. 'And you, Gradlon's daughter, why do you come here?'

'I may be Gradlon's daughter,' replied Dahut evenly, 'but I am not of the new faith. I came here to ask your help.'

The priestess looked again at her companion. The other woman merely looked at the ground, and shook her head slowly. For the first time she spoke, in an unsteady and aged voice.

'How can we help you? We are old. Few follow us now. The Romans tried to stamp out the old worship, and the Christians are finishing the task. We are too old to change ourselves, and too powerless to change the world.'

Dahut stepped forward and interrupted in her agitation. 'But it need not be like that. Rome is tottering. Soon it will fall altogether, and Christianity will fall with it. Soon I will be Queen in Kemper, and I will not waste my time in bargaining with the murderous priests. Out they will go, lock, stock and barrel.'

The first priestess spoke again. 'Do you not understand? The new faith is everywhere. To be sure, the old gods are still respected in the countryside, but only as local spirits. The new religion's power is the power of one great god. People yearn for safety in these terrible times – for authority, for a universal father and protector for one all-powerful and all-seeing god.'

Dahut stamped her foot in the dust. 'You are giving up!'

'We are old,' said the priestess again. 'Once there were seven of us, the time-honoured sacred number. Now there are two, and one aged blind servant.

Soon there will be no one. As each goes we send her to the Mother and burn her house. Whatever the devotions of the people, they do not commit themselves to the sisterhood of the old faith. When the last of us dies the priesthood will die too.'

'It need not be so,' protested Dahut, but now it was the priestess's turn to show anger.

'Think, you foolish young woman! The new faith covers the whole of Europe, and Asia Minor, and North Africa too. Name one tribe in Europe who have not been converted to it! Go on, name one!'

Dahut made as if to speak, but could not.

'Only the Huns,' I said, and the priestess nodded to me.

'Exactly, and what sort of friends would they have been? The new faith is powerful, make no mistake.'

Dahut was beside herself. 'But what can we do?'

'Do as you please,' returned the old priestess. 'We will mourn the departed.' And the two priestesses turned their backs on us and sat in the dust, bowing their heads. Dahut stamped away, tears of fury coursing down her cheeks. The rest of us followed, a disappointed little band. All the way back to the beach she cursed and complained.

'Those stupid old women! Just sitting there, waiting to die. Better to get on a horse with a sword and fight!'

That would do little good,' I put in.

'Better at least to cut off a few priests' heads than to cut yourself off to no purpose. What a waste!'

There was no reasoning with her, as there never was in this sort of mood. She had hoped for a miracle, and found that they do not happen in real life. Perhaps it was the Celt in her, still searching for the mystery. Perhaps it was the Roman in me that took such a cynical view. Maybe miracles can happen. But not in my life.

Later, as the ship swept back across the water to her city, Dahut cried aloud suddenly: 'Pathetic, forgotten old women! How could I have been so foolish! I of all people should have known! There is no hope, no way forward unless we make it for ourselves. I will make it! I will cut and slash my way through!'

The others looked uneasy. I laid a hand on her arm, but she shook it away angrily.

'We are not cowering old crones, to sit and mourn the past. We will live life, Keri. We will kick those old priests in the teeth yet. I meant what I said. I will be Queen in Kemper, and soon!'

Even Meriadauc and Snorebeard, some distance away, looked perturbed at this outburst. I saw them turn to look.

'Dahut, what do you mean?'

She looked at the alarm in my face. Suddenly she laughed, lightly and insincerely.

'Oh, don't be silly! I didn't mean anything. But my father is only mortal, and have you not seen how he is failing? He has aged, Keri.'

'But he was fine when he came here. Is he ill? Can I do anything?' And, I thought, why doesn't the prospect worry you more?

She looked me straight in my eyes.

'You can do nothing more than I. All we know came from Megan, and I learned as much as you, I think.' Her eyes suddenly clouded over as if a door had shut within her soul. Where once I had been welcomed like a sister I was now shut out, and almost suspect, while servants and rakes and drunks had Dahut's ear.

'I will show those dithering old crones!' she shouted suddenly. 'Tonight we will celebrate! Tonight I will throw the wildest party! Let the priest wail all he likes.'

'And what are we celebrating?' I asked.

I looked at her face. Her eyes were wide, her gaze directed at the horizon. There were spots of colour on her cheeks and her face looked somehow distorted. She didn't notice me shudder and turn away.

The naked girl in the dog mask scrambled around the floor on all fours, miming the search for something. She nosed around on the floor, crawled to each table and sniffed loudly. She cocked her head back and pretended to sniff the air. Then she stiffened, as if she had heard something. The audience of revellers giggled and nudged each other. Then a boy appeared from underneath the long table opposite. He too was dressed only in a dog mask, and began to creep up on the girl, sniffing the air and then the ground. Even I had to smile. As mummers they were very good, catching the manner of the canine species in every detail. However, knowing what Dahut's parties were like, I had an inkling that this was not all there was going to be to it. I was right. The 'dog' suddenly came right to the 'bitch's' rear end, and began to nuzzle it with the mask. She looked around sharply, but then began to make the most suggestive panting noises. The young lad, whose excitement was quite clearly not entirely imaginary by this stage, suddenly leapt on her from behind and they coupled like dogs in front of us all. Dahut was greatly amused by the whole thing, as were some of her guests. Others looked embarrassed. Perhaps, like me, they preferred private pleasure to public entertainment. At all events, one way or another everyone's attention was taken up as I left the table. Some were leaning forward eagerly, shouting the occasional ribald comment. Some threw coins to the panting couple on the floor. Most of them were very drunk, but I rarely allowed myself to become fuddled. A poor midwife or doctor I would be if called out from a drunken stupor!

As I reached the door a cheer went up, and I presumed the proceedings had reached their conclusion, although some of the young men were shouting for more. I closed the door behind me and went up the staircase to the upper floor, where I knew the King's quarters were. He had not been seen in public for weeks now, and I was not reassured by Dahut's bland statements of the afternoon. If he was ill I wanted to be sure he was getting the treatment and the nursing he needed.

The door was not locked, and I pushed it open quietly. There was a dim light in the room, but not enough to see clearly. The bed was some way off, and when I approached I saw that the King was in it, apparently sleeping soundly. I put my hand upon his forehead. It was cold and clammy, but he was still alive. I debated with myself what to do next. If he was ill he probably needed to sleep, but I wanted to speak with him. I made up my mind to hear him speak; I might not get the chance again.

'Your Majesty! Please wake up! It is Keri!'

He only grunted, and rolled over. As he did so his face turned towards me and a better light fell upon it. His pallor was certainly deathly, and his appearance was the worse for several days' growth of beard. I leaned over him and pulled one up one of his eyelids. The pupil was so small that I could hardly see it in the dim light. Surely he must be drugged! My stomach turned over. Only one person could be doing this. Dahut's unconcerned comments on her father's failing health and her own impending elevation took on a new and sinister meaning.

I turned away from the bed and went across to the little adjoining room.

It was obviously meant to be a dressing room. Indeed, two chests adorned with the royal emblem suggested that the King's clothes were still there. However, the room had another purpose. There was a table in it, and on the table were the familiar tools of the medicine woman's trade – the pestles and mortars, the bowls and cups, and the implements for cutting and stitching. I recognised a number of perfectly wholesome substances, too – fresh herbs like yarrow and peppermint. But that was not all. A basket in the corner of the room, covered with a cloth, was filled with the seed pods of a wild flower. I could not see them clearly, so I picked a couple out and brought them to the light. They appeared to be from poppies, but not the cheerful red poppies of the hedgerow. A couple of petals still stuck to one of the pods, and as near as I could tell these had once been white. I had not seen white poppies growing locally, but I had certainly heard of them. Attila's men had drunk a brew made from them, which had caused them to feel no pain, even though they might be cut a thousand times in battle. Travelling herbalists sometimes sold the brew, or the reddish-brown liquid from which it could be made. I had bought some in Kemper, and I knew its power. According to the dose it could bring relief from pain, or sleep for the troubled. But like many medicines it was also a poison if given too generously. And at any dosage, if repeated often enough, it brought a pitiful addiction, with death as the end.

For a moment I stood and stared at the basket. I could not believe Dahut was poisoning her father – I *would* not believe it. She must be sedating him with the drug, keeping him too docile to interfere with her plans, persuading herself that this way he was not really being harmed. *My* conscience was not so easily stilled. The end result would be the same as slipping hemlock in his wine. I had to save Dahut from that. For the sake of our years together. For the sake of the friendship that still might be. My decision was taken. All the palace was carousing and making merry. There would never be a better chance. I snuffed out the candle and went back to the King.

'Your Majesty! Your Majesty, you must wake up!' I shook him and patted his face. He did not stir. I slapped his cheeks soundly, and he came to with a start.

'What? What is it? Who's that?'

'It is me, Keri, Your Majesty. You must get up!'

'Ah, Dahut, my dear, is it time for my medicine?'

Medicine! I shuddered. I had to get him out of this! 'Not Dahut, Your Majesty. Keri.' I dragged him up to a sitting position.

But what was I doing? Where could we go? The city guard would never let us through the gates. The King could hardly walk.

The *Boreas*! Of course! The ship was still in the harbour, the quay not far away. Even in his present state Gradlon could get that far! I had to try it.

I threw a cloak around him, dragged him out of the room and down the corridor. The back stairs were at the opposite end from those by which any of the guests might come, and the servants were mostly busy. I chivvied Gradlon along with whispered injunctions to keep silent and not to let us be discovered. We slipped out by a back door into the stableyard. I decided against horses – the quay wasn't far and I was afraid of the noise. Besides, the King was in no fit state to ride. We left the stableyard by a small door in the wall and hurried as best we could through the dark streets, towards the harbour. At any moment I expected to hear a hue and cry rise over the distant sounds of merriment. But we saw no one, heard no alarm.

Meriadauc, when I had finally roused him from his bunk, was sure I was mad. Even the usually imperturbable Snorebeard looked grave as Meriadauc remonstrated with me.

'I can't leave now. I have a cargo to load tomorrow.'

'You will be carrying the most valuable cargo of your life. He is your king, and his life is in danger. You must help him! Snorebeard! Make him listen!'

The big man shrugged his shoulders. 'Meriadauc is the chief here, little lady. I'm only his employee. Of course, if anyone were to ask me, which they haven't, I'd say we ought to help.'

Meriadauc shook his head. 'Sailing in the dark! It's unheard of. That'll put his life in danger, all right.'

'You need only get clear of the harbour and anchor for now. You can sail on at first light. By then the tide will be out and no one will be able to follow you anyway. By the gods, Meriadauc, you always told me you were the finest sea captain there ever was! Now's your chance to prove it!'

Snorebeard guffawed at that, and even Meriadauc managed a wan smile. He knew he had to help. Then Snorebeard spoke again.

'And you, little lady? You're coming with us, of course.'

'No.'

'But the Princess will know.'

'Not if I'm careful. I left the revelry early. She will assume I've gone to bed like the prim old prude I am.'

He chuckled. 'Well, you know your own way best, I daresay.'

Meriadauc nodded. 'But take care. You're the only daughter I ever had, and I don't suppose there'll be any more now.'

I kissed his cheek, a lump in my throat, and hurried away down the gangplank. Within ten minutes I had gone back the way I had come. I trembled as I entered the stableyard. My mind's eye conjured up a picture of the palace guard, iron manacles at the ready. But again there was no one. With the street door bolted behind me there was nothing to show how the King might have got away. I crept swiftly up the stairs and hurriedly shut my bedroom door behind me, leaning back against it in relief with the sound of my own pulse filling my ears. A few minutes later I looked out at the harbour. A dark silent shape could just be seen slipping away on the tide.

I awoke in the small hours, feeling that some sudden sound had been the cause. For a moment I heard nothing. Then there was a dull thump as if someone had fallen against a closed door. The muffled giggles which followed it suggested that Dahut was being helped to bed by her servant girl, but I soon realised it was not so.

'Careful, my Princess,' said the voice of Sylvanus. 'Let me hold you up.'

'Oh, yes,' came Dahut's voice, 'Hold me up till we get inside.' She giggled. 'Then you can hold me down.'

'Your Highness!'

'Oh, now, Sylvanus, you will not deny that you desire me?'

'I ... well... I don't know what to say. You are the Princess ...'

'And you are a fine young man. Don't you think you might even turn the head of a princess?'

'Oh, Your Highness, I don't know. I would hardly have dared to think ...'

'Dare now, Sylvanus.' And the door closed behind them.

I felt sorry for the poor boy. I could only hope the pleasure would be worth the pain when she tired of him.

I was at breakfast the next morning when the uproar started. I heard Dahut yelling in another room, and then guards ran through the hall where a few other guests were regretting the night before. Dahut herself came through a few moments later, a woollen cloak thrown over her nightrobe. She was kicking the servants aside in her temper.

'Dahut ... my Princess. What is it?'

'It's my father! He has escaped!'

'Escaped?' I asked disbelievingly.

'I mean, he has gone out and cannot be found.'

'He is the King,' I pointed out. 'I suppose he can go where he pleases.

She brushed the comment aside. 'We must find out where he is! He has gone without servants or protection! He is not well. He needs to be looked after.' And she was off again, overturning chairs, chasing servants and slaves, and landing them the occasional clout. It was half an hour before the sound of her voice faded, swearing, and cursing everyone's lack of efficiency. The palace seemed to be full of hurrying people. Only I knew that they were hurrying in vain. Gradlon must have been halfway to Kemper by then.

Later, as I wandered out of the city to go home, I saw Dahut and a company of riders set out on the Kemper road. The city guard was to be punished for negligence, she said, for letting the poor half-crazy King wander off and get lost. No one yet seemed to have connected his disappearance with that of the *Boreas*. I wondered how safe I would be when they did.

A few days later I went for a walk by the sea's edge. I had been treating a number of people for an unusual malady which had been circulating amongst the farms and villages. It was mainly a rash and fever, but it did not appear to be measles, or any of the well-known illnesses. I have noticed that such diseases seem to arise every few years. Perhaps it is the displeasure of some god.

At all events, after working hard with the sick I often find the need to get out in the fresh sea air, and perhaps to bathe. On this occasion there was a cool breeze, and I decided to keep my clothes on. Still, a walk along the water's edge is one of the most relaxing activities, and I set off in the opposite direction to the city. The sun was trying to warm the beaches as fast as the wind cooled them, and the sea was deep blue, with the glint of foam here and there where the wind whipped it up. I pondered on our visit to the aging priestesses, and the fury of Dahut's disappointment. I had still heard nothing further about the disappearance of the King, nor did there seem to be any word from Kemper about his arrival. Still, perhaps they would not announce it until they knew he was fully recovered. I still felt guilty about going behind Dahut's back. We had been friends for so many years – most of our lives, really. Yet it was impossible for me to condone her behaviour. Let her have all the lovers and all the orgiastic parties she wanted – whose business was it but her own?

But the drugging of her own father ...

The seagulls were out in force, I noticed. Further along the beach a large flock of them were attacking something in the water. As I drew near they took off and rose up in widening circles, screaming in their vicious angry way. Something white rolled over in the waves. I stepped in the shallows, my hand shielding my eyes from the sun. The water retreated with a liquid rustling of sand and pebbles, exposing the cause of the birds' excitement.

'Oh, Mother!' As the waves ran back up the beach again the body turned. The gulls had done some damage, but not enough to obliterate the youthful features of Sylvanus. At first I thought he must have drowned himself after a rejection from Dahut.

Then I saw the rope marks on his neck.

Chapter Twenty-Five

There was a time when I would have gone to Dahut and confronted her with what I knew, but no longer. She would eventually work out how the King had got away – if not sooner then later, when my continued absence from Ys became painfully obvious. The truth was I didn't dare face her – not her anger so much as her reproaches at my disloyalty after so many years of friendship. But for some time nothing happened. No one came to visit, or to summon me to explain myself. The world seemed to hold its breath, and I began to wonder if it was ignoring me. Then one morning I found that it had merely been resting to gather strength.

I had been out early, and was making my way back to the house when I heard voices through the trees. The clearing by my cottage was occupied by a troop of horsemen. I faltered for a moment, and then saw the royal emblem on their shields. They were royal guards from Kemper, not Dahut's irregulars. Feeling reassured, I strode openly into the clearing.

'Good morning!'

There were only six of them, though a seventh horse had been tethered to a tree. I presumed its rider was in the house, whose front door stood open. The captain of the troop returned my greeting.

'Good morning. You are Keri, the wise-woman?'

I smiled, uncomfortable as always with the title. 'Herbalist, let us say.'

He shrugged. 'As you wish. We have come from Kemper with a message from His Majesty.'

'The King? How is he?'

'Well enough!' snapped the voice of Corentin. I turned to see him emerging from the door of my cottage. 'Well enough to return and punish the demon-led hordes of paganism!'

I sighed audibly. 'I understand you have a message for me. If you want me to listen, you would do better not to start by insulting my faith. I have never insulted yours.'

He drew in his breath sharply, but then nodded, the nearest he was capable of getting to an apology.

'Very well. Let us walk a little. What I have to say is for your ears only.'

We took the cliff path down towards the beach. Corentin, in answer to my questions, told me that Gradlon was recovering well in the care of the monks. I knew what that meant – one dose of medicine and three prayers with every meal. Still, at least he was being cared for, and making progress.

'Now His Majesty is giving his mind urgently to the question of his daughter's behaviour. It is clear that she is possessed by some demon.'

I snorted at this, and he shot me a peevish look.

'Oh, Bishop,' I said, 'your world is full of demons.'

'The agents of the Evil One are everywhere!'

'Well, continue. What does the King want to do, and why have you come to see me?'

'The King has raised an army.'

'Oh, Mother!'

'A Christian army. But his purpose is not to make war, though he must be ready for it if need be. He believes even now that the situation may be saved. He wants to meet with his daughter and come to an agreement. He would like her to enter a religious house …'

In spite of the serious subject, I burst out laughing. Corentin glared.

'Oh, Bishop, I'm sorry! I really don't mean to mock you. But have you no idea of Dahut's feelings? She would die first!'

'That's as may be,' he said stiffly. 'I am the King's emissary; it is my duty to pass on his message.'

So Corentin didn't think it would work either.

'His Majesty does not want her to become a nun, only to stay in their spiritual care for a time, and repent of her past wrongdoings. She could return to public life when the cure is complete.'

I shook my head in disbelief. 'She will never agree.'

'She might. If it were put to her in the right way. Perhaps by someone she trusted. Someone she knows well.'

'Oh, no, Corentin. Not me!'

'You are her lifelong friend. Who else could do it? Any messenger might deliver the terms, but who else can persuade her to accept?'

'After my helping the King to escape, I don't think I stand too highly in the Princess's estimation right now.'

'Then it must be war,' he said simply. I shuddered at his calm acceptance of it. We had reached the sand by this time, and had begun to walk along it when something caught my eye.

'What's that?' I said suddenly, glad of a diversion.

'What? Just some seabirds. I don't see – sweet Jesus, have mercy!'

We staggered forward. Bile rose in my throat but I willed away the urge to vomit. The gulls rose in alarm as we approached, shrieking their unearthly cries. They were big birds, and menacing, but I steeled myself to come closer and look at the scores of bodies which lined the water's edge.

'May the Lord smite them in their cruelty and sin,' intoned the Bishop.

For a moment I thought he was talking about the dead, and then his meaning penetrated. 'What do you mean? Surely you don't ...'

'Look at them! Look at all these pitiful wretches! There is hardly any that does not wear the crucifix. Look at their hands! They are tied! This is no act of god. This is murder – mass murder, a second slaughter of the innocents! She has raised up a new Sodom, but the Lord shall destroy her, as he did that ancient city of evil.

'To Hell with you!' I raged suddenly. 'Yes, she has done wicked things, cruel things. Yes, she is dissolute, and a drunkard! But who made her so? When I first knew her she was a kind, loving person. She was my only friend. I loved her. What happened to her as she grew, Corentin? I'll tell you. You happened.'

He waved a hand at the scene of carnage around us. 'You seek to lay this at my door?'

'You brought her to this! You and others like you took a passionate and high-spirited girl and tried to force her into a box! Brother Emrys lied to her, misused her emotions. *You* threatened her with divine vengeance for wearing jewellery and wanting to sing! As for Johannes ...'

I tailed off, afraid of saying too much, but Corentin pounced. He seized my shoulder and shook me.

'Yes, tell me about Johannes! We have never heard the truth about his death, have we?'

It was out before I could stop it.

'He killed her child!'

Corentin lurched back as if I had struck him.

'Child?' he breathed at last. 'She had a bastard?'

The secret was out. One sentence and it was enough. Relief surged through me and I found my voice again.

'Do not speak of her like that. The Princess had a daughter by Prince Riwal. Megan acted as foster mother.'

'The woman who was burned?'

'Yes. And the child with her. The King's grandchild, Corentin.'

'God preserve us!'

My anger flared up again. 'Don't you think you and your god have done enough damage? You have blocked her at every turn. You sent Johannes after her here. You harried her at Kemper. When at last she escaped to her own city by the sea you followed her! You got the King to make her build the church before she could have the sea gate. You sent Fracanus to spy on her! You made it impossible for her to live a natural life ---'

'Natural?'

'A life that was natural for *her*. You tried to break her spirit!'

'It was for her own good!'

Now it was my turn to point at the bodies lying around us. 'Yes. I can see it all turned out for the best.' And I turned away.

'Is that the answer you give your King?' growled Corentin. 'There is little time. The main force is only a day or so behind.'

And I kneeled down on the sand and gazed through my tears across the bay, to where Ys lay bathed in sunshine – clean, beautiful, and totally corrupt.

I shook my head. 'No. Tell me all that His Majesty wants. I will do whatever I can.'

We returned to the clearing shaken and fearful. As Corentin spoke to his captain I brooded on the bitter turn of events. How could Dahut have sunk so low? I knew she was plagued by the same depressions her father had once suffered. Each time her spirits rose there was something to dash them down again – often something trivial was enough – and each time she fell deeper into the abyss. Each time the darker side of her nature came more strongly to the fore. I shuddered. Where would it end?

My thoughts were interrupted by a distant rumbling. The soldiers looked up, their hands going nervously to their weapons. They exchanged anxious glances, and those who were not already in the saddle mounted at once. Corentin too.

'We will return when the main force is here,' he said, 'and see what you have been able to achieve.'

I nodded.

Suddenly a troop of about thirty riders burst into the clearing, pennants flying. Nodens, Dahut's steward, was at their head. At the sight of the King's men he help up his hand and his ragged troop drew to a halt.

'So, wise-woman,' he called to me, making the title an insult. 'Consorting with the enemy, is it?'

I turned to Corentin. 'Go. Get your men away!'

'Will you be safe?' It was the first time I had heard him express any concern for me.

'Will I be any safer if you stay and get killed? Go!'

He saw the sense in that, and muttered to his captain. They began to edge away towards the only other path.

'My visitors came uninvited,' I called to Nodens. 'They are just leaving, but they have left me important information.'

He looked sceptically at me. The King's men were almost out of the clearing and he was obviously unsure about whether to attack. If he recognised Corentin

I was certain he would not hesitate. Dahut would surely heap rewards on anyone who brought her the hated Bishop's head.

'Leave them,' I urged, walking forward to distract him. 'They are of no importance. Besides, the main force is close by and you would soon be outnumbered.'

There were mutterings among his men at this. They were not regular soldiers, and their bravado was easily dashed. Nodens made his decision.

'Never mind. We have no instructions about engaging the enemy. Yet.'

'Listen,' I said, 'I told you I have important information. It is vital that I see the Princess as soon as possible!'

He smirked at this.

'Why do you think we are here, wise-woman? We came for you.'

I stood again in Dahut's hall, but this time I was not on the dais with her. The hall filled with Dahut's friends and hangers-on as we waited for her to appear. One or two of them were openly contemptuous – one actually spat as I went past. For the first time, I realised that some of them had feared my influence with Dahut, and were glad to see me cast down. What a simpleton I was when it came to palace politics! I thought of myself as a healer. I had failed to understand that these people saw me as Dahut's confidante and therefore as a rival. The sight of manacles on my wrists must have given them much pleasure. I had protested against being chained, for there was little prospect of my running away, but Nodens had insisted. We both knew it had less to do with security than humiliation.

The door from the ante-room opened, and Dahut swept in. She seated herself in the carved throne and avoided looking at me, which sent a pang through my heart. She was heavily made up, which was unusual for her. But I knew her of old, and I could see the pallor which she had tried to disguise. She wore a robe of Roman purple, which surprised me too, although it shouldn't have. The purple was the royal badge of office. To wear it was against the King's law, and virtually a declaration of independence in itself. I thought of the King's plan, and wondered what he would think if he could see his ambassador in chains and his daughter in the royal colours.

'Silence!' came the voice of Nodens, and his staff of office banged on the tiles. The murmuring of the crowd gave way to a silence tinged with anticipation. Nodens began.

'Your Highness, you see before you Keri the wise-woman …'

'I know who I see before me,' said Dahut quietly. 'I see the friend of my childhood. She grew up with me, shared my bed, my table, and my innermost thoughts. She accepted my generosity. And how was this generosity returned?'

The question was addressed loudly, to the assembly in general. The crowd began to murmur again until Nodens banged his staff for silence. Dahut looked directly at me with an expression of great sadness. To an onlooker it probably seemed convincing.

'Oh, Keri,' she said, 'how could you do this to me? Have we not always been friends?'

I found my voice with difficulty.

'Not in this, Your Highness. Your Father was – is – King. My first duty was to him.'

'But he was ill. I was nursing him!'

'I know what you were doing. I know what drug you were giving him. Can you name a god who would look upon that with favour. Or a goddess?'

She smiled mirthlessly. 'So, as always, you know what is right, what is best for everyone?'

'Your Highness, I would never claim that. But I know that opium kills.'

She waved my comments away imperiously. 'Such nonsense. I gave my father medicine to dull the pain of his rheumatism. You persuaded him that I meant him harm. You persuaded him to run away! You turned him against me!'

Her slender fingers hooked themselves under the arms of the throne. She leaned forward suddenly to emphasise her words.

'You betrayed me!'

There were more angry mutterings from the crowd, and Nodens banged for silence yet again. My spirits plummeted. She was sick. She really believed what she was saying. Her eyes, only a yard from my own, were burning as brightly as they had done on the day she killed Tiernan. I shivered, and felt cold sweat running down my spine. I tried to speak, but only a mumble came out, and Nodens interrupted me easily.

'Your Highness, there is more.'

'More? What could be worse than this?'

'Your Highness, when we arrested the woman she was openly consorting with Your Highness's enemies.'

He had already reported to her, of course. This was for public show. She signed to him.

'Go on.'

'She was speaking with troops of the King of Kemper, Your Highness. They rode away as we approached, but there was no doubting who they were. His device was on their shields.'

'I see.'

With an effort I stopped my trembling and found my voice again.

'Your Highness, I was visited by troops of His Majesty this morning. I did not send for them. They called uninvited.'

'Why would the King's troops call on you?'

'They called with a message from your father. His Majesty asked me to speak to you on his behalf.'

'And?'

'Your Highness, the terms were for your ears only.'

She banged the arms of the throne. 'I rule here! Speak!'

'Very well. Your father wants you to acknowledge him publicly as King. He will not interfere with your rule here, if you will reaffirm your loyalty to him.'

'Indeed! Anything more?'

I dreaded telling her. In private would have been bad enough, but here ... she would never agree to terms in front of all these people.

'Well?'

I found myself babbling.

'The King wants you to go – just temporarily, of course – into a religious house ...'

I got no further. She let out a bellow of genuine laughter. She rocked in the throne, and the crowd joined in sycophantically.

'Oh, Keri,' she managed at last. 'The poor man has no idea.'

'That's what I told them,' I said.

'The idea's ridiculous.' She wiped a tear of mirth away from her eye, and all my hopes of peace with it.

'Burn her!'

The words dropped into a silence. But death by burning had fearsome associations for Dahut. Instantly her anger flared up again and she sprang to her feet.

'Who said that?'

A red-faced young man became painfully visible as the crowd parted, separating itself from the object of Dahut's anger.

'I will rule here! I will decide who dies, and how! Guards! Take that man and burn his hand for him. Give him a little of what he is so anxious to deal out to others!'

The man was seized and dragged away protesting. The crowd was stunned by the cruel and arbitrary decision. A few sidled out. Dahut in this sort of mood was unpredictable and dangerous. Slowly, she sat down again and returned her attention to me.

'What am I going to do with you?' she sighed.

Nodens edged forward. 'Your Highness ...'

'Not now. You may give me your advice in private.' She gestured towards me. 'Take her and keep her safe until I decide further.'

Without another word she rose and walked out by her private door. I felt hands settle on my arms. The guards, former members of Gradlon's palace guard, knew me well.

'I'm sorry, *Domina*. You must come with us.'

They might know me, but I was not going to rely on getting any help from that quarter. A soldier sells his conscience for a piece of gold and a salt ration.

Gradlon had thoughtfully provided the palace with a prison. A few cells opened off a central room where prisoners might be interrogated. At least, I hoped that was what it was for. I seemed to be the only inmate. The guards handed me over to the care of the keeper and took their leave. Even when a jailor is busy his life is still sedentary by the standards of any peasant. This one was fat as a result, and morose into the bargain. He grunted at me and shoved me into one of the cells. My only consolation was that he took the manacles off me first.

The cell was about ten feet by six, with the door in one end wall and a small barred window high in the other. There was a stone bench which served as a bed, and a straw palliasse with a blanket to put upon it. The only other item of furniture was a chamber pot. By prison standards this was luxury; many a peasant or poor monk fared worse. But I hoped I would not have to spend a winter in these quarters.

My mind was in a whirl. My 'negotiations' with Dahut had been a farce. I had failed the King, and seemed to have failed my friend as well. There was every prospect that my transgression might be too much for her to forgive, and there could be only one outcome if it was. I knew that Nodens would be urging my death upon Dahut, and I had no friends in this court to speak up for me. I wondered whether our long friendship would be enough to stay her hand. We had gone our separate ways for some time, and other friends had taken my place. With my head full of such thoughts as this, I fell asleep.

When I awoke it was still only midday. The jailor stood by the open door.

'Food,' he said simply, and laid a bowl of soup and a hunk of bread on the floor by my feet. 'Make the most of it. There's only one meal a day.'

'Thank you,' I said, sitting up. I saw him look me up and down, but ignored it.

The soup was a thick army-style broth with vegetables floating in it. I would not get fat on it, but it would keep me alive, especially with so little activity. Afterwards there seemed to be nothing else to do, so I fell asleep again.

In the evening the jailors changed shifts, and a younger man came on duty. He was thin and scrawny, but I only saw his face through the grille in the door. He left me alone. A drunken soldier was brought in to sleep it off, and put in one of the other cells. He sang and shouted obscenities for most of the evening, before exhaustion and alcohol finally overtook him and he slept.

In the morning the fat man was back at his post. He unbolted the door to let me out.

'Slop out your pot,' he growled, and showed me where the drain was. I found the now sober soldier standing over it, relieving himself. He nodded to me incuriously, and finished what he was doing before sloping off to face his commander. I emptied the pot and returned to my cell, my thoughts once again turning to Dahut and the seemingly inevitable war. The jailor came to shut the door again, and found me sitting on the bench staring at the floor.

'There, there,' he said, in what seemed like an attempt at kindness. 'Things aren't so bad, you'll see. It's not much here, but the basics are looked after. Of course, there are ways of improving things.'

I looked up at him, and he took a few steps closer.

'They only give me enough to keep you alive,' he went on. 'But a little gold or silver, now, that could improve things a lot. I could send out for food, whatever you like.'

'And take a little for yourself?'

He smiled. 'Well, now, of course a man's got to look out for himself in this life, but you wouldn't lose by it.'

I didn't care about the conditions. They were adequate. Greater things were on my mind.

'I have no gold,' I told him. Not exactly true, but I wasn't going to tell him where to find it.

'Hmm. Well, now, there are other things a man values besides gold.'

And he sat down beside me and put his hand on my thigh.

I leapt to my feet as if I'd been stung, and retreated into the corner.

'Suit yourself,' he said. 'I could take you by force, anyway. No one cares what happens to you down here.'

Memories of the Saxon flashed through my mind. With them, only half-admitted, was the awful realisation that I was tempted to give in. After all, I was no innocent virgin, and it would give me some influence over him. Why not? But what guarantee would I have? This man would take what he could and give nothing in return. Who was to stop him? Then something happened which took all of these conflicting thoughts and drove them away.

Suddenly the room seemed brighter. I drew myself up straight. I was a good three inches taller than him, and he was sitting. I saw him as he was – a pathetic, despicable little man, feeding on the misfortunes of others. I compared his grubby proposition with the youthful ardour of Cynan and the experienced, considerate affection of Coel. How could I, who had shared the Mother's gifts with these men in joy and in pride, think of debasing them with this wretch? Once again I was a servant of the Mother, and I felt Her power pulsing in joy in my veins. I stepped forward and pointed directly between his eyes.

'Stay away from me! Do you not know who I am – what I am? If you harm me you bring down the Mother's curse upon yourself. Your blood will flow from you, your manhood fail, your senses grow feeble. Your life will wither and fade like a flower torn from the stem. You may forget yourself, but She will not forget, and your penance will be awesome to behold!'

I kept the finger pointed at him, and his resolution crumbled.

'I didn't mean no harm ...'

'Get out!'

He backed away to the door.

'Yes, *Domina*.' He paused at the door. 'Sorry, *Domina* ...'

He gestured towards the bolt, as if he were afraid to offend me by sliding it.

'Bolt it! What difference does it make to me? If the Mother wills it I will burst through your bars and bolts as through parchment!'

He scuttled away, muttering to himself. I couldn't hear much, but the word 'witch' figured several times. Well, perhaps it could be a useful label after all. I almost laughed out loud at my renewed spirits. I might have forgotten the Mother in my misfortunes, but She had not forgotten me, and when I needed Her most, She was there.

I stayed in the prison for three days. I still had to slop out the night soil myself, but the food improved. It also began to come three times a day, as the jailor stopped diverting most of it to himself. Proper washing bowls appeared, and a comb when I demanded it, and these did more for my spirits than anything; if you can't look after your appearance you lose more than just cleanliness.

Then, on the evening of the third day, the bolts were drawn unexpectedly. A couple of the guards stood there, looking very uncomfortable.

'Sorry to disturb you, *Domina*. I am commanded to bring you to Her Highness at once. I think ... I think they're ready.'

Chapter Twenty-Six

We passed across the palace courtyard and in by the kitchen door, as I had once returned after smuggling the King away. There were people in the great hall. No doubt Dahut was going to see me there and give judgement in public where it might serve as an example. I could hear the sounds of singing – not drunken carousing but a quiet sentimental chorus. Dahut must have brought in a professional singer, although his voice was lost amongst the others. I thought miserably of Coel, and wondered where he was, and if I would ever see him again.

When we reached the hall doors, we did not go in, however. The guards led me up the back staircase to Dahut's own quarters. It seemed that this time our deliberations were not to be in public after all. My heart skipped a beat as the leading man knocked on the door, and Dahut's voice immediately bade us enter.

'Your Highness …'

She waved the man to silence. 'Yes. I know who it is. Let her enter.'

I stepped into the room, and Dahut dismissed her men with another wave. They hesitated, but she knew she had nothing to fear from me.

'Go!' she ordered peremptorily, and they went.

She was sitting in a chair by the window, gazing out over the sea, and she looked dreadful. Her beautiful face was bloated and puffy, as if she had been weeping. Indeed, her eyes were bloodshot and somehow there seemed to be no life in them. Beneath them purple shadows told of poor sleep. Her hair was unbrushed. She had a black woollen shawl draped around her shoulders despite the blazing fire in the hearth, and an undyed linen shift beneath it. She looked like a peasant woman in poor health.

'Dahut,' I began. 'Are you well?'

She did not comment on my familiarity, but turned towards me and held out her arm. 'Oh, Keri, come here.'

As we had done when we were children, we fell into each other's arms and our tears mingled.

'I'm sorry,' I found myself sobbing. 'I never meant to betray you. I should never have left you. I should have stayed here where I could help.'

'No, no, you were right. You were never intended to be a court official. You had your own path to follow.'

'But what has happened? Dahut – all those poor people …'

'Ah, yes. If you had been here you would never have let me. Remember what you said, the day we killed Tiernan? You were right. I have become a monster.'

'No, Dahut!'

She held me at arm's length and looked straight into my face.

'Keri, I once said I would burn all their damned churches and hang all their priests, but it isn't enough. The Church is its people. While they live, it lives. Perhaps I have become a monster, but it seemed to be a terrible necessity. If only here in Ys, I must be certain of all those around me.'

I could almost find myself accepting the logic, so greatly did I wish things to be as they once were between us. But I saw in my mind's eye one particularly pathetic little bundle, no less dear a child to its mother than Morgan had been, tumbling in the surf. Suddenly my tears stopped, and I stood up, drying my face on my sleeve.

'Dahut, what on earth are you going to do? There cannot be much time now. They said the main force was close behind when they asked me to mediate between you. I still want to, if I can. Your father doesn't want to fight his own daughter, any more than you want to fight him.'

She sat forward in the chair, pulling the shawl more closely around her. 'I don't know what I want. It came to me suddenly yesterday, as I was reviewing the city defences. Why is this happening? War? My dearest friend in prison? Where did I go wrong? I didn't want to fight the new religion, only to preserve the old ways alongside it. But these newcomers won't accept that. It is all or nothing as far as they are concerned. I did not seek the killing. They started it.'

'And Sylvanus?'

She sighed.

'Foolish boy. He thought a night's pleasure gave him rights over me. He should have realised that he was serving my needs, not the other way around. He forgot I was a princess. I told Nodens to see he was reminded. I didn't know until afterwards what had happened. His body had been sent out on the tide.'

'I know. The sea has its own laws though, Dahut. The bay below the cottage was littered with dead on the morning you had me brought here.'

She shifted uneasily, pulling the shawl tightly around her.

'Keri, don't judge me! I told you why that had to be done. Besides, we can't afford to waste food on traitors. We'll need all our resources in the days to come.'

'Dahut, can you really withstand a siege here?'

She stopped abruptly, 'A siege? Who said anything about a siege? If it comes to it, we shall fight!'

I was flabbergasted. 'You can't mean it! Fight? In the open? With that motley lot of peasants? Your father's troops are trained in the Roman tradition. The best of them fought Attila, and survived. That makes them the best there is! Your army wouldn't last ten minutes!'

She shook her head again. 'Not in the open. We'd use the tactics the Germans used against the legions. We'd harry and run. We'd pick them off a few at a time. My people know this country like the backs of their hands. They could go on for years without giving in. How many years will my father live?'

'And if he dies, how sure are you that you will inherit his throne? And the loyalty of his army – a largely Christian army these days?'

She shrugged. 'We shall see. I'll cross that bridge when – or if – I come to it.'

She stood up and faced me. 'Keri, let's not argue any more. I've decided what I'm going to do. I'll give word that you can come and go as you please. I know you won't betray us.' She didn't say 'again', but the word hung there in the air between us. Before either of us found a way of breaking the silence, there was a knock at the door.

'Ah,' said Dahut, 'I heard the singing finish. Let him in.'

I went to the door and opened it. I thought it would be Nodens, Dahut's steward, but it was another. A big man with greying hair and a beard flecked with gold. I was so unprepared that for an instant recognition failed me.

'Coel!'

My sense of relief was so palpable that I actually went weak at the knees, but Coel swept me into his arms and lifted me off my feet. I just clung to him for a while, until he gently set me down again, keeping one arm around me.

'You've lost weight. You've not been eating so wisely, wise-woman.'

'Oh, Coel, you've no idea how glad I am to see you! I've missed you so much. But I thought you'd be away till next Beltane. What brought you back so soon?'

'Ah, well, I didn't enjoy it much in Roman Gaul. And a little bird told me there was trouble here, and maybe my grizzled old head might not be a totally unwelcome sight. Then again, maybe I just couldn't keep away!' He drew me closer to him as he spoke. He could still work magic. I felt my strength returning by the minute.

'But how did you come to Ys?'

'I came to look for you, foolish girl, what else? I ran into the King's army, and heard you had been brought here. So naturally I followed.'

'Naturally' indeed! He had risked his life for me, without even noticing how brave it was.

'Oh, Coel, you took such a risk.'

'Ah, no, I've told you before – a bard can go anywhere. In fact, that's what makes him useful.'

There was a twinkle in his eye.

'Useful?'

'Yes. When you failed to return the King asked me to mediate for him – to make a last attempt at peace. He was also prepared to ransom you, if necessary. A matter of honour, he said. He knew I was much in sympathy with the Princess. I was really the only person for the job. Anyway, I think we've the bones of an agreement at last.'

'Oh Coel!'

'If I may interrupt the lovebirds,' said Dahut. 'I should point out that I'd already decided on your release. I wanted to talk to you alone for a while, so I got Coel to sing to the company in the hall. I knew you'd have no time for me once you saw him.'

And she looked away sadly, as if remembering a time when she too waited for a man to return.

'Don't worry,' I said. 'Surely everything will be all right now that an agreement's being negotiated.'

She smiled weakly. 'We must hope so. My father hasn't heard the new terms yet.'

'I shall try to persuade him,' said Coel. 'You do acknowledge him as King, and that's the most important thing. He will want to make peace more than he will want to send you to a nunnery. That was Corentin's idea, I'm sure.'

She nodded. 'Don't underestimate him, though. Corentin won't stop scheming while there's breath in his body.'

'Then the sooner I get going, the better,' Coel announced. 'We agreed I would try to get back to them tonight.'

'Where is the army?' I asked.

'Behind your cottage, almost. On the hillside. I suppose it's an easily defensible position. Anyway, that's where I agreed to meet the King.' He squeezed my hand. 'You'll come with me, of course?'

I looked at Dahut. She was half turned away, staring out of the window, rocking slightly in her chair, the very picture of misery. My heart went out to her, and when I looked back to Coel he saw it at once.

'I understand.'

'I'm sorry, Coel. She needs me too. I don't think anyone else ...'

He put his arms around me. 'I really do understand. I'll wait at your cottage after I've seen the King. Come when you can.'

He kissed me firmly, and feeling his lips pressed on mine was almost enough to weaken my resolve.

'Oh, how I've missed you!' I whispered to him. 'I'll be there as soon as I can.'

He hugged me and gave one of his gravelly chuckles. 'I'll be waiting.' Then he spoke up. 'With your permission, I'll go now, Your Highness.'

She turned to us. 'May the Mother go with you.' She looked at me quizzically as Coel went out alone.

'I'm staying for the moment,' I said, 'If I may, that is.'

She smiled thankfully at me. 'I couldn't ask it, not after all that's happened. But there's no one I'd rather have with me.'

To my alarm she began to cry. I ran to her side and put an arm round her.

'Hush, Dahut! It's going to be all right.'

'I don't deserve you. Stay with me a while. Talk to me. Tell me about Coel, about your work. You know, since you've not been here there's no one I can talk to – not about normal, ordinary things.'

We talked for a long time. I found it a strain, to be really honest. Nothing is more difficult to maintain than an air of normality when all around you is decidedly abnormal. Still, it helped to calm Dahut. Eventually, she allowed herself to be persuaded to undress and go to bed.

'Won't you share the bed with me?' she asked. 'It'd be just like the old days again.'

'I will,' I said, 'but I want to take a walk first. I've been indoors for three days, and I'm not used to it.'

''I know, I'm sorry.'

'Never mind. It's over, but I still need a little fresh air. I'll be back in half an hour.'

'It's dark. Do you want someone to go with you?'

'It's all right. I'll walk back by myself. Your men all have work to do. Besides, what can happen to me here?'

She nodded gravely. We embraced and I reached for my cloak. The truth was that I felt as if I had been visiting the sick, as I suppose I had. As if often did, the experience had left me feeling shut in, and in need of air and space.

The dark streets were almost deserted, and my feet clattered on the cobbles as I walked along, deep in thought. In spite of the turn things had taken, I could not shake off a sense of foreboding. I could not see why. War must surely now be averted. Gradlon would withdraw the threat of a nunnery, I felt sure, in return for Dahut's public allegiance. No doubt there would be some public penance, but she could live with that if it meant retaining her beloved city.

Yet still I felt in my bones that I would never walk the streets of Ys again.

Perhaps because of this I decided to pay a last visit to the harbour. It was dark, but I was not going for the view. The weather was not cold, but the wind was gusting hard, as if a storm was brewing. Beyond the harbour wall the waves were crashing on the shore, and fine salt spray floated on the wind. Within the harbour all was still. I walked out along the quay, pulling my cloak tight about me. There was a little stone building near the sea gate, and a dim light was flickering within it. I had almost reached the place before I noticed. I knew the harbourmaster used the building during the day, but who could be there at this hour?

As I drew level with the door it opened, and a man came out. I caught only a brief glimpse of his face in the guttering candle light, but it was enough. For him too, evidently.

'The witch-woman!'

'Budic!'

My mind hunted for meaning in this bizarre encounter. What was the King's guard commander doing here? But he was also Corentin's chief henchman! The delay was nearly fatal. He lunged at me and seized my wrist in a grip of iron.

'What in God's name are you doing here, woman?'

'But, what do you mean? Why are you here?'

'Being spied on by you, it seems!'

'Spied? No, no. I am here on King's business.'

He laughed aloud. 'A likely story!'

'It's true. He asked me to mediate between him and the Princess. Because of our old friendship.'

'That was days ago. You didn't return. Anyway, it makes no difference. It's past time for talking.'

And he began to drag me towards the hut. He pushed the door open and threw me inside, in spite of my protests.

The interior was bare, except for a table and chairs. A candle stood on the table, and there were two other men. They were much younger than Budic, but no less hostile. Dumped in the corner were the bodies of two guards, the usual occupants of the building.

'Who is this woman?'

'A witch-woman. A spy, and a traitor. A blasphemer.'

Oh, Mother preserve me! Was there to be no end to it? A chill ran through me that was nothing to do with the weather. I had seen faces like these before. On the night that Morgan and Megan had gone to their terrible deaths. Faces with wide eyes and bared teeth. And I knew that Corentin hated me, and his desire to rid himself of me might overcome his respect for the King's orders. I ducked between two of them and ran, but a foot flashed out and tripped me headlong on the floor. Then strong hands gripped me.

'Don't run away, little lady,' said Budic. 'The night is yet young.' Again they all laughed coarsely, and dragged me to my feet.

'Come along,' Budic went on. 'Come and see the nice bishop.'

They dragged me out and bundled me along in the direction of the sea gate. The wind was already stronger as we struggled along. I had given up protesting. It was no use. These men were not acting for Dahut or for Gradlon, and my threats were fruitless.

Further along the sea wall someone had put a ladder reaching down to the beach. The water was already lapping at the foot of it. Budic pointed down, saving his voice in the wind. I climbed down quickly, hoping for a chance to run, but there were others at the bottom. I could hear the sound of hammering. Someone was doing something to the sea gate. There was a flash of lightning, and I glimpsed a number of men. At first I thought they must be battering the gate down, but they seemed to be hammering wedges into its enormous jambs. My ankles were awash. Another man grabbed me and led me a few yards up the beach to where three armoured soldiers were huddled in conference with a gaunt figure in a monk's habit. Corentin letting the common folk get their feet wet, I reflected sardonically. The Bishop turned and saw me. Budic shouldered his way past and spoke to him first. I knew what his version would be.

Corentin was beside himself with anger.

'Vile witch!' he screamed above the wind. 'Would you seek to thwart the will of the Lord?'

'What Lord?' I yelled back. 'You are thwarting the will of your Lord the King. This is mutiny, treason!'

Behind him his men were still busy at the gate, now knee-deep in the foaming tide, which was rising at a frightening rate. As the waves ran back the undertow threatened to whip their feet from under them. Each new wave crashed against the gate and sent spouts of water flying twenty feet in the air. One of the men fell, but was dragged to his feet again by the others. Then they turned as one and waded back through the water to the Bishop's side.

'It's all we can do, Father,' said the first, and the others muttered assent. 'The sea will do the work for us now, in any case.'

The Bishop took his attention off me for a moment.

'Very well, my sons. You have done well. God asks no more of you.'

'And what about her?' asked Budic.

The Bishop turned back, to look me up and down.

'The Bible says we shall not suffer a witch to live,' he said gruffly.

'Where does it say that?' I demanded, tossing the hair from my eyes. 'In between the bit about loving your neighbour and the bit about not killing?'

He slapped me across the face, and the stinging brought tears to my eyes.

'Do not profane those holy words with your pagan lips,' he growled slowly.

'In the sea with her, is it, Father?' asked one of the men. 'Or should we save her for the fire?'

Oh, Mother, not the fire! I waited for no more, but made a second lunge for freedom. The man who was holding me was caught unawares. I left him with my cloak in his hands, while I raced for dear life along the beach with my hem held above my knees. I risked one glance back, and saw that I had only gained a few yards, and the gap was already narrowing. I was lighter than the soldiers, and they had the weight of armour to carry, but they were used to running. One sprinted ahead of the rest and began to overhaul me on the landward side. The foam or the flame, was it? Then I would rather choose the foam, and sink or swim as the gods willed it.

Still running, I pulled my shift up over my head and flung it behind me – I would rather be seen naked than dead – and ran into the shallows. The breakers loomed ahead, curling towards me in a wall of white foam. There seemed no chance. Yet I knew that beyond the line of the surf the water was always quieter, and a person might swim in comparative safety. But, by the gods, the water was cold! Taking a deep breath, I ran forward and plunged into the heart of the great wave.

My body nearly froze with the shock of water all around me. The noise was deafening. Then I felt as if a huge hand had gripped me and thrown me back to the land. In a moment I was flung on the beach in a cauldron of bubbling froth. The men quickly spotted me again, and leapt forward. There was nothing for it but to try again, but this time I gambled all. I threw myself into the retreating surf, knowing the undertow would draw me away with more power than human hands. The sand stung as it whipped past my skin in the grip of the tide. I must have been cut a hundred times by sharp stones. Then I was in the heart of the wave, turning over and over as the roaring waters rolled around me. I tried to struggle upwards, but the current was too strong. It held me down, sucking me further out under the tumbling wave crests. My lungs were bursting. Death was very near, but I was not ready for it yet. Years of living by the sea had made me a very strong swimmer. It stood me in good stead now. Almost at the point of giving in, I felt the current's grip on me lessen. Seconds afterwards my head burst through the surface into the night air. It felt like breathing fire, but never has pain been so welcome. I filled my lungs, and concentrated on keeping afloat and recovering my breath. Turning towards the land, I could see nothing for a moment. Then the wave in front broke on the beach, and another lifted me up, so I could see better.

Unfortunately, so could the men on the beach. I could not hear them shout above the roar of the surf, but I could see them pointing. Dark the night might be, but I probably showed up against the white foam which topped each wave. I turned again, and swam as strongly as I could manage away from the city, keeping parallel to the beach. It was clear they were determined to stop me escaping to the city to warn them. Of what I didn't know. Two men followed my progress along the beach. Budic and another were trying to launch a boat.

The fishermen of these coasts make coracles of pitch-coated hide, like the men of Britain. One of those would have been too light to push through the surf. They knew this, though, and had settled on a small wooden boat of Roman style, pointed at both ends. They might manage that, and as I watched, they did. The pointed prow of the boat appeared above the wave tops, tilted as such an angle that it looked as if it might turn a somersault. Then it was over the crest of the wave and down the other side, both men rowing for all they were worth.

Oh, Mother, had it come to this? To be chased and speared like a fish? I swam, but I could not swim fast enough. I had already done more than most women could do, and it was not enough. Helplessly, I watched as the boat gained on me. One man, clearly Budic, had shipped his oars and now knelt in the prow of the boat, spear poised. He would not rest until he had killed me. Then as I saw his arm go back, ready for the throw, I dived. In the blackness I could not see the boat, but I made for the direction I thought it lay in, and luck was with me. I came up next to it, and immediately grabbed the side and made as if to haul myself aboard.

The man who was rowing cried out in alarm. More importantly, the boat tilted towards me, and Budic fell over. His helmet and spear went overboard. With a roar he scrabbled half to his feet and lunged for me. It was a fatal act. His weight and mine combined nearly upset the boat altogether, and he flew past me into the black water. With his armour and leather tunic he was lost, and sank like a stone. His comrade picked himself up to find me aboard, and the boat half-full of water.

'Bail!' I yelled at him, but he looked blank. 'Your helmet, man! Use it to scoop out the water!'

He dimly took in the situation, and taking off his helmet he set to work. Fear of drowning drove him harder than any desire to kill me – at least for the moment. As he bailed, I took the only oars left and rowed us further out to sea. He didn't seem to notice.

'Mark this!' I shouted at him through the noise of wind and water. 'If you make one move against me, or if I even think you do, these oars go over the side, and so do I. And you know what that means!'

He nodded, and carried on bailing, his bald head flashing at me each time he bent down.

'Give me your cloak!' I yelled, and he stopped for a moment and took it off. It was sodden, but it would cover me. I shipped the oars briefly and wrapped it around me. Good woven wool, it was, and surprisingly warm in spite of the water in it.

'Why are we going so far out?' asked the man anxiously.

'Have no fear,' I called to him. 'We have to row out, but the current will take us in.'

And when I judged that my little cove was opposite I turned the boat towards the shore. I could hardly row by now, but used the oars to steer the boat, and keep its prow pointed towards the shore. If it turned side-on to the waves we would be overturned in a moment.

'Are you a Christian?' I asked the man.

He nodded.

'Then swear me an oath.'

He looked startled. 'An oath?'

'Swear by your god that you will not harm me or hinder me once we are ashore.'

He hesitated.

'Swear it! Or join your friend.'

'I swear it. May God strike me dead if I break my word.' He paused for a moment. 'You could have killed me, but you didn't. I will keep my word.'

'Very well.'

Minute by minute the sound of the pounding surf grew louder. Our little boat went up one side of each wave, rode briefly on the crest, and then lurched down the other side. We were drenched with spray, but it seemed I had judged the currents right. This time, though, it would be live bodies floating in on the tide. As we drew nearer to the line of thundering surf the soldier began to look anxiously over my shoulder towards the shore.

'Sit down!' I called to him. 'Hold on tight, and we will ride in.'

Well, it was not quite so easy as that! We seemed to be nearly there, riding the crest of a huge breaker, when the boat struck a submerged rock and turned over. We were almost at the beach, though, and a few seconds' tumbling in the thundering surf found us staggering waist-deep in the shallows. I felt the wave begin to turn and its creeping fingers beginning to tug at me.

'Run!' I called to the soldier, who was only a few feet away, holding his head in both hands. 'Run, before the undertow takes you!'

I grabbed his arm and we hauled ourselves through the retreating water, which rushed lower but faster as the next wave gathered. I was naked again, but past caring. The poor soldier's head had been hit by something heavy, and blood was flowing from the cut. Still, we both came to land alive, if exhausted. The man wanted to sit and recover, but I would not let him.

'If you rest you will sleep,' I told him. 'And this beach is covered on a normal high tide. The gods alone know what it will be like tonight.'

Somehow we climbed the cliff path, taking it in easy stages between rests. The soldier's head injury had temporarily knocked the wits from him, but his feet obeyed my instructions. I was frozen by now, and in terrible need of food and a hot drink. But at last we reached my cottage and slipped the latch. The blessed warmth flowed over us both, and the poor soldier sank to the floor.

'Gods above and below!' There was a tremor in Coel's voice, as well there might be.

True to form, though, he asked no questions until he had fetched blankets and put a pan of wine on the fire to warm.

'What on earth has happened to you?' he demanded as he rubbed the life back into my tired body.

'Have you seen the King yet?'

'Yes. There was a man here, waiting to take me to him. The King was delighted with the news, of course.'

'Poor man!'

Jerkily, half-sobbing with exhaustion and cold, I told him what I knew.

'We must warn the city!' I finished up. 'I don't know what Corentin is doing, but it must be sabotage. With the gate wedged they will not be able to use the harbour to provision against a siege.'

Coel shook his head thoughtfully. 'They could moor against the wall itself and unload in good weather. No, I don't ...'

I felt his grip tighten through the blanket.

'What is it?'

'Keri, when they were building the gate, didn't they say it needed the weight of water in the harbour behind it? I don't understand these things, but didn't they say that the water behind holds it up against the sea?'

'Yes,' I breathed, 'and Corentin's men were wedging it shut at low tide. The gate will have nothing but air behind it when the tide comes in! Oh, Coel, it was rising fast even while I was there!'

Abruptly he got up and reached for his cloak.

'I'll only be a few minutes,' he said. 'The King's army is just up on the hill. They can ride to the city and warn them. There is still hope!'

He raced out into the night.

I got on some dry clothes, and then – as much out of a need to be busy as anything else – turned my attention to the soldier. He was exhausted, poor man, and allowed himself to be half-dragged to the fireside, where I tended his head injury and helped him change our of his wet things. Warmth is the best treatment for shock; dry blankets, a warm fire, and hot wine.

Coel seemed to be gone for an age, but at last I heard the cottage door slam shut, and the stamping of his feet in the outer room. He came in, wet and bedraggled.

'I saw the King,' he said simply. 'They are on their way. It is in the hands of the gods now, Keri.'

We paced the room. No conversation seemed adequate. I drank enough hot wine to drive the cold away. The inactivity was stifling.

'Coel, I can't just sit here!'

'What else can we do?'

'I don't know. Let us at least try.'

Understanding man! He knew it was pointless, but he knew better than to argue. We grabbed blankets and his cloak and wrapped ourselves up in them.

The weather erupted in our faces as we opened the door. Still, the rain was lighter now. The wind was gusting almost strongly enough to blow a man over. We followed the clifftop path. The furious waves were crashing on the rocks below, and the spray reached us. Then we came to a place where an outcrop gave a good view across the bay.

The lightning was flaring almost continuously now, not mere forked lightning, but sheets which flashed and crackled from cloudbank to cloudbank. The scene below was almost as clear as day. We saw a group of horsemen approaching the front gate, one of them carrying Gradlon's personal standard. They were let through almost at once, and soon we saw them in the square between the church and the palace. Down to the left the empty harbour lay like a pool of menacing black shadow, while the waves crashed in fury against the sea wall, surf flying over the top into the darkness. The tide was fully in.

Coel pointed back to the square, and we saw the palace doors open, spilling a pool of light on to the cobbles. Figures with torches came out and assembled on both sides. Then between them came a figure in a white nightdress with a red cloak thrown over it. That could only be Dahut. For a moment the King and his daughter hesitated then they clasped each other firmly in their arms.

'Oh, Coel,' I whispered, and the wetness on my face was not just rain.

Then the sea gate burst.

I heard a strangled yell from Coel, and looked for the cause. The sea gate had cracked in the middle, and was flung aside. The raging waves rushed through the gap, a wall of water more than twenty feet tall. As the water ran through it must have undermined the walls on either side, and whole sections of it fell. The greedy waves poured over into the harbour. Most of the boats were engulfed, but one ship was caught by the onrushing wave, and lifted bodily. As the roaring water hit the quayside, it simply flowed up over it and into the city.

'Oh, Mother. See the people!'

There was panic in the streets. People ran from their houses in nightclothes, or naked and were pounded in the raging water. I looked back to the palace, and saw Gradlon take Dahut on to his horse. They turned for the city gate, but then the water reached them, and I could see only spray. Still the sea poured in, tearing down more of the sea walls. The remaining ship rode up over the quayside and was carried into the town. It careered right up into the square, where it hit the wooden church and they dashed each other to splinters. I saw houses fall under the onslaught of the sea. Part of the cliff behind the city collapsed, adding to the chaos. The waves ran on, eventually crashing into the landward city wall. The guards were flung over it on to the mud. A handful of others escaped through the city gates, before the waters rushed through and flooded the plain outside them. We watched in helpless horror while the proud city fell into ruins. Even the stone palace did not escape. Rocks hurled by the waves destroyed part of it, and a section of the collapsing cliffs did for the rest. Within minutes almost nothing of Ys was left to show above the water. Outside the gates a handful of survivors struggled through the rising water on to firmer ground.

There was no sign of the King. And no sign of anyone in a red cloak.

Chapter Twenty-Seven

The storm, the worst within living memory, continued unabated for three days. When it was over there was little left of the City of Ys. What remained was a source of irritation to Corentin, and he led a band of Christian volunteers to dismantle what ruins there were, mainly parts of the palace and the city walls. After a few more stormy winter seasons on that coast not the slightest trace of Dahut's jewel by the Ocean would remain.

But there would still be bodies floating in the surf. Hundreds came ashore in the days after the disaster. Bones and wreckage were to carry on being washed up for years, until the bay of Ys became known as the Bay of the Drowned, and people spoke of it fearfully, in undertones. Christians or not, they still had a healthy Celtic respect for the ghosts of the unquiet dead. Out of that fearful respect has grown a legend. So, some say the streets of Ys were paved with gold, but of course they were not. Some say it was the fairest city in the world. As to that, I have never seen Rome, but from what I have heard it must be fairer, with its statues and buildings of marble. Ys had none of those. Some of the Christians have concocted the story that Dahut fell in love with the Devil and gave him the key to the sea gate, but, of course, it had no key. I have heard it said that the priestesses of Sena invoked sea-spirits to build the sea walls of Ys in only one night – those unhappy, powerless old women!

None of these things happened. There were no spirits, no devils, no magic. There were only people, with all their faults, blemishes, and good intentions. I know. I was there.

I was lucky to escape. Corentin knew that I was the only witness to the entire story. He would have silenced me if he could, but the Mother was with me. Coel and I gathered anything we could carry and allowed the peasants to lead us away across country. Those loyal people were glad to repay me for all that I had tried to do for them in the Mother's service. They brought us safely to Kemper, and my step-father's house.

The *Boreas* sailed gently on a finely rippled sea. The angry waves were gone. I gazed over into the deep blue waters and let the flowers fall, one by one, from my hand. They scattered, and made a trail on the surface as we glided along. Coel and Meriadauc stared fixedly at the distant bay. For the first time in my life I saw a tear in Snorebeard's eye. I could not cry, for there were no tears left, not for Dahut, not for Gradlon, not for Ys. Not even for the old religion, and its few pathetic priestesses who waited to die on Sena, to the south of us. I had spent almost twenty years in Armorica, and I had learned that there were worse things than Saxons or Scots.

'May your soul find rest,' I said as the last flower fluttered to the sea.

There was a gust of wind, and the sails filled suddenly as the *Boreas* quickened her pace towards Britain.

More books available for the Amazon Kindle:

Berlin Rendezvous

Book 1 in the *Century of Turmoil* series

What would you risk to help a stranger escape a tyrannical regime: your marriage, your partner's career, your own freedom?

Diana arrives in West Berlin, bride to a British Army officer — and a fish out of water. The Army operates by 19th century standards; wives conform. Don't these women have lives of their own? Are shopping or affairs their only outlets? Does no one care that an officer is beating his wife? But the officer class will hear no criticism from a woman who doesn't know her place.

As tensions grow, Diana receives a risky proposition. Dare she gamble so much in a city full of danger and intrigue? One man is already dead…

At the same time, terrorists are about to attack the British military community, aided by rogue elements bitterly opposed to the reforms sweeping the Eastern bloc. Why is Diana's husband the target?

Written by an author who lived in West Berlin for ten years, this novel evokes the atmosphere of a vibrant city surrounded by walls and fences, patrolled by tanks and helicopters: a city under international military occupation since 1945. Following the 30th anniversary of the collapse of the Berlin Wall, here is a story to bring that unique period to life for another generation.

The Devil's Issue

Book 2 in the *Century of Turmoil* series

Is Susan Jessup mad? Certainly, she sees things that cannot exist, things that never could. Is she paranoid, or just plain crazy? Even she isn't sure. And if she isn't crazy, she certainly sees some crazy things.

This story is set in England in the early 1990s, shortly after the opening of the borders between the old Soviet Union and the West. It was a different world back then, before mobile phones and the Internet.

It wasn't just the technology that was different. Although the Soviet Union had effectively collapsed, Russia's attitude to the rest of the world was quite unclear.

Several stories emerged that caused Westerners' hair to stand on end. Some of the plots dreamed up by communist bloc military strategists had gone beyond the most paranoid Western imaginings of the Cold War. "People said we were too paranoid," said one commentator. "Looks like we weren't paranoid enough!"

What might follow in the wake of the collapsed Soviet empire? To Western security services, many of the political changes were welcome. But with them came insecurity and a sense that they had to be ready for every possibility.

This story is based on one of those possibilities…..

Look out for:

The Checklist

A stand-alone novel of the turbulent life of a diagnosed psychopath. But can we really diagnose a man's personality condition on the basis of a 20-item checklist? Frankie Lowe says not, and he doesn't like the people who do it.

But he wouldn't, would he? He *is* that man…

Coming soon

For news of this and other new books, why not join my mailing list? Your details will be held in strict confidence, and not used for any other purpose than to bring you news of my work up to four times a year.

Just send an email to: rawriter@rawriter.myzen.co.uk with "subscribe" in the subject line.

Printed in Great Britain
by Amazon